Writing Lines

The Complete Words of G G Wentworth B Sc

Selected and edited by

Tony Stuart

authorHOUSE®

AuthorHouse™ UK
1663 Liberty Drive
Bloomington, IN 47403 USA
www.authorhouse.co.uk
Phone: 0800.197.4150

Published by AuthorHouse 10/03/2016

ISBN: 978-1-5246-3444-5 (sc)
ISBN: 978-1-5246-3442-1 (hc)
ISBN: 978-1-5246-3443-8 (e)

Print information available on the last page.

Any people depicted in stock imagery provided by Thinkstock are models, and such images are being used for illustrative purposes only. Certain stock imagery © Thinkstock.

Photograph courtesy of Roy Shepherd www.discoveringfossils.co.uk

This book is printed on acid-free paper.

Contents

Episode 1

9ᵗʰ January 2005

Loath as I am to take up your time at this busy stage of the school year, I feel you ought to be fully acquainted with the facts about the incident on the ski trip over the Christmas break which led to that typically low and flashy *News of the World* headline *"Toffs' Teacher in Nun Slaughter Horror"*. Further, the idea that I was arrested for the poor woman's murder is a gross exaggeration. Naturally, I 'helped the police with their enquiries' and I will admit that there were some sticky moments initially until the full explanation emerged after the forensic team's investigation. This, I am happy to report, completely exonerated me from any culpability in the nun's tragic death. The truth is as follows.

You will, no doubt, remember Pete Hull's rather desperate e-mail communication just before the end of term for someone to join the trip as a last-minute substitute for the teacher who discovered she was pregnant with twins (belated congratulations to our bigravid colleague here!) and so could not go after all. I was happy to step into the breach despite not having skied since the early 1960s when still a schoolboy myself. Eventually, Pete conceded to my pressing offer of assistance and, just after St Stephen's Day, we set off for the Austrian alpine fastness that is Löwefahrt.

After Pete's assurance that 'all the kit will be provided' the only item I selected that I thought appropriate for such a trip was the splendid meerschaum pipe that was a gift from my late-lamented uncle Reginald. Many of you will perhaps have noticed this on display in its usual place on my mantelpiece: I emancipated it from there to allow it to breathe again in its native mountain air. It really was a superb example of its type. The bowl was decorated with a wonderfully grotesque caricature of a face, a hinged chased silver lid surmounted it; the stem was of stout gunmetal with a fine white porcelain mouthpiece. Certainly, it was not small – "like a dustbin on a stick" was Pete's observation when I first poured in a couple of ounces of Balkan Shag and lit up – but I feel it gave me a certain something, helped me to fit in if you know what I mean. Unfortunately, the weight of the pipe was something I was unused to and this led to a soreness, which, in that cold, dry Austrian air, itself led to a small degree of chapping of the lower lip. I bought a simple lip-salve and applied it liberally whenever outdoors as a prophylactic which, thankfully, seemed to help prevent the condition worsening.

I must say that Pete's ski trips are a wonderful tonic to the system and certainly earn the epithet 'sybaritic'. Though the caviar-and-champagne 'on tap' in the staff suites was a welcome novelty, I took to having lunch in a *kneipe* in the pretty town square while the other teachers were helicoptered up to the more rarefied meals available in the new El Bulli-bulli franchise atop Mt. Klingschaubel. After we had arrived, I only encountered the pupils twice: once I caught a whole lot of them skulking in one of those dubious 'tourist shops' in the village which sell the sorts of things silly schoolchildren all think wonderful such as fireworks, flick-knives and saucy post-cards – and I quickly shepherded them out and ordered them to get some fresh air into their lungs; and second during the high jinks of the New Year's Party celebration which the rest of the staff left me (as 'senior man') in charge of while they went to the casino. For the rest of the time pupils were either skiing with the ski-school or in the care of the PGL group to which Pete had sub-contracted that part of the trip.

And so, the Old Year gently ticked into the New, bringing that fateful Sunday with its death of a nun on the cobbled square amongst the bunting, clamour and colour of a religious festival.

That morning was, for me, just as usual: a solid breakfast (though I could not get used to salami and cheese amid the other offerings of prunes, knobbly breads and fresh pineapple – have they never heard of kedgeree?) followed by a couple of slides down the gentle 'green runs' I favoured. I always skied extremely carefully and paused frequently after a couple or more snow-plough turns to take in the views. Up until that day, other skiers I had found rather brusque – sweeping past with a loud hoot at something or other, or shoving past without eye-contact in the queues for the chair-lift. But that morning they all seemed more cheerful and welcoming, smiling and nodding at me quite often. I just applied a little more of my lip-salve and smiled back at them, surmising that the New Year had produced a resolution amongst them to look on their fellow-man more kindly.

At about mid-day I parked my skis and settled down at a table on the pavement outside the *kneipe* and, after ordering a coffee from a waitress who gave me a curious look and then a broad smile, lit up my first pipe of the day and relaxed under the shade of the awning. Then I heard the singing. Processing slowly from one end of the square and towards the charming little church on the other side was a choir in green behind a pair of nuns and all led by a pastor who was resplendent in canary yellow cassock and snow-white surplice and carrying in two hands before him an enormous golden cross. My coffee arrived and I took a sip then replaced the cup in its saucer. Shortly afterwards, a nun lay dead.

Just as the pastor was drawing abreast of me, I observed a crescent of bright red lipstick on the rim of my coffee-cup. Irritated, I was about to call the waitress when I noticed that there appeared to be something adhering to the mouthpiece of my pipe. In the shade of the awning I couldn't clearly see what this might be so, clamping the lid of the pipe down with my thumb to keep the tobacco 'in', for illumination I pointed the stem out into the sunlight beaming down on the square. Unmistakably, there was lipstick of the same shade on the mouthpiece. At that moment the pipe went off. A jet of scalding dottle shot from the stem and hit the pastor's surplice like a brown paintball. He staggered and the golden cross slipped from his hands, toppled over, and an arm of it sliced through the nun's wimple, her skull and her hold on life.

As I say, the facts that led up to this sorry event emerged during the police investigation. They seemed to be at something of a loss about the customary 'ragging' that English schoolchildren accord a favourite teacher, but the forensic evidence finally convinced them that my part in the death was wholly accidental. I must admit, despite the sombre final outcome, to a sneaking admiration for whichever pupil it was who, during that New Year's Eve Party, had substituted the balm in my lip-salve with a cylinder of vermilion lip-stick (no doubt employing skills imparted in the Design Department by our peerless Phil Shikespier!). This caused harmless amusement at my expense though, of course, one should never encourage such a thing. Extracting the gunpowder from a firework, however, and putting it amongst the tobacco in my pipe was utterly irresponsible. When this powder exploded the blast was channelled into the narrow confines of the stem so turning the pipe almost into a hand-gun with the terrible consequences described above.

Although I wanted to challenge the *News of the World* for dragging my good name through the stews of its pages, the Head has persuaded me that 'least said, soonest mended' and so I hold my peace - and may that blameless nun rest in hers.

Episode 2

Friday 23rd June 2010

Email to Sixokes Staff involved in the teachers' CAN DO! concert

I hope that you will join with me in scotching the false accusation that I hear is spreading amongst the pupils that I am a secret 'cross-dresser'. This scurrilous canard seems to have started doing the rounds merely on the so-called 'evidence' of the very public exposure on the stage of the Playfair Hall last night of the lady's red silk underwear I happened to be wearing at the time.

Of course, I was happy to volunteer to perform in the concert in aid of charity. I was confident that my appearance would delight and entertain in equal measure – and would, I felt sure, be memorable in the sense that few, if any, of the pupils would have seen or heard anything like it in their lives. Hence my insistence on keeping the nature of my act to myself until the night itself: any inkling of the treat to come would have robbed it of the immediacy a genuine surprise produces. This did mean that I had to take 'pot luck' with the place in the order that my act was scheduled for (as Colin Greening, the chap who'd put himself in charge of the concert told me with a shrug) but this was a small price to pay.

An hour or so before I was due on stage, I slipped into the dressing room in the Belling Theatre. I knew I would have it to myself - the others in the cast were changing in spare rooms dotted about the Hall itself. I had decided to wear black tie which, I knew, would not only raise the sartorial standard more than somewhat (having seen some of the ill-advised 'casual clothes' other members of the cast had adopted in the vain hope of appealing to youth) but would also immediately impress with gravitas and polish. I always liked 'dogging up' (as we used to say about formally dressing for the evening) and welcomed the chance of airing the old rig one more time.

It was as I stepped into the trousers that I noticed the fit was far snugger than it really should have been: the button holes at the waist could barely be reached and the material in the upper leg region was positively clinging. I breathed a small reproach directed at Pearl in the Catering Department. She was always giving me a smile, a wink and ladling out extra portions of puddings and this generosity was now pressing fulsomely on the black barathea. I'm not really sure why it is that Pearl has taken such a shine to me but it may well have been over an incident one lunch-time last winter. I had arrived fairly late for lunch and joined the 'P E Boys' at their table. The young and chirpy Sean Golden put a tumbler in front of me and filled it with wine that he'd brought from some hospitality event put on by the kit suppliers to the School (a company whose pantechnicon-sized vans, as I'm sure you will have noticed, are forever blocking the drive as they deliver yet more stuff most mornings) and urged me to 'drink up to keep out the cold'. It proved a most convivial and rather protracted lunch. It was while carrying my tray back to the clearing area that I inadvertently stumbled over the 'Henry' vacuum-cleaner that Pearl was using and fell towards her. To save her from the trayful of crockery, I threw it boldly to one side. Unfortunately, this led to an even more catastrophic loss of balance and I ended up clutching her sturdy frame in my arms with my face pressed close to her crisply permed ringlets. Be that as it may, the trousers were just too tight.

Glancing around the dressing-room, my eye alighted on the wicker props box. Inside I found the elasticated red silk bloomers that had featured so prominently in Jimmy Grint's audacious pantomime version of *Hamlet*. (Though not universally applauded in the English department, I for one enjoyed the pupils' enthusiasm as they yelled 'Behind you' as the ghost appeared on the battlements and the wonderful interplay with the cast: 'To be or not to be, that is the question', 'Oh no it isn't!', 'Oh yes it is!' I doubt they'll repeat this sort of participation when they go to a more formal production in later life.) It was the work of a moment to fish these bloomers out and, discarding the rather thick wool-mix combinations I favour, slide into them. As anticipated, the thinner fabric together with the slippery texture allowed the dress trousers to sheath my lower half much more comfortably.

*   *   *

I stood tiptoe in the wings as Greening announced me: "And now, with something but I'm not sure what, which he tells me he will accompany himself with, your very own Mister G G Wentworth!" I walked carefully to centre stage where there was the chair and microphone I'd requested. You could have heard a pin drop.

This silence was only to be expected. Two reasons would have been that, firstly, seeing a revered figure usually clothed in tweed 'n' twill absolutely resplendent in black tie would have been a surprise; secondly, no-one knew that I had any hidden talent to reveal and so this would be another surprise. However, a third reason was the rather sombre – almost grave - mood that the previous two acts had engendered: Alex Smithley with an acoustic guitar had given a throat-choking rendition of Eric Clapton's *Tears in Heaven* and this had been followed by a wonderfully poignant version of the *Pearl Fishers Duet* by Helen Tabby and Phoebe Best. But, like an old trouper, I got on with it. Raising a foot onto the seat of the chair, I whipped my spoons out of my jacket pocket, gave an introductory clatter with them between palm and knee and launched into the song at the top of my voice:

My old man's a dustman; he wears a dustman's hat
He wears gorblimey trousers and he lives in a council flat!

At this point I attempted a pretty tricky percussive manoeuvre with the spoons only to find one of them flying out of my hand, bouncing and skittering off the stage and hitting the egregiously foolish Peregrina Atkins squarely on the forehead. I gesticulated at her to lob it back to me and she threw it, demonstrating an aim that was as wild and inaccurate as her prose, and causing me to turn quickly and fall awkwardly over the chair. The sudden bending double was the last straw for the trousers which promptly ripped apart and the red silk underwear was displayed through a vast rent for all eyes to see. There was a short silence before huge gusts of laughter filled my ears. Turning to face the wildly-appreciative crowd, I edged sideways off the stage.

Thus, my act was not the celebration of music-hall times that I had planned. But, given the 'cross-dresser' rumour, I would appreciate it if you, like me, insist that it was, in fact, a deliberate 'comic turn' rather than anything more damaging to my dignity.

Episode 3

Wednesday 6th March 1995

"What's it all about, then, this 'appraisal' nonsense? I've got the Headmaster coming in to my lesson on Friday to what he calls 'observe my teaching' whatever that entails. I don't know what business it is of his, really. Any of you chaps got an inside line?" I looked around the table. We were enjoying a pleasant and leisurely lunch in the staff dining room and had just been served the cheese and coffee by the ever-attentive catering staff – with a couple of us, with no period six to teach, supplementing these with some of the fine old madeira that Oliver Cooper, the Bursar, had recently unearthed and acquired for the School's cellars.

"Another dismal import from the world of commerce," sighed Richard Hansum, doyen of the English department. "No doubt soon we'll all be assessed for our 'productivity', 'customer relations' and 'targeted aim–fulfilment'." With his characteristic world-weary languor, he tapped the ash from his cigar and continued. "It seems that the best future for education lies in turning it into a 'business' whereby knowledge, like soap-flakes, is homogenized, optimized, super-sized and merchandised. We teachers are to be the operatives, the hirelings, who dose the machines, stamp the boxes, hawk the –"

"Yes, yes, Richard," cut in Frank Englishe, "Do give that hobby-horse of yours a rest for just a few minutes and tell Dob here how you actually handled your 'lesson-observation' part of the appraisal." He poured a little more madeira into Hansum's glass and the latter acknowledged it with an airy gesture of the hand.

"Well, to give the Headmaster his due, he was on time and sitting quietly at the back of the class when I arrived at my desk and faced the usual array of the pusillanimous, the lack-lustre and the damned that is my 5th form class. The Headmaster seemed to take no notice of me, merely started scribbling onto a page on the clip-board with which he had so thoughtfully come equipped. 'Reading lesson!' I announced. 'Go to the library, collect a book of fiction and return here in 10 minutes time.' They all trotted off obediently enough and I pulled a few essays out of my briefcase and started marking them. The pupils were back in the specified time and the rest of the period was spent in silence save for the occasional susurrus of the turning of a page and the sound of my pen decorating margins with insight." Hansum paused to sip from his glass and take a gentle inhalation of cigar-smoke. "When the bell went, so did the Headmaster. And a perfect stillness followed in his wake."

Thursday 7th March 1995

I recounted the gist of Richard Hansum's 'lesson observation' to Alex James, the handsome and charismatic Head of Biology this morning and he was vehement that I should not repeat the same sort of thing when it came to the Headmaster's visit to my lesson tomorrow afternoon.

"Don't even think of it – he's already gunning for the Biology Department and we need to make sure he sees us in a good light. Look, the lesson he's coming into is your 4th form isn't it?" I nodded. "Well, why don't you come into my 4th form lesson later on to get a few ideas?"

"If you think it might help, there'd be no harm I suppose," I replied though it all seemed rather a fuss about nothing. Teaching has always come naturally to me and I could see little point in sitting through another teacher's performance in class. However, for the sake of smooth relations, I was attending dutifully at the back of Alex's class at the start of his lesson (the double period just before lunch) where, as he'd told me, he was going to start the topic of photosynthesis.

The class filed in quietly and settled on their stools at the benches. Alex waited until there was absolute silence and then began.

"You'll remember that last lesson we finished looking at how mammals breathe, how they exchange gases between their bodies and the environment. Today, we are going to see how that other great kingdom, the plants, go about this gas exchange..."

I must say that, despite myself, I found myself getting interested. Like the pupils I began to hang on his every word and, when he finished his short introduction and got them to start noting down a few sentences, felt like getting some paper and writing it down myself. The lesson went gently and painlessly on: after some short notes he put an acetate of a leaf cross-section on the OHP and the class dutifully copied it and added colour while Alex passed between the benches adding encouragements and individual questions to the pupils.

There was only a brief disciplinary matter that cropped up and Alex handled it beautifully. A boy started talking to his neighbour while Alex was telling them about the density of stomatal pores on a leaf epidermis – a particularly striking analogy where he got them to picture each member of the class spread equally over Dyke's Meadow and waving a flag: this certainly provided a vivid and memorable illustration. Anyway, he stopped and got the talking boy to stand up.

"Now, what were you saying, Stratford?" he asked politely.

"Please sir, I was just –"

"Don't mind me or what I'm saying, do go on," Alex urged.

"Yes sir, I was going –"

"Am I interrupting you when I start talking? Do go on."

"But if –"

"I think talking over you when you are speaking isn't going to get us very much nearer what you want to have heard, do you?" asked Alex.

"Not really sir, and –"

"No." There was a pause. Alex raised his eyebrows and Stratford nodded and smiled ruefully, his lesson learned. "Please sit down again and listen to what I say." Stratford opened his mouth but then closed it and smiled again.

The last half-hour was given over to practical work – the extraction of chlorophyll from a leaf and testing it for the presence of starch. I was impressed by his organisation and attention to detail; the way he avoided a scrummage over equipment-collection; his emphasis on the care required to switch out the Bunsen flames before bringing removing the test tube of ethanol from the boiling water-bath; his insistence on protective glasses when handling iodine solution; the efficiency and effectiveness of the clearing-up afterwards. In the final few minutes, he tied the practical work into the theory, set them a stimulating exercise for homework, and dismissed them with a smile. I almost broke into applause.

Afterwards, in the prep room, I told him that I was full of admiration. He accepted my praise and pointed out that it all came from the preparation of a good lesson plan. I was interested in this novelty.

"A lesson plan, eh? What's that when it's at home?"

"Simple really – my lessons all follow a basic format to fill the double-periods we have in the Middling School. As you saw, I settle them down and start with a few minutes of linking the prospective lesson material with the past; then some note-taking and diagram-copying, followed by half to three-quarters of an hour on practical work, and finally a brief round-up and homework-setting. Easy as pie."

"Do you know, I'm going to give it a go," I said slowly. He looked pleased and slapped me on the back.

"Good for you!" he cried.

In fact, I decided to reproduce exactly Alex's lesson with my class tomorrow as it had been such a fine example: how could the Headmaster be less than greatly impressed?

Friday 8ᵗʰ March 1995

I might have guessed that my 4ᵗʰ form would make a mess of things: talk about spanners, grit and flies!

First off, rather than the quiet and purposeful entry into the classroom that Alex's class had effected, my lot burst through with a great deal of pushing, shouting and arm-punching. That is until they all noticed the Headmaster sitting solemnly at the back of the room. This squared them up and they sat whispering amongst themselves while I took charge and started the lesson.

"You'll remember that last lesson we –"

"Ooh yes, the dinosaur chase, sir," called out Atkins gleefully. "You were chasing Temms around sir."

"Really?" I said, "What was that all about?" For some moments I was genuinely puzzled until it dawned on me that this indeed had happened. We had been in the middle of the topic 'Diet' and somehow we had got onto the subject of dinosaurs and how formidable they were as predators. To illustrate this I had stomped menacingly around the room roaring like a *Tyrannosaurus*. Temms had started from his stool and, with mewling cries, pretended to be my prey, so I chased him around the room to the great encouragement of the whole class. I was pleased they had remembered it. I threw back my head and gave another *Tyrannosaurus* roar (an ability I am rather proud of having) and they all responded with roars of their own. This might have gone on some little time but I noticed the Headmaster was looking a trifle impatient so I moved on.

"Now the leaves of a plant are like the lungs of an animal when it comes to gas exchange and so forth," I went on and, like Alex, gave them a couple of introductory notes.

"Now I want you to copy down the diagram I have on this acetate," I said to them as I held it up in my hand and switched on the OHP. There was a lot of immoderate laughter because some miscreant had drawn a large red phallus on the glass of the OHP. I rubbed at it with the cuff of my jacket but this had no effect. I rubbed harder.

"Careful it doesn't shoot off, sir!" someone shouted. I must say, I found this inordinately funny and nearly collapsed in giggles – my prep school humour came rushing back! Wiping a tear from the corner of my eye I asked for a bit of quiet but to little effect - understandable really: it was a very funny comment. I was rather jealous of the stony countenance the Headmaster maintained despite what must have been a tumult of laughter going on behind it.

Then I remembered that there was ethanol for the practical so, dabbing some up with my handkerchief, I rubbed out the offending member and put down the acetate for them to copy. I wandered around the classroom trying not to look at the pinkish smear on the screen which threatened a return of the giggles.

"You said the leaves are like the lungs, sir?" said Temms thoughtfully.

"Yes, Temms, that's right," I answered, pleased with this opportunity to show the Headmaster how I could handle the off-the-cuff parts of lessons.

"Does that mean the epidermis is like the ribcage?"

"Well I suppose you might say that," I replied. "But really the –"

"And this xylem sir, is that the bronchiole?" butted in Atkins.

"Don't be stupid," said Temms, "that would be this phloem (he pronounced it 'fleem') thing. The xylem is more like the pleural fluid I'd say. And that would make the diaphragm the...the...the spongy mesophyll!" he finished triumphantly.

"Anyway," I interrupted hurriedly "the whole class will notice that the stomata are the pores through which the gases are exchanged. There are lots of these pores spread about on the leaf. You might be wondering what the density of them is. Well, imagine the class up on Dyke's Meadow waving flags –"

"Are there flags on leaves sir?" asked Temms

"Don't be an ass, Temms," I said testily.

"Can we go up to Dyke's Meadow to try waving flags, sir?" said Minton with hope in her voice.

"Density, sir, density – we've done that in Physics. It's all about mass times volume," chirped Atkins.

"Volume divided by mass, you mean!" shouted Mason.

"Just be quiet and get on with colouring your cells in," I said and, surprisingly, they all obediently fell in with this suggestion.

A minute or so later, out of the corner of my ear, I heard some boy talking and rounded quickly to see Grubridge saying something to the Headmaster while the latter looked over his exercise book.

"Silence!" I shouted. A hush fell as the class stopped what they were doing and turned to look at Grubridge at the back. I told him to stand up.

"Now, what were you saying, Grubridge?" I asked with the icy politeness of Alex James.

"Please sir, the Headmaster was just –"

"Don't mind me, do go on," I urged.

"Yes sir, he asked me –"

"Am I interrupting you when I start talking? Do go on."

"But if –"

"I think talking over you when you are speaking isn't going to get us very much nearer what you want to have heard, do you?" I asked.

"Not really sir, and –"
"No." I paused.

At this point the Headmaster had to stick his oar in.
"I had merely asked the boy to show me –"
"Oh please, do go on."
"As I said, I merely –"
I stopped him by raising a hand and both eyebrows. After a few seconds he turned away and began writing furiously on the paper on his clip-board. A strong contrast there with the good grace of Stratford I thought to myself!

After all this chit-chat, my introduction to the practical work was inevitably rather hurried and I admit I did overlook the great emphasis that Alex had put on switching off the Bunsen burner before removing the test tube of ethanol from the boiling water bath. Predictably, it was Mason who lifted out the test tube with tongs only to find the ethanol fumes caught light to produce a foot-long tongue of flame. Equally predictably, rather than quietly putting the tube back into the beaker, he dropped it with a loud cry. The ethanol poured out of the tube and along the bench in a flaming line, causing several of the exercise books to catch fire. This caused consternation amongst the other pupils and two or three more test tubes of ethanol caught fire and were thrown to the ground. Keeping calm, I pressed the fire alarm bell and then took the carbon-dioxide fire-extinguisher and, aiming it at the flaming exercise books, pressed the handle on the nozzle. The jet of gas blew fragments of flaming paper into the air to catch more ethanol fumes alight and soon there was a fair conflagration going – including the surface of the OHP I remember noticing with some impressive clarity of mind. It was unlucky that some stray ethanol spilled into the Headmaster's lap but a prolonged blast from my extinguisher soon quenched the flames. It was hardly my fault that the very low temperature of the carbon dioxide gas had such a severe chilling and hospitalizing effect on what Martin Starr called 'The Headmaster's family allowance'.

Later, once the fire brigade had declared the shell of Biolab 4 to be safe, Alex James looked around the charred and blackened remains of the laboratory and assured me that I had "given an unforgettable lesson". I suppose he was right: it seemed a fair appraisal.

Episode 4

From his diary: Thursday 20th May 1968

What a terrific game of cricket! The recollection of the tenseness and excitement that occurred in this evening's thrilling game has made the adrenaline course through my veins once again – my heart is beating hard, my mouth is dry, I can scarcely hold my pen (which, I notice, has once again been leaking slightly so that my fingers are slightly blackened. I must take it back to the shop and get it put right. You would have thought in this day and age that a decent ink pen could be manufactured. A quill would be more reliable!). Having just put a shorter résumé in my letter to Mother, I can now dilate on the day's events: how we so nearly famously vanquished our great rivals!

*   *   *

Was it only twelve hours ago that Duncan Gownsend approached me through the fuggish clouds of cigarette smoke as we sipped our morning break-time sherries in the Masters' Common Room?

"Ah, Gownsend," I said, guessing that he had come to me to complain about my punishment of one of the bone-headed boys in Dark Grange, where he is the Housemaster. "I can tell you that Pawson's behaviour in class really was quite intolerable and thoroughly warranted my –"

"Never mind all that, Wentworth," he cut in in his high-pitched, quavering and slightly querulous voice, "I've got something far more important to ask you." I bent my head intelligently towards him. "As you may know, I am captain of the Obelisks and I'd like to invite you to play for us this evening. I know this is late notice but I've been told you're a damned decent player and poor Doubleday has had to cry off at the last minute because his wife is having certain complications with the birth of their child." His expression took on the puzzled look of someone not entirely able to credit a man missing a cricket match for something merely domestic such as this. "Will you play? It's one of our most important games – cup match against Tinbridge School."

What an honour! I knew that the staff cricket team ('The Obs') played at a high level of excellence, with two ex-county players and several at league standard. And, of course, our local rivals, Tinbridge, boasted an ex-international in their ranks. Although uncertain how my record as a cricketer – a few inter-house matches while at prep school – had got parlayed up to 'damned decent player', I was not one to let the side down. "Delighted to, Gownsend," I said and we made arrangements about getting to the ground later.

*   *   *

I'm afraid my Biology classes were rather neglected for the rest of the day – I got the boys copying out notes from the text book as I day-dreamed about the game to come and practised a few of the shots I'd seen batsmen playing. In the last class of the afternoon, some of the more perceptive boys noticed this and offered to bowl balls of crunched-up paper at me. I was game and soon all the boys had joined in and a positive blizzard of paper balls was coming at me. With a handy yardstick I slashed and hooked, sliced and pulled with much vim and vigour, shouting encouragements and imprecations while the boys roared for 'wickets', 'catches' and 'LBs'. All of a sudden, the paper balls ceased to fly and, surprised, I looked back at the class (my eyes having been following a particularly juicy square cut towards the skeleton fielding on the boundary). They were sitting meekly at their desks with expressions of rapt attention on their faces. Then I noticed the Headmaster and five or six prospective parents were frowning in through the window. I waved the yardstick in their direction and smiled cheerfully – I knew the Headmaster would applaud this extra practice I was putting in for the good of the team – but he merely turned away and briskly shepherded the parents towards the newly-erected temporary huts that currently constitute the Language Block.

*   *   *

Later, I stood by the practice nets taking in the perfection of the ground – The Header – laid out like an emerald green carpet before the magnificent chapel and other imposing buildings of the venerated school that is Tinbridge. Knots of boys in boaters and tails were slowly moving to swell the ranks of spectators on the slopes where I could pick out butlers serving champagne and canapés to the great and the good. Out on the wicket, a single bent old groundsman was applying a besom reverently to the crease. The air was clear, still and scented with freshly-mown grass; the sky a soft and pearly blue. I was entranced.

"For God's sake, Wentworth, what the hell are you dressed as?" Gownsend expostulated.

"It's the only sports kit I have at the moment," I replied. He looked at my collarless white shirt, black knee-length footer bags and grubby plimsolls. I realised that my apparel might introduce a slightly jarring note to the peculiar beauty of a cricket match on an English summer's evening, but I had had no time to borrow a more fitting costume. I'd used my Old Beckhamians tie as a belt around the bags but this touch was not enough to rescue me from Gownsend's strictures. He hustled me back into the changing room and, from his own kit-bag, gave me a pair of cream trousers and an 'Obs' cricket sweater. They fitted pretty well once I'd turned up the cuffs of legs and sleeves a few times. This second changing that took place meant that, unfortunately, I had had no chance for any warm-up in the nets and so no-one on the team had any idea of my abilities with bat or ball.

Sixokes were in the field first and we strolled out to a smattering of polite applause. Gownsend approached me, nonchalantly tossing a new ball from hand to hand. He smiled.

"You look fine, Wentworth. Look, sorry about snapping earlier – was a bit keyed up, don't you know?" This was handsome of him and I nodded appreciatively. He drew a little closer and became rather conspiratorial.

"These Tinbridge chappies know our team inside out usually - but you will be an unknown quantity, old man. I want to spring a surprise on them by having you open the bowling. What's your style?" He looked at me expectantly.

"I can do over-arm," I said, modestly.

For some reason, this made him laugh out loud and, throwing me the ball, he said "That's good enough for me!" He went about setting a field while I eyed up the pitch. It looked a long way to the set of stumps at the far end. Indeed, the stumps themselves appeared to be an especially diminutive toy set.

A great cheer went up as Tinbridge's opening batsmen strode commandingly towards us. Freddie 'Stonewall' Walston, who had opened the batting for England on many occasions in the 1950s, took guard and glanced imperiously around at the field. The umpire looked at me and said, "Right arm over?" Unsure what he meant, I nodded, unable to trust myself to speak. I was quite petrified at that moment and, ever the good captain, Gownsend gave me a reassuring pat on the back and murmured that Walston was rather susceptible to the lifting delivery early in his innings and so he was going to position himself at leg-gulley. "Right-ho," I croaked. The umpire called, "Play!"

I took a couple of shuffling steps and lobbed the ball towards Walston. It bounced twice before reaching him. Just after I'd released it, he'd given the ball a surprised look, then he waited. And waited. After the second bounce, with exaggerated care he played an immaculate forward defensive and the ball came trickling back up the wicket and into my trembling hands. Both batsmen – indeed, all the players on the ground – were laughing at this, the Great Man's response to Sixokes' surprising sally.

When my second ball followed the same trajectory, Walston stepped forward and dispatched it back over my head for six. He gave me a thin smile. Gownsend rushed up to me.

"Stop messing around now, Wentworth – send down the quick stuff," he ordered.

"This is the only way I can bowl," I said. He was aghast.

"But I was told you took 4 for 25 in the Varsity Match last year..." he said with a desperate note in his voice.

"I was at Birmingham," I told him quietly. "And I've not played very much cricket." At this he actually smote his brow and, with something I didn't catch, started to rearrange the field taking away all the close fielders and scattering them to far-flung corners of the ground. Walston scored 22 off the remaining 4 legitimate deliveries. There were also 4 wides. So, after the first over, Tinbridge were 32 without loss: not the best of starts for us. It got worse.

Gownsend decided to apply maximum pressure on Tinbridge's other batsman and stationed all fielders close to the bat while Ernie Graves marked out his preternaturally long run-up. I was put at short mid-wicket. Graves swept in and sent down a fearsome yorker on leg-stump. The batsmen got a leading edge and the ball ballooned up towards me. I snatched at it; snatched a second time; finally, the ball dribbled along the ground at my feet. While I was dropping this dolly, the batsman had decided to run – indeed, he had got a third of the way down the wicket when Walston, leaning casually on his bat at the non-striker's end, calmly called 'No!' In turning, the batsman stumbled. Three stumps were fully exposed and I swooped on the ball to throw down the wicket. Gathering the ball up smoothly, I hurled it with all my strength. With a cry, Falconer at fifth slip collapsed clutching his knee and the ricocheted ball sped away to the boundary for four. Having Falconer stretchered off was a terrible blow – our best batsman retired hurt without facing a ball. Tinbridge were now 36 without loss; Sixokes down to ten men.

One sees the point that thinker johnny made about 'adversity necessitates nobility' (a phrase drummed into us at school by 'Joff' Brown, our Latin master though I can't for the life of me remember the name of the chap who said it first, or indeed, the actual Latin tag. I can almost hear Joff now, making that curious humming noise of his before pronouncing with a sorry shake of his head, "Wentworth, Wentworth, what are we to do with you?" Funny thing, memory.). Anyway, here we were, facing top-notch rivals; facing a superb batsman who had just carted the ball to all distant points; facing the loss of one of our own crack players; in short, facing defeat. We had plenty of adversity; Ernie Graves stepped in with the nobility.

Graves was furious. Throughout the time it took for poor Falconer to be carried back to the dressing room he paced and fumed, grimaced and glared, the epitome of rage. Finally, when the ball was thrown to him, he almost seemed to take a great bite out of it has he stamped back to his mark and then rushed back in to hurl the ball down the wicket. The stumps were flattened. A new batsman arrived: the stumps were flattened. Another batsman: an edge to the 'keeper. Dot ball. Last ball of the over: edge to second slip. It was magnificent bowling – 4 wickets in the over and Tinbridge now on 36 for 4. I didn't join in the muted and steely celebrations among the rest of the team from my position at deep fine leg but the hushing of the nearby crowd during this procession of wickets was like a charge of electricity down my spine. We were well and truly back in the game!

It was cat and mouse stuff for the rest of the Tinbridge innings. Every time they seemed to have started to establish a partnership with the adamantine 'Stonewall', a wicket would fall and the runs would dry up for a time. Walston himself was magnificent and, at the start of the twentieth and final over, had scored 91 out of his side's 122 runs.

Gownsend brought himself on to bowl that last over and, again, set an aggressive field to limit the scoring: five close fielders with three others patrolling the boundary. I was one of those three, alert and alive at long-on. Gownsend's first ball was a cunningly drifted off-break which dipped in at the last moment before cutting viciously off the pitch. Walston took a pace down the wicket and hit a terrific off-drive, the ball flashing past Gownsend and hurtling straight towards my ankles. Instinctively, I leapt out of the way and the ball thudded into the boundary boards behind me. The momentary self-congratulation at my speed of reaction to danger was soon over-ridden by embarrassment due to the laughs and jeers of the boys in the crowd. As my cheeks reddened, someone threw me the ball which, unfortunately, I fumbled and dropped which provoked even more laughter. Much chastened, I lobbed the ball back towards Gownsend who was standing at the wicket with his hands on his hips.

His second delivery was a quick, darting ball, cleverly disguised, which speared in on Walston's pads. Walston took a pace back into his crease and crashed the ball back past Gownsend and, again, towards me at a stupendous speed. Shutting my eyes, I knelt down in its path and held out both hands, palms-first, in the direction of the ball. There was the sound of the ball thudding into the boundary boards behind me. Sheepishly, I retrieved the ball before anyone in the crowd had a chance to throw it, ignoring the unflattering comments that were thrown instead.

I noticed Gownsend waving me in so I trotted back with the ball. He took it from my hand without a word. Then, teeth clenched, with a gesture of his head he indicated that I should field back at short mid-wicket once again. While he re-set other fielders at other positions on the square, I worked out his ploy: Walston was now on 99 and would be keen to get his century and the field was set to block the singles by which he might easily achieve it.

Gownsend's third delivery was a peach – a slow arm ball which completely deceived Walston and was taken just past the leg stump by our redoubtable 'keeper, Tony Gray, who immediately whipped off the bails with a tremendous 'howzat!' The square-leg umpire (who was Tinbridge's captain) pushed out his lower lip and shook his head. After nodding his appreciation at the bowler, Walston took guard again.

The fourth delivery was even more subtle. It looped up, hanging invitingly in the air before hitting the wicket where the overspin caused it to scud at ankle-height straight at the stumps. Walston was just about equal to it; jumping back into his crease and jabbing down on it, sending the ball harmlessly back up the wicket to the hard-eyed Gownsend. It was wonderful stuff!

A couple of players afterwards told me that they'd never seen anything like the fifth ball which was an absolute jaffa. Apparently it described as sort of 'S-bend' in the air before dropping like a stone and fizzing off the wicket into Gray's gloves. Walston then did something extra-ordinary: he walked down the wicket to Gownsend and shook him by the hand as a gesture of admiration. What a sportsman! A great cheer and thunderous applause came from the crowd, and all we Sixokes fielders joined in.

We settled down for the final delivery of the Tinbridge innings. What did Gownsend have up his sleeve? It turned about to be a totally innocuous slow ball without an ounce of spin or guile - one not unlike my own efforts at the outset - not a peach or a jaffa in sight. "Isn't it odd how it is these fruits that are singled out to mean a superb delivery? Obviously, 'he bowled him a banana' or 'a pineapple' wouldn't work as these are not very ball-like fruits, and cherries and watermelons are the wrong size even though they too are very juicy. But 'a lemon' might work just as well – or better still, an apple. 'He bowled him a russet' has a certain ring to it…come to think of it, isn't 'pippin' already…" I must admit that, instead of concentrating on the play at this juncture, thoughts such as these were going through my head as Walston struck the ball. Suddenly, I saw it was whistling directly towards my head! With a yelp, I turned rapidly to one side and threw up my left arm for protection and immediately experienced a searing pain in the palm of the hand. Shocked, I looked down to see what damage had been done and there, wonder of wonders, I discovered a cricket ball: I had caught the great Walston! There was a stunned silence for a moment, then something like a hushed groan from the crowd. Walston merely tucked his bat under his arm and walked slowly off the square. As he passed me I said 'Great knock, sir!' He paused ever so slightly with his eyebrows raised, then gave me a second thin smile before continuing onwards into the rising tumult of applause echoing around the ground.

*   *   *

Our team was subdued but determined: there was some confidence that we could achieve the daunting target of 131 runs in the 20 overs to win the match and go on to the next round of the cup. True, Falconer could not walk, let alone bat, but we still had Warding, who had played for Hampshire, and Gray who had hit 50 off just 68 deliveries in a match against Ode Hill. Gownsend promoted himself up the order to open with Warding and our innings began. The chatter and gaiety of the crowd soon began to abate as the metal score-board plates began to be changed swiftly and Sixokes' score rattled along with no wickets falling. We were on 90 without loss at the end of the twelfth over, Warding on 48 when I was told that it was now my stint as umpire. In cup games, the usual feature of umpiring being done by the batting side is adjusted with one 'neutral' umpire officiating. Since I was down as last to bat, I could easily be spared to umpire. I put on the long white coat and returned to the middle.

I held out my left arm while Warding tapped a couple of times at the wicket and then returned to his crease. He looked up, I dropped my arm and the bowler bowled. It was not an especially good delivery – several inches wide of off-stump, medium pace, easy bounce. Warding, his back leg close to the stumps, swung his front leg up and around and, cross-batted, attempted a brutal square cut. Unfortunately, the ball caught the lower edge of the bat and crashed into the pad of his back leg. Since it would clearly have gone on to hit the middle stump, I raised my finger and said 'That's out!" There was a stunned silence at this sad dismissal when so close to his half-century. Gownsend, standing next to me took the blow badly, no doubt shocked that Sixokes had suffered this reverse just when things were going so well.

"There hasn't even been an appeal, you ass!" he seethed. The delighted bowler politely enquired:

"Might that be given out?"

I remained calm and spoke in an even but severe tone that carried down the wicket,

"A gentleman should walk when given out by the umpire, Gownsend." Warding, with some show of good grace, trudged off slowly shaking his head at Gownsend's poor form in challenging the umpire's decision. Gownsend went half way with him, called out to the dressing room and Beamish ran out to take over the umpiring duties from me "You'd better go in and pad up," he said quietly, shrugging into the coat. I was nonplussed at getting quite so much applause as I trotted back to the changing room but the crowd were proving to be rather an odd lot.

This reversal of fortunes in the course of the match seemed to reinvigorate the Tinbridge team and the runs dried up as wickets fell regularly. Gownsend was out soon afterwards and I started towards him as he paced back towards the dressing room but Tony Gray grabbed my elbow and advised me not to commiserate just yet. I sat quietly on the boundary bench and watched the game unfold.

It was Gray himself who batted with his customary brio and brought Sixokes back to the brink of victory: 7 deliveries to be bowled, 2 runs to win, 1 wicket in hand. That wicket was mine and I sat, tense and thrilled, pads buckled, gnawing on the green rubber spikes on the fingers of my gloves.

The last ball of the 19th over was bowled and Gray struck it superbly towards deep mid-wicket. The Tinbridge fielder, showing the speed and agility of a panther, flung himself at the ball and plucked it from the air – Gray was out!

I walked as calmly as I could towards the wicket. Young Busby Beamish came to meet me and patted my shoulder.

"No panic, Wentworth," he said. "You can afford a sighter or two. Just lay a bat on something and look for a run then I'll finish it off with something to spare!" I wish I could say his confidence was infectious.

Since he and Gray had crossed before the latter was caught on the boundary, I was to face the first ball of the last over. I took guard tentatively and looked up the wicket. It now seemed absurdly close – I could almost touch Beamish and the umpire with the end of my bat. The Tinbridge bowler ran in and hurled the ball towards me. I closed my eyes and held out my bat. To my surprise, the ball hit it and ran out towards point. Beamish was looking enquiringly in my direction and I suddenly realised it was my call.

I accept that, to the purist who insists on sticking to the letter of the Lord's Coaching Manual, my call was not as crisp and clear as it might have been: "Yes…No…Yes…Wait…Get back, you fool!" but, to my mind at least, Beamish was rather careless in backing up quite so keenly. He was easily run out and so we had narrowly lost the game. The crowd, at least, was appreciative.

*   *   *

As I say, a terrific game of cricket to be a part of – no doubt in the Common Room tomorrow there will be a great buzz of excitement and clapping of backs in appreciation of our valiant efforts. For now though, I'd better go and wash the ink off my hands: a quotidian end to a sensational day.

Episode 5

Two letters sent following an incident at the school

June 1998

<u>To the Chief Fire Officer, Sixokes Brigade</u>

Dear Sir

I thought your comment in this week's *Sixokes Sentinel* newspaper was unworthy. I refer to your statement about your call-out to the school being the result of "the silly antics of a daft old buffer who should have known better". Quite apart from the gratuitously insulting tone, my antics were not in the least 'silly' and were, in fact, the result of aspiration and physical endeavour, two qualities I would have thought a public servant in your position might applaud rather than disparage. Let me explain the circumstances and you will then see that you are in the wrong and, I should hope, as a consequence feel honour-bound to issue a public apology.

Since you are not a teacher, you will be unaware of the utter drudgery of exam invigilation. Here, the fine minds of highly intelligent people are trapped in a large room with arrays of repellent adolescent faces poring over exam scripts with nothing whatever to do. The boredom is crashing. However, the staff at Sixokes are nothing if not resourceful and, to make the purgatory of invigilation less dire, we have devised a host of challenging games for which we either score or lose points. The points are recorded in a league table, with the top scorer at the end of the exam period winning a case of champagne. As an illustration, two of the games (played during different exam sessions of course) involve putting out too little paper for the candidates – say one or two sheets when they will need at least three or four. The first game is called 'Paper Chase' and we gain points for being the teacher to supply the candidate with paper when, inevitably, they raise their hand for it. I score well in this game – showing my physical fitness is not in doubt. The second game is called 'Diehard' and here the teacher *loses* points if they hand out paper – one has to steel oneself to ignore the often frantic arm-signalling of a candidate desperate for more paper. Many of my colleagues 'crack' quite soon in this game but, modesty aside, my steely resolve has never given way. I only mention this to illustrate that my fortitude is not to be doubted – fortitude which led to my being stuck at the top of the climbing wall when your men rescued me. I had taken up an invigilation game challenge to ascend and descend the wall in the Gym in the shortest possible time for a large number of points – something which would put me in an unassailable position at the top of the league table.

I hope that this short explanation demonstrates that you need to publicly revise your views of my character and my behaviour,

Yours faithfully,

G G Wentworth

To the Chair of Staff Common Room

Dear Chair

Before getting to my complaint, might I point out the ridiculousness of this appellation? It sounds as if I am addressing a piece of furniture (along the lines of the vocative *'mensa'* – used when making a verbal declaration to a table, a construction which was laughable when I was a schoolboy doing Latin, and is equally laughable now). I am aware that 'Chairman' contains 'man' and, to those with a limited awareness of the source of meaning carried by words, appears implicitly to insist that only men could be worthy of holding the post: 'sexist' in other words. This interpretation is as senseless as thinking that, since 'king' is in 'thinking' only kings can think! As you will remember, my opposition to the change was robust but doomed to being ignored due to the baseless sensitivities of a certain very vocal section of the Common Room. Your acquiescing to the change was spineless, in my view – and you now reap the reward of being classified with an item made merely to be sat on (though, I might add at the risk of being 'politically incorrect', being one which is also highly decorative!).

My complaint is your decision to dock me 50 points from the total I had accumulated in this year's Invigilation League. From my position leading the field, I am now trailing in amongst the 'also-rans' with no realistic chances of overhauling those in front of me. I acknowledge that my actions in the A- Level examinations in the Barley Gym led to massive disruption and invited the interpretation that the League was disreputable, but I feel your action is draconian and should be totally rescinded.

As you know, this year's new game 'Eiger Tiger' had drawn few takers – I, for one, seeing it as too divisive a game since its physical challenge would naturally exclude many of the staff. However, several factors combined to encourage my picking up the gauntlet. The first was that, due to the timetabler's machinations, I was allocated to the Barley Gym at the same time as Geoff Gibb (my closest rival for heading the League) who told me at the start that he was going to take on this year's best time for the ascent, ceiling touch, and descent of the climbing wall at the back – a record then held by the estimable Paul Flashett. A second factor was the very small number of candidates sitting the two exams going on there – 2 doing Greek and 3 doing Electronics – which meant that even a lengthy attempt would have minimal effect on one's invigilation duties. A third was the speed with which Gibb completed the task, seeming to ghost up in hardly any time at all and then having the panache to descend head-first with an occasional leg-kick of insouciance on the way: he made it look all too easy. The fourth and final factor was my being driven to the back of the gym due to the uncanniness of the three Electronics pupils. I would swear I'd never seen them in the school before. They looked identical with pasty faces, small tufts of hair sticking straight out just above the right side of the forehead, and eyes that moved independently. Unnervingly, they all seemed to be writing identically too – reaching the end of lines and pages at the same time. I checked to see if they were, in fact, triplets but no – the names on the sheet were Berke, Preston-Pangbourne and Tadd. I retreated to the back far corner of the Gym and assessed the knobbly hand- and foot-holds screwed into the wall. How hard could it be?

Afterwards, I must say that I got very little sympathy even though my ordeal, frozen with quite justifiable fear on the wall just below ceiling level, was both substantial and prolonged. I think Gibb was admirable when, after having joined me and attempting to coax me down with whispers (so as not to disturb the exam candidates), he recognised that this was not going to work and hence summoned the fire brigade, suspended the exams, cleared the candidates from the Gym and informed the school and exam authorities.

Docking me points for this is unreasonable and counter-productive. Unreasonable because I had done nothing illegal in terms of the rules of 'Eiger Tiger'; counter-productive in that such a penalty will deter others from joining in challenging new games in the future and the Invigilation League (the only thing worth looking forward during the exam sessions) may well wither on the vine. I insist that you reconsider your decision, particularly as you yourself are not entirely without guilt in this regard (unpenalised guilt I need hardly add) with your gaffe last year in awarding one of the language assistants "25 points for sustained and superior gurning during the 'Straightface' game" when, of course, she had been blissfully unaware of any such game being played during her invigilation duty (and equally unaware of what 'gurning' meant until some kind soul explained it to her) leading to her outburst of passionate wailing whenever catching sight of you right up until her departure from the school.

On the subject of 'Straightface', could I ask you to rule that no 'props' are brought in to assist in attempts to make other invigilators laugh out loud? I think that the usual contortions of face and body - and even the more elaborate mumming as in Sundip Patel's Cleese-worthy 'silly walk'; Matt Judd's 'space invader' performance; Ian Thompson's mime 'man trapped in a glass box'; and Alan West's sequence of balletic movements including his arabesque, entrechats, pas-de-deux and the ambitious if ill-advised échappé sauté which resulted in a broken desk and ankle – are perfectly acceptable here. But the bringing in of extra materials is unfair in my estimation. I am thinking particularly of Ralph Ruler's use of a noose looped through a basketball hoop to assist in his 'execution scene' and the astonishing sequence of hats (including a fez, beret, pith helmet, boater, mitre, Tyrolean trilby, flat cap, sombrero and baby's bonnet) that Paul Happiman took out of his briefcase and wore as he paraded along the back of the examination hall.

I think the case I have made here is compelling and look forward to a reversal of your decision so that I can claim my title as League Leader once more.

Yours sincerely,

G G Wentworth

Episode 6

Email to Sixokes School Teaching Staff

3rd September 2003

If our much-admired Underhead, Mike Holdon, had not been so pressing, I'm sure that Paul Happiman and I would never have joined him in Snowdonia during August's Gold Duke of Edinburgh's Award Expedition. Then, we all would have been spared the embarrassment of that unfortunate photograph which, I am told, has attracted a massive number of 'hits' by a great number of both staff and pupils since it was posted on the website of the local Welsh Hills sheep-farmers' gazette, *Topped Up*. Those of you who have seen it and read the accompanying article (unattributed as I am sure you will have noted!) will have only a highly misleading account of the 'Mountain Rescue' in which we were involved and the circumstances that led up to that unflattering picture entitled 'Erring and Straying Teachers' in which we three chubby middle-aged men appear full-frontal and stark naked apart from our walking boots and wristwatches. Here are the facts.

It was one evening last June during our usual Statesmen's Club Dinner in the local hostelry that, by chance, we found that we were all going to be in that area of Wales at the same time: Mike with the D of E; Paul in his on-going homage to Ruskin; I for a visit to a small museum in Dolgellau housing a rather rare plesiosaur fossil.

Mike insisted that we all meet up for a 'day in the mountains' and painted an enticing word-picture of the glories of the rugged natural beauty to be experienced in an untouched corner of the Snowdonia National Park. Being in a warm and wonderful mood, we heartily agreed to meet at the Boys' Brigade campsite at Diffryn Ardudwy (where Mike, other Sixokes staff and the D of E participants were camping) on the morning of the 28th August - then called for more brandy to toast the success of our future expedition to the peaks of Rhinog Fach and Rhinog Fawr.

Though Mike had invited us to 'rough it in the tents at the camp', Paul and I instead chose the cosy warmth of a B and B in Dolgellau. After serving us a splendid breakfast, Mrs Evans sorted out a picnic lunch for us: cheese-and-pickle and ham-and-tomato sandwiches in home-baked bread; a couple of her small meat pasties; two generous slices of lardy cake; two crispy snack bars; some dried fruit; a couple of juicy apples. She wrapped them all in grease-proof paper and I stowed them carefully in my daysack – Paul was happy to have our 4 litres of water and our spare jumpers in his – and we were ready for our day in the hills.

We caught an early local train which took us down the estuary and then along the Cardigan Bay sea front. The two-carriage train was packed with people and animals all off to some market or other further up the line. Paul said it reminded him of bus rides in Afghanistan where, on one occasion, a goat ate his whole briefcase with the exception of the brass fittings and a bottle of ink. Nothing quite so untoward happened this time save when a ferret escaped and caused quite a few panicky chickens to roost nervously up on the luggage rack and we had to stand to avoid eggs (or worse!) dropping on our heads. We arrived at Diffryn and walked down to the campsite to meet Mike. The weather was grey and cool.

"The forecast was not very encouraging, Mike," Paul said glancing up at the slate-grey clouds edging about above us.

"You don't want to take any notice of those national forecasts," Mike assured us. "This little corner has a micro-climate all its own. Let me tell you that today's going to be a scorcher!" This was a great relief. I was glad that I'd had the foresight to put my sun-block cream into my daysack along with some other necessaries for our day out. "We can set off straight away – Harry Coote is going to give us a lift out and will pick us up again at 4 o'clock this afternoon. Climb aboard!" Paul and I scrambled into the back of the minibus, Mike in the front, and, with a cheery grind of clutch and gears, we were off.

Not being a driver myself, I was full of admiration for the way Harry barrelled down the narrow country roads, totally ignoring the odd stones he clipped out of the walls with the wing-mirrors. He had a rather neat arrangement stuck in the middle of the wind-screen – a sort of wire rack in which he had an open book of crossword puzzles. As we sped along he read out some of the clues to us. Mike and Paul knew lots of the answers and Harry filled them in with his red biro explaining the letters were 'a bit shaky because I'm right-handed naturally'. He paused briefly as we rattled over a cattle grid, then finished filling in the clue before turning round and saying to me:

"Is Koff alright back there with you two?"

Koff is Harry's lovely dog who goes everywhere with him. Her usual place was on the front seat with her nose pressed against the windows and barking at anything that moved. In the back with us, she kept struggling to get back to 'her' seat, scrabbling away at Paul, me and the daysacks that got in her way - I decided to keep a firm hand on her collar.

Very soon, we arrived at the head of Cwm Nantcol and disembarked pulling our daysacks with us. After a smooth nine-point turn during which the bumpers bore the brunt of most of the impacts, with a wave from Harry and a bark from Koff, the minibus roared away into the greys and greens and we surveyed the magnificent soaring peaks of the Rhinogs in front of us. Our adventure was about to begin.

We strode easily along the well-marked *bwlch* (Mike gave us this local name for a path) that runs between the Rhinogs for half a mile or so and then turned sharply south to follow a trail uphill past Llyn Cwmhosan and Llyn Hywel which would lead us to the top of Rhinog Fach. We decided to drink some water before tackling the ascent. Paul and I sipped from our water bottles but Mike scoffed at us.

"Pure mountain spring water at your feet, you duffers – no need to carry that extra weight!" Kneeling down by the stream gushing down beside the trail, he dipped his face into the water and drank deeply.

"Delicious – it has that freshness and flavour you can never get from a bottle," he declared, smacking his lips with relish.

We climbed over a small brow in the hill about ten yards upstream and encountered a dead sheep, in a fairly advanced state of putrefaction, lying across the stream. Mike looked at it thoughtfully while Paul and I exchanged a glance.

"The wool will have filtered out any nasties," Mike said confidently. We carried on climbing.

It was tough-going, especially the scree slope past the wind-plucked grey surface of Llyn Hywel and the last sharp ascent from there to the peak. Unfortunately, the weather started closing in just as we arrived at the cairn of stones at the top. Fine drizzle in a thick mist whipped along by the brisk wind made us hurry over onto the lee-side of the hill and huddle in the shelter of a boulder. Mike checked the map and decided to 'take route one down'. By this he meant ignore any sign of a path or sheep-trail and plunge downhill in a straight line. "Nothing to it, really – and it will get us out of the mist and we can orientate ourselves easily," he assured us. Paul and I had, of course, total confidence in him and happily followed as he embarked on the descent.

Several precipitous outcrops barred the planned straight line option and we had to jink about quite a bit to find negotiable alternatives. Meanwhile, the mist got thicker and the rain got steadier. After about three quarters of an hour, we arrived at some levellish ground and paused to consult Mike's map. The wiry grass yielded easily beneath our feet: it was marshy and the black, peaty water rose over the welts of our boots. Visibility was now down to about ten yards or so; the rain seemed to have a grim and unwelcoming determination about it. Mike stabbed a finger at the map. "We must be just here," he said. "If we head due north we'll pick up the forest edge and can then take the *bwlch* on the other side of Rhinog Fawr. After that, if the weather clears we can get up that peak – or just contour round it to get back to the minibus in Nantcol later." I asked him if we should use a compass to get the direction. "Well, I don't bother with one myself - luckily I'm like a homing-pigeon when it comes to a sense of direction – have you got one though?" he asked. Pleased to be able to show that I had come well-equipped for all eventualities, I pulled off my daysack to get out the compass I had packed into it earlier along with the sun-cream etcetera. A shock was in store: it was not my daysack. I pulled out the contents - some dirty laundry, a first-aid kit, a packet of dog-chocs, a book of mind-games (all completed in red ink), a torch (dead), a faded red cagoule (ripped), a footpump and a tatty old sleeping bag. I must have picked up Harry Coote's daysack by mistake after the Koff kerfuffle in the back of the minibus!

"No compass," I said regretfully as I repacked the daysack.

"And no picnic either," observed Paul sadly.

"Never mind!" Mike said cheerily. "Like me, you could both stand missing a meal," he slapped his belly and laughed. "And we'll be back in time for a cream tea if we press on sharply!"

We trudged north and, an hour or so later, got off the marsh and into a mess of scree, heather and boulders. Mike was delighted.

"Just the terrain I expected," he told us. "And since we are west of the forest all we need do now is contour round to pick up the trail to Llyn Du."

Like me, Paul is not as experienced in hill-walking as Mike certainly is, and, as ever, keen to learn new terminology, he enquired about this 'contouring round' idea.

"Simple technique if you are not absolutely sure where you are to the exact square metre," Mike informed us. "All you do is walk on a contour – not going either up or down – and this will take you around the hill until you reach the path you want." Like all the best ideas, once you had had it explained clearly to you, it was obvious.

I must say that the following couple of hours were not pleasant (apart from Paul attempting to keep up spirits by coming up with the translations of the forty words that the Welsh have for rain – from 'Drizzle's Kiss' to 'God's 'rods'). The rocks we had to scramble up, down and around to maintain the contour route were all very slippery and many were very sizable indeed – not too much of a struggle for the taller Mike and Paul, but much more of a challenge for me. The heather occasionally gave way to stunted gorse which proved thornier than usual and the patches of slaty scree slipped beneath our feet at every step. The rain dripped off my hood and crept up the sleeves of my waterproof jacket. The ever-thickening mist was disorienting in magnifying shapes which loomed ahead of us. Occasionally we put a foot into an unseen shin-deep pock-hole of stinking water. We stopped and sat on some boulders for a rest and Mike pulled out his packed lunch – a couple of flabby lettuce sandwiches – and shared it with us.

"I've been thinking about this 'contouring round' thing," said Paul carefully. "What if the contour we are following is one which is *above* the path we want – won't it just mean that we go right around and get back where we started?" I must say that the same thought had been niggling away at the corners of my mind too. Mike shook his head and showed us the map.

"Can't happen," he said flatly, pointing to the centre of the map. "We must have started here at this level – which brings us neatly around to the path." Paul considered this as he gazed at the map.

"But if we were just a few meters lower on *this* contour line," he said slowly and touched a place slightly different from Mike's, "we would miss going around the Rhinog, miss the path and end up..." his finger followed the contour. "...well to the north of Cwm Bychan and nearly half-way to Harlech." He raised his eyebrows and looked at Mike. I thought Paul was on to something with this analysis. Mike smiled and put us right.

"Perhaps I can't have explained the principle carefully enough," he said gently. "When we mountain leaders resort to contouring round, it is because we are confident in our position, are aware of the map-terrain confirmatory actualities, have taken on board the climatic, physiological, geographic, vegetational and geological factors, and..." he paused with a serious look on his face before allowing a broad smile to spread across it "...know how best to get to our cream tea!" Reassured, we scrambled to our feet and pressed onwards around the mountain.

At 8 o'clock, with darkness gathering, hours after the time we had arranged to meet Harry and the minibus, we were still in the scree/heather/rock stuff that we had been in for what seemed, to me, like a life-time. Mike had stopped consulting the map because he had noticed that every time he did, Paul seemed to get more disconsolate. We stopped for a rest and Mike had another idea to help get us to the path to Nantcol. While Paul rooted in my (well, Harry's) daysack for the dog-chocs which he thought might raise his blood-sugar level, Mike took out the map and said, "assuming our rate of travel has been about one and a half clicks and that we are now more or less here, if we climb up for a couple of hundred meters, we will run into this stone wall – and we can simply follow it down to Nantcol. Should be there in an hour easily." Paul sucked gingerly on a dog-choc for a few seconds then spat it out. Apparently it tasted more of dog than choc. Wearily, we climbed after the irrepressible Mike through the teeming rain and deep-grey clinging fog, the vision of scones with jam and cream and a nice hot round pot of tea spurring us on.

An hour later we encountered not a wall but a largish body of water. Mike was triumphant.

"Now we will know exactly where we are!" he crowed as Paul and I puffed up alongside him. "This lake will tell us precisely where we are once we've identified it on the map." We all crowded around the map to look. To my untrained eye, there were rather a lot of little lakes around: not just Cwmhosan, Hywel and Du – but also Morwynion, Perfeddau, y Bi and Gloyw lyn.

"The shape gives it away, you see," Mike said. "Let's all take a rest and I'll sort out the position and the best way home." We settled on a patch of turf right next to the lake. As we were all quite cold, I had the idea of using the old sleeping bag in Harry's daysack as a cover for our legs as we sat around. I pulled it out and we all snuggled together under it while Mike did his planning. After a couple of minutes, I started feeling rather itchy. At about the same time, Paul and Mike began scratching at their heads and necks. I looked closely at their faces and saw small dark specks moving on them. Then I looked down at the sleeping bag – it must have been Koff's and was alive with dog fleas! The others had noticed this at the same time and, jumping up, we could feel the fleas crawling down into the warmth beneath our waterproofs.

"Quick – into the lake!" called Mike, tearing off all his clothes and boots and immersing himself. Of course, we were quick to follow his example. It was very cold – but effective in clearing us of the fleas. We rinsed out our boots and put them back on. Our clothes, however, were still crawling with the little beasts. I had a bright idea.

"Fleas are attracted to warmth so all we need do is build a fire and put our clothes near it. The fleas will jump towards the heat and so leave our clothes flea-free. All we need is some dryish heather – the stuff near the base should be alright despite the rain. And we can get warm while we wait," I added.

Half an hour later we had got together quite a mound of heather but it was rather damp. "What I need to help light this stuff, chaps,"

I said, "is some spunk." A horrified expression appeared on Mike's face but Paul's lit up at once.

"D'you know," he said, "I've not heard that word used verbally in that way before. I came across it in *Kidnapped* – 'spunks of decency'. Where'd you get it from?"

"At University," I replied. "We had some talk about bracket fungi that could be used in the preparation of tinder. The lecturer referred to these as 'spunk' and it stuck in my mind," I replied.

Though the complete absence of trees ruled out this material for lighting a fire, I suddenly remembered the first-aid kit in Harry's daysack. I took out the bandages and tore off the cotton wool padding. This was highly flammable and burnt at a high temperature. With a few sparks from my penknife on a handy stone, I soon had a good crackling blaze going. We crouched around it, welcoming the warmth. It was then that we heard noises sweeping close by and a voice call out "Here they are!" We stood up all together and turned towards the person calling out. It was at that precise moment that a blinding flash struck our eyes – the flash of a camera capturing us in that awkward pose.

The Mountain Rescue Team assured us that the photograph was merely for 'training purposes' but, as you have probably seen, this was unreliable. At least they had the decency to pixelate our generative organs although, as Mike said, he would rather they had pixelated his face than the other feature since 'no-one on Earth would recognize me from *that*!' Spoken like a true leader. (Oh, and excepting the apples, Koff scoffed our picnic.)

Episode 7

From his diary

17th September 1983

Naturally enough, one expects a new Headmaster to stir things up a bit, if only to justify a 'presence' in the School. Hence, I was unsurprised to be summoned to his study for what was billed as 'a little chat about your position' by the new man who took on the job last September, Richard Broker. I spoke of this summons beforehand to Tony Cobberly, one of our most senior masters and notable for finding any sort of authority irksome, and he gave me some advice.

"Don't let him tread all over you, Dob. He has hardly anything academic in his background, so you needn't feel he has any sort of intellectual superiority even over you. He's just a manager – and full of all that guff about running a school like a business. He uses a manager's tricks to keep us on our toes – or our knees. Stand up to him. Fox him with knowledge he cannot have; don't immediately do what he asks; don't let him get one up on you."

Mustering myself outside the Headmaster's study, I squared my shoulders and, turning the door-knob smartly, threw open the door and stepped in. Rather deflatingly, the room was empty. I went out again only to be tapped on the shoulder.

"Come back in, Wentworth," said the Headmaster in a somewhat weary and resigned tone. He led the way back into the room and went across to the window overlooking Carriage House lawn where he stood with his back to me rubbing his nose.

"Sit down, won't you?"

I thought this a management ploy – by my sitting down he would remain on his feet and hence in a more authoritative position.

"I think I'll stand actually," I said, trying to put some airiness into my tone.

"As you wish."

He turned and slid into a comfortable chair a few feet in front of me. Immediately, I felt like an errant child stood before a forbidding father and wished that I too was seated. My feet seemed huge and I had no idea what to do with my hands. He watched me like a snake, apparently relishing this discomfort.

"Quite a few staff left last term," he observed.

I kept silent since he obviously expected a comment from me.

"A good independent school needs the best management," he went on. "And the best management cuts away whatever is useless, Wentworth, whatever isn't pulling its weight."

He paused and I tried to consider what he had in mind in the School that 'pulled its own weight'. Perhaps he was thinking of the new scrummaging machine? Or had he confused me with being a Physics teacher where, I know, they do pulleys and things? While I was wool-gathering in this way he went on:

"The School cannot afford any dead wood."

He looked over my head and allowed his gaze to become fixed. I wondered what it was that had captured his interest and craned around – perhaps it was a picture, or some exotic insect he wished to draw my attention to?

While the back of my head was towards him he went on in a dreamy sort of voice, "Are you dead wood, Wentworth?"

Blast the man; he had managed to put me completely on the back foot with this staring manoeuvre. I went on the attack:

"Not dead wood, Headmaster, heart wood," I said crisply.

As I had anticipated, being a non-biologist he hadn't a clue what heart wood was. It was a term I'd heard a botany lecturer use when I was at University and, thinking myself in love with Monica Stimpson at the time, it had lodged in my mind. Seeing his incomprehension, I gave him a small but quite sympathetic smile.

"Heart wood? What's that?" he demanded. My mind went blank. What *was* heart wood?

"It's…well…as a biologist speaking to a layman, um, well it's ah-"

"You *are* a teacher, Wentworth," he interrupted silkily, "and I am not *wholly* unintelligent so I think you can venture a description of this *heart wood* and expect me to grasp it." Clutching at a few wisps of knowledge that crept from the memory I stammered, "It's…it's the material at the centre of a…well a … fine, mature tree. Very tough … gives it strength … solid." My tongue felt like a dry foam-rubber sponge. "Good for making chopping boards," I heard myself blurt out at last.

The Headmaster allowed a long silence to grow between us before saying very quietly and slowly, almost to himself, "Good for chopping boards…" After a few more interminable seconds he suddenly reached out to the table beside him and picked up a report slip before turning back to me.

"I'm concerned about our reporting to parents, Wentworth, and I want to produce something to help guide staff in their report-writing such that parents identify our academic and pastoral input and throughput as both maximal and optimal. Currently, I don't feel all staff share this approach. Read this out, will you?" He hardly extended the hand holding the report slip so I had to bend forward in a sort of obeisance to take it from a hand that remained unmoved throughout. I straightened and then read out:

"Your son is an ass: work-shy, thick-headed and obstinate. His marks are woeful; his prospects dim."

There was a fairly long pause.

"One of yours, Wentworth, I believe," he drawled.

This was one of my finer efforts in my humble opinion: pithy with both insight and truth together with a touch of schoolmasterly humour. I hurried to acknowledge it.

"Certainly, Headmaster." I felt some self-confidence surging back. "I think it accurately sums up Atkins and his performance in Biology" I said briskly, with what I considered some justifiable pride and then handed the report back to him.

"And what do you think Mr and Mrs Atkins made of this... report?" He raised his eyebrows but, having been in the game for nearly 20 years, I recognised a rhetorical question when I hear one and kept quiet. "They'll think that we are not doing our job." I noticed the plural and was feeling grateful until he went on: "Or rather, that *you* are not doing *your* job, Wentworth."

He got up and slowly walked around the room until he was behind me. I was at a bit of a loss here – was I meant to keep swivelling on my feet to keep him in view? Or prowl about alongside him? Obviously, this was one of his management techniques to unsettle the opposition. I took the initiative and strode to the door saying, "Righto, Headmaster."

"Where the hell do you think you're going?" he called, clearly rattled at this display of self-assurance.

"Oh, had we not finished?" I said brightly, hand on the door-knob.

"No we have *not* finished," he said testily. "I want reports from teachers to be always positive and encouraging. I want nothing negative in them at all." Seeing that my expression was one of non-conviction he went on smoothly, "Parents nowadays expect teachers to show *care* about their child's academic progress, mental development and character formation. They expect – indeed, they pay to expect – reports that single out something special and praiseworthy in their child, reports that reflect a deeper concern for their child's well-being, reports that–"

"Don't tell the truth?" Feeling he deserved it, I was blunt.

"Don't be obtuse, Wentworth. You know perfectly well that modern schooling requires modern methods. Since you are, if I may say so, perhaps the biggest dinosaur on the staff in this respect, I want you to lead the change to more sympathetic reporting."

He paused and I warmed to the man a little. Being singled out as comparable to a dominant leader of one of the most awesome and successful groups of creatures ever to roam the Earth was a noteworthy compliment and I unbent towards him.

"Of course, Headmaster, I will always wish to help keep Sixokes in the forefront of education –"

"So," he cut across me swiftly and laid a hand on my shoulder. "I want you to produce a guide to all staff which spells out the terms that should be included in reports." I opened the door and felt him gently pushing me through it.

As I walked slowly and dispiritedly away he called out.

"And Wentworth…chop, chop, eh?"

Tuesday 18ᵗʰ September 1983

When I recounted the gist of my interview to Cobberly and Richard Hansum they cheered up no end. "We'll help you produce the guide, Dob old chap. In fact, leave it all to us and we'll put your name to it and that'll get him off your back for good." I reflected gratefully on what it was to have such friends. They put their heads together and came up with the advice below which I sent to the

Headmaster and for which he telephoned through his gratitude for what he described as 'probably the best I could hope for'.

Staff Guidance on the New Report Writing Style

What you write	**What you mean**
Industrious	Works without thinking
Reflective	Thinks without working
Independent	Friendless
Lively	Excessively noisy
Personable	Smarmy
Eager to please	Dim
Focused	Blinkered
Open-minded	Empty-headed
Diligent	Pedestrian
Able	Good enough
Capable	Not nearly good enough
Writes fluently	Sentences too long
Writes clearly	Sentences too short
Occasionally struggles with…	Dim
A leader	A trouble-maker
Expressive	A show-off
Creative	Doodles a lot of the time
Inventive	Dishonest
Finds some of the work a challenge	Dim
Perceptive	Cocky
Willing	Biddable
Participative	Rowdy

Assertive	Lippy
Should ask more questions	Dim
Should participate more in class	Bored a lot of the time
Eager	Juvenile
Confident	Arrogant
Sensitive	Precious
Popular	Excessively chatty
Witty	A clown
Delightful	No trouble
Thoughtful	A dreamer
Individualistic	Uncooperative
Tenacious	Obstinate
Conscientious	Ponderous
Clever	Glib
Excellent	Good
Very Good	Fair
Good	Acceptable
Fair	Pathetic
Poor	Abysmal

Episode 8

Two extracts from his diary plus an inserted letter

Sunday December 1ˢᵗ 1999

I felt a little humbled this afternoon after reading a note that had been pushed through my letter-box. It was from the Bensons and contained an apology for their 'little Billy' coming into my garden through the hedge to retrieve his football, together with an invitation for me to spend this coming Christmas lunch with them. I suppose they must have read the obituary in the *Sixokes Sentinel*. I regretted having peppered the boy this morning with a mouthful of dried peas from my pea-shooter from my vantage point in the back bedroom when I saw him sneaking through the hedge yet again despite my objections about this in the past. I went around to accept the invitation and, to show that bygones were bygones, returned the arrows, tennis and cricket balls, kite, Barbie doll, trainer, soldier on a parachute, boomerang, plastic bucket and spade, toy fire engine and model fort that I had confiscated after they had sailed over from their property into ours during the last few months. We all solemnly shook hands. I admit that for the rest of the evening I was rather misty-eyed.

*   *   *

Wednesday December 25ᵗʰ 1999

Never having had a Christmas day that wasn't spent quietly as just Mother and me before, I can say that the way that it was approached by the Bensons was something of a revelation: they treated it as a riotous excuse for all sorts of excessive behaviour.

I had made due sartorial deference to the special nature of the day by wearing a bow-tie rather than a neck-tie when I presented myself at their door punctually at 1 o'clock, but was wholly unprepared for the licence the Bensons allowed themselves in this regard. They were all in fancy dress costumes. I was greeted by a Cleopatra 'well past her sell-by date' (an apposite phrase I had overheard one of the Third Form pupils using with reference to her tutor, Miss Fittock, recently recruited to add gravitas but, alas, not pulchritude in any form, to the History Department) wearing an alarmingly low-cut flowing silk number (the maiden aunt, Dorothy or, as she giggled "Just think of me as Dotty, pet, everyone else does! And here's a 3-pint head in a ten-gallon hat!") waving forward... a General Custer complete with spurs and sword (Mr Frankie Benson with a "Where did I put my little big-horn, wifey!") while throwing an arm around... a Liza Minelli in black sequined cocktail dress, black-plumed headband and fish-net stockings (who was Mrs Rhoda Benson belting out *"What good is sitting alone in your room?"* with greater success in terms of sentiment and gesture than tunefulness) and pushing forward 'the kiddies'... a Batman rather tinier and more chocolate-stained than the original (Little Billy offering a handshake with a concealed mild electric shocking device); a Living Dead who was just black, white and red all over (Nancy with a convincing sickening leer and a disarming curtsey); and an Elephant (Little Freddie in cardboard mask and howdah shuffling and stomping in the narrow hallway). I presented my offering of the home-made Christmas pudding to Liza and, after being symbolically dubbed 'Sir George of Number Twenty-Eight' by the inordinately chuckle-headed General Custer with his wavering plastic sword, we pressed on into the sitting-room for 'another gargle or two'.

"Now then, Mr W – or can I say George? – no, I can now say SIR George!" shouted my host in a fit of laughter and cheers from the others (and an 'Arise Sir George – oh no, he's already standing up!' from one of the 'kiddies' but I wasn't quick enough to round on them to catch which) "What's your tipple? What's your fancy? What will whet your whistle and tickle your tonsils?" He lightly punched my shoulder and gestured expansively with his gauntleted hand at a stunning array of beverages arranged on a side table by the wall. I looked at them searching for something familiar amongst the plethora of bewildering shapes and colours – a few there that stick in the mind were: 'Granny's Egg-nog and Dubonnet' in a violent red and yellow twisted bottle; 'Zummarrzet Zider, Peppermint and Vodka Cocktail' in a ring-pull can; 'The Original Rat's-Arse Ozzie Chardonnay' in a battered cardboard box – before settling on the plainest on offer.

"I think a small scotch, thank you," I said, helpfully pointing at the bottle of Bell's towards the back of the crowd.

"Och aye, the noo!" roared the General. "And there's no wee in this hoose, I'll have ye knoo!" This sally produced more gales of laughter from the others as he seized a tumbler and glugged it half full. "Did you hear aboot the alcoholic teacher, Sir George? His life was ruled by Bell's!" I smiled as pleasantly as I could and accepted the glass while looking around the rest of the room trying to find a compliment.

This proved difficult. Apart from the table of bottles, every surface was festooned with the tackiest array of 'Christmas decorations' I have ever seen gathered in one place. Anything that did not glitter of its own accord winked in the barrage of flashing multi-coloured lights suspended from hooks around the ceiling; the massive tv screen (on, of course, but thankfully muted) was wreathed in silver-effect holly and ivy; a quarter-size, wall-mounted, battery-driven, motion-sensitive, crimson-suited Santa kicked up his black velvet booted legs as he roared 'Ho-ho-ho! Here's a reason to be jolly!'; and in the furthest corner of the room a small herd of helium-filled inflatable reindeer jostled shoulders with each other and a vast cotton-wool snowman wearing a rakish top-hat with 'Merry Christmas One and

All!' written on it. Finally, I raised my glass towards the tree crowded behind the fake polar-bear skin bedecked sofa.

"Someone has put in a lot of effort there," I said. The green plastic branches positively dripped with shiny, tasteless baubles in the most garish colours imaginable and prompted a wistful recollection: the subdued, gently resinous tree that we always had; *Carols from King's* on the wireless; Mother and I sharing the decorating; the small red wooden apples and understated woven corn angels and snowflakes, the silver-glitter-glued cardboard star I had brought home as a child from primary school sitting on the top; sherry, a couple of crackers and an exchange of gifts. A powerful blow between the shoulder-blades nearly knocked me off my feet and it took some acrobatic ability to avoid spilling my whisky.

"Bless you, Sir George!" the General shouted. "It came all pre-done! All we had to do was pull it out of its box and straighten the branches!" Having no comment to make, I sipped the whisky. Then, thinking of the next couple of hours ahead, took a more substantial mouthful. Liza came in rather superbly with more of her rendition:

"Start celebrating/Right this way your table's waiting!"

"Lunch is served," said Cleopatra and, slipping her arm through mine, she tugged me into the dining room and settled me down in a chair next to hers. I will gloss over the meal only noting the novelty of the Benson family's approach to the tradition of Christmas Dinner. It seems that Mr Frankie 'General Custer' Benson is the Retail Outlet Supervisor at Gatwick Airport and 'uses his pull' to secure 'special seasonal' airline ('BA too – nothing but the best of British, Sir George') dinners in individual microwavable plastic trays. We even used disposable plastic knives and forks ('which saves little Liza from anything like loading the old dish-washer') as we speared and cut ineffectually at the uniform slices of pressed turkey breast stained with clots of cranberry jam and what is generally called 'all the trimmings': a crisp and gluey gob of stuffing, bullet-like sprouts, flaccid carrot batons, soggy roasted potatoes, all gripped in a viscous brown gravy. Copious quantities of generally fizzy drinks were offered and consumed by the others while I stuck doggedly to the whisky.

I had hoped that the Christmas pudding that I had brought – made by Mother in early November as she always did – might allow some small semblance of tradition to intrude. We had always enjoyed the ritual of the flaming brandy, the rich scents of fruits and spices, the anticipation of the lucky sixpence. I mentioned the possibility to Cleopatra as she came around the table shovelling the trays with their knives, forks and ruined remains of the main course, into a black bin-liner.

"You got no chance, pet," she said, not unsympathetically. "Rhoda always gets in chocolate trifle – the kiddies can't stand that old pudding muck – just spit it out. Trifle is what we'll be getting."

She was just about right: a fat pot of 'Mrs Sugar's chocolate-flavoured tastelicious fruit-free trifletto' with a scoop stuck thoughtfully on the underside of the lid was plonked in front of each of us by Liza with:

"Put down the knitting, the book and the broom/It's time for a holiday!"

After this final course had been summarily dealt with, we all returned to the sitting room 'for a bit of a game and some more gargling'. As I was their 'honoured and most honourable of honoured guests' I was invited to suggest the game we might play. Without having given this enough thought, I said the first thing that came into my head: "How about charades?"

Of course, none of them had ever played the game and I had to spend a few minutes rather impatiently instructing them about the rules and principles involved. Then, of course, it took several more minutes for paper and pencils - in most households, household items – to be gathered together in sufficient quantity for everyone to write down their book/film/etc. on a slip of paper, fold it and place it in the snowman's top-hat – which made me just a little bit more over-wrought. Furthermore, of course, at their unanimous insistence, I had to be the first to act. I plucked out a slip and opened it carefully: 'Lady Chatterley's Lover' stared up at me.

It didn't take too long for it to penetrate that I was going to act out a three-word book and film. Nor very much longer for them to twig that I was going to act out the third word which had two syllables. I had chosen this of the three since, with even the barest modicum of knowledge of literature, 'something something lover' would be easy to get. The six of them sat expectantly waiting for my performance. I acted out sniffing a bunch of flowers, then sank to one knee and pursed my lips in a kissing movement while offering the flowers in supplication.

"Interview!"

"Fish-face!"

"Cattle-prod!"

"Arise Sir George!"

"Kisser!"

At my looking approvingly at this last offering from Cleopatra and a 'come-on' hand gesture they began to elaborate:

"Snogger!"

"Frencher!"

"Lip-smacker!"

I frowned and shook my head sharply.

"Deep throat!"

For some reason, this produced huge laughs from the adults. I decided to cut my losses and indicated that I was going for the second word, three syllables, instead. I decided to do the 'chatter-' and the '-ley' separately: first I bent my knees, scratched both armpits, and mouthed excitedly like a monkey; then began chopping viciously at the air as the great karate fighter Bruce Lee would do.

"King Kong!"

"Jungle Book!"

"Planet of the Apes!"

All this accompanied by wholly immoderate hilarity.

Annoyed at their boneheadedness, I held up my arms and indicated that I had abandoned the second word and was going to do the first word, two syllables. Reckoning that even they would have seen Oscar Wilde's play, I minced imperiously around the room swinging an imaginary handbag just like Lady Bracknell. This brought no guesses whatsoever as they were all in paroxysms of laughter with tears streaming down their faces. In my justifiable irritation I'm afraid I swung my arm with the imaginary handbag rather too wildly in the direction of the helium-filled reindeer and set them loose. One of them drifted over the sofa towards the tree and Little Freddie swept at it with his elephant's trunk. In moving to do this, his cardboard howdah jabbed Little Billy in the eye. Billy fell back and pushed Living Dead off the sofa and brought her nose into a collision with the side table supporting the family's homage to liquor. In jumping up to save the bottles, General Custer caught his feet in the snowman's top-hat, lost his own hat and careered into the sofa which, on being violently pushed, caused the tree to topple over sideways. The flashing angel on the top of the tree fell onto his exposed head slicing into the soft bald skin the hat had concealed. Meanwhile, in simultaneously crouching forward to avoid the descending tree, Liza and Cleopatra violently bumped their heads together. All-in-all, there was quite a bit of blood.

Fortunately, my first aid at work training came to the fore and I soon had them all treated and they sat swathed in bandages, grateful and subdued in the wreckage of the sitting room. I thanked them and said it was time I was going. Liza struggled up and went and got the Christmas pudding I had brought.

"You take this with you, Mr Wentworth," she said and, as their front door slowly closed, I heard her singing softly: *Life is a cabaret, old chum/Come to the cabaret..."*

Back in the quiet and comfort of home, I wondered what I should do with the pudding – would it keep? Did I need to freeze it? I knew where to find the answer: *Delia Smith's Complete and Utter Home*

Cooking – Mother's culinary bible. I pulled it off the shelf and fondly brushed the ends of the several pieces of paper and card that she had put in as additions to and amplifications of the recipes. I looked up 'Christmas pudding' in the index and then turned to the right page. To my surprise, there I found a plain white sealed envelope with 'Georgie' written on it in Mother's hand. I sat at the kitchen table and opened it.

Dearest Georgie

I want to tell you a secret. I have given a good deal of thought over the years about whether to tell you this but have always thought it best not to. Now that I know that I will soon be gone, I have been thinking about it all over again, but cannot really make up my mind. Should I say nothing at all and let sleeping dogs die? Or write this letter and leave it to you with my will?

Neither of these seems right to me so, as you have already probably guessed, I have decided to do my usual and leave it in the hands of chance. When I have finished writing, I shall seal the envelope and toss the sixpence. If it comes up 'tails' I'll leave the letter with the will. If it comes up 'heads' I'll put it somewhere not-too-obvious where you may, or may not, ever find it.

Here, my dearest boy, are the truths I have kept secret from you and I hope and pray will not shock you too much. I have never been married. The man in the photograph that is always on my bedside table is not of your father but of someone I do not know. Your father knows nothing of your existence. Your 'Uncle Reggie' is unrelated to either of us. My surname is not Wentworth.

What is true, and has always been true, is that I have loved you from your first breath and will love you until my last.

I met your father (your biological father I suppose you would say) on the 15th June 1945. What was so special about that day for everyone was that this was the night when all the lights came back on after the war. It is hard to imagine how we had to put up with so much darkness in our lives (let alone the prospect of losing to the Germans) for so many years. At 8 o'clock, when all the lights were switched on, masses of people were on the streets and cheered and cheered. We hugged strangers, laughed, cried, shouted – it was wonderful!

I had been out with my friend Mavis (in Hastings – that part about my life before Birmingham was nearly all true, including my parents dying in a bomb-blast in Croydon and my being fostered with the Clitheroes. Except that wasn't their real name, sorry) but we got separated and I found myself next to a nice-looking man who slipped his arm around my waist and gave me a quick kiss. At just 19, I wasn't at all experienced with men but, well, I can't really explain it, Georgie, there was something about him and the night air and the atmosphere of the crowd that sort of swept me away.

He really was a very nice man. He said he was called Gordon Howard and that he was the younger brother of Trevor (you remember him, the actor – he was 'Alec' in *Brief Encounter* with Celia Johnson as what's-her-name). He did have a sort of resemblance to him too, and just the same sort of manner. He seemed quite the gentleman. I wanted to believe him. (It wasn't true, by the way – I soon found out that Trevor Howard was an only son.) He was in the RAF – told me he flew Spitfires (but I expect that wasn't true either). Anyway, later that evening we ended up in his hotel room and now I can tell you the truth about the sixpence.

When I told him my surname was Tanner (yes, that was my real surname) he laughed and started calling me his 'lucky sixpence'. He really was quite a lovable man, Georgie - jolly, kind, interested in me. He told me about how he had a silver sixpence sewn under his wings on his jacket – apparently this was what the aircrew all did for good luck. Well, in the morning when I woke up there was no sign of him – his clothes, bag, everything, were all gone. But there, on the bedside table, was the sixpence – the George III one, 1816. He must have taken it off the uniform and left it me for luck. But, of course, that wasn't all he left me.

I didn't try searching for him, not even when I realized that I might be pregnant. In the September, I went to the doctor's for a test. I had to go back a week later for the result. I remember sitting in the waiting room and picking up an old copy of *Punch* and reading a story in it about a man called Wentworth. The name stuck in my mind for some reason. The doctor was very severe when he told me I was pregnant (and really, I quite agreed with him) and, rather than going home, I went and sat on the front with the sixpence in my hand and had a bit of a cry. A couple of men walked behind me and I heard them talking about the pools and I thought to myself 'why not? You never know'. I'd never played them before but knew it was simple – just choosing matches where there would be draws. All I needed were 8 numbers. I chose my date of birth (27 and 5 and 26 from '1926'), the 'lucky' date when the lights came back on and I met Gordon (15 and 6 and 45), and the date of the sixpence, the lovely, lucky sixpence (18 and 16). And I won, Georgie, I won. £24, 139 16s 5d – a fortune in those days.

Luckily, I had asked for 'no publicity' and, as soon as the cheque arrived I ran away! I left everything behind at the Clitheroes in Hastings and took a train to Birmingham. Taking on a new identity was easy enough with all the turmoil of the war still making a mess of people's lives. I opened a bank account in the name of the widow Mrs

Wentworth, bought our house in Starling Road, found a likely-looking photograph of a man in a junk shop who I pretended was my poor dead husband, Arthur Wentworth, and devoted myself to my darling baby George (after the lucky sixpence) Gordon (after his father).

The money meant I could afford to send you to a good prep school and then on to Beckham Grange. It was a wrench when you went off as a boarder, but I thought you should have a lot of male company to balance out being an only child with just your poor old Mother the rest of the time! I was so pleased that one of them – your Mr Brown – became something of a father-figure for you and helped you to get to University. I was so proud of you, Georgie! That and making such a good life for yourself at Sixokes and, I'm sure, being a wonderful teacher.

One last fib to own up to is 'Uncle Reggie'. He was a rep for the clothes we made in the factory. He took a shine to me and we became friendly. I knew he had a wife and family in his home town (Barnard Castle he told me) but I didn't mind. We saw each other for a couple of days every month and, every summer, we took a holiday together – and you went to stay with the Chambers family. We always went to a little cottage in Portreath except once when we went to Austria to see the alpine meadows because I'd seen *The Sound of Music* and said, just casually, wouldn't it be nice to go somewhere like that? Reggie fixed it all up without telling me – he was such a nice man like that! Do you still have that great pipe he brought back for you? We didn't think about smoking being bad for you back then. It was after that trip that Reggie dropped out of my life. I've no idea why. He must have changed jobs or something. Anyway, I've never heard from him since. But my memories of him are all fond ones – I know you liked him too, Georgie, and he really was like a proper uncle wasn't he?

I will close now. The doctor said the cancer is inoperable – all those silly ciggies! – and that I haven't got long. I thought it best to keep it from you and go quietly. Least said, soonest ended, after all.

With all my love always,

Mother

X X X

PS I have put the lucky sixpence in the Christmas pudding I made for you just before I went into hospital. I always knew where it was so I could be sure you got it in your portion – there are two almonds together on the edge right next to it.

M. X

Sure enough, the sixpence was in the spoonful next to the two almonds. I wiped it clean and placed it gently on the letter next to Mother's final kiss. I closed my eyes and made a wish.

Episode 9

Draft of a letter to the Chairman of the Governors of Sixokes School

March 22nd 2001

Dear Lord Sackbut

Being precipitately and heavily rugby-tackled to the ground in the mud and rain by a burly member of the Royal Protection Squad as I chatted easily to Duke of Edinburgh was a shock. Seeing the film of it later on the *News At Ten* was something of a humiliation especially when, during the accompanying interview, the Headmaster spoke of my behaviour as being 'both fatuous and misguided'. I will admit that this construction might seem the obvious one to put on the events leading up to the disruption of the Royal Visit to the school yesterday, but, given the background, I think history will vindicate me when the attendant circumstances become better known.

It all started in January at the beginning of term Staff Meeting in the Common Room. My usual chair is a lone survivor of the 'makeover' that was forced upon us last year. Its partners, together with the maroon flock wallpaper, history-soaked brown carpet, running bar, full-sized billiard table, cigarette and tobacco machines, and range of sporting magazines on the old scarred tables, were, apparently, not good enough for a vocal section of new staff who swept all this away in favour of chintz and chemical air-fresheners. Be that as it may, at least grudging respect was paid in allowing my favourite chair to be tolerated in the dingiest corner of the room. It was in this chair that I settled down to doze through the administrative drudgery that the Staff Meeting always consists in. What I was unaware of was that a colleague (my good friend Busby Beamish) had rigged up a remote-control device to the underside of my chair. The device, manufactured with all the ingenuity and engineering skills one associates with the German nation and called *Der Großvater*, allows the controller to deliver an extremely realistic simulation of the breaking of wind at the push of a button. During the meeting Beamish delivered half a dozen short blasts at just those moments (he told me later) that I appeared to be nodding off completely. The last one happened in the interval between the end of the chaplain's prayer of blessing on the term ahead and the general 'Amen'.

The relevance of this is the splendour – and, I must say, the limitations – of *Der Großvater*. Beamish showed it to me during the lunch break. The splendour was in the range of possibilities that it offered: there were three separate dials for settings marked (thankfully not in German!) *pitch* (ranging on the dial from 'peep' to 'gruffler'), *volume* (from 'hiss' to 'blaster') and *duration* (from 'sneak' to 'ripper'). He let me borrow it and, as you can imagine, I spent a most enjoyable evening exploring its full range of possibilities and learning the controls in anticipation of using it in my classes to simultaneously disconcert and amuse the pupils. This harmless diversion was summarily scotched by an edict from the Headmaster. Some tomfool Low School brat brought his own *Der Großvater* to school and had it confiscated almost immediately by his officious and humourless tutor who passed the information about the existence of such a device on up the chain of command. A notice went out banning it from the school premises and, in all good conscience, I reluctantly had to abandon my plans to use it to spice up my lessons.

With Beamish's permission, however, I took on the task of improving the machine. As I saw it, the limitations were in there not being any variations during the actual delivery of the sound – no way to modulate the controls to produce, say, a quietish, gentle beginning that could increase in volume as it decreased in pitch. In short, it could be made even more realistic with some adjustments, especially with regard to beefing up the power. In my garage workshop, having borrowed a few tools and the necessary equipment from Phil Shikespier in the Design department, I set about effecting the changes. It was more difficult to achieve than I had anticipated and I must have spent about 50 hours of my spare time on it. Eventually, however, I soldered the final connection and stuffed the box, now with its attachments of bigger battery and external loudspeaker, into my briefcase to bring to school. As ill-luck would have it, this was yesterday - the morning of the visit of the Duke of Edinburgh for the ceremony to officially open The Knobbe.

Like everyone else, I think the school can be justly proud of this bold, futuristic, soaring, central building. I know that a few people find the name of it rather unfortunate but I think the governors were absolutely right to associate this very contemporary structure with the fact that the school is an ancient foundation, established in the mid-fifteenth century and mentioned so honourably in his *History of the World* by Walter Raleigh: *'Verily, for Schooling that doth furnish the great Doore of opportunity, Sixokes is the Knobbe'*. This smooth and imaginative linking of tradition and novelty is, of course, a hallmark of the school.

With all due deference, I might interpolate here that the occupancy of the building has not been wholly uncontroversial. At least two senior members of staff argued that it should house important educational departments to reflect on their central importance to knowledge and culture both in the school and in the world – specifically English or The Classics departments. There was a good deal of bitterness and cynicism expressed when it was announced that instead it would house Marketing, Finance, Administration, The Old Sixokesians Suite, the school uniform shop, lost property, a fresh juice and coffee franchise and, in its sub-basement, an occasional meeting room containing a massive oval table.

But to return to my arrival at the school yestermorn. As usual, I had a full English breakfast in the dining hall and, while walking out afterwards, was waved over by one of the catering staff, Pearl. She whispered that she had 'something special for me' and pulled me into one of the storage rooms in the kitchens. This 'something special' turned out to be a half-dozen mille-feuilles crammed into a plastic air-tight box. Pearl knows that these sweet and creamy delicacies are a particular favourite of mine and she had acquired a few of them from the buffet lunch being made ready to celebrate the Royal Visit. "You share these with that nice Mr Beamish, Mr Wentworth, sir," she said softly in my ear.

You will appreciate that I was put in a difficult position: to take the pastries would be to condone a bit of mild pilfering, but not to take them would be to upset a kind and thoughtful member of the school staff. I decided that the best thing would be for me to take the box and then surreptitiously put back the pastries on the tables at the lunch. I tucked it into my briefcase, gave Pearl a warm smile and some hearty thanks, and went over to The Knobbe to have a look at how the preparations were going prior to the ten o'clock ceremony.

Understandably, there was a fair bit of activity going on in the atrium, but I had time to gaze up at the vast floor-to-ceiling wall-hanging that first greets the eye of the visitor: the collage of gorgeous materials in a harmony of pinks and greys that shows Sir Walter Raleigh with one hand negligently on a great globe (artfully tilted to show Sixokes at the centre), reaching out with the other towards the handle of an impressive door partly open to show the broad and sunny uplands of future prosperity beyond. And, of course, beautifully appliquéd beneath in Elizabethan script, the relevant quote from *History of the World*. It was at this moment that I heard stern voices behind me and I turned to see several police officers at the door where they were demanding that bags were to be searched. I'm afraid it was here that I panicked rather. My feelings of guilt about being discovered with the pilfered pastries were, on reflection, out of proportion given the circumstances. Nevertheless, I hastily hid my briefcase on the floor between the wall and the skirts of the wall-hanging and, with a show of nonchalance that disguised the tumult within, left the building and headed for the library telling myself I could retrieve it after the Visit was over.

Half an hour or so later, mille-feuilles forgotten, I was idly turning the pages and looking at the pictures in *Palaeontology Now!* when the alarm bells went off – and I can honestly say that I made no connection between that and my briefcase: why on Earth would I? Like the rest of the school, I made my way to the designated Dyke's Meadow assembly point for such bomb alerts, and stood there in the persistent rain.

Here, I think some praise is due for the speed of thinking involved in the hasty rearrangements so that the opening ceremony was not abandoned altogether. The Duke's limousine being redirected to the Meadow; the Bursar's idea of carrying the large papier-mâché model of The Knobbe there as a substitute for the real thing, together with some silver gift-wrap tape stretched across it and stuck down with Sellotape, plus a pair of nail-scissors borrowed from a secretary for the Duke to snip with at the appropriate moment; Martin Starr's production of a megaphone for the Duke to use in his address – all of these were inspired in my opinion. It was unfortunate that the rain on the papier-mâché caused the model of The Knobbe to slowly subside into a very flaccid position during the Duke's speech and that rainwater in the megaphone made it work only intermittently so that the final words reaching the bulk of the crowd were "very happy to have…this prominent…and magnificent…Knobbe!" Of course, the

Duke carried off these difficulties with the nobility and grace that are so characteristic of our incomparable Royals.

Shortly after declaring the building open, as the Duke skirted the sad remains of the collapsed model, he inadvertently stepped on my foot (unsighted, I dare say, by the umbrella some gormless flunkey was mis-handling at the time) and stopped to apologise (*such* good manners!) and then he fixed me with a penetrating glance.

"We've met," he declared. "At the Variety Show at the *Palladium* – terrific act. Laughed till my sides were sore." I tried to correct him, explaining that he must be confusing me with Arthur Askey, but he just shook his head and said "Terrifically funny – loved that bumblebee thing – and what was that one about the pier again?" Getting mildly confused by this, and just a little flustered by this surprising attention, I began to ask him for a good place to stay if I were to come to see the Tattoo (he is Duke of the place after all, so I thought he might have something to recommend) and reached into my pocket for my diary to get the dates right when I was felled from the side by the Protection Squad Officer, rapidly hand-cuffed and hustled away into a police van and then to Paddington Green police station for interrogation as a suspected terrorist.

The puzzling pieces which led to this only emerged later: the discovery of my briefcase behind the wall-hanging close to where the Duke was to have performed the opening ceremony; the portable X-ray machine showing battery, metal boxes and wires together with an airtight box seemingly packed with six slabs of plastic explosive; the identification of my being the owner of the briefcase; the radio message from the Bomb Squad in The Knobbe to the Royal Protection Officer on Dyke's Meadow; this Officer's being told in reply to his question to the Headmaster about the identity of G G Wentworth; then, the Officer thinking me a potential assassin and, seeing me reach into my coat while being so close to the Duke...it all made sense but, as I hope you will now appreciate, I really was absolutely blameless.

Yours sincerely,

G G Wentworth

Episode 10

Ten hand-written missives of different sorts from Monica Stimpson tied together by red string and found in an unmarked large white envelope. All are undated but can confidently be placed in the spring and summer of 1966. They appear to be in chronological order. There was also snapshot (of Wentworth sucking up a drink) on the back of which is written 'May Ball 1966'. The missives are followed by a diary entry from Wentworth.

Letter

Dear Mr Wentworth,

Thank you for your splendidly formal letter of the 13th inst. requesting the pleasure of my company for a cinematic experience. I accede to it and will meet you outside at 7pm.

Yours sincerely,

M. Stimpson (Miss)

Note on page torn from a spiral-bound notebook

Tremendous hoo-hah at breakfast – the neighbour outraged by what she called 'a caterwauling geek clattering spoons on his knee' outside her window last night. It was the description of the pink velvet hipsters (gorblimey!) and floral corduroy waist-coat dimly perceived in the streetlight that raised just the mildest suspicion that perhaps a slightly lost Whizzer (my troubadour!) was the one!!!

Tell me later,

Your

Mo

Note on page torn from a spiral-bound notebook

Had a lovely laugh over your 'love poem' – some great doggerel moments. Lucubrational strains evident – introducing the hairdresser who 'crimps on' and 'primps on', for instance. And how could you rhyme 'Monica' and 'doctor'?! Should have told you that I had a short spell peri-puberty of calling myself 'Monique'. Far more scope there:

> *Monique, Monique,*
> *So sleek, so chic,*
> *My pulse gets strong while my knees get weak...*

Here's one in return for you:

> *There was a young fellow from Brum*
> *Who lived at home with his Mum*
> *When one night at the flicks*
> *One of those forward young chicks*
> *Allowed him to fondle her gently*

Yes – a pity I couldn't find a rhyme to end it. Perhaps you could help me out later?!

See you soon,

Mox the Dox

Birthday Card [pictured on the front is a hand-coloured psychedelic treatment of a group of nuns]

Happy Birthday to my Gee Gee Whizz from your utterly, utterly, Ut Mo St xxx

Letter

Dearest G,

This may be hard for you, but it is for the best, I'm sure. I'm finishing our relationship.

Looking at the horizon beyond finals it seems hopeless to me to try to keep up with any sort of tie here in the UK. I want to be free of all that - to concentrate on the work with the ICRC which, I need hardly tell you, has inspired me more than anything else - even you, you funny little thing.

I've thought a lot about 'relationships' and what really matters in love and what really matters to me about a person. I know this might sound funny but I couldn't really love someone forever if he lacked, for want of a better word, nobility. I guess that sounds a bit old-fashioned but for me it isn't at all – it's really important. I want to explain this to you because, well, because you've been quite a distraction to me over the last few months. More than a distraction, of course, I mean you have taken up quite a space in my life. I don't want to be harsh, G, but you'll be the first to agree with me that you aren't naturally noble. And, having been with you and got to know you well, I don't think you'll ever become noble either – it's just not you.

Is nobility the sort of thing you can get more of? I remember we had a debate about this at school. My English teacher (yes, the one I had a crush on but I can't see why on earth you are so jealous!)

told us about Kyd, a man so far ahead of his time that he thought human nature could be changed rather than being fixed (like all other Elizabethans seemed to think). This included becoming noble – and he points the way in his *Hamlet*:

> *Aye, noble's born to few*
> *And few make steps to know*
> *True noble's light. Yet golden rays*
> *Can plainest man imbue*
> *Sure-settled, clear, well-stamped trow:*
> *Thou livest must close good all ways.*

Could you do that, G? I don't think you could ever live with this ennobling sustained self-sacrifice, could never do good in secret. And that's why this is goodbye.

Monica (ex)

P.S. No regrets!

Note on page torn from a spiral-bound notebook

Do stop sending flowers. They make me sick. And so do you.

Monica

Note on page torn from a spiral-bound notebook

Alright, alright – come around this evening at 6 and we'll talk.

Mo (x?)

Shopping List on an oblong of card cut from a cereal box

Sliced bread (1 loaf will do)
Tin of sardines (biggish) (tin not sardines!)
See if you can get anchovy paste, if not, never mind
Macaroni (large pkt)
Tinned tomatoes (the peeled plum ones, 2 tins)
Tin of condensed tomato soup
Ditto mushroom
Cooking oil (small bottle)
Garlic (??!?)
3 large onions (not the red ones and make sure they're firm)
Mince (a couple of pounds, pref. beef)
Bottle of gin
Orange squash
Plonk (3 big bottles. Try to get French)
Long red candles
Joss sticks (shop next to haberdashers)
Tampax (the green box size – may need to ask at counter)
Soap (NOT coal-tar this time!)
Washing up liquid
Serviettes (same red as candles?)
Apples
Oranges
2lb sugar

Postcard showing a picture of Magellan's ship entering port. It has a triangular stamp featuring a hippo.

Hot and busy night and day. Horrible, horrible diseases and conditions. Smallpox, yaws, kwashiorkor, beriberi. People radiant when not sick or grieving. Other dox great. Best thing for me.

Mo
x

Aerogram

Dear George,

As this is the last time I will write, I suppose I owe it to you to really spell out how futile it is to see our relationship as anything but dead. It was your last letter that finally convinced me of the mistake I made allowing us to start up again. That and the fact that I've decided to stay here and work for at least another year.

Let me say that I do appreciate your trying to change. The H-bomb accidentally lost off Spain from that B-52 bomber seems to have been wonderful for CND recruitment in general – and you in particular - and I admire your gumption in coming up with a great idea for your ban-the-bomb stunt. Certainly, if it hadn't gone wrong, it would have been brilliant. However, reading between the lines, I think that the reason for its failure was not down to 'pure bad luck' as you seem to think. For one thing, your referring to your fellow conspirators on the day as 'those two other stooges' rather gives away your attitude towards them and the cause.

Some of us actually watched the game – we took a few hours off and drove into a hotel in Malanje where they had a black and white television set. So, even though, as you know, football is a waste of time in my view, I did witness at second hand what you call the 'indescribable excitement' of the match but can't really see why this should have distracted you so much from the stunt. Yes, your plan was 'ingenious' – whoever thought of going on crutches which could then act as supports for the banner once unravelled from its hiding place under your coat deserves credit there (though you must have been sweltering swathed in banner and your winter coat on what looked a hot day for Britain – perhaps that's why you all 'quaffed beer perhaps a little too liberally'?). But why wait until so near the end of extra-time before getting out to demonstrate? Surely any fool would know that such pressure of time would only conspire towards things going wrong? Your account of one of the crutches getting so entangled with the fence around the pitch that you had to abandon the banner altogether despite your 'desperate attempts' comes across as rather farcical. And then running on the pitch with the idea of laying down in the centre-circle in the shapes of 'C' and 'N' and 'D' was doomed. No-one had a clue what you were there for – indeed, the commentator summed up what anyone else would have thought about it when he said something like 'There are people on the pitch – they think it's all over!'

But the good credit mark you might get for your 'noble commitment to a noble cause' is more than wiped out by your telling me about it. Remember the *'close'* in *'close good all ways'*? To become noble your finest acts must stay secret.

No, G, you haven't any nobility in you and never will have. I cannot love you which is why it is all over. Try to remember our good times and to forget me.

I will always be fond of my memory of you.

Best wishes,

Mo

Tuesday 5th September 1966

Flew back this morning, crushed and desolate. With my scalpel I excised the pages for past 5 months and 15 days and took them into the back yard. In an improvised crucible, I burnt each page one by one. The smoke made my eyes water but, at last, it was all over for me too: my love story just ashes in a dustbin lid.

Episode 11

A copy of an essay submitted to Beckham Grange School magazine, *Grange Rover*, as an entry for the competition for an essay entitled *'My Last Schooldays'* which was open to that year's cohort of leavers.

Added to the bottom of the essay in Wentworth's hand is: *'This was not published but was awarded 6th place. 26th May 1964'*

<u>My Last Schooldays</u>

Though Beckham Grange be not in the first rank of the country's schools, it will always be, for me, a worthy also-ran and a source of memories – most of them good. I will focus on just two characters – one a master, one a boy – to illustrate the more memorable parts of my life here as I come to what will be 'my last schooldays'.

I arrived at its gateposts (the gates themselves having been sacrificed for the War Effort and still awaiting replacement then, as now) in September 1959 resplendent in my stiff new school uniform, face and shoes shining, hair greased flat, palms sweating and heart beating just a little fast. I gazed along the drive to the red-brick pile that is so familiar to us all and little thought of how, one day, I would be looking back fondly over a shoulder as I bid it farewell.

"Get a move on, shrimpo!" said a rough voice, as its owner barged me out of the way.

These were the first words spoken to me by another Beckhamian. It was true that it had been, perhaps, a little foolish of me, having been the first off the bus bringing us from the local station, to have stood stock still just outside the bus door, but I soon learnt to associate this bustle and straight-forward talk with all that is best about the place. The boy so keen to get past me was none other than Colin Berressford – 'Squeaky', of course, to all us boys – whose shrewdness and talent deservedly led him to the position of Head Boy this year and it was a pity that he had to leave the school so suddenly before completing the final term.

It was Berressford himself who bequeathed me the nickname that you all know me by. It came from our roll-call of names in our very first lesson: Latin with Mr Brown. My name was last on the list.

"And finally, Wentworth G G!" he called.

"Here, sir!" I piped.

"G G," he intoned and then paused before casting a droll eye around the classroom. "Let us hope that you are not a *Trojan* horse, my boy." Naturally, this specimen of wit brought forth joyous laughter with which I genuinely tried to join in. Behind me Berressford called out that I was not big enough to be a horse, I was more like a Shetland pony! And so the nickname 'Shets' arrived. As now have the two Beckhamian characters in my personal history.

I'm afraid I was a grave disappointment to Mr Brown in one regard as I never got to grips with Latin. I gave it up when I moved into the Senior School and my A-levels but he told me that he still quotes affectionately my translation of the first line of Caesar's *De Bello Gallico* (*Gallia est omnis divisa in partes tres* as you will all know) as 'All Gaul is quartered into three halves' as one of the best howlers he's encountered. It is pleasant to know that one's name will linger on in such ways. I will return to Mr Brown later, but first want to recall a couple of incidents in which Squeaky Berressford and I figured as they mark, for me, some milestones in my life in the school.

The first one occurred at the start of the summer term at the end of our first year when we were both at the cricket trials in the nets. I had had some very modest success in our French cricket matches at prep school and was keen to get into the Shell Eleven; Berresfford was far less keen – in fact, he'd openly told us that he was looking forward to Saturday afternoons free from playing games so that he could easily 'sneak off for a good smoko'. I must say that I was rather shocked and deprecated his lack of gamesmanship.

"Don't be snooty, Shets," he shot back at me "It'll mean you'll have more of a chance to get in the team!"

Inwardly, I acknowledged the justice of this observation.

Back then, the master in charge of Shell cricket was the Physics teacher Mr Ponsford and he rapidly put us through our paces in the nets. I'm afraid my having broken my glasses made my own batting and bowling efforts rather more miss than hit but I did witness Berresfford's turn at batting. Up until then, he had been muffing catches, bowling wildly and asking Mr Ponsford inept questions to show his ignorance: 'And does the wicket-keeper change every over, sir?'; 'Should we have a fielder at silly pointless, sir?'; 'Can we have two bowlers bowling at the same time, sir?' After several more such questions, Mr Ponsford poked Berresfford's chest several times and told him to 'belt up and pad up' as he wanted to see him batting. Nonchalantly, Berresfford wandered down to the wicket and patted the crease with his bat.

"Hold the bat with two hands, you cretin!" shouted Mr Ponsford who was preparing to bowl. Berresfford obeyed and the ball was bowled. Eyes closed, Berresfford took an almighty swish in the general direction of the ball. It came straight out of the sweet spot and whistled past Mr Ponsford's ear like a rocket. He tripped over me as he ducked sideways and fell heavily into the dust with a fearsome oath. Meanwhile the ball sped through the air and struck the bulldozer on the other side of the Bothy with a tremendous clank. (Some of the younger boys may be wondering about the bulldozer. It was there for the excavation of a pit for the swimming pool which, due to the Appeal being unsuccessful, was abandoned – and why the Biology department got their own wildlife pond when the abandoned pit flooded during the winter. It was here that I found my first diving beetle, *Dytiscus marginalis* – a rather splendid male, in fact.) After a cuff to the head, Mr Ponsford sent me to fetch the ball while he tried to get the worst of the dust off his suit. When I got back he had called everyone in to announce the team for Saturday's match.

"Batsmen are Toop, Crossly, Bannerman, Noorland and, the captain, Westering," he paused and gave 'Sunny' Westering a nod of approval. "Wicket-keeper is Crubey – but don't keep your knees together when you crouch, boy, it looks queer," he said severely. "Bowlers are Jenkins, Brotherton, Ngogo, Chert and Darlington-Smith." There was a long pause as Mr Ponsford glared around. "We will have two reserves who will not play but will attend to sort out the kit, change the scoreboard and generally fetch and carry," he consulted the piece of paper in his hand. "Wentworth and Berresfford." Then he turned smartly on his heel and strode across the Bothy towards the school.

I, of course, could hardly contain my excitement at being selected as reserve. Berresfford, on the other hand, was incensed and flung a pad into the ground as he stared at Mr Ponsford's figure diminishing in the distance. While the rest of us packed up the kit and trudged back to the changing room, Berresfford remained rooted by the nets.

My first flogging was a painful experience but, though I knew it was undeserved, I felt a sort of pride in this initiation into a Beckham Grange tradition. I know that there are stories of other schools having far less corporal punishment – even wild assertions of flogging being banned in some - but this seems inconceivable to me. How else can proper discipline be instilled? A short, sharp reminder of your deficiencies teaches you the required lesson effectively and efficiently. 'Taking one's six' like a man is an honour as I'm sure all true Beckhamians will agree – even Squeaky Berresfford, famed for being the least-flogged Beckhamian ever!

The Master gave me my first six after the keys to the bulldozer had been discovered in my desk. Unable to give any explanation for their presence there, I was punished as 'a probable accomplice' in the destruction of the cricket square which, since restitution of a pitch takes years of work, meant that no cricket has been possible at the school for the last five years. But I can honestly say that I was as shocked as everyone else at the discovery, the morning after the Shell eleven trial described above, that someone had started up the bulldozer during the night and scraped away the whole square with two great sweeps of the mighty scoop at the front of the machine. The silver lining of this act of malice was that, instead of cricket, the school introduced the alternatives of softball or the Summer Run – and in the latter I was often an integral part of the reserve squad which led to my receiving, with great pride it goes without saying, a ringing endorsement and my House colours for my 'doggedness and punctuality'.

Besides sport, another admirable feature of the school is the great range of opportunities it provides for developing interests and broadening horizons – from the Philately Society to the Origami Club, from the Brass-rubbing Group to the Hand-bell Association: a rich choice indeed! But I know that many of you, like me, will best remember the chance of foreign travel, the excitement of trying an elite activity, the novelty of being with one's peers but not in school, which the annual ski trip to Austria afforded. I went two years ago but, as you may know, the skiing for most of us who were complete novices was rather a wash-out. I know that many people blame me for that but it was hardly my fault that the unseasonably warm weather meant that the nursery slope where we were to learn the basics of skiing could only be maintained by the nightly spreading of snow from a giant snow-machine situated at the base of the slope. It was true that the various bits and pieces surrounding the nursery slope were a trifle demeaning for we chaps who were well out of 'la kindergarten': the plastic gnomes and fairies; the banners with figures from Grimm's tales; the jolly piped music of nursery rhymes that blasted out from the speakers. Berresfford, for one, was totally disenchanted as we were introduced to it on our first day standing amongst the groups of toddlers and babbling kiddies while the more experienced members of the group jeered across at us as they made their way to the lifts.

After a first morning of laborious hefting out of the slushy snow, of collapsing as the 'button' thumped into us as we waited to be dragged up the slope, of the humiliation of seeing three-year-olds sweep past our careful snow-ploughs with a verve and confidence we could not emulate, Berresfford suggested we have a break and try something more interesting.

"Let's see who can sit on top of the snowman," he said, pointing to the figure at the top of the slope.

The eight of us eventually managed to get dragged up by the button and then, having taken off our skis, slogged up even further to the white rounded plastic snowman. It was immense – at least eight or nine feet tall – and the roundness of its smooth sides made climbing it out of the question. Berresfford however, showing that Beckhamian spirit and determination, refused to be defeated. He looked around at us and gave a quiet smile.

"We can all boost Shets up, I bet!"

Though rather nervous about this, I felt proud to be thought capable of being the one to conquer the snowman. The others exchanged glances and agreed to be my supporters in the endeavour. Chert, Phipps and Clooney went on their hands and knees, Shipley and Homerton-Teste stood on their backs, Wisley stood on their shoulders. Berresfford hoisted me up onto his shoulders and I was man-handled from their up the human pyramid to where I could get a grip on the contours of the plastic scarf around the snowman's neck. With this grip secure, I pulled myself upright and reached for the rim of the top hat. I heard a creak and there was a slight lurch which, at first, I thought was my footing slipping. Hurriedly, I flung both arms around the top hat and this violent shift of my weight, I suppose, caused the snowman to be uprooted. I heard cheers from the others as it tipped forward and threw me into deep drift of snow before beginning its ponderous roll down the slope. Horrified, I watched it pick up speed, scattering screaming kiddies from its path, until it crunched sickeningly into the snow-machine causing both a good deal of damage – indeed, the snow-machine was inoperable for days and that meant no more skiing for the novices that week.

As I say, not really my fault at all – but at least we all got proficient at 'Chase the Lady', a card-game Berresfford taught us that we played for hours at a time during the rest of the holiday.

Having recounted a memory from my first and my third year at Beckham Grange, I will now turn to the influence that Mr Brown has had on my choice of the direction in my career to come. Although, as I mentioned already, no great shakes at Latin, I always enjoyed his lessons – especially the 'catch-phrases' that he loved. I'm sure we'll always remember his cry of 'schoolboy error!' whenever any of us made a mistake in translation; his 'hearing it out of the corner of my ear'; and, his particular favourite, 'I'm afraid that you seem to be in the dark, boy – and I'll warrant it's nearer Stygian than Cimmerian!' But what I most appreciated was the interest he always took in my well-being and progress. It was he who helped guide me in my choice of reading Biology at university by encouraging me in my beetle-collecting and helping me out with a clear writing style. It was Mr Brown who lent me the net with which I caught and identified the diving beetle in the pond. Even more generously, he would allow me up into his flat in the top of the Old School building where I set up three tanks for my live collection (my Mother being scared of 'creepy-crawlies' as she calls them in her ignorance) so that I could study the life-cycles of some of the beetles I had collected from meadows, wood-piles and woodland in the school grounds.

It was while I was returning from one of my solitary beetle-hunts one week-day evening last summer that I came across Berresfford and the sequence of events leading to his one and only flogging came about. Since he is well clear of any of our school rules now, I can reveal that we met in the woods near the edge of the Bothy and he told me that he was on his way back from Town (strictly out of bounds, of course!) where he'd been to 'the Offie' for his 'usual supplies'. With this, he opened up his jacket to reveal the neck of a bottle of whisky and a packet of fifty Senior Service cigarettes.

"Should see me through the tedium of the weekend," he said wearily.

I was surprised at his coolness.

"But you'll get a terrible flogging from Chester if you get caught with that stuff, you know," I told him earnestly.

Berresfford tapped the side of his nose.

"The thing to remember with contraband, Shets, is never to hide it in your own room. If it's ever discovered by some suspicious eye, you haven't a leg to stand on. What you have to do is hide it in a more public room – that way, there's no link to you. Anyway, what have you been hunting as if I need ask – got any man-eating ones?"

I brought out a collecting bottle. "This one's quite fierce," I said. "It's a bombardier beetle, *Brachinus crepitans*."

He squinted at it for a moment. "Not carrying its rifle, I see." It struck me then that perhaps Berresfford had already taken a swig or two from his whisky bottle. "Or does it carry bombs about its person?"

I explained that the beetle didn't have weapons like the Corps. He broke in with: "Don't talk to me about the Corps – the only good thing I learned there was when Corky Jones taught me how to do roll-ups." [Note to editor, please delete this bit if you think if might get Staff Sergeant Jones into trouble – we boys all know he's been a bit unpopular with The Master since accidentally shooting his dog.] I told him that the beetle did have weapons, but chemical weapons.

"It has a sac of acid which it can squirt out of its back-end," I explained. "If it feels threatened, it can fire hot jets of acid in any direction for up to about two feet – which is enough to put off any attacker."

I felt pleased to be able to tell the sophisticated Berresfford something he didn't know.

"Hold up!" whispered Berresfford urgently, gripping me by the upper arm and putting a finger to his lips. He nodded towards the edge of the Bothy where we could see a pair of legs in corduroy trousers stretched out on the grass. With exaggerated footsteps, Berresfford approached to see who it was (though I had already recognized the trousers as being Mr Brown's) and then returned to me with an excited grin on his face.

"It's Joff," he whispered. "Spark out asleep with his mouth wide open, as usual."

I made a move to go and wake him up to show him my new additions but Berresfford roughly pulled me back.

"Not so fast, Shets. Come with me, and," here he looked at me fiercely, "don't make a sound."

Stealthily, we got to the tree beneath which Mr Brown lay asleep. With the trunk between us, and at Berresfford's physical urging, I climbed up first and he followed close behind. We got to a branch above Mr Brown's prone form and Berresfford quickly reached into my jacket pocket and pulled out the bottle with the bombardier beetle in it. Swiftly taking off the cap, he whispered "Bombs away" and tipped it upside down.

It was either a really lucky or a really unlucky shot, depending on how you look at it. The beetle struck a couple of leaves and twigs in its descent and then dropped smack onto Mr Brown's nose and bounced into his open mouth. This woke him with a start and, almost immediately, I would guess, the beetle must have fired off its bombardment of acid. Just as Mr Brown began roaring and spitting, I felt myself slipping so grabbed quickly for a firmer hand-hold. Unfortunately, this happened to be Berresfford's leg and I must have dislodged it so that he lost his balance and, with quite a bit of crashing through intervening vegetation, thumped onto the grass next to Mr Brown. The whisky bottle and cigarettes spilled out from his pockets and with a shout worthy of Stentor, Mr Brown scooped them up with one hand, hauled Berresfford upright by the ear with the other, and then marched straight to The Master's study for the flogging.

Naturally, Berresfford didn't peach on me for my part in this sorry incident showing that 'Beckhamian spirit' that the school inculcates in us all and which, I am sure you will agree, will influence and guide us as we make our several ways through life in the future – as illustrated in the fifth verse of our great school song:

> *Life's journey's path lies all before*
> *Our youthful steps are light and free*
> *Where will they bend once past your door?*
> *O Beckham Grange, we'll bend with thee!*

And with that, I cry '*Valete!*'

Episode 12

From his diary

Friday 25th June 1986

The usual select group settled snugly around our table in the staff room and the talk turned to the long holiday ahead. Busby Beamish was full of optimism about his trip to Mexico where he was booked in for all of England's World Cup matches.

"Lineker's at the top of his game and the squad's full of beans… and the rest of the tour looks pretty entertaining too – there'll be the Mexican wrestling day, Acapulco and a lot of night club talent, no doubt –"

"I take it that Maggie's not accompanying you," commented Tony Cobberly drily, "And you will be bypassing the cultural artefacts of the ancient civilisations?"

Beamish, who was swilling back a beer, merely raised his eyebrows over the glass.

"You, no doubt, will be off to Crete?" put in Richard Hansum tapping cigar ash into the special receptacle he'd had attached to his chair. Cobberly nodded – he always spent several weeks in the summer sorting and cataloguing archaeological finds on that island and enjoying the rather sumptuous hospitality of the government department in charge of the stuff.

"And you, Hansum?" enquired Cobberly politely.

"Same as last year – back to that little house near Langeais where we're going on with our odyssey into Balzac. It's to be the provincial life this time – accompanied by some more of those delightful Loire wines I was pressing on you last autumn – and the delights of the incomparable countryside of the Touraine. You going anywhere special, Dob?"

"Why would anyone not want to be in Sixokes in the summer?" I replied, rather pleased with this subterfuge where the inference disguised the truth.

At this point the newish maths teacher John Surgery marched over and butted in.

"I don't know why you chaps don't get off your fat backsides and do something a bit more adventurous for a change. You'll be old before you know it!" he shouted cheerily but with some aggression - he almost waved his fist at us.

While the rest of us thought to ignore his crass and boorish behaviour Hansum, ever the gentleman, invited Surgery to pull up a chair and give us some ideas. Needing no more encouragement than this, Surgery sat himself down and recounted an amazing string of foreign trips he had undertaken including climbing in the Hindu Kush, circumnavigating Australia, camel riding the ancient Silk Road and canoeing down the Yangtze.

"And there's plenty to be done even for you stay-at-home types," he said, fixing me with his rather wild blue eyes. "A couple of years ago I hired a Harley-Davidson and visited every county town in England in a week. I can tell you that it was a pretty mathematical problem sorting out the shortest possible itinerary to achieve it…and this summer I'm going to finish walking the length and breadth of the country!"

He explained how this was literally true. He had consulted the maps and found the two longest grid lines that run from north to south and from east to west. He simply walked as close to these lines as possible and had already completed the shorter east-west one.

Beamish observed that for most of the time, Surgery must have been walking on private land and that the going would have been challenging too.

"That's the adventure of it!" yelled Surgery feverishly, a trace of spittle collecting in the corner of his mouth. "Crossing motorways and railway lines – to say nothing of the larger rivers – makes calls on your resourcefulness and courage that goes without saying. And, of course, there are some people who objected when I climbed over their fences and walls or went through their hedges to walk through their gardens on my way but," here an expression of self-congratulatory low cunning crept over his face, "I'd planned for that. I mocked up this." Delving into a side pocket of his shabby jacket, he produced a plastic-coated card on a ribbon. He passed it around and we saw it had a passport-sized photograph of him and, under the imposing letters 'BBC', an authorisation that he, John Surgery, was pioneering the route planned for a forthcoming television programme '*The People the Length and Breadth of England*' conducted by Michael Palin.

"I've also got what looks like a portable tape-recorder and a microphone. As soon as they see that pass and I offer to record their voice and name and dangle the prospect of meeting that bloke Palin and of being on tv, they are eating out of my hand," he guffawed. "They practically fall over themselves to offer me a meal – or even a bed for the night. The family who live at the intersection of the two grid lines in Castle Bromwich took me out for a night on the town and have given me a standing invitation to join them on their caravan holiday in Frinton.'

"You said 'looks like a tape-recorder'" said Beamish with a smile.

"Oh it's just a black metal box in an old Grundig leather cover. I keep my stash of mint-cake in it actually," he added dismissively.

As coincidence has it, this evening Mother also brought up the subject of a summer holiday. Her trip to North Wales with her old 'Brum Chums' has been cancelled due to their worries about radioactive rain and not being able to eat a nice lamb chop there.

"When you get back why don't we have a holiday together for a change, Georgie?" she said brightly.

I wasn't enthusiastic. But, on second thoughts, reflected that perhaps I owed it to her: she had been under the weather recently and, after all, she was my mother.

"Perhaps a few days in Norfolk?" I suggested. Her face fell a little.

"I was thinking of Cornwall," she said. "I've had lots of happy times there. Let's toss for it!"

She took out the sixpence and flipped it into the air.

"Tails!" I called. It was heads.

"East is least and West is blessed,

And the wrong one you have chose!" she warbled tunelessly. "Cornwall in the summer with my Georgie!"

She gave me a hug and then skipped friskily out to make the cocoa.

"Oh well, never mind," I thought to myself.

*   *   *

Sunday 30th August 1986

Sometimes I despair at the state of British journalism. I know that this is the 'silly season' and that they have to fill up their grubby pages somehow, but surely there are vastly many things more important that the story splashed on the front page of 'The Sunday Times' today? And that photograph and the headline 'The Whirly-bird catches the Worm!' that so delighted Mother just made me feel sick and weary at the memory of it. No doubt I will be the target for a storm of ribaldry about it once term commences. At any rate, I can record the proper facts in these pages.

(And I was right not to take the diary with me on the holiday as Mother let something drop which makes me think she might not be averse to a bit of a Paul Prying. On the beach one afternoon a black family settled down not far from us and soon after, the father trotted over with a camera and asked me to take a picture of them. Naturally, I obliged and, when I got back, Mother muttered something about seeing 'a picture of you with your piccaninnies'. I simply froze and said nothing for a long time. I guessed she must have found the photograph in my drawer. Reluctantly, I burned it this morning.)

I won't give a blow-by-blow account of the whole week but just concentrate on the concatenation of circumstances which led to my dangling beneath the rescue helicopter clutching a twelve-foot-long plastic earthworm.

That said, I feel I ought first to note one or two highlights of the first few days of our Cornish venture. Pasties! What a discovery this was – meaty, crisp, hot, peppery and delicious – a far cry from the limp and insipid simulacrum of that name proffered on the shelves of Waitrose. The woman in the local bakery dismissed anything not made and consumed in the county as not worth the trouble: 'what we do call a pull-through pasty – they do just stuff in tatie and onion and then pull a bit a gristly meat through un on a bit o' string to give it a bit o' flavour.' And the rock pools! I spent hours of wonder exploring them. And, of course, I had a good chance to use my old fishing rod (but caught nothing but a titchy green shore crab). However, it was the evening of our penultimate day in Portreath when, looking back, the first link in the chain was forged.

It was Mother's idea that we should take the coach trip to the Mynack theatre to see *Macbeth*. I guess what prompted this had been my comment during the previous evening's Scrabble match recalling the brilliance of Hansum when he had played with us last May after dropping in to borrow my smaller spokeshave and finding the board set up ready on the kitchen table. He and Mother had a small disagreement straight after his – and the game's - first word: 'raguly'. She said that this wasn't a proper word and so wasn't allowed under the rules. Hansum, gentle and polite as ever, explained its meaning to her. She said that she bet it wasn't in the dictionary and, rapidly leafing through the Collins Pocket we keep to hand, proved it. Hansum pointed out that the Collins was not the 'standard dictionary' in which are to be found the words that the rules of the game say are permissible. She argued that 'standard' means ordinary – as in standard eggs – and that the Collins was about as ordinary as you can get. Hansum argued that in this context 'standard' means that to which all can be compared – as in the Oxford English Dictionary. I, of course, agreed with Hansum and Mother just pinched her lips and kept quiet. (I've just checked back on the rest of that game in my Scrabble Record Book and here are Hansum's words: raguly (20); pUisne (38); mOxa (26); sPaHis (38); coRyza (42); mouSmee (25); and, it comes flooding back because I had just made a bon mot about my bon mot 'nick' getting rid of 'my 'k' in the nick of time!' when he completed the game magnificently, spanning the two triple-word squares and using all his letters with pr(u)iNose (54 + 50) – what a player!) Anyway, after Mother had waved away my praise of Hansum and muttered a disparaging comment about 'that wordy old poof' I told her severely that she knew nothing about it and just try to find something better than the 'purty' she had been trying to pass off as good English.

Well, it was the next day that she surprised me with the tickets to the play and "This will give you something to talk to that Hansum about, Georgie!" and added "Where's there's a will, there's a play."

This last made me a bit snappy especially as I was still in something of a sour humour after discovering just one of a pair of my favourite socks had been packed. All Mother could say was "A sock in the hand is worth two in the wash" in that blithe way she has of diverting anything unsettling. I told her not to be such a ninny and, when she gave me her gormless expression in response, called her 'a tiresome old trout'. She looked sad for a fleeting moment then replied:

'Trout? Trout? Doubt that the stars are fire…" and just gazed at me in that soppy fond way of hers. I just pushed past her to root through the laundry for something to wear on my feet.

Anyway, I wasn't really displeased about going to the play. I had done it at Beckham Grange for my O-level and recollected Puffing Billy Dockery telling us that it was 'the shortest one that Shakespeare wrote so it will not be without some merit in your eyes.'

The coach picked us up just before three o'clock in the afternoon and, with some stops on the way to collect more people, bustled its way along the roads to the Lizard. Everyone on board was very cheerful and friendly with there being quite a buzz of fun and excitement. It was heartening that so many of them were of the younger generation too – something to stick in Puffing Billy's pipe for him to smoke! The weather was good if rather cool which was another bonus given the outdoor nature of the theatre with its steeply-raked seats a la Cobberly's Greece. I'd bought a programme and soon saw that Mother had made a huge bish as I read the notes in it.

'The Pink Shakespeare Company [it begins] *is committed to bravura performances of the Bard's works as interpreted from a gay perspective. In our production of Macbeth, we see Duncan, the old quean, unable to choose between the charms of the rivals for his affections and his seat (of power!), Macduff and Macbeth. This duo's relationship develops against the twin foils of mystic fatalism and the tragic figure of Lady Macbeth as, embittered and disillusioned, she despairs of any 'straight' love from the puissant man she thought she had married...'*

I groaned out loud as I read this but was trapped: with a crash of a hammer on a sheet of metal and flashes of blue-white lights, three lithe and androgynous actors minced to stage centre and, after a lot of lascivious body movement amongst themselves, one of them sobbed with camp longing in its voice:

"When shall we three meet again?"

It was a load of filthy old tosh but Mother seemed to find the whole experience wonderful though no doubt it was all way over her head (I didn't let her read the programme). Shortest play or not, it was dark by the time the final scene (quite disgracefully portrayed as consisting of some sort of sodomy challenge thrown down by Macbeth as he lay on his stomach on his 'warlike shield' and poked up his rump to call 'Lay on Macduff and damn'd be he who first cries hold, enough!' before, I suppose, literally dying for love) which is why I didn't see the thermos flask of hot coffee. Stupidly, the woman next to me had removed the top after pouring herself a cup and just put the flask down while she drank it. In my hurry to quit the theatre and get a good seat on the coach, I accidentally kicked the flask and the rest of the contents was precipitated onto the backside of the man in front who, like me had just stood up. From his howls of anguish, it was clear that the coffee was still at a painfully high temperature. What was even more unlucky about this was that the man turned out to be our coach driver and, given his scalded posterior, he was incapable of driving the coach back. It seemed to take an age for the coach company to produce a substitute for him and it was a much less cheerful group that finally boarded for the return journey. Indeed, no-one so much as spoke to me as if this was all my fault. The consequence was that Mother and I didn't get back to our cottage until past 3 o'clock in the morning. This explains why it is that we both overslept the next morning - which was that first link in the chain I mentioned.

Our over-sleeping meant that we missed our bus for what I had been anticipating as one of the main attractions of our holiday: a trip including a tour of a couple of blowing–houses, lunch in an original piskey-factory, a guided exploration of an old tin mine with, afterwards, the opportunity of panning for tin in a stream before being treated to a lavish Cornish cream tea. No, we missed all that because neither of us was awake in time. And, since we had anticipated eating out, this meant we had to make a decision about what to do for lunch – which led to the second link in the chain.

We were on the pavement beside the sea-front and in discussion. I favoured buying pasties and pastries from the baker's and a bottle of dandelion-and-burdock and having a picnic on the beach. Mother favoured a sit-down meal of dressed crab in *The Wreckers Arms* nearby with a healthy glass or two of gin and tonic. She fished out the sixpence and gave it a good spin into the air.

"Heads!" I called but I was wasting my breath. Mother failed to catch it and, after a twinkling bounce on the granite kerbstone, the sixpence shot through a slot in the drain-cover beside us and disappeared into the blackness within. Uttering a sharp cry, Mother dropped her basket and was immediately on her knees pulling at the cover to get her precious sixpence back. After a few unavailing tugs, she applied an eye to a slot and then shouted with triumph:

"I can see it, Georgie! I can see it! It's stuck on the ledge just down there. Here, you look!"

I must say that it took quite a bit of struggling on my part, together with that of a helpful passer-by, to lift the cast-iron cover to reveal a crudely brick-lined well with, about ten feet down, a disc of dirty grey water. There was a narrow ledge about five feet down the sides and, on this ledge, was a large glistening dog-turd on the surface of which was nestling the sixpence. The helpful passer-by was a resourceful chap.

"I reckon if you take off your jackut," he said to me slowly, "I be able to hold you by the legs and you can reach down an' get un. Me, I'd get stuck in th' ole but you'm the right sort o' build arn' 'ee, boy?"

The thought of putting my fingers into that dog's mess was not a pleasant one. I matched the man's resourcefulness.

"Mother – give me your tweezers," I said as I removed change from my trousers and slipped off my jacket. She soon found them and handed them to me. Taking a deep breath and trusting to the brawny arms of the passer-by, I edged head-first down the drain. Somewhat surprisingly, there was no mishap and it was something like triumph that I was hauled out of the drain with the soiled sixpence (tails, of course) pinched between the jaws of the tweezers. I took my fresh handkerchief out of the jacket Mother was still holding and carefully wrapped the sixpence and the tweezers deep into its folds: we would put all three into a bowl of hot disinfectant when we got back to the cottage. Stowing the handkerchief back into the inner pocket of my jacket, I nodded towards *The Wreckers Arms* and invited the passer-by to join us for a well-earned drink.

The passer-by turned out to be something of a celebrity of the town: a coalman called Bonzo Johns who had played in the front row for Cornwall in a famous victory against a touring All-Blacks rugby team.

"You'm a hero, you are!" he cried "Took a lot o' guts to trust I'd not drop 'ee fer the fun of it!"

He insisted on my having a 'special' to brace me up. He spoke quietly to the landlord and soon both he and I had a pint of cloudy brown liquid with small islands of foam on their surface presented before us on the dark-stained bar counter. Mother got her large gin and tonic and we all toasted each other and Bonzo nodded in my direction and shouted 'Bottoms up!' which had us all in stitches of laughter. I took a good swig of the drink to match Bonzo and he looked at me quizzically and asked quietly:

"What do 'ee think, pard?"

I nodded thoughtfully and gave it due consideration.

"I'm getting green fruity notes and just the hint of elderflower blossom," I said carefully. "Good grip at the edges; good attack; long-lasting finish. Rather fine altogether." I'd heard Hansum say something of the kind at the last *Pro Probus* evening. Bonzo roared with laughter.

"That's our local rough cider, my 'ansum. 'Devil's Piss' we do call it – saving your presence, ma'am," he added, touching his forehead at Mother. She smiled back at him and sipped some of her G and T.

"Ill waters run deep," she said in her gnomic way.

I took another slow sample and washed it around my mouth. It seemed remarkably innocuous, just like squeezed apple juice with a hint of heat. As we lowered the cider I told Bonzo about how doctors used to taste their patient's urine to help in diagnoses.

"And what might this 'un be sufferin' from?" he asked, resting a tanned forearm on the bar. "Too much brimstone, mebbe!"

The conviviality continued over a homemade and giant-sized pasty lunch and, I think, one (certainly no more than one and a half) more pints of the delicious local cider for me and rather more than that for Bonzo. Mother kept pace gamely. Thus it was that, around about two o'clock, I emerged blinking in the sunlight outside *The Wreckers Arms* just rather more squiffy than I might have been and, thanks to the rather large lunch bill, rather shorter of cash too. Link number two (and three perhaps).

If I hadn't been so light-headed, it would never have occurred to me to hire an earthworm – something which became link number three (or four if we are counting the other way).

Mother and I decided we should have a nice rest on the beach for the afternoon. She had our bathing costumes and towels in the basket and we took these out and sat down on the shingly sand with the sparkling Atlantic embraced by two arms of turf-capped cliffs of shale that formed Portreath bay at our feet. But it was draughty – there was quite a brisk breeze (an off-shore wind, I think it's called) whipping occasional white horses from the surface of the ocean.

"Be a darling and get us a wind-break, Georgie," said Mother as she stretched out on her towel muttering "Easy breezy, lemon and squeezy" for some reason probably known to no-one on the planet.

I trudged up the beach to the garish temporary hut that hired out or sold various things for the beach: wet-suits, surf-boards, buckets, spades, rubber rings and other inflatables, kites, swing-balls, beach balls, and, of course, wind-breaks. The girl in charge was reading a book but seemed happy to put it down and attend to me. She was remarkably pretty (not unlike a more youthful Mary Boyne) and gave me a very wide smile as she handed over the wind-break. It was then that I noticed that I'd left my jacket with my money in it back by Mother.

"I'll trust you," she said with a laugh. "You've got a good man's face. You take it and then you can pay me when you bring it back."

By the time I had banged in the half-dozen poles of the wind-break, Mother was turned on her side and very gently snoring in her sleep: the pasty and gin had cast their spell. I looked at the sea: it was a blue and white enticement. People were sporting in its skirts, yelping as the chilly waves swept over their knees; surging on boards; flinging beach balls; cavorting on inflatables. I decided I was going to join them. But first, I was going back to that girl in the hut. I picked up my jacket.

She was reading her book again but gave me the same lovely smile.

"Are you enjoying it?" I asked, gesturing towards the book she had laid on her seat as she had got up.

"Well, it's on my reading list and it seems appropriate here," she said with a laugh and pointed up at the sign which advertised 'Beach Shop and Hire'. I must have looked puzzled because she pointed to her book which I now saw was Keats' Collected Poems and then looked at the corner of the advertising board where I read 'prop: B. Keats'.

"Oh yes, Keats and Keats," I said with what I thought was great witticism, and chuckled heartily. She looked at me keenly.

"Even better, he's called Basil Keats!" she said conspiratorially. I hadn't a clue what she was on about but did my best.

"Rather a faulty sort of name!"

She looked blank for a while but her face soon cleared and she smiled at me again.

"I bet you want to hire one of Basil's favourites."

"And what might that be?" I asked with a debonair expression that I conjured nonchalantly onto my countenance.

"Why, one of these special lilos," she replied sweeping her hand towards the back of the hut where banners depicting various inflatables emerged. I squinted at them (my glasses seemed to have got a bit blurry). On the pictures were featured a dragon, a banana, a crocodile, a frog and, right in the centre, an earthworm.

"The earthworm seems a bit exotic," I said.

"Yes. Basil told me the story behind the idea," said the Beach Hut Girl winningly. "The company he was buying the lilos from said that if he put in a good order, they would make him a special one with any animal of his choice. So he asked his daughter Polly (just seven years old and a little darling) what her favourite animal was. And do you know what she said?" I shook my head, enchanted.

"She said a worm because 'it does no harm to anything but does all good for everything'. Isn't that the cutest thing?"

I was about to tell her something about Darwin and worms but before it got to my lips from my brain she went on:

"So here we have a lilo made out of transparent plastic with, running down its middle and on out into a long fat tail, an earthworm. You just snuggle into a hollow in the worm and away you go!"

Delighted by her warmth and enthusiasm, I said I would hire the largest one available. She hauled out a rolled cylinder and attached it to a nozzled hose near her shin. In a trice, the earthworm lilo was inflated and under her arm. It was over twice my length.

"Together with the wind-break, that will be eight pounds with a ten-pound deposit for them both," she said spoiling things slightly with this element of commerce.

I had just a ten-pound note and some loose change – well short of the sum required. She looked rather doubtful now - despite my 'good man's face' I reflected. Then I remembered the sixpence.

"In this handkerchief," I said, pulling it out of the inside pocket, "there's a Georgian silver sixpence worth at least a hundred pounds – you can keep that as a deposit if you like," I told her. She was still looking at me askance so I carefully unswaddled the tweezers and the sixpence in the folds of the handkerchief.

"I'm afraid it fell into some dog's mess earlier but, as you can see," I said pushing it towards her. She recoiled with a look of disgust.

"As you can see, it's dated 1816 and genuine silver and worth a good deal."

"Alright, alright – just wrap it up and put it up on the shelf there," she said indicating a plank behind her on which rested a collection of echinoderm skeletons. "Here you are!" She thrust the earthworm lilo into my arms and, picking up her book, slumped back onto her chair and resumed reading.

If I hadn't been feeling so cider-spirited and at peace with the world, I suppose I might have felt rather conspicuous as I made my way back to our wind-break – especially as the wind kept whipping at the tail of the worm and threatening to slap the other beach-goers. I stumbled over the sharper pebbles scattered more thickly at intervals in the sand. Mother was still fast asleep so, keeping a wary foot on the lilo at all times to stop it blowing away, I slipped into my trunks and then jogged athletically down to the surf with my 'cutest thing' of a lilo and plunged with it into the maw of the sea.

God knows what number link I'm up to now. It doesn't matter really because there are a few more links to come before I'm on the front page of The Sunday Times.

I pushed out beyond the gently collapsing waves and then bravely breasted the lilo. The head (sporting a rather silly-eyed expression that was biologically incomprehensible) to the mid-section of the puffy segments of the 'worm' was hollowed out to allow a body to squeeze into its confines while the transparent oblong section of the rest of the lilo provided stability. The tail of the beast trailed behind and, if your legs were long enough, or if there were others to disport themselves, could be used for extra buoyant support. Clutched snugly in the shiny fat segments, I lay back and contemplated the sky. It was all patched with tufts of cloud and I closed my eyes. Wavelets gently rocked me up and down and from side to side; up and down and from side to side. The happy cries and laughter from the beach began to fade; kept on fading. Feeling ineffably sleepy, I drifted off…

The silence was profound and the choppiness of the waves more insistent when I opened my eyes. I had drifted off. Raising my head I saw the coastline was what seemed miles away. I suppose that what is described as a 'wave of panic' would have swept over most people at this point but, oddly enough, all that swept over me was a great feeling of calm. Shortly after that came the wave of panic and I struggled to raise myself up from the clutches of the earthworm which had ferried me out into uncharted waters to be engulfed in the slavering jaws of a monstrous fish hurtling up from the depths to consume this grossly enticing morsel! I called upon my better nature to be calm: earthworms were not bait for sea fish. As long as sea fish knew that, I was quite safe.

However, this calm reflection did not wholly dispel the seriousness of my predicament: I was adrift at the mercy of the Atlantic. On the other hand, I told myself, Mother would doubtless be awake by now and, noticing my absence, have alerted people on the beach and hence, even now, my rescue would be under way. (I was totally wrong about this as I found out later. Mother awoke after two or three hours from her sozzled snooze and immediately assumed that I had gone back to the cottage or off to find more pasties to eat and so had just wandered up and down the beach idly beach-combing for interesting shells. By which time, the two RNAS Culdrose Sea-king helicopters had been scrambled and a full-scale emergency rescue had begun.)

I reviewed my options. I could just sit tight and wait for the rescue. I could make a noise to attract attention. I could wave and hope to attract the attention of any walkers on the cliffs. I could either paddle the lilo with my arms or slip off it and kick with my legs to get me back to shore. Finally, I could abandon the lilo and strike out for shore unencumbered.

I gave each of these some thought and decided that, since the wind and current that had taken me this far were clearly moving at a faster rate than anything I could propel myself at, neither swimming alone or with the lilo was a sensible option. Gauging the distance to the beach was a couple of miles, shouting or whistling would be pointless. Thus, I combined by first two options by sitting up on the worm and waving both arms about.

It is surprising how tiring arm-waving can be. Furthermore, the sky had become more overspread with cloud, the wind seemed to be gusting and changing direction and, what with the occasional spray, I was getting rather cold. And thirsty too. How soon might exposure and hypothermia begin? I felt the building of another wave of panic when, with vast relief, I heard the steady beat of an engine approaching me from behind: I was saved!

The small fishing-boat chugged towards me and, just a few minutes later, I was grabbing at a sort of hooked pole and was soon hauled up into the well of the back-end of the boat which I shared with a couple of lobster pots and a cheerful pair of rough-handed Cornish crabbers, Dave and Tom.

"First time this fisherman 'ave caught a worm!" said Dave and they both roared with laughter as he hooked my earthworm lilo out of the sea.

"Now, my luvvur," he went on turning to me, "Tell us what made you set sail in this dobby li'l craft?"

I explained about relaxing in it and then falling asleep. They both shook their heads in sorrow, obviously thinking I was very foolish tripper indeed. I thought I might be looked on more favourably by mentioning the local celebrity I'd shared lunch with.

"You bin drinkin' with Bonzo?" shouted Tom with joy. "Not that Devil's Piss I hope?"

When I acknowledged this they were again shaking their heads but this time laughing.

"I mind Bonzo and me 'avin' a fair few pints o' that brew once," said Dave. "I don't mind much else but I tell 'ee that when I looked in the mirror next mornin' I 'ad eyes on me like a myxy rabbut!"

There was a bit more of this bantering before Dave noticed me shivering and took me into the tiny cabin-like box. I mentioned that Mother might have raised the alarm about my being missing.

"No, my 'ansum, there've bin nothing on the radio 'bout any missin' men. Or worms come to that."

He gestured at the ship-to-shore radio mounted next to the steering-wheel thing.

Pushing and shoving things about in a low cupboard he soon dragged out a blue jersey that he gave me to wear.

"I'll leave you to put that on while Tom an' me puts out the last couple o' pots. Then we'll 'ed back to th'arbour and you'll be as right as sixpence!"

I was pulling the jersey (which, I might add, reeked of diesel, fish-guts and lanolin) over my head while he went on:

"I'll just give us a bit of way and set the wheel..."

By this time my head had emerged and I saw him flicking a switch or two on the dashboard (I suppose there will be something a bit more nautical for it but, to the plain man, that's what it was). He joined Tom at the back of the boat and, while Dave hefted a pot up onto the railing, Tom dropped some sort of fishy bait into it and lashed on some rope at the other end of which was a bright yellow buoy. With something of a heave, Dave threw the pot.

I suppose the next few moments were indeed just moments – but it all seemed to pass in slow-motion. As Dave was heaving the pot I noticed part of the rope had looped round the plastic of the worm's tail so, to save it from going overboard, I grabbed the head end and pulled hard. It came free much more easily than I had anticipated and this meant I fell backwards into the cabin. I put out my hand to save myself and grabbed a handle. At the same moment, the boat jerked forwards. The jerk caused Dave to overbalance and topple into the sea. Tom, who had turned quickly towards me as I had plucked the worm away, didn't see Dave's departure but, in his hurried turn some fish-bait slopped out of his bucket next to his Wellington boot. Finally, as the rope from the sinking pot pulled on the buoy which Tom was still holding. This tug made him step onto the slippery bait and, with a whirl of arms and a harsh cry, he too fell over the back end.

Although never immodest, I must record that I am rather proud of my coolness and rapid reaction to this potential disaster. To save them from drowning I unlashed the white cylinder marked 'life raft: pull lever and throw overboard', pulled lever and threw overboard. Gratifyingly, the raft self-inflated and was soon bobbing on the surface of the sea like a friendly rubber mushroom. I watched while Tom and Dave swam towards it and heaved themselves in. That was part one dealt with. Now to getting the boat under control so I could go back and pick them up and get us all back to harbour safely.

This is where things came unstuck. Not, of course, due to anything I did wrong. Rather, because, quite naturally, I had no idea about the controls of a boat. I was blissfully unaware that the handle I had recently inadvertently pulled was the accelerator-thing and, though the boat was rushing along at several miles an hour, decided that I could easily use the steering wheel to take the boat near the shore and raise the alarm. However, the steering wheel seemed to be locked in position – no doubt there was something on the dashboard to allow a course to be fixed to allow the fishermen to get on with some work while the boat puttered merrily along by itself. I eyed the dashboard warily: there were four switches in down positions, two more up, and a red button in a recessed metal rim. What was the worst thing that could happen, I asked myself. My heart beating rather fast, I gingerly flicked one of the switches. Immediately there was a deafening sound of a foghorn. I flipped the switch back down and, mercifully, the keening wail died out.

Before trying another, I thought I'd take a breath or two and looked back at the life raft. It seemed to be over a mile away now and it was then that I noticed the wind had shifted and was propelling the raft towards the rocks at the base of the cliffs. Meanwhile I was surging in the opposite direction – probably towards America. No doubt I'd run out of fuel well before then but it was a chilling thought. Stepping back into the cabin I reached out and pressed the red button. The engine coughed once and stopped.

Ironically, I was adrift again.

The option for sending a distress call was, this time, feasible: I had the radio. I picked up the handset, pressed the button on the side and intoned "May-day, May-day," in a pretty exact imitation of Jack Hawkins in that navy film Mother and I had watched in the cottage one rainy afternoon earlier in the week.

"Hello May-day. This is the Coastguard Service. Please identify yourself, over," came the reassuringly smooth and authoritative reply.

"Well, it's George Wentworth, actually –"

"Please identify your vessel, sir, over."

"Not sure about the name. It's a little fishing boat. White picked out with a blue trim. Catches crabs and whatnot. A couple of chaps called Dave and Tom –"

"The identity of the vessel will be on the radio, sir, two letters and three digits, over."

"Oh yes, so that's what that is. Righto – have you got a pencil and paper handy? Here they are: P for Percy, H for Henry then three, three - that's two threes, one after the other - two, got that?"

There was a short pause.

"Papa, Hotel, three-three-two, sir, over?"

"That's it," I said. "Well done."

"What is your position, sir, over?"

"I'm a schoolmaster – Biology you know. Never really fancied being a headmaster. Rather a good school in Kent. Sixokes to be -"

"I mean your whereabouts at this moment, sir, as precisely as you can manage, over."

"I'm in the cabin part, facing forwards. In fact, the boat seems to have shifted around a bit and I can see a cliff ahead now –"

"Are you off Portreath, sir, over?"

"Clever of you to guess that. Yes, about a mile or so. You see, I accidentally drifted out to sea from the beach and Dave and Tom kindly plucked me from the sea into their boat – this boat, that is. Then they fell over the side while the boat took it into its head to speed up. They're alright because I threw them the life raft. But I ought to tell you that after they got into it I noticed the wind was blowing it towards some rather nasty-looking rocks. I pushed a button on the dashboard here and the engine cut out. Now it looks like I'm drifting towards another set of nasty-looking rocks. Bit of a problem all-round really which is why I thought of calling you chaps –"

"Can you re-start the engine, sir, over,?"

"Haven't a clue about that, I'm afraid. Can't even drive a car although –"

"Right, sir. I am sending two rescue helicopters, one for you and one for the life raft. You will see them within ten minutes approaching from the West. Meanwhile, you could help expedite the rescue by making the vessel more visible. I will keep this channel open for any further communication. Is that all clear, over?"

"Perfectly," I replied. "Over and out." It doesn't take me long to pick up the lingo.

I turned my attention to becoming more visible to the helicopters. The obvious thing would be to light a fire.

The blue jersey that Dave had lent me, if its rank smell was anything to go by, should burn beautifully and I felt sure that, in the emergency, he wouldn't mind my sacrificing it. But what could I use on the boat to start a fire? Then another scene from the Jack Hawkins film popped into my mind: distress flares! If I could find one I could lash it to the top of the cabin wrapped in the jersey and then set it off. I started hunting around in cupboards but then the earthworm caught my eye: here was another eye-catcher! It was the work of a moment to open the popper and then, with some judicious rolling, squeeze out the air. Now I had a twelve-foot orangey-brown flag which I began to wave over my head as the pair of helicopters loomed over the cliffs in the near distance. Regrettably, there was no need for the fire after all.

Soon a man was winched down from a helicopter to join me on the boat. He turned a key on the dashboard that I had failed to notice in all the excitement and the engine started straight away. He spun the steering wheel to point the boat out to sea and then set about putting me in the harness to take me up to the helicopter. Seeing me clinging to my rolled-up earthworm he tried to tell me that I must leave it behind. I refused point-blank. I guessed that Beach Hut Girl might not return the deposit – including Mother's lucky sixpence up among the sea-urchins – if I didn't return the damn thing. Unfortunately, just as I was nearing the door of the helicopter, the worm unravelled and, I suppose, just at that moment, a photograph of this was taken by someone in the second helicopter - or perhaps it was some journalist or other on the cliffs – of me clutching the silly head end of the worm as the rest of it streamed out in the down-draught from the rotor blades.

At least John Surgery might find my story close to the sort of holiday adventure he thinks it sensible to undertake: a slim silver lining to a fat black cloud.

Episode 13

From his diary

Friday 13th November 1997

Having lately qualified for an important golf match, Alex James, my Head of Department, asked me to fill in for him in his regular 'Oxbridge' session after school today. I don't do such things usually.

"What sort of thing goes on?" I asked him.

"Well, a dozen or so of our brightest and best pupils who are aiming to do Biology at Oxford or Cambridge come along and the idea is to give them something that is intellectually demanding – a sort of seminar, I suppose. Tommy's frightfully keen on them. What I do is give a 5 to 10 minute introductory talk on a topic that is unfamiliar but which has interesting links to things they do know about. Last week's was on 'the aquatic ape theory' and the week before that on 'what limits a skeleton'."

I nodded as if these things meant something interesting to me.

"Then the pupils chip in with questions or observations and I keep the ball rolling by challenging their thinking." He detected a look of apprehension on my face and patted my arm. "Why don't you do something in the dinosaur line?" My face cleared immediately – here was a subject both close to my heart and one in which I had a good deal of knowledge.

"I'll do that!" I said.

"Just put up the title of your talk on the door during the day so the pupils have some idea of what to expect, G G – and thanks!" he said before taking the rest of the day off to put in some practice for his match.

In bold black felt tip pen I wrote: '*G G Wentworth's Oxbridge Seminar: Why Dinosaurs Were More Than Terrible Lizards*'. I miscalculated the size of the paper and had to finish the notice on a second sheet but, with a bit of extra blu-tacking, the larger than usual notice soon adorned the door to Biolab 1. I was rather proud of it.

After school, as pupils drifted into the lab, I noticed that the second sheet of paper forming the notice had gone – leaving just '*Why Dinosaurs*' but before I could say anything about this, rather to my consternation, Tommy Coxswain himself came through the door. Since becoming Headmaster, a salient feature of Tommy's leadership was to develop what he called 'greater academic rigour' in the school.

"Saw your notice earlier and was intrigued," he said in his rather breathless way. "Why dinosaurs indeed! But must let you get on. Don't mind me." He glanced quickly around at the five or six pupils sitting waiting and settled himself down on a nearby stool and looked up at me expectantly.

I decided to ignore Tommy's presence and placed a few of the plastic models of dinosaurs I had collected from gift shops on my travels to different museums on the front bench. I put some plastic trees down to represent a small forest. Picking up a *Diplodocus*, I gave it a sort of rocking motion in my hand to represent it moving slowly towards the trees.

"This is *Diplodocus*, a vegetarian, plodding on its way towards its food," I said in a sort of sing-song voice as if telling a story. I made it peck at the top of one of the plastic trees. "Munch, munch – tasty lunch!" says *Diplodocus*.' In my experience, pupils always respond well to visual aids especially when combined with good story-telling. I was just reaching for a *Tyrannosaurus* when one of the pupils rudely butted in with a question.

"Mr Wentworth, sir, those trees look like horse chestnuts – deciduous angiosperms, sir – they were surely not around at the same time as these early dinosaurs?"

"That's as maybe, Chakraborty. Let's just overlook that pointless detail and stick to the scenario I am developing shall we?" I replied testily and aimed the predator at *Diplodocus*. Chakraborty is in the Multinational Centre, our 6th form boys' boarding house and, like many others there, too clever by a quarter.

"Now, the mighty *Tyrannosaurus* lets out a roar!" I threw back my head and roared in my spine-chilling imitation of the great *T. rex* and galloped the model at its prey. While I engaged the plastic models in a very realistic struggle for life (or a meal, depending on your point of view) again Chakraborty butted in.

"Sir, I was reading that it seems likely that *Tyrannosaurus rex* was almost certainly homoiothermic and –"

"Chakraborty," I cut in quite kindly but firmly, "A schoolboy error, I'm afraid. You see, dinosaurs were reptiles and, by definition, reptiles are cold-blooded so there is no possibility of *T. rex* being warm-blooded." I looked towards Tommy to exchange a glance of appreciation of a superior mind using iron logic but noticed that all he had on his face was a bit of a frown. I sought to clear up his puzzlement at this high-level biological talk but he waved aside my introduction to the classification of back-boned animals and asked a question of his own while looking around at the pupils with an eager expression.

"You'll excuse me steering you in a slightly different direction, Mr Wentworth, but can we get onto the intriguing question of 'Why dinosaurs?' It seems to me that the question cuts to the heart of the evolutionist/creationist debate – why put dinosaurs on Earth merely to extinguish them? Or what natural forces create or extinguish life forms?"

'Yes, indeed, Headmaster, sir," said Chakraborty, "whether there is some necessary direction to evolution by natural selection (though

I am sure you will not think this in any way teleological)," he smiled quickly before carrying on. "Or indeed whether such life-forms are unique in the sense..."

'In the sense of phylogeny as opposed to mere category," finished Tommy with an approving nod.

Both he and Chakraborty turned to me at this point but I was unable to say anything because, while they had been talking I had picked up a baby pink *Stegosaurus* and, while idly nibbling at one of the vertical plates along its spine, had got it stuck in that small gap between my two front teeth. With some mumbling and gestures I indicated my inability to enlighten them for the time being. Fortunately, another pupil piped up with an observation so attention moved away from me as I made my way over to the sink. Using a drop of liquid soap I rubbed it around my teeth and the plate of the *Stegosaurus* and, after some little time and the use of a handkerchief to improve my purchase, managed to lever the thing out. Then I spent several minutes trying to rinse the taste of the soap out of my mouth.

All this time the discussion raged on and I relaxed and let it wash over me. They were intent on the question of biological change and how its significance is decided upon – Tommy was burbling about 'parameters and paradigms' when I coughed and pointed out that time was up.

"Next week's session will be with Mr James again," I told them and, with a pleasing show of reluctance, they filed out of the lab. Tommy was extremely animated.

"That was excellent, George – they are a good bunch, I must say. Their views on the classification of creatures were most illuminating, most stimulating, most engaging..."

"There isn't a lot of classification on the syllabus though, Headmaster," I told him (for good reason: we teachers and the pupils all find it deadly dull. I kept that bit to myself). Tommy looked appalled.

"But it is essential! I am minded to get in touch with the Board immediately about this dereliction! George, I need a few ideas from a specialist though – could you do me a paper? Nothing too long – say a couple of sides. Typed, of course. Let me give you a title." He thought for a moment while I took out my pen and drew a sheet of paper towards me. *'Taxonomy: the intellectual justification for its more prominent place in the curriculum'* he dictated. "I look forward to reading it on Monday," he said and, with his characteristic smile and wave, swept energetically out of the door.

Saturday 14th November 1997

First period this morning I was with my 6th form class. We were on the topic of Human Reproduction and I set them the task of copying out drawings of the appropriate parts while I mused on the dratted paper Tommy had asked for. I had the title in front of me but nothing of any use came to mind. After 20 minutes or so, I wandered slowly around the benches to give them a bit of encouragement.

"Very nice pencil-work, Miss Lyter...Excellent work Miss Limward, admirable labelling style." Absently, I tapped the drawing of the boy sitting next to them, and said mildly, "Mason, your penis is too small." This provoked some stifled giggling from the girls and, realizing what I'd said, I started to colour with embarrassment.

"Never had any complaints before, sir' remarked Mason with that annoying insouciance of his and a sidelong glance at the girls. This provoked more giggling and my face became even more deeply suffused, my tongue absolutely tied. Mason is one of those boys who have an uncanny knack of homing in on any sign of a master's weakness, like a shark scenting blood in the water.

"I'm sorry you find a small penis disappointing, sir," he went on smoothly. I was totally inarticulate with embarrassment and anger and at a loss to know what on earth I could do to shut him up. Naturally, he just kept on.

"I couldn't help noticing you were very complimentary about the *girls'* genitals, sir" This was too much!

"Enough, Mason!" I shouted. "Enough! Your behaviour is totally unacceptable and you will write me a thousand lines!"

"But, sir, that's not fair, sir, I've done nothing wrong sir!" he protested.

"Mason, as I have told you before, you might find fairness in a face but never in life. You will learn that lesson!" Seeing that the Misses Lyter and Limward were looking a little shocked at this eruption of authority, I started to calm down a little and to think that perhaps I was being just a little harsh on Mason on this occasion. But I wasn't going to let him off scot-free. A better idea struck me.

"Alright Mason, perhaps so many lines might be inappropriate. I'll commute it to an essay."

"But sir –"

"Be quiet, Mason, and take down the title," I cut in. He made no effort to conceal his crossness, bashing his notebook onto the bench and noisily selecting a pen from his pencil-case.

"'*Taxonomy: the intellectual justification for its more prominent place in the curriculum*'," I said slowly, giving him time to write it down. "That will help you learn a bit more Biology as well as acting as something of a deterrent with regard to your wayward and inappropriate remarks in my classroom. Two typed sides, please, Mason – by Monday morning. Now then, class, we can move on to the delights of oogenesis..." I was back in my stride.

Sunday 15th November 1997

Spent practically the whole day toiling over Tommy's blessed paper. The opening line was easy: 'According to the Oxford English Dictionary, taxonomy is the science of classification.' I had got that far by lunch time but the rest of the two sides were blank – a good reflection of my mind on the matter! Luckily, I had the idea to phone Alex James and, after his commiserations about Tommy's demand

and a blow-by-blow account of his golfing victory, he gave me a good few pointers about what I might put into it. I noted these pointers down, thanked him, and then buckled to it. With a few pots of strong tea behind me, I finally reached the end of side two. I saved it onto a floppy disc ready for printing at school tomorrow and will go to bed pleased with a job well done.

Monday 16th November 1997

On my way to the Copy Shop first thing this morning to get the paper for Tommy printed, I was passing Miss Lyter who then smiled and paused in front of me, holding out a typed sheet.

"Mason asked me to give you this, Mr Wentworth," she said. "He's got his driving test this morning and thought you'd want it sooner rather than later."

This was both unexpected and encouraging – Mason doing what he was told, on time, and with concern for his teacher for a change.

"Good stuff!" I said, taking the sheet and tucking it into my briefcase. For some reason, Miss Lyter coloured slightly before turning and demurely walking away. With an inward sigh about why more of the boys couldn't be like more of the girls, I went into Carriage House and into the hot and dingy room that is the Copy Shop where one of the ever-cheerful ladies took my disc and got on with churning it from digits to words on one of the machines. Meanwhile, I checked over the new bits of stationery on the shelves – they had some very pretty new coloured plastic sleeves and some natty paper clips that caught my eye.

"Here you are, Mr Wentworth," Pammy said and handed me the paper.

"Could you let me have a box of those assorted paper clips, Pammy – and what about that snazzy A4 wallet?" The latter I had just noticed, nestling behind some very dull-looking box files. The ladies in the Copy Shop are used to my stationery fixation and, after a happy few minutes, I left with Tommy's paper and a few other items stowed in my briefcase. I set off for the Common Room and the pre-school cup of tea I had earned.

The usual faces were there and showed some interest as I fished out my new A4 wallet to show them. Spotting Mason's punishment essay in the briefcase, I crunched it up into a ball and tossed it in the air towards Busby Beamish who, with that marvellous talent he has, headed it unerringly into the waste-paper bin with a cry of "One more for the Gunners!" I mentioned I'd had to spend hours on a paper for Tommy but got little sympathy – nearly all the others had had similar requests for papers on topics like 'Whither Keynesianism?', 'The Plate Tectonics of the Humanities' and 'The Art of Nature'. In fact, they rather sneered at my having to do just two typed sides so I changed the subject as I tucked the paper into one of our internal mail envelopes and added in Tommy's initials, TLC. "Any more ideas of what the 'L' stands for?" I asked. This old favourite rekindled a repetition of previous guesses and one or two new ones: "Leonard… Lasher…Lysistratum…Lionel…Loblolly…Lamplighter…Litlun!" and so on until, much cheered, we were summoned by the bell for first period. I put the envelope into the wire basket for the porter to deal with, washed my hands, had a quick read of the daily notices, then strolled across to my first class.

*   *   *

Just after school, I happened to be in Carriage House again and the duty porter handed me an internal mail envelope. I noticed it was the same one I had used that morning – GGW immediately below my TLC. It was my paper returned from Tommy with, written across the top in purple ink in his neat italic hand, 'Rather unexpected. Is this a joke?' I must say, my first reaction was intense irritation to this comment on all my hard work. Then I started reading.

The title was mine but the rest consisted of the following set of sentences repeated ten times to fill up the two sides:

'According to the Oxford English Dictionary, taxonomy is the art of stuffing. There is nothing like a good stuffing, something of particular importance in Biology where, without a lot of good stuffing going on, life would end. I would like a good stuffing. A good stuffing is not to be confused with getting stuffed. Getting stuffed is something you want to happen to someone else, especially someone else who has no stuffing of their own. They should be stuffed with the right stuff. The right stuff for someone lacking stuffing of their own would, I suppose, be good stuff. Here good stuff would make them better stuff. But probably not the sort of stuff you would ever like to have a good stuffing with. If they asked, you'd want to tell them to get stuffed just because they were the stuff of nightmares. Or a stuffed shirt. All stuff and no sense. I wouldn't ever want a stuffed shirt but would always welcome a stuffed blouse. That sort of stuff could lead to other sorts of stuff. Like a good stuffing. I really and sincerely doubt you've bothered to read this, sir, so I'll end now. GGet stuffed.'

Mason's essay, of course. No doubt my own was still nestling in the bin in the Common Room. Never mind – I still had the floppy disc on me and went into the Copy Shop to get another one printed off to give to Tommy.

The Copy Shop ladies were all looking rather fraught as they stood beside a few mounds of paper, facing the task of preparing a special 'letter-to-parents' with information about a new move in the curriculum which affected all pupils. "Four different sheets in thirteen different categories of pupil," Pammy said with as near a moan as I ever heard from her. "We'll be here for another two hours!" She was happy enough to break off the letter-job and run me off another copy of my paper for Tommy which I put carefully in another internal mail envelope and dropped in the mail for TLC.

Who should I run into as I left Carriage House but Mason – strolling nonchalantly along the path chatting to Misses Lyter and Limward.

"Mason!" I called. He looked at me quite cheerfully. "Going anywhere special?" I asked casually.

"We're heading into town to celebrate my passing my driving test, sir" he replied, the grin broadening on his face.

I wiped it off with a quiet: "I read your essay."

He shuffled about uncomfortably at this but, sensibly, said nothing. "I have a punishment for you which will take you an hour or so. Come with me."

I took him into the Copy Shop and told the ladies that I'd found an assistant to help them. The girls, who had followed us in, then said that they too would like to share in Mason's punishment. Who can fathom the female mind? I waved at the piles of letters to be put in envelopes and turned to the boy.

"A little job you might appreciate, Mason – stuffing envelopes!"

Leaving them to their task I set off towards the Biology Department to put my plastic dinosaurs in the dishwasher – they had all looked a little dusty on their recent outing – when I saw Chakraborty coming towards me with an earnest and inquisitive look about him. I turned sharply on my heel and hurried to the refuge of the Common Room where the cup that cheers and a read of the *Sun* proved far more congenial than some dreary discussion with a nit-picking ninny. Tea and page 3: hot stuff both!

Episode 14

From his diary

Tuesday January 10ᵗʰ 2007

This morning I communicated a stiffish email to the Chair of Common Room about the continued non-return of the stapler that I left in the Interview Room at the end of last term. This was in reply to his own offhand and rather insulting response to my last one - which, I might add, ran to seven paragraphs. I reproduce it here verbatim, including his stylistic idiosyncrasies (or should that be idiocies?):

> hiya george. sory abt yr missing staplr but am i yr staplr's keepr? prhps yr GGW on it made it a trophy *chuckle* sure itll turn up soon ;)

And this man is aspiring to be Head of English!

I feel embattled on two fronts what with this stapler business remaining unresolved and the next-door fencing dispute now poised at an apparently critical juncture. When that all started last summer I had no idea it would prove so contentious and time-consuming – leafing through my file on it I see that we have exchanged 14 letters on the subject (12 substantial ones from me and 2 from her) – so, since this is looming quite large in my life, I'll summarise the state of things here rather than trying to glue in copies of all the missives as that would make this diary overly bulky.

When the Family Benson outgrew the house and departed from number 26 several months ago, I was optimistic that the next occupant would be less troublesome. The continuous thrashing row of Little Billy's drum-kit late into the night, to say nothing of the weekend barbecue parties of 'Gatwick Guys 'n' Gals' that sent thick gusts of burnt meatsmoke and frivolous chatter over the hedge between us are, thankfully, fading gently into distant memory. And knowing that the occupant in question was to be 'Call me Dotty!' Benson, the maiden aunt I'd met one ghastly Christmas years ago, was reassuring – surely a spinster would be less noisy, less brash, less exuberant? In that, I was gratifyingly correct. But, true to form, she had a cat.

Though possessing no pretensions towards being a Monty Don or a Bob Flowerdew (let alone a Bill Sowerbutts!) I am quietly proud of my efforts in the garden and I had to object when her cat – a monstrous ginger-and-white thing – scratched up half a dozen of the African marigolds I'd only just planted along my 'sunburst' border. Although she didn't choose to formally reply to my letter on the subject, she did deliver a verbal apology along with a trayful of plants (a quite inappropriate collection of pansies in blues and purples which could have no place in 'sunburst' – and there was no room for them in 'azure', of course) and a suggestion that 'we do something about the hedge to keep Mr Tibbs from straying'. I had my own idea about that.

Her first note to me was, frankly, hysterical. Accusing me of cruelty to animals and threatening a report to the police merely because she had seen me with my catapult and a few old squash balls attempting to deter Mr Tibbs from entering my property through a gap in the privet hedge was wholly disproportionate in my view. I pointed out that, as a biologist I knew something about animal behaviour and that pain was a splendid teacher. I got no reply.

I also got no replies to my objection to the large piles of faeces Mr Tibbs took to leaving under the mahonia; to my objection that such excreta was proving the attraction to snails from her garden into mine and these snails were ravaging my begonias; to my request for compensation for snail-damage after having proved the snails provenance by marking a dozen I'd collected and dabbed with red paint and thrown back into her garden, some of which subsequently returned to mine; to my riposte to her cry from an open window 'perhaps they are homing snails!' concerning the habits of gastropods; to my request about stopping the caterwauling at night; to my suggestion that any animal-lover would have a cat put down to save the lives of wild birds attracted to my bird-bath.

Her second brief note informed me that she intended to put up a fence 'to prevent all animal traffic'.

She replied to none of the subsequent five letters I sent her at intervals over the next few weeks: about the extent of the hedge boundary on either of our properties; about disturbance to garden plants (including my half of the privet hedge) in the erection of her fence; about possible fence treatment products such as creosote harming plants and wildlife; about her fence contractors' noisy singing, whistling and blasting radio tuned to some inane 'music station'; about the style, colour and type of wood she had chosen for her fence. It almost seems pointless trying to engage with such people.

Wednesday 11ᵗʰ January 2007

I found a note from next-door on the mat this morning.

Dear George,

Thank you so much for putting up with all the disturbances while the fence installed. I'm assured that the colour will soon become weathered to a very natural tone. By way of celebration, would you like to join me (and Mr Tibbs!) for supper some time this week?

Yours,

Dotty

She must be a very strange woman – as if our repeated clashes during the past months were a mere nothing to be passed over as too trivial! I will give my response some thoughts before drafting a reply.

This slight air of despair with regard to the behaviour of the world was alleviated by my engaging with the 'Command Structure' that the new Head has 'rolled out to successfully drive the School to greater future peaks'. Fortunately, I can consult the glossy pamphlet that was sent to us all and so reproduce the magnificent system of management that now controls the School's destiny. At the pinnacle of it all is, naturally, the Head. Below that we have the Deputy Head for Internal Affairs, the Deputy Head for External Affairs, and the Chief Executive Officer. On the next tier down are: Pastoral Executive Officer; Academic Executive Officer; and Extra-curricular Executive Officer. Each of these ('execs' as they are referred to) has three Superintendents ('supers') reporting back to them. So, for example, the Academic Executive Officer oversees the Superintendent for Academic Development, the Superintendent for Academic Implementation and the Superintendent for Academic Assessment. Now here we have a little blurring of the strict hierarchy (not helped by the lines of demarcation getting folded into the spine of the pamphlet) as it is unclear whether the Superintendents are above or below the thirteen Commanders that we have: Commander of Marketing, Commander of Admissions, of Information Systems, of Accounting, of Tertiary Education, of Day Pupils, of Boarding Pupils, of External Examinations, of Materials, of Buildings, of Administration, of Physical Well-Being, of Parental Liaison. These thirteen Commanders each controls a team of two Assistants to the Commander. Naturally enough, there are several Squadrons of Secretaries (with their five doughty Squadron-Leaders) to do the donkey-work for all of the above. Oh, and I nearly forgot the seven Heads of Year each of whom has a Deputy Head of Year. And, of course, the Cadre of Comms-Pilots whose sole job it is to facilitate and integrate communications between all elements of the Command Structure.

Naturally, all these groups required budgets and these were created from the scrapping of the budgeting system based on the old departmental structure the School suffered under. The last penetrating and candid audit described most of these old budgets as 'confections of fudge and fiction' which, of course, was only to be expected by having people in charge without the training, skills, organization or aptitude for the precise science of keeping accounts.

In my first lesson this morning with my Upper Sixth, I was using the departmental calculator to illustrate the value of finding the standard deviation for data as well as the mean (the data I was using were their marks from a recent test) when the battery ran out. I went into the office to get a replacement when my head of department, Brenda Whipple (who, despite her other sterling qualities, is a bit of a stick in the mud when it comes to grand visions for change) told me, quite rightly, I would have to use the new system. Given the drop-down menus and the electronic reporting forms, this was pretty straight-forward but, since the calculator was being used for teaching ('the value of standard deviation') as well as involving pupils' marks ('data from test results') I had to apply to both the Superintendent for Academic Implementation and the Superintendent for Academic Assessment as well as, naturally enough, to the Academic Executive Officer, the Commander of Accounting and (since a calculator is classed in the same category as other electronic equipment) Commander of Information Systems. Given that my request involved more than three Superintendents and/or Commanders, the Chief Executive Officer was automatically incorporated into the request.

By this time, I thought I'd better get back into the classroom (where the noise level was getting pretty intolerable) and to the lesson. An appeal to the pupils produced a battery from Temms and, once installed, we got on with things. As Brenda told me when she heard what I'd done, this meant more applications re the battery: to the Superintendent of Teacher-Pupil Interactions, the Commander of Day Pupils and the Commander of Parental Liaison. And since now there were more than six Superintendents and/or Commanders involved in the request, both the Deputy Heads for Internal and External Affairs were copied in to help smooth over any 'turf wars' that might ensue.

With any luck it shouldn't take too long for all parties involved to agree to a decision about the precise weighting of the cost that each Section should shoulder to cover the amount incurred and then for a cheque to be authorized, a courier sent with it to the bank to bring back the 82p in cash that will reimburse Temms for the battery.

I reflected with satisfaction on how this rational and structured ordering of the School, with its 69 'drivers' is a massive advance on the situation which obtained when I joined the School four decades ago when everything was decided by just three people: Tim Naylor, Byron Craggs and Di Daley - a recipe for muddle and misrule if ever there was one.

In the peaceful hiatus of a post-lunch free period I was resting in my chair in the Common Room when Richard Hansum floated in. He was wearing a dark suit and a black tie and I surmised that he had just got back from Tony Cobberly's funeral.

'Yes, it was all quite nicely done, Dob,' he said, languidly flicking at a stray piece of lint that had found its importunate way onto the leg of his sharply-creased trousers. 'Though it was rather a pity that the vicar brought up the subject of the only book old Cobberly ever managed to get into print. It would have been far better, in my view, to have glossed over his continual difficulties with the publishing world. Alluding to his one victory just pointed up the complete lack of success with the slew of other offerings he made.'

I remembered Cobberly proudly presenting me with a signed copy of this singular book which he described as 'a stocking-filler aimed at a narrow pseudo-intellectual market'. It consisted of a compendium of the oddest ideas promulgated by the Ancient Greek philosophers that were now totally ignored (such as the world being all water, or movement an illusion) and had the title *Thunk Without Trace*. I still haven't opened it but will do so when time allows: I suppose I owe him that much.

'I did meet his brother, an associate professor of orthodontics at Brixham University,' Hansum went on, 'and he told me rather a good story that Cobberly kept from us concerning a spat he had that finished off any chance of his getting a foot-hold on the ladder to fame and recognition that comes with appearing on the small screen. This happened in the mid-seventies when Cobberly was granted the opportunity of participating in a television program called *Mastermind* hosted by a great Icelandic personality.'

I nodded at Hansum to indicate I was familiar with it. To myself, I registered some surprise that Cobberly had been one of the show-offs keen to parade what they think of as their intellectual superiority for the sake of winning a cheap glass bowl. I thought I'd known him well but here was a facet of his character that had been hidden from me – something bearing out Hugh Pollen's observation, I suppose.

'It seems that Cobberly had acquitted himself faultlessly on his specialist subject of Homer's *Iliad* and *Odyssey* and was several points clear of his nearest rival, a well-nourished retired librarian of the female persuasion who had done rather well herself on the subject of *The Webbs and Post-Revolutionary British Marxist Schisms*. I expect you know that there follows a second round of general knowledge questions?' I nodded again – I usually manage to get one or two of these myself if they are on the subject of Angola or Biology.

'Our librarian fared moderately well on this round and was the one possible obstacle to a Cobberly victory as the other two contestants had achieved only the humiliation of single-figure totals. But her final score was a modest seven ahead and, given his earlier showing, no-one could doubt that the obstacle presented by the librarian was anything more than mere dust soon to be crushed beneath Cobberly's triumphant chariot wheels. But things went very differently.'

Hansum's face changed and, with that wonderful gift for mimicry he has, he played out the scene of Magnus Magnusson's questioning and Cobberly's replies. I could almost have been there myself.

'"Tony Cobberly, schoolmaster and scholar, you scored eighteen points on your specialist subject on the works of Homer. Your target to beat is twenty-five points. You have two and a half minutes on general knowledge and your time starts now. Which of Christ's twelve apostles was a doctor?"
"None of them."
"Wrong, it was Luke. Where –"
"No, Luke was not a doctor –"
"Where in the body would –"
"I have to insist, Mr Magnusson, that Luke was not a doctor. That is a very common misconception. It arises from a misinterpretation

of the particular Codex used by Aquila of Pontus. In the oldest Codex, Luke is referred to as what is best described as 'healer with herbs'. Aquila, in his notoriously haphazard way, rendered this as what approximates best to 'healer of men'. Jerome who - as every schoolboy knows – failed to go to the primary sources and merely translated Aquila's Greek bible into Latin, chose the term which modern usage agrees to be 'physician' for Aquila's 'healer of men': hence the mistake. The best description of Luke's profession would be 'apothecary' which, as you are no doubt aware, is very different from a doctor. Your researchers should have checked that more carefully –"

'At this point a distressed floor-manager breaks in and approaches our noble contestant clutching a clip-board to his narrow chest.

"Cut, cut! Mr Cobberly we really can't have this sort of back-chat! Just answer the question or say 'pass'. We'll have to start you off again. Just wait for Magnus to do the intro and –"

'Our *Marxist Schisms* expert gets off her chair and waddles into the argument.
"That's not fair. Why should he get another chance just because he didn't know Luke was a doctor? And he's had some practice in the chair with general knowledge now – none of the rest of us had that. He should just retire as it's all his fault that the program has gone wrong –"

'Here I'm afraid Cobberly was rather short with her and dismissed her with a reference to one of the general knowledge questions she had stumbled over.
"Just you 'Mungo Park' your backside where it belongs and leave us men –"

'This brusque dismissal brings the quick-tempered husband of the librarian into the fray. Leaping from his seat in the front row of the audience he rushes up to the group which now includes Cobberly who has vacated the forbidding black leather chair and, with a good deal of belligerence, shouts in his face.

"Don't you talk to my wife like that you fat slap-head!"

'Cobberly turns to him coolly and, employing one of the choicer phrases from his never-published compilation *Insults from the Ancient World*, calls him 'a goat-herd's shite-wipe'. This is in Greek, of course, but the man evidently gets the gist that it is pretty nasty.

"Oh yurr!" he jeers, displaying a lamentable lack of good breeding and dentistry, "Suck on this!" and takes a mighty swing at Cobberly's jaw. Cobberly ducks and the fist slams into the unsuspecting floor-manager behind him who collapses like a demolished chimney-stack taking with him the impressive form of the librarian. Her legs begin waving in the air like a pair of monstrous pink caterpillars and reveal altogether far too much of her surprising underwear which the pugilistic spouse attempts to hide by bending and linking his brawny arms around her knees. Cobberly is about to sink a judicious boot into the posterior that fate has kindly presented but, at this point, a second floor-manager steps into the melée and hustles Cobberly off the stage, off the program, out of the building, and out of the limelight of television's fame. Poor old Uncle Tom,' on these words Hansum's voice cracked a little.

I was chortling at the story and this caused me to slide forward a little on the leather of my chair. I grasped the arms to push myself back into the seat better and my right hand slipped down between the side of the arm and the cushion. I felt a hard object. It was my stapler. How on Earth had it got there? While Hansum was carefully wiping his eyes with his handkerchief, I surreptitiously got the stapler into my pocket. I would have to throw it away later – I didn't want to look a fool.

Episode 15

From his diary

5pm Friday March 20ᵗʰ 1975

I doubt that I'll have time later to complete an account of the day's events given the thrilling evening ahead of me, so will just put down what has led up to this moment while Mother takes the time to press my evening suit and iron my dress shirt. Suffice to say, brain and body are both in a highly-elevated state of anticipation!

True, today did not start off all that auspiciously in my double lesson with 1Q first thing. I was washing through the complete sheep's gut (from oesophagus to anus – no half measures!) I had got in from the abattoir after having stretched it out for the pupils to appreciate 'the real thing' and prior to the dissection I had planned. (And although, yet again, half a dozen of the pathetic little things either fainted or were sick at the sight/smell, I maintain in the face of general opposition from my colleagues in Biology that this is a fair price to pay for the experience.) Despite my having sent a stern note to the Reinstatement Department last week about the faulty tap over the sink on our raised teacher's bench, nothing had been done and when I tried to turn it off the tap just went round and round while the water continued pouring out. Unfortunately, some of the gut (I later identified it as the appendix and part of the colon) blocked the sink outlet and, as a consequence, the rather foul washings, together with a fair length of intestines, overflowed and cascaded down onto the front pupils' bench ruining several exercise and text books as well as one or two of the furry gonks that children that age like to bring in with them. There were a couple more fainting attacks and a general screaming exodus from the rest but, once the mess had been attended to by our stalwart lab technicians, I think I can safely say that the educational benefit outweighed any of the trauma suffered.

The rest of the teaching day was without incident apart from having to reprove Mason for putting several small boys on the branch of the pine tree outside the library. He has grown into something of a hulk now that he is in the Sixth and had lifted them easily up the eight or nine feet above the tarmac where they sat, keening and snivelling, when I came out from lunch and spotted them. The reason he gave for this bit of tomfoolery was 'to elevate their prospects while providing ornamentation for our eyes'. I made him catch them as they jumped down one by one and then waved him away to his lesson while adding a bon mot to the effect that one day the size of his *brain* would catch up with the size of his *frame*. To his credit, he turned and smiled and nodded to acknowledge this piece of wordplay and wisdom.

Perhaps the underlying inspiration for my rhyming quip came as a result of the conversation I'd just been having over a leisurely lunch with Richard Hansum and young Busby Beamish. Busby had surprised me with an invitation to join him for a romantic Equinox Supper at the newly-opened Langan's Brasserie in Mayfair. Hansum had coughed and raised a laconic eyebrow and Busby hurried to make it clear that this was with 'a couple of gorgeous girls from the Maths Department at Rainham College'. When I asked who these might be, Busby said, "Blind date, Dobbin, blind date." Then he broke into song in his pleasing baritone:

There'll be one for you, and one for me;
A couple of couples that's what we'll be.

We'll kiss and dance by the light of the moon;
Laugh and love, get married in June."

"Rather a rushed romance you are planning, Beamish," said Hansum with a wry smile, tapping the ash from his Russian cigarette. "But I do so love the linguistic kitsch of popular songs – the sighing and crying, yearning and burning, lovey-dovey, art's-sake, heart-breakiness of it all…" He sipped the last of his cognac and, having placed the glass carefully back in the small indentation it had made on the table cloth, glanced quickly at us both. "Before your lover's tryst later this evening - with the no-doubt numinous and numerate little numbers that will be adding their charms and dividing the attention of the other clientele at the Brasserie - why not drop in to my modest book-launch party?"

He gave us the august address of the rooms where Faber were launching his latest volume of poems *Vision and Visions; Volitions and Velleities* and I think that young Busby shared my sense of privilege in being afforded some admission to the high-flown world that Hansum inhabited. He waved away our burbles of thanks and admiration and, with a self-depreciating smile, told us that he was sure we would contribute towards the colour and amusement of the event and that he looked forward to our being there prior to our 'late-night spooning'.

I am nervous! I am excited! I am alive!

Saturday 21st March 1975

I am fed up. Mother has just beaten me by 4 games to 1 in our usual Saturday Night Scrabble Match and won't stop crowing about it. Occasionally, due solely to her having fluked some good letters while I have all vowels or similar, or when I take the risk and allow her access to the triple-worders not expecting a lucky 'quiz' or 'boxer' that she plonks down with a cry of triumph, yes, occasionally she takes the odd game off me, but she rarely wins our 'best of seven' weekly head-to-head matches. I have to say that, unusually for me, my heart wasn't in it all evening due to my brooding over the events of yestereve and thinking of what might have been. I suppose the silver lining is that her chances of catching up with me in our league (where she finally has a few more points from her score in the 'W' column to go with the 2 in the 'D' where a power failure and lack of candles, and the discovery of the missing 'V', stopped matches mid-session) are pretty small even if we do have 52 matches a year for the next 50 years!

In fact, now I think about it a bit more, the evening in London had its memorable moments despite my romantic hopes being dashed when I spoke to young Busby at lunchtime today and he handed me a plastic carrier-bag containing my watch, dinner jacket, dress shirt and bow tie together with the sodden remains of my shoe and said, "When Maggie and I got back to the flats in the early hours, Mary just opened her door and pushed the bag into my hand and told me to 'give these back to your friend the filthy little pervert' and then slammed the door in our faces. What the hell happened, Dob? Look, you'll have to tell me later – I've got to take the Firsts away." With a half a smile and a puzzled shake of the head, young Busby hurried off.

Perhaps painful though recounting the events may be for me, I will keep the faith. This is what happened.

I admit to some trepidation as we ascended the shallow marble staircase of the Athenaeum. Young Busby, on the other hand, seemed totally relaxed, keeping up a steady flow of comments on the surroundings which he was comparing unfavourable with the décor of the school's administrative block, Carriage House. "Pity they have this Greek statue when you could have a vase of dusty plastic flowers...Why have plush crimson pile carpet when scabby brown lino is available?...Notice the dullness of the hand-painted bosses and motifs on the walls compared to the greasy grey shoulder-marks from innumerable rubbings…Oh look, a dreary old Reynolds painting instead of a faded photograph of a boy failing at the high jump…" We reached the room and were ticked off on a list on a clipboard held by a rather harassed-looking woman.

There were about a dozen people inside, all in a circle being addressed by a long-haired chappie in a beige suit who had his back to us. Hansum noticed us and came across to shake hands and lead us to a small drinks table. Unable to fulfil young Busby's request for a pint of mild, he looked a trifle put out until Busby reassured him that he'd love to try a Campari and soda instead. I chose a dry sherry. He took us across to the circle murmuring that he thought Busby might know the man in beige, a last-minute guest brought in by a Faber executive.

"So I dropped a nut on that ponce Keegan and the ref -" the man in the beige suit didn't get to finish the sentence as he caught sight of us approaching and gave a great shout of delight: "Beamer!" He followed this up by hugging young Busby and the two of them then performed a sort of shimmying dance at each other which included foot-tapping, hip-wagging and head-nodding (rather like the courtship ritual of the red grouse). It turned out that the man had played football in the same team as Busby – Islington Schoolboys – and was now a professional with Arsenal. I was introduced to Charlie George. Busby pointed at Charlie's hand which was liberally covered in specks of red paint.

"What's the story there, Charlie?"

"You're looking at the reason I won't be in the team to play Spurs tomorrow, Beamer mate. I got caught red-handed!" he laughed immoderately before going on, "You know our arsey manager? Well he's been right snotty with me for months now. Earlier in the week he bought himself a new black Jag – right proud of it too. Well, this morning at the training ground I turn up late and go to the car-park first with a spray can of red paint, find the Jag and write 'Bugger Mee'

– that's M-E-E of course - down both sides of it. Chuck away the can and trot out onto the pitch and he calls me over for a dressing-down about lateness – and then tells me off for not even washing my hands properly. Later, when he sees the Jag he puts two and two together and nabs poor Charlie," he paused to swig back a large amount of drink. "Reckon it's the transfer list for me."

He and Busby went on to reminisce about past games and larks while Hansum introduced me to a man who made hats in Kensington. I can't remember his name but he talked non-stop for about a quarter of an hour and kept touching my arm. Nor can I remember much of what he said except it was about the iniquity of miners getting a 35% pay rise and how he hoped the new leader of the Conservatives would 'stamp a stiletto or two into Arthur's comb-over, the gobseckery old git' whatever that meant. I haven't the time for politics and so just nodded and smiled my way through the harangue. I was rescued by Busby and Charlie who combined to pull me away saying we all had another engagement. We hastily said farewell to Hansum who, apparently very taken by him, pressed a copy of his new book into Charlie's red hand with a hope that they could meet in the future to hear his opinions.

After a 'couple of quick ones' in the 'nearest boozer' it was decided (though I had one or two reservations but kept them to myself) that Charlie should join us at Langan's to meet the 'Rainham talent'. By the time we got there, we were nearly twenty minutes late and, before they caught sight of us, were both looking rather cheesed off. My heart started thudding: one of them was merely attractive; the second was absolutely stunning. Busby whispered in my ear that the stunning one, Mary, was my date. I gulped and felt my legs turn to the consistency of jelly.

Luckily, Charlie proved a great ice-breaker, embracing both girls and throwing wild compliments at them. Busby smoothly slipped an arm around the attractive one, kissed her quickly on the lips and introduced her to me: "Maggie Mayfield". She shook hands and then Busby said, "And this is her co-calculator, Mary Boyne. Mary, meet the perfectly formed master of all things dinosaurial, George Wentworth – but everyone calls him 'Dobbin'." Mary gave me a dazzling smile and a gentle hand. God, she was beautiful! I think I managed to mumble 'Pleased to meet you, I'm sure' while we all settled down at the table and Charlie called for 'a bottle of champagne, no, make that two bottles, mate – I'm thirsting for the wine of love!'

Like me, Mary scarcely got a word in as Maggie, Busby and Charlie kept a lively conversational ball ricocheting across the table: it was terrifically entertaining and marvellous to be a part of. The meal and wine was ordered and consumed and in that couple of hours all I managed to discover that the lovely Mary was from Ireland, loved tea, knew nothing about football teams and had perfect table manners and a superb smile. Was I falling in love?

At this moment – about 10 o'clock or so – another party came into the Brasserie and settled down at a table several yards from us. They attracted a good deal of attention because one of the couples there was particularly famous: Rod Stewart and Britt Eckland. They made all heads crane in their direction.

"You watch this Beamer," said Charlie quietly, beckoning to a waiter and ordering four bottles of champagne to be sent over to the Stewart/Eckland party. The bottles were duly delivered and, as they turned to us to see who was being so generous, Charlie lobbed a bread roll at Rod Stewart and cried "On yer 'ead, son!" Stewart immediately leapt to his feet and headed the bread roll into an ice bucket with a shout of "One more for the Gunners!" Then, with a huge grin and a running skip, he dashed over and wrapped his arms around Charlie and lifted him off his feet.

"Charlie George, as I live and breathe!" he shouted. "Why aren't you home in bed getting some beauty sleep – I'm expecting you to stick a couple past Jennings tomorrow, you reprobate!" Charlie explained about his being dropped for painting the manager's car. Stewart was delighted with the story and laughed uproariously. Then his brilliant gaze swept around our table. Charlie made the introductions as Britt Eckland stepped languorously across and took Stewart's hand and kissed his neck.

"This is Busby Beamish who was on the Gunners' books for a couple of years, and these are..." Busby smoothly stepped in and pointed at each of us as Charlie looked a bit lost:

"Dobbin, the gorgeous Mary Boyne, and the light of my eyes, Maggie Mayfield."

At this last name, Rod Stewart smiled and threw back his head and started to sing.

"Wake up Maggie, I think I've got something to say to you
It's late September and I really should be back at school
I know I keep you amused, but I feel I'm being used
Oh Maggie I couldn't have tried anymore."

At this point in the rendition, it seemed like the whole of Langan's Brasserie joined in with the song (except me, of course, as I haven't the time to keep abreast of popular culture and so knew none of the words). I must say I found the colour creeping into my cheeks as I glanced at Mary lustily singing:

"All you did was wreck my bed
And in the morning kick me in the head."

The volume was immense, the gaiety enormous as the song drew to a terrific close:

"You stole my heart but I love you anyway..."

At the finish, amid the wild cheering, whistling and yelling, Stewart turned to Britt Eckland and gave her a searching kiss; Busby took Maggie's waist and kissed her deeply on the lips; I looked into

Mary's eyes and she smiled encouragingly at me: I shook her hand warmly.

As normality returned, Rod Stewart took Charlie George's arm and suggested that, since he was free, why didn't we all 'split this gaff' and 'hit the mean streets for a night of partying'? Charlie was immediately enthusiastic, as were Busby and Maggie. I demurred, thinking that Mother would be concerned if I didn't return home in good time – and, of course, I had a full teaching load the next day. Mary said that she too would give it a miss and we both sat down as the others boisterously collected the champagne bottles from the Stewart/Eckland table and, with the others in their party, crushed out of the door raucously singing:

> *"Champagne Charlie is my name, by golly,*
> *And rogueing and stealing is a game"*

Mary and I sipped the last of our wine and I asked her if I could see her back to her flat in Rainham. She smiled and said that would be very nice. I called for the bill. The waiter came back with our bill and was accompanied by the manager with another. The manager asked me if I was 'Mr Beamish's friend George'. I said I was and he handed me the bill for six bottles of champagne. I drew out my cheque book and suppressed a sigh – together, the bills came to something like a month's salary. But I wasn't going to let that take the shine off the fact that the beautiful Mary Boyne was slipping an arm through mine as was stepped out into the street.

A taxi and a train ride later, we arrived at the front door of a fine Victorian building in the salubrious environs of this popular London district and she invited me inside for 'a special cup of tea'.

On the train journey, she had told me about her novelty tea-pot collection but I was unprepared for its extent: the sitting room had shelves on all walls, and on all shelves there were tea-pots. It was quite bewildering to the eye: there were arrays of 'famous faces' tea-pots; tea-pots in the shapes of buildings from cottages to palaces; monuments from the Eiffel Tower to Cheops' Pyramid; tea-pots in the shape of insects, mammals, fish, crustaceans, birds; there was a tea-pot with two spouts marked 'tea for two and two for tea'; even a chocolate tea-pot 'though I don't ever use that one' Mary assured me with her stunning smile.

"But this is the one I think is just right," she said and lifted down a large purple tea-pot. It was not a bad reproduction of a brontosaurus with the long neck and head forming the spout although, as I pointed out, the long tail which curled over to form the handle was anatomically impossible. She laughed and lightly touched my cheek saying that Busby had been right about my being a dinosaur expert.

My heart was galloping as I sank into the plush velvety sofa while Mary went to the kitchen to make the tea. When she returned, all went along wonderfully. She was warm and witty and laughed easily at my small jokes and frequently patted my knee with approval and a knowing look. The conversation got around to her time at a convent school back in Ireland 'where the only males we ever got close to wore their collars the wrong way'. At this she mentioned how she'd put in an entry for Rainham School's magazine *Cyclops* which was running a competition for a short story in less than 250 words. I said I'd love to read it and she immediately went over to her desk and handed me a typed sheet of paper. As I read it, she sat down close to me and read it too, our thighs and shoulders touching, her rich blonde hair tickling my cheek.

For The Love of God

She waited under the tree at the end of the road where the curate lodged. She'd be late for school but what did that matter? Ten more minutes passed. Then, on his bicycle, soutane rippling, he swept around the corner. She called out a greeting and he braked hard stopping at her feet.

'Hello,' he said. His voice was low – husky even. Were his emotions as strong as hers?

'Touch of catarrh,' he explained. His voice had fallen and, conspiratorially, she moved her head a little towards his.

'In fact,' he went on, 'last night in bed I coughed and coughed then suddenly found myself with a great clot of phlegm in my mouth.'

She stopped breathing at the thought of it: slick, warm and alive, pillowed on the red velvet of his tongue.

'I got up to go to the bathroom but Mrs Barlow must have been in there: I saw the light under the door.' He paused. Shadow patches fluttered over him and a fleck of the sun rested briefly on his dog-collar revealing a faint but ancient stain.

'So I'm afraid I opened my bedroom window and spat it out onto the path beneath. When it landed it sounded very loud.' His eyes held hers. 'But, do you know, when I went for my bike just now there was no sign of it anywhere. I wonder what happened to it?'

She, too, wondered.

I hadn't a clue what the point of it was but said it was great. I also made a mental note about suggesting to Jane Pensword that Sixokes could run such a competition and I could put in something about the life of a dinosaur – but which one? Such a tough choice…perhaps a series? While I mused along these lines and tucked Mary's story into my dinner-jacket pocket, I felt a need. The champagne, wine and cupfuls of tea, had run through the system so I excused myself and entered Mary's bathroom.

It was exquisitely decorated in a combination of chocolate and cream: dark velvety brown wall-paper; cream tiles; dark lavatory seat beneath a period elevated cistern and ceramic handled chain; creamy bath and wash-basin; brown laundry basket; cream towels on a rack. I glanced at myself in the mirror and smiled at my reflection: I felt on top of the world! So cruel of Fate to send it crashing all around me! It began with my pants.

This was the first time I was wearing a new-fangled item of underwear. Hitherto, I had always stuck to my tried and trusted white Y-fronts but, in honour of the occasion, I had decided to slip on a pair of the 'briefs' that Mother had bought me last Christmas. Their rather daring shade of pale blue had made me feel young and adventurous at the time. Now, having unbuttoned my fly and lifted back the lavatory seat (which only just reached the vertical), I found briefs lack an opening as per usual in Y-fronts. It meant having to hoick down the elasticated waist with a left-hand thumb while guiding the *membrum virilis* over the top with my right. I started urinating and was in full flow when the lavatory seat began to fall back towards the pan. I grabbed at it with my left hand to save it getting sprayed with urine. However, this allowed the elasticated waistband of the briefs to spring upwards against my whatsit and hence cause me instead to spray urine in an arc over the wallpaper which darkened very noticeably.

After a bit of manoeuvring (and a short thought on how lifting lavatory seats and finding them ill-fitting is never a consequence for the female of the species) I completed the evacuation of my bladder and looked at the dark arc on the wall. Taking some of the toilet paper I scrubbed at it vigorously. Unfortunately, the effect of this was not only to remove the urine, it also removed quite a bit of the colour in the wallpaper and now I was looking at a pale swathe which was even more noticeable than the dark arc. Dropping the toilet paper in the pan, my eye swept along the shelf above the bath looking (far more in hope than expectation) for something to save the situation. It seemed that, after all, fate was on my side: there was a bottle of hair dye advertising itself as 'chocolate brown' and right next to it was a basket of cotton-wool balls. I took a couple of balls of cotton-wool and, having unscrewed the bottle of hair-dye, applied them to the opening while shaking it. I put the bottle down on the edge of the bath and carefully swabbed the hair-dye over the pale swathe on the wall-paper. It had some masking effect, but another coat was needed. Reaching for the bottle I accidentally knocked it into the bath where it emptied itself in a moment, producing a large brown pool. I dabbed up some of it with the cotton-wool balls and applied a bit more colour to the wall. Though by no means invisible, it wasn't a bad match.

Dropping the stained cotton-wool balls into the pan, I now turned to cleaning the bath. The obvious solution was to take the shower attachment in hand and hose the hair-dye away. This shower attachment was hooked high up above the taps and just out of my reach. I stepped onto the lavatory seat to get at it. But I had forgotten about the rickety fixing of the seat and, when I put my weight on it, it shifted suddenly to one side and I slipped and plunged my foot deep into the U-bend. As I was falling, I clutched at the chain and my weight broke it off in my hand but not after emptying the cistern.

With my foot jamming the U-bend, the water from the cistern rose high in the pan. My violent yanking on the chain before breaking it off seemed to have caused the cistern to continue to allow water to flow and, in just a few seconds, the pan was brim-full of dilutely urinous water in which floated brown-stained squares of toilet paper and cotton-wool balls. Now it began to overflow. Cursing my luck in having two plumbing obstructions in a single day, I acted. Clearly, to remove the blockage, I would have to untie my shoelace, slide out my foot and then pull the shoe clear. But to untie the shoelace would mean plunging my arms into the panful of water.

Hastily, I removed my watch, dinner jacket, bow-tie and dress shirt (cursing the fiddly dress studs and cufflinks which took agonising seconds to undo) and flung them (together with the useless lavatory chain) towards the other end of the bathroom. The steady overflow from the pan was increased as I put both arms deep into the water and scrabbled at the shoelace. I couldn't find the ends and the pain in my foot was nigh-on intolerable as I bent to the task. It occurred to me that the pain there might well be causing swelling which would make extrication even more difficult to achieve so I'd better hurry up.

It was at this point that I heard banging and muffled shouts. The occupant of the flat below had noticed water flooding through their ceiling. Casting round for something to help mop up the steady flow over the pan, I seized on the packet of sanitary towels between the lavatory and the bath. I ripped it open and spread the dozen towels as best as I could around the base of the pan. They were soon soaked and sopping. I needed something more. Reluctant to use Mary's fresh creamy bath towels, I hit on the idea that there might be used ones in the laundry basket. I had just knocked off the lid of the basket and pulled out the first couple of things on the top when there was some furious knocking on the bathroom door. Holding one of the items in my right hand, I put the second one from my left between my teeth so I could stretch a hand towards the bathroom door key. It was barely reachable but, with a tremendous effort, I managed to turn it. But while turning it I overbalanced and fell backwards. My foot was forcibly and painfully wrenched free of my shoe in the pan and I fell flat on the floor winding myself.

The door was slowly pushed open and Mary's face appeared and took in the devastation of the scene. There was the soaked floor and brown pool in the bath, the wrecked toilet seat and chainless cistern, and there I lay shoeless and gasping amid sodden scraps of soiled toilet paper, cotton-wool balls and sanitary towels, stripped to the waist, fly gaping, in my right hand her brassiere and with the gusset of her knickers stuffed in my mouth.

I must have cut rather a poor figure.

Episode 16

From his diary (including a letter gummed therein)

Thursday 8th March 2004

Amongst the usual trash that pours through the door, this morning I found something of a treasure and a curiosity in the post: a personal letter with real (though rather childish) handwriting spelling out the address. It was addressed not to me but to Mother – or, rather, "Ms Elizabeth Wentworth". Here it is:

13b Staindrop Street
Barnard Castle
Teesdale
Durham

3rd March 2004

Dear Elizabeth

Sorry if this is a shock for you but my grandfather Reggie Boothby died just after Christmas last. He died peaceful and in his sleep. He was cremated in a very nice service. I have the ashes on my mantelpiece in front of me. I am writing to you because of the shoebox in his wardrobe. On top of the personal stuff in it I just found your card saying your change of address

*from Edgbaston to the one I sent this to. Because of what is in
the box I thought you would like to know this.*

Yours,

Diana Boothby

Naturally enough, although it has been well over four years
since Mother, to use her favourite term "dropped off the perch", this
communication did give me food for thought. What was in the box?
To illustrate how greatly this question distracted me all I need do is
recount an incident with my 4th form – or 'Year 10s' as they like to call
themselves nowadays – during period two. After a piece of silliness
from one of the boys and then cleaning the board of some nonsense
or other, I wrote up a load of notes for them to copy and then, with
a quiet cup of tea, sat thinking at my desk while they got on with it.
Sometime later, I became aware of quite a buzz of noise going on and
demanded the meaning of it.

"We've all finished, sir," said Atkins looking brightly up at me
from the solitary 'naughty desk' right the other side of mine.

Sure enough, a quick check of a few books confirmed that a
good half an hour must have passed while I was pondering on the
contents of the letter. I still had ten minutes of the lesson to fill up
so thought I'd write up some more notes for them. I went to pick up
the board-duster from the old oak teacher's desk in front of me but
it was immovable. When I say immovable, I mean it – at one point
I scrambled up onto the desk and, with the board-duster squarely
between my feet, wrenched on it with all my strength. It didn't
budge. Not to be defeated, I jumped down and went to the prep room
and came back with a hammer and chisel and, with a few judicious
blows, separated duster from desk. They all cheered my efforts as I
brandished the board-duster above my head. Then the bell went and
they all crowded out of the door.

"Sounded a very popular lesson!" Barbarella trilled as she swept
through the classroom with an armful of exercise books. "Oh no

– what happened to your desk?" She had paused and was looking down at the gouges in its surface – several largish splinters from the desk had come up with the board-duster after my efforts with the chisel. "I bet they super-glued it! They can be little blighters can't they?" she threw over her shoulder leaving me with something else to think about besides the contents of the shoebox.

During lunch, I mentioned to Hansum that I had something personal that was puzzling me and, considerate as ever, he immediately invited me around to his apartment earlier this evening to help "sample a '96 that should be ready for broaching" and that we could "discuss the matter in rather more comfort and confidence than this hell-hole" with a pained expression as our colleagues noisily shovelled away their food with much more haste than discrimination.

"After Mother died I found out that she'd been having an affair with this man Boothby – a man she knew was married with a family." I told Hansum. "I knew him as 'Uncle Reggie'. I liked him."

"Well," he said, pushing the letter towards me across the occasional table on which rested our glasses of claret, "I can see why you are suffering some disquiet, Dob." He relaxed in his chair and rolled his fingers on the arms a couple of times. "Love letters would be the obvious thing she says are in the box – though doubtless your mother would have had to send them somewhere other than to his home … but then, why doesn't our dear Diana say that they are letters if that's what she means by 'personal stuff'? Perhaps the contents are merely innocent nothings steeped in sentiment – like a piece of court plaister and the leadless end of an old pencil, for instance … On the other hand, there is that last sentence with that 'because of what is in the box' bit which could have a sinister interpretation … but" he added briskly, "since your mother is dead, there is no question of anything in it being an embarrassment to you, Dob, nothing like any sort of blackmail if that what was worrying you!"

"I hadn't really thought of that," I said. "I'd just thought it would be letters. And that she might have mentioned me in them, that was all."

Hansum set down his glass and looked at me seriously.

"My advice is never – never – think that what anyone says of someone else behind their back is any better an indication of the truth than what anyone says to someone's face. If you want the truth –". At this moment there was a knock at the door. It was Tony Cobberly fresh from his detention duty.

Hansum held up the bottle and Cobberly squinted at the label and raised his eyebrows. "Worth a try, certainly," he said as he hitched at the front folds of his gown before slumping into the depths of a fine leather armchair. After some fairly stertorous sniffing and slurping he finally swallowed some of the wine that Hansum had presented to him. He turned to me:

"One of the joyful band with me this evening was Atkins as usual. I saw from the crime sheet that you'd put him in for 'having sticky fingers', Dob – does that mean you caught him misappropriating?"

I explained about the supergluing of the board-duster and the damage done to the desk as a consequence. I was putting my glass back onto the table and, clumsily I acknowledge, spilled a little wine onto its surface. Hansum leapt to his feet and, plucking a snowy handkerchief from the sleeve of his jacket, wiped it up.

"My French polisher insists on it," he explained giving it a final caressing touch.

"Nice piece of Tunbridge-ware," observed Cobberly nudging the table with his toe. "Goes well with your side-table there. He looked across at the glossy piece of furniture beneath a rather startling large oil painting in a style I call 'modern'. "Jean and I are thinking of getting something in this line. Expensive?"

It was clear that, like me, Hansum thought this sort of question rather vulgar. However, his principle of good manners trumped his principle for discouraging poor taste.

"The two are insured for £10 000," he said abruptly and changed the subject while I inwardly shook my head on the silly amounts of money spent on so-called 'antiques'. Why buy anything other than the robust and efficient flat-pack furniture available in Pikea? Not only is it stylish and cheap, you get the added bonus of using craftsmanship in assembling it yourself. It had been a real delight to get rid of Mother's clutter and replace it all with Bunni shelves and cupboards, Looksi tables and chairs, Plebbi beds and wardrobes. I tuned back in to what Hansum was saying.

"Given the likes of Atkins, one does sometimes wonder why it is that we expose ourselves on a daily basis to the crudity and ignorance of the adolescent mind," he said. "The recompense is meagre in every sense."

Cobberly pensively drank more of his wine, then spoke.

"Though they can be a trial, occasionally a pearl can emerge from the swine, you know. I'm thinking back to last week when I was trying to get across the nature of approximation that comes with the task of translation. I was emphasising the problem involved in capturing the intentional rather than the literal meaning of words and phrases. Young Temms added a pertinent insight to the translating business by pointing out that the translator himself may be deliberately biased and hence unfaithful. He produced a splendid example that I'd not come across myself – something he'd picked up in Jon Dory's class. According to his account it seems that Montaigne's *Essays* were first translated from the French into English by a John Florio. In one place Montaigne writes of '*Nos Allemans noyez dans le vin*' which" (and here he nodded at me for some reason) "simply translates into '*Our Germans drowned in wine*' but which Florio gave as '*Our carousing, tosspot German soldiers, when they are most plunged in their cups, and as drunk as rats*'."

Hansum chuckled and we all took an appreciative sip of our fine French wine.

"You know," he said in that careful, reflective voice he keeps for anecdotes, "I had a similar experience of such a pearl being disgorged (rather than emerging from elsewhere) just yesterday. We were reading over some of Keats' *Lamia* and the line "*Philosophy can clip an angel's wings*" came up. As you probably know, Mason is frightfully keen on Philosophy and he immediately bridled at the idea that his pet subject could be regarded in a negative light. Naturally, I pointed out that it was likely that what Keats had in mind was what Disraeli characterised as the emptiness and fruitlessness of much of the scholastic tradition in philosophy – seas of ink wasted on how many angels could dance on the point of a pin. I even allowed myself the modern trope" (he paused to smooth the lustrous waves of his hair) "philosophical argument being like two bald men arguing over a comb" and added that Apollonius might well have been one of them. He paused and chuckled but, I think, like me Cobberly hadn't a clue who this Apollonius might be so we non-committally sipped some wine. Hansum went on:

"I'd never even considered whether there was anything deeper in it than the good Benjamin's dismissal but Mason – and I say this with true academic humility – put me right. He said that arguing about the possibility of angels on pins was of fundamental importance to the questions of dualism and transubstantiation – not just of angels but also the human soul and God Himself. The point at issue is whether supernatural beings are extended or not – if they occupy space physically. Angels are supernatural and yet, on occasion at least, become visible (and sometimes audible) through interacting with the physical world – which requires them to be physically present in that world. However, if they are physical in this way then the question arises of whether they have to obey physical laws too. If they are physical then there is a limit to how many could occupy the tiniest area of space imaginable - that to be found on the point of a pin - whereas if they were non-physical an infinite number could easily occupy that space. I must say that this insight prompted me to a good deal of reflection on the matter and it has been most rewarding."

I kept quiet. The only questions outside the syllabus that *my* pupils seem to find interesting are ones like Atkins came out with in the first part of the lesson this morning: do girls fart or not?

Friday 9th March 2004

After writing up yesterday's entry, I noticed that, after all, Hansum hadn't finished off the advice about what I should do about the letter. The end of his sentence was obvious to me as a scientist though: "If you want the truth, establish the facts." I wrote a short letter to Diana Boothby telling her about Mother's death and asking if I could come and see her. I dropped it in the post on my walk to school.

*   *   *

Tuesday 20th March 2004

Naturally enough, my trip also involved the pleasures of travelling on trains and buses: up to Darlington with what I always think of as good old British Rail and then an enchanting bus ride through the burnished crags and velvety dales of The North to my destination: Market Cross, Barnard Castle.

The language of the man behind the counter in the newsagent's proved impenetrable (I surmised that he was probably of Polish extraction) and, proffering him a pencil and the address on a sheet of notepaper, I performed an elaborate mime to indicate that he should draw the directions to it rather than trying any more words. Better than that he took me to the door and pointed.

"Tharyarmun!" (or something) he shouted, clapping me on the shoulder. Beyond the broad tip of his stubby finger, right opposite us, was a sign saying "Staindrop Street". It took only a little more detective work to bring me to a tired grey house with a plywood door next to which were three doorbell buttons. I pressed the middle one: 13b.

Although the room in which we sat was tiny, terribly over-heated and extremely cheaply furnished, it was very clean and the tea was hot and strong. There was a garish plastic urn on the mantelpiece: Uncle Reggie, no doubt.

Diana was in her early twenties and had the appurtenances I'd expected: three tattoos on her arm; two rings in her face; one child born out of wedlock. But, these apart, she totally confounded my prejudices and proved to be just like her grandfather: warm, kind, garrulous and with what is known as "a heart of gold". After a few minutes – in which I explained the background to Me, Mother and Uncle Reggie – she "opened up" as I think she herself put it and sketched out her own family background while her daughter buried her face in her lap between occasional glances of wonder in my direction.

In outline, Reggie Boothby's professional life was simple: he was in the Army for twelve years then left to become a salesman – first for Kestens "the undergarments of choice for ladies of discrimination" and then for the pharmaceutical company just outside the town. Diana laughed as she recalled Reggie's own favourite summing up: "I started as a trained killer then travelled in ladies' underwear before ending up peddling drugs."

The family history proper came next: Reggie married Daisy ("that's dear old great-gramma, poppet" to her daughter, giving her a bounce on her knee) and they had two children, Bobby and Stan. Bobby was sickly and died of measles when he was five ("aaah, the same age as you, poppet" giving her a hug) but Stan ('grampa') was big and strong and married Doris ("who was my mother and your…" "Gramma!" said the girl. "That's right, poppet, you are so clever!") and they had four children ("Uncle Adrian, Uncle Brian, Uncle Colin and…now who was the next uncle I wonder…?" "Mummy!" shouted the daughter, tugging at Diana's shoulders and rocking with delight).

"Whenever she had the bread-knife in her hand, Mum would wave it at Dad and say "And this saved us from any little Erics and Freddies and Glorias and…" it was a family joke to keep on to the end of the alphabet – Zebedee off the Magic Roundabout," Diana said with a broad smile so reminiscent of Reggie himself.

She went on with more details about each of the family but I must confess, I rather lost track of which uncle worked in Scotland, which was the breeder of budgerigars, which was the professional wrestler (and, thinking back, one of the uncles alone might have fitted the bill) and whether it was Australia or America her parents went to live "for the sunshine". What I do remember was her saying how Reggie and Daisy had sold their house to pay for Daisy's treatment which "made her no better and things a lot worse" and, once Daisy died, Reggie lost all heart and, within the year (2003), he too died.

All this was sombre stuff and I thought I should lighten the mood so clapped my hands at Diana's daughter and asked her her name.

"Poppet!" she cried with a grin.

"You certainly are – but what's your name?"

"Poppet!"

Here, perhaps noticing just a trace of irritation on my face, Diana hurried to explain that Poppet ("no, not Poppy") was indeed the girl's name. I felt fresh prejudices curdling within me. Soon she would be at school full time ("though not at a big school like Mr Wentworth's") and then "Mummy could go back to doing some shop-work at Merryson's again".

While Poppet trotted out to replenish the plate of biscuits (chocolate Hobnobs, a particular weakness of mine) Diana said not to mention a Daddy of any kind – apparently he had "skipped off, good riddance too!" well before the birth. She chatted some more about Reggie: the hours spent fishing; his love of a flutter on the horses; his funny stories. I brought up how he loved good furniture and auctions.

"Auctions?" said Diana. "That's a new one on me. And the furniture too, really."

"He took Mother and me to at least two auctions when I was just a little lad. I remember him saying he loved having beautiful old furniture around. In fact, he bought two pieces and left them at our house so he could enjoy his visits even more, he said. One was a Tunbridge-ware occasional table and the other was a bow-fronted sideboard. My main reason for coming to see you was to ask you what you want done with them?"

She looked perplexed.

"I mean," I went on, "as Reggie's real kin, they belong to you. I would have brought them today but I came up by train."

She gestured at the room. "There's no space for any old furniture here – you keep them, Mr Wentworth!"

"Well, I'd like to keep them, of course – they have a lot of sentimental value for me as I'm sure you'll understand. But I wouldn't feel right about not paying for them. Will you let me buy them from you?"

"Don't be daft, I'd never have known any different if you'd not said anything! You enjoy them."

"No, it wouldn't be right," I said solemnly and paused for some thoughts. "I suppose I could sell them and send you the money…"

"But you love them, Mr Wentworth, don't you go selling off things you love! Have them with my blessing."

"No, Diana," I said drawing out my cheque-book. "I insist on buying them from you – then I'll feel they are mine all honestly acquired and above board – which will keep them all the more precious in my eyes."

"If you don't mind me saying so, you are a funny old thing!" she said. "Alright then if you really think that's best!"

I started writing out the cheque. "A fair price will be the amount I have them insured for," I told her. I finished writing and handed it to her – and took the opportunity of snaffling up another chocolate Hobnob with my hand on the way back.

She made a bit of a fuss for a while but, as I explained to her, Reggie had paid hundreds for them at the auctions back in the 60s and, after all, as a teacher at the great Sixokes School, my salary was munificence itself so £10 000 would make hardly any difference to my pocket or my life.

"Well, it will make a big difference to ours!" she kissing and hugging Poppet to her. I saw it was time to leave and hastily retreated to go and catch the bus back to Darlington. Just as I was closing the door, Diana came clattering down the stairs.

"I nearly forgot to give you this," she said.

It was the shoebox.

Wednesday 21st March 2004

I was so tired after the long journey to The North and back that I hadn't the energy to bring yesterday's entry to completion. And today's trip to Hastings didn't pass off wholly as I'd planned either. But I have fortified myself with a good strong pot of tea and will bring everything up to date before snuggling down into my Plebbi. So, Barnard Castle to Sixokes.

On the bus to Darlington I sat with the shoebox on my knees. Now the thing was physically in my possession I was actually feeling quite fearful about rummaging through it so just gazed at the sodden grimy fields through a hole I had wiped in the condensation on the window. Despite the rather uplifting encounter with Diana and Poppet, my mood was now flat.

I was the sole passenger. The miles passed.

Soon I recognised the approaches to the train station and, feeling like a thief, I lifted the lid of the box slightly and sneaked my hand just inside it and pulled out a card that rested on the top of what felt and sounded like tissue paper. It was one of the yellow change of address cards that Mother had sent out announcing she was no longer at 62 Starling Road but now resided (I remember her chuckling to me about this word making her sound "as grand as a piano") with her son at 28, Powell Road, Sixokes. Underneath this, in her own very familiar hand-writing she had added "Even a worm will learn" which I couldn't make much sense of – especially as the bus had by now hissed to a stop and the driver was craning round to urge me off. I crammed the card back into the box and hurried onto the platform and, with great good luck, my train was there waiting for me. I stepped through the doors and felt the usual wave of optimism that comes with being on the railways.

The train ride was spoilt for me by one or two trivial things.

Having settled into a window seat and put the shoebox on the table and congratulated myself on having a bit of space and solitude ahead of me, a couple of teenagers unceremoniously plumped themselves down opposite me. They were jointly linked by wires from an ear to a small white box which was churning out a tinny din with a dull metronomic beat behind it. They munched open-mouthed handfuls of stinking oval-curved pre-formed crisps shaken from a big tube. On occasion (usually when one or other of them had swallowed down a gobful of mashed fat and flavoured carbohydrate) they would snog noisily. My looking daggers at them and frequent tutting had no effect whatsoever. With a very pointed "Please excuse me, won't you?" (which, of course, was totally ignored) I went to drink tea in what in greater days would have been the dining car. Now it announces itself as the "Snackeroo Bar". We pulled into York and, with some thought of moving to another seat, I returned to my place.

My first feeling was one of relief as I saw the teenage couple pass the window on their way down the platform. My second was one of panic as I looked at the table and saw that it was now empty! I rushed out of the door and ran after the couple shouting at them to stop. A whistle sounded: shrill, distant but insistent.

It was then that I noticed that neither of them was carrying the shoebox so, in the very nick of time, I re-boarded the train and hurried back to my place. It was then that I saw that the table opposite to what I thought was 'my seat' was littered with crisp-shards and a gutted tube. And the shoebox. I have noticed recently more than once that my erstwhile sharp-as-a-razor memory for space and time has been blunted in this way. With a nod towards mortality's reminder, I sat down again, tapped the box reassuringly and, I suppose, nodded off because the next thing I knew was hearing the announcement of "all change" as we were back in the smoky purlieus of the capital once more and, to my chagrin, I had missed my usual game of trying to correctly guess the number of cranes thrusting upwards into the London air.

It was on the last leg of the journey home that I suddenly was struck with exactly what to do with the contents of the shoebox, the contents which somehow linked Mother to romance and memories. As I dodged amongst the others crowded on Charing Cross concourse I looked up at the information board for platform six to see that my train, the Sixokes train, terminated at Hastings. Gratifyingly, my memory still showed itself to have an edge and now it cut sharply into my consciousness: Mother said in her last letter to me that Hastings was where she was born and where she grew up – and where she met my own father. I decided in that moment that I would travel there first thing next day (today in fact) and lay the box to rest to complete a circle for her. I would leave the contents undiscovered. I was now sure it was what she would have wanted.

And so it was that, just before noon today, I stood at the end of Hastings pier as the watery light of the struggling equinoctial sun probed through the brisk and hopeful clouds that were lifting the curtain on springtime. With an inward picture of Mother smiling tenderly, I cast the shoebox into the sea with a heartfelt echo of her favourite ironic farewell: "Goodbye, good luck and good riddance!"

As the box (which I'd secured with string to keep the contents united) splashed into the choppy waves and sank, a firm hand clapped onto my shoulder from behind and a stern voice said "I arrest you!"

Irritated beyond measure at having this poignant moment interrupted, I swivelled round to see a tall and shabby figure fixing me with a sharp blue eye.

"I am making a citizen's arrest for flagrant littering!" he cried transferring the hand on my shoulder to a grip on my elbow. Clearly, he was a nutter. The thing was, he was a strong nutter and nothing I could do or say could stop him as he marched me back the length of the pier (past several people who made no attempt to intervene in this fiasco despite my hurried appeals to them) and out through the iron gates.

"Ah, there is a policeman!" he said stopping abruptly and pointing to a man of the law in the distance who had removed his cap and was idly polishing the peak with the sleeve of his jacket.

I then realised what the nutter was up to. He wasn't interested in making a citizen's arrest – all that he wanted was for me to offer him some money. I called his bluff.

"Well then, let's go and you can have me charged, my good man," I told him.

Curiously, this didn't seem to disconcert him a bit and, with something like a snort, he gripped my elbow even more firmly and stalked with me to the policeman.

"Officer, I have made a citizen's arrest of this man for wanton littering!"

The policeman put his cap back on and slowly looked at the pair of us.

"Did you not put your litter in a bin, sir?" he asked me quietly.

I explained that I had been interring the sentimental remains of my deceased mother in the place where she had been born and known happiness.

"It was an old shoebox tied up with string!" expostulated the nutter. "Not even ashes! He's obviously lying – you should arrest him and fine him now!"

The policeman twitched his lips, paused for a while and then nodded.

"Right," he said. "You leave him with me, Howard, and let me deal with this."

Howard the nutter reluctantly released my arm and, with a "litter-bug!" hurled at me with some venom, turned and strode back towards the pier.

The policeman held up a hand to stop the flow of my justifications and complaints.

"He's harmless enough, sir - and was just doing what he thought was right. You must agree that he had a point at least."

I told him that the man had no such thing, that such an intervention would only be acceptable if there were reasonable grounds, that the solemnity of my demeanour and the clear integrity of a fellow-citizen –

But here he held up his hand again.

"Just pass along will you sir. Pass along now."

Clearly, he was not interested in doing any sort of job as a public servant and just wanted to idle his way through his shift. This made my blood boil. Turning from him I ran after Howard the nutter and grabbed his elbow.

"I arrest you!" I cried. I dragged him back to the policeman.

"I have made a citizen's arrest on this man for wrongful citizen's arrest," I told him thinking that this would make him sit up and take notice. Not in the least. All he did was sigh deeply then turn on his heel and walk away.

Howard and I were equally outraged by this behaviour. In fact, a short discussion discovered that we were quite kindred spirits on the matter and soon we were shaking hands forgiving each other (with full agreement on both our parts) for hastiness and expressing heartfelt understanding of the position of the other. He invited me back to his emporium for a cup of tea which I accepted with gratitude.

This 'emporium' (a largish garden shed on the promenade close to the pier) sold junk advertised as 'antiques and bric-a-brac'. As I sipped the ebony brew he handed me (in a chipped mug with a painting of a canal-boat on it, "sorry no milk") I idly looked around while he wittered on about the general degradation of the town and rolled himself a stingy cigarette. I was reflecting on the fire-hazard he presented when something on a worm-eaten chest of drawers at the back of the shop caught my eye. Propped up against a dusty glass decanter was a brownish photograph in a badly foxed cardboard mount with a varnished wooden frame. It was priced at £10 and, with the swiftest thanks and a twenty-pound note, I left Howard with his canal-boat mug and hastened home with it. It's in front of me now.

The photograph shows an adolescent girl jumping in the blurred loop of a skipping rope. Her long dark hair catches in the wind. Behind her is a restless sea and the stark steel girders of the pier; in the foreground are a couple of spiral strands from a spool of barbed wire. Mid-leap, she is smiling openly at the camera, all happiness and innocence. In the right-hand corner of the picture is written in italics: *"Hastings: Spring 1940"*. I'm sure it's Mother.

Episode 17

From his diary

Wednesday 24th June 1972

A bit of a blow from the Headmaster at break this morning in one of what he jokingly refers to as his 'weekly staff updates' (an excuse for a lot of self-congratulation and the piling of extra work onto us poor toilers at the chalk-face) when, with a huge grin around the room as if he were handing out a great treat, he announced that all teaching staff would be required to assist in the running of the Great New Sports Day on Saturday. I could barely stifle a groan as he maundered on with what I thought was totally unwarranted enthusiasm about how this, on the last day of term, would be a triumphant culmination of the year, one at which the whole Governing Body was to attend not least to witness our appreciation of the superb new running track they had funded.

After he had left, I soon found sympathetic voices around me.

"How can watching a bunch of spotty kids pointlessly labouring round and round a track be regarded as 'triumphant' let alone a 'culmination' as if the whole point of the school is to build muscles rather than minds?" moaned Tony Cobberly as he plucked at his gown before flopping disconsolately into a chair.

"It's nothing to do with a Sports Day," opined Percy Gorval. "It's because he wants to tap even more money out of the blessed governors. Of course, it's his first year and he wants something public to show he's innovative and actually doing something to earn his corn. Just a pity he couldn't do that without totally mucking up my holiday arrangements which I had confidently arranged to begin straight after lunch."

I silently acquiesced in this – I had planned to make a start on my packing then too.

"And our prowess on the athletics front is hardly a strength. It could well be a humiliation and an embarrassment to see the likes of Phipps having to limp the final laps of the slowest mile on record clutching at his terrible stitch as the owls begin to hoot..." Richard Hansum was observing when the massive figure of Martin Starr, Head of Games, loomed over us.

"I am looking forward to you gents joining me that afternoon." He said slowly. "I'm sure I can rely on you to snap to it with a will." He paused and idly tapped the edge of the billiard table with his knuckles. I could swear that all the balls jumped. "Full training for your roles will be given so you need have no worries there. And..." here again he paused before breaking into a broad smile, "Pimms will be served to all officials throughout the afternoon." With that, he turned and walked away airily swinging his massive bunch of keys.

Hansum spoke: "At least the pill is being sugared," he sighed. "And, who knows, the day may be one of sunshine and glory. And one might hope for a glimpse of something lithe and graceful from one or two of the boys..."

"Yes," said Gorval brightly, "And with such a show of willingness on our part, no doubt the annual pay rise should be a fat one..."

As I left them with a wave I reflected on the characteristic willingness, optimism and good-heartedness of my colleagues.

Thursday 25th June 1972

A note in the internal mail giving me my duties for Sports Day seems to be all I am to get with regard to the 'full training'. This is it verbatim:

> *GGW. Timekeeper. Press the tit on the stopwatch at the start of the race. Press it again at the end.*

Am I being over-sensitive to read a hint of condescension in it? Then again, in all honesty, this may well be par for the course for P.E. teachers. In any event, it should be a piece of cake.

Took a couple of hours this evening starting to sort out the packing then I wrote to Mother thanking her for the flight money and bringing her up to date with my important new role at the ticking heart of the School's Sports Department.

Friday 26th June 1972

At luncheon today a remark from Busby Beamish started a disagreement and ended with a gratifying bruising for that preening nincompoop, Shadwell. As he reached for the brandy, Beamish casually asked "Do any of you need to borrow any P.E. kit for tomorrow? We've got quite a bit in lost property if you haven't – though there will be a bit of a premium on the larger sizes available…"

"Surely we aren't expected to expose ourselves in any such ludicrous costume?" cried an appalled Gorval. "I'm proud to say that my legs have not seen broad daylight for several decades and I do not mean to shock them by having them parade before the pitiless gaze of the massed pupils let alone their parents!"

"If the weather's fine, I'll be in the tennis whites," said Shadwell with that annoying half grin of his, one that makes one of the drooping limbs of his Zapata moustache twitch like a dog cocking its leg. "Real cool, man."

"I think young Beamish is teasing us," said Hansum pleasantly as he sniffed appreciatively at the Stilton. "Personally, I shall be in my panama and Henley blazer – perfect for Pimms."

"It's a pity that convention makes such a fuss about men in dresses," mused Shadwell as he smoothed the length of one of those ludicrous hirsute excrescences sprouting from the sides of his face. "A light frock or skirt must be just the thing in the summer, don't you think Hansum?"

There was a brief silence during which Hansum's face momentarily froze and his eyes narrowed ever so slightly. Almost before I could notice this, the customary urbanity and fluidity returned to his features.

"Now why would you want to wear a dress, Ian?" he asked politely, fixing him with his eyes whilst slowly crumbling a Bath oliver over his plate.

Shadwell twitched a little uncomfortably in his chair. "Oh, you know, equality of the sexes and all that." His face – or what you can see of it amongst the hair – was reddening.

"There is no need to insult us with any championing of feminism here, young man," said Cobberly sternly. "Some of us have chosen this bastion of the sterner sex precisely because we wish to keep the hysterical clamour of the female world at more than arm's length. And as for feminists -"

"With their hairy shins and plunging dugs," put in Gorval.

"And as for feminists," Cobberly went on with the merest nod in Gorval's direction. "I have no objection to women wishing to be on a level with men. However, I do object to that having to be achieved by men grovelling on their knees." With that he violently twisted his napkin and threw it, like a gage, on the table as he leaned forward and stared across at Shadwell. I gave a hearty chuckle, nodding in agreement, pleased to see this hostility directed Shadwell's way: it was gratifying to see the worm being skewered. Hansum moved in for the kill.

"I can only surmise that dear Ian," he said very quietly, "Our *dear* Ian has been rather too influenced by a touch too much intimate contact with one of the jewels – or perhaps, one should say one of the pearls - in the Catering Department." As if on cue, the young girl from the kitchens with whom the scandal-mongers had Shadwell having a passionate liaison, came in through the door and cleared away some of the dishes and glasses. The silence while she did this was enormous. It seemed that all eyes sought to avoid all other eyes. After she had left the room, Hansum went on in the same quiet tone: "It would be such a pity if the Headmaster got to hear of any such unprofessional conduct amongst the staff, wouldn't it Ian?"

Shadwell's face, from being flushed, went deadly white. Abruptly he rose to his feet and, clearly furious, spoke to Hansum through clenched teeth but almost at a whisper.

"That was beneath you, Richard. I am saddened. And I am sorry." He left.

Surprisingly, given the rout he had inflicted, Hansum himself showed no pleasure but merely shrugged uncomfortably before quickly popping some cheese and biscuit into his mouth.

Saturday 26th June 1972

The weather forecast was for changeable conditions so I had both sun-hat and umbrella with me as I walked towards Dyke's Meadow for the Sports. My path was interrupted by the arrival of Lord Sackbut's Rolls Royce which ponderously negotiated its grey elephantine way into the parking space marked 'reserved for the Chairman of Governors', its gleaming front bumper nearly touching the short retaining wall at the foot of the grassy slope leading up to the running track. It seemed that the other governors must have already arrived as all the other spaces there were occupied. Naturally enough, the governors were accorded the privilege of parking here so they had the least distance to walk: staff and parents in cars had to scramble for the left-overs elsewhere.

As I waited, I was joined by Hansum and together we toiled up the long slope, the buttercups scattering pollen onto our shoes.

"I'm on time-keeping," I told him between breaths. "What are you doing?"

"Ah, ever perceptive, Mr Starr has chosen to employ my talents on the Tannoy," he said. "You will hear my studiously-trained and honeyed tones used merely to call for somesuch inanity as boys to go to the sand-pit or announce the distance that someone has managed to throw a heavy weight." He sighed. "At least the Pimm's will succour and soothe."

At last we breasted the apex of the slope. We paused to gaze at the splendid backdrop to the new running track: Powell House, home of the Sackbuts for over four centuries, couched comfortably among scattered handfuls of oaks, with, here and there on the open well-turfed clearings, occasional groups of fallow deer grazing peacefully; and this all spread beneath scudding white clouds in a pale blue English sky. The perfect tranquil beauty of this landscape was spoilt by the fat form of Phipps occluding the foreground and excavating a nostril with greater concentration and diligence than he ever shows in my lessons.

Hansum and I moved on and parted company near the finishing line and I crossed the track to where Starr was handing out stopwatches from a box.

"Better late than never, Dobbin!" he cried pressing a large time-piece into my hand. "Hundred-yard dash, no, no, what am I thinking of, hundred-metre sprints are about to begin, gentlemen. If you stand in height order – that's it, Dob, you at the front-" he arranged us in Indian file in line with the finishing tape "then the tallest, that's you of course, Ian," he nodded at Shadwell who was parading himself in a set of dazzlingly-white tennis clothes of which the shorts were the skimpiest imaginable. "And, if I might say so, it was good of you to wear those so we could all see your religion…yes, the tallest times the winner, then, next in line – Arthur – times second and so on until Dob here times sixth place. All clear? Right, first race coming down."

With that he waved a white flag towards the start and I saw six boys crouch. There was a bang from the starter pistol and the boys were up and running. After a momentary fumble I pressed the button on my stopwatch. Eagle-eyed, I watched the runners sweep up to and past the finish, clicking the button as the sixth runner came abreast of me. I was feeling rather breathless myself – it was more exciting than I'd thought it might be.

Tony Gray, the track judge, had written down the names of the boys in their order of finishing and now, holding his clip-board officiously, came over to us to get the times.

"First?" he said, pencil poised.

"13.2" said Shadwell crisply. Gray recorded it.

"Second?"

"13.4"

"Third?"

"13.7"

"Fourth?"

"14.6"

"Fifth?"

"14.9"

"And sixth?"

"Well there seems to be something funny going on with this watch," I said. "I've got 10.6 seconds."

Gray looked up at me. "I think that would be a world record for this age-group." The others were all laughing. "It was fairly close. I'll call it 15.4."

"Ready for the second race, are we?" called Starr. I looked down the track to see another six boys crouching. Starr waved his white flag and, shortly afterwards there was a bang. I was pleased with my reaction, reckoning I pressed the button on my stopwatch almost straight away. After the finish, Gray came over with his clipboard again.

"First?"

"13.0" said Shadwell.

"Second?"

"13.3"

"Third?"

"14.3"

"Fourth?

"14.9"

"Fifth?"

"15.2"

"And what do we have for sixth?

"26.6," I replied confidently. Again, there was a good deal of laughter.

Gray looked at me. "Did you, by any chance, forget to zero your watch?"

I was surprised. "Doesn't it do that automatically? Pretty poor sort of stopwatch isn't it?"

While Gray was doing the mental arithmetic and writing down a time of 16.0 for my runner, Gownsend kindly told me that I needed to press the button twice to get the timer back to zero.

"Third and final sprint, now gents," called Starr. "Big boys. Might set a South East Division record if Atkins is pushed." He waved his white flag again and I fixed all my attention on the six crouching figures held like greyhounds in the slips a hundred metres away. Almost exactly on the bang of the pistol my finger reacted. The senior school boys thundered impossibly quickly towards us, Atkins and Lenten straining for the front, apparently neck and neck. It was nip and tuck, tuck and nip. In the last few yards, with a huge effort, Atkins lunged at the tape to win it by just a few inches. In the heat of the moment, I pressed the button on my stopwatch: I had timed the winner rather than whoever was in sixth place.

Starr, having shaken hands with both Lenten and Atkins, came over to us at the same time as Gray to hear the times.

"First?"

"11.2," said Shadwell.

Starr groaned. "Just a tenth outside the record."

"Actually," I said with quiet authority, "Atkins got a time of 10.9 seconds." I held up the face of my stopwatch towards Starr.

"That's rubbish!" said Shadwell. "The fool hasn't a clue what he's doing."

Keeping calm I used cold, clear logic to refute him.

"You will notice that Atkins won the race in the shortest time, Shadwell. Hence it follows that my time – obviously the shorter of the two – must be more accurate."

"Yours is shorter because your reactions are slower, you idiot!" he yelled.

Still icily calm I spoke quietly.

"On the contrary, I pressed my button almost exactly when I heard the gun –"

"You see, you see!" he cried, turning feverishly to the others, "He didn't even go on the smoke! And, no doubt, he anticipated the finish to boot! Can't you see the man's incompetent! Martin, take him away before it's too late." He gestured towards the lines of parents on the other side of the track and the neat line of governors in their chairs near the tea-tent. "Spare your department and the school any more embarrassment at least!" With that, the flaming great nit flounced away towards the Pimms jug set out on a small table a few yards away and poured himself a beakerful which he tossed off in one go.

Starr shook his head and then took me by the arm and led me in the opposite direction. Conspiratorially, he bent his head close to mine. "You can see he's all het up, Dob, and I know that you've every right to feel like sticking one on him, but I'm going to ask you to do me a big favour." He squeezed my upper arm and I felt the blood supply get cut off. The man had no idea of his own strength. The stopwatch I'd been holding dropped to the ground. "As a personal favour to me, I'd like you to swap with Jack Natter who's on the shot." He nodded down the track towards the starting-line.

"Of course, I'm happy to help you out," I told him, tapping at the ground with the point of my umbrella. "But I've no experience of fire-arms so operating the starter-pistol might –"

"No, no, oh no," he said with a grin, "It's the shot-put that Jack's doing." He pointed to the far end of the grass on the inside of the running track. "That's where the javelin and shot-put happen, Dob. You trot on down to Jack and ask him to come up here as a time-keeper. As a bonus, the field events won't start for another three-quarters of an hour or so and there's another jug of Pimms down that end too." He released my arm and scooped up the stopwatch. I felt some life coming back into my hand again. "Cushy number, Dob. Jack'll tell you all you need to do – we've got ten minutes or so until the next race because all the jumps need putting out. See you later!" With that he gave me an encouraging push between the shoulder blades and turned away to supervise the positioning of the hurdles.

The way Natter explained it, supervising the shot seemed to be the simplest job imaginable. While he was running through the main points, I reflected on how the senior staff got the easiest ride while relative novices like me were loaded with the more onerous and complex tasks like time-keeping.

"So, just to summarise, summarise, you know," said Natter through one of his sunniest smiles. "Just the six competitors; each of them has two throws; mustn't step out of the front of the circle; mark the distance with a steel pin; record the better distance of each competitor on the clip-board here. That's it. As there's only one measuring tape you may as well wait until Gorval has finished doing the javelin before you start. Safer that way too. Everything you need is here – including the Pimms, lovely Pimms! Best of luck, Dob. See you later at the tea, no doubt!" With a curious sort of scurrying run – more of a fast creep than anything else – Natter headed for the finish-line and I silently wished him well wrestling with the intricacies and attempting to avoid the pitfalls that awaited him there.

I poured myself a beaker and sat in the shade of the hawthorns on the outside of the running track. Hardly anyone else was at this end – the crowds of spectators and non-competitors were massed near the tea-tent and finishing-line. Sipping quietly at my drink I tried to soothe the feathers that that furry ferret Shadwell had ruffled. I may even have dozed a little because next time I looked the javelin was in full swing just twenty or so yards away.

I went over to the shot-put circle just to check everything one last time – the sort of professional approach any good teacher possesses naturally. There by the circle were the dozen shots ready to use. I picked one up with the idea that I might have a go myself. I soon changed my mind: the thing seemed far heavier than the 8lb that Natter had told me it weighed. I dropped it with a thud and instead picked out one of the steel marker pins from the bucket. It was nearly a foot long, like a giant nail with a number in white paint on the head. Taking the chance to refill my beaker, I carried them both back to my spot under the hawthorns and sat down again to take in the Sports Day scene. A javelin was arcing gracefully through the air nearby; at the other end I could make out some boy running then performing a sequence of spastic movements before landing in a heap in a sand-pit; over by the finish-line crowds of boys and parents were cheering as another race finished. Setting down my empty glass, I pushed the steel pin into the turf. Except I didn't: with all the dry weather, the ground was rock hard. Here was a problem for me! Old Gorval had no such problem as the javelins were doing their own marking. I bent my mind towards a solution.

Next thing I knew, Gorval was shaking my shoulder and thrusting a large tape measure towards me. "Wakey, wakey! Here you are, young Wentworth. Heard you're doing shot." Briefly, he looked over his shoulder and then turned back to me. "I've done my bit and, if I scoot off now, should miss most of the traffic and get on with my holiday. Don't tell anyone I've gone early will you, old chap?

See you in September!" With that he dashed away through a gap in the hawthorns on his long trek to the staff car-park.

His place in front of me was almost immediately taken by an apologetic-looking Mason.

"Sorry to bother you, Mr Wentworth, sir, but could we start the shot now?" He gestured behind to the circle where five other boys were doing stretches and pushing shots up and down. "All but one of us are needed for the relays coming up and we have to do this first." He explained. Another difficulty heaped on me I thought to myself – now I was under time pressure! As is often the case, when under the greatest strain, the brain comes up with the neatest solution. I knew exactly what to do. A great wave of self-congratulation swept over me. (It must be how the Headmaster feels during his updates.)

Briskly, I strode over to the circle and picked up the clipboard. On it were the competitors' names, numbered one to six.

"Right, listen carefully, you lot. This is going to be carried out with an efficiency and precision you've probably never experienced, but get used to it." I barked this at them in my best Corky Jones manner. "First, line up the shots behind the circle." The boys did this smartly and, taking some chalk from my jacket pocket (what teacher doesn't have a few such stubs?) I chalked numbers on each shot: one to six and then one to six again. I stood to attention and, perhaps unconsciously, so did the boys. "Now, listen carefully. Each of you will, in turn, throw a shot with your number on it. Follow the rules about not stepping out of the circle and whatnot. Then you can get off to run in your relays while I do the measuring. Any questions?"

"Aren't you going to mark the distances with the pins, sir?" said Mason.

"Schoolboy error, Mason, a schoolboy error – you've not noticed that the ground is like iron. Useless trying to get a pin into it. I've tried that. The chalk markings will tell me whose shot is who's and…" I held up my hand to stop him interrupting me, "…and, no, the chalk won't come off because the grass is bone-dry."

"But won't it –" he was saying when the smooth tones of Hansum's voice came through the air: "All competitors for the relays should report to the marshal by the finishing-line immediately. That's all relay-race competitors, final call."

"Just get on with it, Mason, and leave the thinking to me. I know what I'm doing." I said sharply. Standing in front of the circle (but well to one side, of course) with my clipboard I called the boys in turn to the circle in turn and checked the legitimacy of each of their throws or puts or shots whatever they are called. It took less than a couple of minutes. I hurried them away, pleased to know that later, when Starr heard of my ingenuity and how I had not held up the relay races, I was in for some well-deserved praise to make up for the time-keeping difficulties.

I set about getting the measurements. Now that I was alone, I felt calm and self-possessed: a man getting on with a good job well. My first task was to pick up the shorter shot of each competitor and get them out of the way by rolling them back to the circle. This took more effort and time than I'd anticipated. Next came the measuring. Here a bit more of the Wentworth ingenuity was called for. Securing one end of the tape at the front of the circle while I unwound the rest of it from the spool to each of the remaining six shots was a problem - immediately solved by pushing a pin in the crack between the concrete of the circle and the turf where it had shrunk away! My brain was running like a well-oiled machine. Tying the tape to the pin (the odd few centimetres that this took up could hardly matter as a proportion of the total distance that the shots had been put, I told myself) I went about measuring and carefully recording the six competitors' distances. Finally, for a neat, professional job, I rolled all the shots together by the circle, wound up the tape and put it with all the pins in the bucket next to the shots.

As I was thus engaged, the final relay was sweeping around the track to a good deal of noisy excitement. Binns Major trotted up to me. "Mr Starr's compliments, sir, but could he have the results for the shot?" I handed him the clipboard and asked if he knew the state of play.

"It's really exciting sir. Temms is leading at the moment for the *victor ludorum* cup – he got the school record for the long jump, sir – but if Mason wins the shot, then he pips him for it, sir. Must go sir, Mr Starr's waving at me!" Sure enough, up by the finish Starr's massive arm was waving a come-hither. Binns sprinted away and I followed at a far more leisurely pace, bidding adieu to the last of the sun as a mass of thuggish grey clouds began to shoulder their way overhead. The groundsman's tractor went past me towards the shot and javelin end and, up ahead, there was a general exodus of the crowd as it trooped down towards the Dining Hall for the high tea: Sports Day was over.

The exception to the exodus was the formidable figure of Starr who was staring at the clipboard that Binns had given to him. He scratched his head; he shook his head; he turned his head my way. Then he ran at me.

"What the hell happened here?" he shouted, pointing at the distances I'd written neatly next to the competitors' names. "These are impossible – five of them break the school record and one would beat the world record by about four metres!"

Despite the fearsome expression on his face, I remained calm and collected.

"I can use a tape measure, Mr Starr – and those are the distances the shots went." I said.

"But Lenten could never beat Mason!" he expostulated.

"Well," I replied patiently and gently, "He did today. His technique was far better than Mason's, that's all. Mason went for chucking it up miles in the air so after its first bounce it hardly went anywhere. Lenten went for a lower trajectory and, on this hard ground, it rolled much further. Hence his winning shot or put or throw whatever it is," I ended with, I must say, a fair bit of nonchalance at taking the wind out of his sails in this way.

Starr's jaw muscles bunched to the size of eggs as he clenched his teeth. His lips moved and I noticed he was counting to ten. His muscle-and-bone fists twitched horribly at the periphery of my vision. Finally, to my relief, he took a huge breath and let it out slowly.

"Right, Dob, here is what will happen now. You will go back to the shot circle and stop the groundsman taking away the shots, bucket and tape. You will stay there and wait for the six boys to come up. You will then allow them two puts each. You will mark the point on the ground with a metal pin. You will use the hammer in the bucket to knock the pin into the ground. You will mark where the shot *lands* and not, **not**, where it ends up. You will get two of the boys to measure the distances and you will write down the results. You will then send Lenten with the clipboard down to me at the double. Is that all clear to you?"

I nodded, deeming it wisest not to regale him with my chalk-marking idea. He went on:

"I'd do it myself but I'm supposed to be at the tea right now sitting next to Lord Sackbut as this Great New Sports Day is all down to me." He shook his head. "But anyway, I'll send up the boys smartly and I'm sure you won't cock it up again."

Playfully, he punched my shoulder and ran off with lithe, ground-eating strides. I massaged the spot under my lapel ruefully whilst walking back to the shot circle. There, under a few pins in the bucket, I saw the outline of a lump-hammer. An insistent heavy drizzle began to fall and, pushing my sunhat into my pocket with the chalk, I put up my umbrella, tucking it under an arm as I polished my glasses.

The groundsman was unsympathetic as I outlined the programme for a re-run of the shot-put. Sliding javelins onto the trailer behind his tractor, he paused to consult his watch.

"It's just gone four now and I finish at five," he pointed out.

"So there's plenty of time then," I said.

Oh yeah, how'd you work that out?" he replied with what I felt was a note of belligerence.

"Well, this re-run will only take ten minutes or so once the boys get back – which will be in just a few minutes – then loading up the trailer with the shots and so on won't take long and we can get the boys to help there, so you'd be all loaded up by half-past four at the outside."

He stabbed the last javelin into the ground and leant on it.

"Then what?"

"Um, well, we all go home," I said brightly.

"No. We don't all go home. I have to drive the tractor and trailer down to Willy's Store, offload everything and put it away, then park up the tractor – and then I've got my 15-minutes hand-washing time before finishing at exactly 5 o'clock," he told me. I was getting fed up with having stuff spelt out to me like this and decided to allow myself a touch of asperity.

"It doesn't take quarter of an hour to wash a pair of hands!"

He plucked the javelin out of the ground and turned it to bring the point mid-way between our faces.

"It's what the law says, Shorty. Law says I get 15 minutes washing-up time and 15 minutes is what I take."

I decided not to continue this fruitless conversation any further and turned to go. I felt the point of the javelin tap a couple of times on my umbrella.

"Now, don't be in such a hurry," he called. "You tell me what you're thinking of doing with the shots and stuff once you've finished with them, that's all."

"I'll leave them here," I said. "You can pick them up first thing Monday."

"Kind of you to think of that," he said slowly. "Trouble is, first scheduled job on Monday is tractor maintenance. Can't break the schedule – union rules. You'll have to bring the stuff down yourself. There's an old wheelbarrow over there by the grass-clippings, you can use that." He gestured towards a hillock of grass half-hidden among the hawthorns. "If you work quick, you might even get it down to Willy's before I get to hand-washing."

With that pleasantry, he shot the javelin onto the trailer, swung up onto the tractor and chugged away. At that moment, the six competitors came jogging up. I took charge.

"Right, as you may be aware, there was a slight mix-up with the results in the shot so Mr Starr thinks we need a re-run for confirmation. Similar routine but this time I'll be using the pins as someone has now found the hammer. Get cracking!"

All went perfectly smoothly though I had to abandon my umbrella to tap the pins in to the places where the shots pitched. The drizzle had turned to rain. A cheering moment came when Mason's second put – the last of the long, long day – was measured and found to have outdistanced Gormington's by a good half-metre or so and this put him in first place and, as a consequence, meant that he'd scored the points needed to win the *victor ludorum* cup. It was hard to resist the joy with which the boys danced around him slapping him on the back and cheering while Lenten rushed away with the clipboard and the final results. My heart warmed to them.

It soon cooled again as the others began to jog away in Lenten's wake. "Hey, get back here you lot!" I cried. Once back in front of me I waved an arm to encompass the pins, the shots, the bucket, the tape. "All this needs clearing away."

"But we can't sir, we can't" they whined. Of course, as they feverishly explained to me, Mason had to rush back for the presentations and the others all had parents waiting for them at the tea. I sighed inwardly. Perhaps it was only just that I should have to do the clearing up. In all fairness, I had not covered myself with glory in the Sports Day. I waved them away and trudged over to get the wheelbarrow.

It had seen better days. No, it had seen better years – perhaps even, better decades. There were several holes in the body, where the metal had rusted through. It would have to do. On its spongy tyre, I wheeled it over to the shot circle and hefted the bucket in. I took the lump-hammer and knocked out all the pins and put the lot into the bucket. I corralled the twelve shots and dropped them in, then put the tape measure on top. By this time, I was wet and pretty cold.

Defeated, I furled my umbrella and laid it on top of the other gear, gripped the chilled and slippery handles of the wheelbarrow and lifted. It was heavy. Briefly, I considered taking two trips but, given the rain and cold, given the fact that the groundsman would be gone by the second, and given that, after all, once I was off the track it was downhill all the way, I decided once was enough.

I wobbled unsteadily along the hundred metres of track then turned and paused for a rest at the top of the slope. I looked with some envy towards the Dining Hall where a splendid high tea was even now being tucked into: scones with jam and cream; fruit cakes and pastries; tea cakes dripping with butter; hot tea – hot tea! Calling myself to arms, I lugged up the handles of the wheelbarrow, pointed it down the slope and pushed forward. I had been right – the going got smooth and easy. I had time to notice the now sodden and drooping buttercups rushing past my feet in blurred spangles before it dawned on me that the wheelbarrow was going rather faster than I liked. In fact, I was getting close to a run as I plunged down behind it.

Through the smears of rain on my glasses below me I could see Martin Starr leading the party of governors back towards their cars. He must have seen me at the same moment and assessing the situation in a moment, he signalled frantically with both arms for me to steer the wheelbarrow to the left, away from the cars lined up below me. I must say to my credit that there was a cool centre in my brain which gave this some consideration. Clearly, I needed to steer one way or the other to avoid the parked cars, the question was, was Starr right to indicate the shallower slope away to the left rather than the steeper slope to the right? Reason told me he'd got it wrong: the steepness to the right would stop the wheelbarrow much more quickly. That cool centre even told me that turning to the right was the *adroit* manoeuvre and mentally lodged that bon mot in my memory to recount later. I wrenched the handles to force the wheelbarrow to the right.

Unfortunately, all that happened was that the wheelbarrow tipped over on its side and the twelve shots, like a pack of frenzied dogs, sped bounding down the forty or fifty yards of slope between me and the governors' car-park. I went as cold as if I were lying in snow. Almost in slow motion I watched the first shot leap off the grass on top of the retaining wall and snap the spirit of ecstasy on the front of the Rolls before crashing onto the grey, water-slicked bonnet and, a moment later, shattering the windscreen. In quick succession, the other eleven shots wreaked a sickening havoc among the cars. It was quite a scene of devastation. I picked up my umbrella, unfurled it and, sheltered from the rain at least, went down to say sorry.

I was grateful when Starr put a brawny arm around my shoulders as his own shook with emotion. He whispered to me: "Never mind, Dob, never mind. This will go down in the annals as 'The Golden Shot', you mark my words."

The Bursar was less charitable as he totted up the damage: wings, bonnets and windscreens of three Mercedes; crushed headlamp on the Daimler; and the car that had taken three hits, the Rolls, where one shot was still lodged deep in the radiator – which the Bursar asked me if I knew were always individually hand-made? I thought it best not to reply as he made a mental calculation of the thousands of pounds claim that the school insurance company would have to take.

Shadwell strolled up and gave a low whistle. "I'll go and get my camera, Bursar – you'll want some evidence for the insurance, no doubt? And a silver lining at least will be that I can have some of them made up into slides to show my class when we study the Battle of Trafalgar – a pretty good illustration of the effect of a broadside even at a slow speed."

He turned and gave me his sly half-grin. The dog cocked its leg.

Episode 18

From his diary

Thursday 1ˢᵗ July 1967

There was a new notice on the 'teaching posts' section in the careers centre: 'Newly-qualified graduate required to take up the post of teacher of Biology at Sixokes School, Kent from September this year'. Unpinning it, I took it over to the desk and asked for some more information. Apparently the position was being advertised so late due to a some mishap or other there – a teacher had gone hiking in the Scottish Isles during half-term and had simply disappeared and hence this last-minute advertisement. As I was very well aware, all the plum jobs had been snapped up ages ago. There had been nothing to take my fancy on the board for weeks now. Tucking the details of where to apply into my jacket pocket I decided that perhaps this could be just the place for me. Granted, the name of Sixokes School was a total unknown but I quite liked the idea of living in Kent. I wrote a short letter of application and posted it on the way home earlier this evening.

*   *   *

Thursday 8ᵗʰ July 1967

Letter from Sixokes: I am to be interviewed for the post tomorrow! I asked Uncle Reggie who was staying the night on one of his flying visits if he had any tips and, of course, he had a real nugget to offer.

"What you need to help get the job is to stand out from the crowd, have something striking or unusual that gets you noticed and gets you remembered by everyone when they meet up at the end of the day to make their choice. So, a flashy silk handkerchief tucked into the sleeve that is whisked out with a flourish every now and then – or a smart walking-cane, perhaps. Anything that helps catch the eye is all to the good – it gives them a point of reference because, of course, no-one remembers the names. 'That chap with the bright silk handkerchief' or 'the one who tapped his cane so smartly as he walked' will help you make your mark, George. And all the very best of luck, my boy!" he finished, gripping me warmly by the hand.

I feel it deep in my bones that a new door is opening in my life.

Friday 9ᵗʰ July 1967

The train journey down to that quiet, fairly smug, little town in Kent was uneventful enough. I had brought with me the Independent Schools Register and Review so that I could mug up on a few details in preparation for the interview. The entry on Sixokes School was very dry and dusty except for the final paragraph which promised to be more flowery. I decided to learn it to show the depth of my knowledge and interest. I've never been particularly adept of this sort of rote-work but I toiled away at it and was more-or-less word perfect on the first sentence which, as the train was slowing for Sixokes, would have to do I decided.

I took a taximeter cab up from the train station (the cabbie trying it on with a charge for 'extra luggage' which I refused to pay. I hope that this grumbling specimen isn't typical of the town's type) and arrived with perfect punctuality at 11 o'clock at the door of Carriage House, the nerve centre of the School. The Headmaster's secretary was all of a dither behind the slew of papers that washed around the prominent typewriter on her desk. She riffled beneath one of the piles and drew out a slim buff file which, I saw, had my name on it. Getting up she said "If you'd like to leave that in the corner, I'll take you in now, Mr Wentworth," and ushered me into the adjoining study saying: "This is Mr Wentworth, sir, for the Biology job." She laid the file on a pristine desk and left us, quietly closing the door behind her.

A tall, dark-haired man who had been gazing at something written on the huge blackboard that covered nearly all of one wall - and which was itself nearly covered with jottings at various angles and of varying sizes of words - whirled around and advanced towards me holding out his hand.

"Pleased to meet you, Mr Wentworth. Welcome to Sixokes. Naylor's the name – Vernon Kitchener Naylor in my Sunday best - but everyone calls me 'Tim'!"

He waved me to an armchair and made as if to walk to the study door.

"Hope you had a good journey here - would you like anything to drink?"

"Well, it's a bit early for me," I replied politely. "But you go ahead."

Momentarily nonplussed he then gave a deep chuckle.

"Very good. How about a tea or coffee instead?"

I thanked him but refused. I didn't want to run the risk of spilling anything during the interview ahead. I tried to ignore the faint worry that the man might be a dipsomaniac.

Rubbing his hands together he began pacing energetically around the room as he quizzed me about my schooling and interests at university. After some minutes of this, he picked out a sheet of paper from the buff file.

"There's a line here somewhere…ah yes." His alert blue eyes met mine. "This reference from your Latin teacher, a Mr…" he glanced down to check the signature. "…a Mr Brown, says that you are 'dogged, clean and enjoy collecting beetles' – but you've not mentioned any of this beetle-mania (if I may so describe it), Mr Wentworth! Come on, don't hide any lights now!"

I explained that I had moved on to greater things and that dinosaurs had supplanted the *Coleoptera* as the focus of my interests. This seemed to catch his imagination. He strode to the blackboard and tapped at the words 'Field Study Centre - Wales?' that were written in one corner.

"Could you set up some sort of exploration for the boys for dinosaur fossils in Wales?" he asked with some keenness. I explained that this was a particularly barren area for dinosaurs, that South America or China were the best places. His eyes lit up immediately and, seizing some chalk, underneath the 'Field Study Centre' entry vigorously chalked in 'S. Am??' and then 'China!!' He gazed at this last word, enraptured it seemed, for some little time, before turning back to me.

"After your experiences, won't joining us in this back-water in Kent be too retiring for you?"

To show him I'd done my homework, this seemed to be a good time to express my willingness to make the best of teaching at his obscure little school. As I'd guessed, it put him on the back foot and, no doubt, put up his respect for me a few notches.

"I think it could well be stimulating to do my part in guiding this struggling craft into smoother waters," I said modestly. He frowned.

"What do you mean by that?" he said - with a touch of asperity I thought.

"Oh, you know," I said with nonchalance. "That entry in the Register and Review: '*Sixokes is a tin-pot tramp steamer struggling in the wake of its mighty neighbour the majestic cruise liner that is Tinbridge School*'." I smiled to put him at his ease. "But I'll be happy to put my hand to the wheel, splice the mainbrace, scrub the decks – even pump the bilges – to keep the vessel afloat, Cap'n." For some reason, Naylor looked appalled at my having discovered this slightly unflattering (if perfectly honest) quote about the school. Just then, a soft tap at the door preceded the appearance of a handsome head around it.

"Ah, Byron," breathed Naylor softly.

"Time to swap, Tim" said the man who turned out to be the Nethermaster, Byron Craggs. Stepping smoothly into the room he brought with him the person who turned out to be my only rival for the teaching post – a chap called George Benson-Briars.

Craggs led me to his office which was on the other side of the secretary's. As we passed her, she suddenly leapt up.

"Oh crikey, I forgot his file!" she cried, pulling out another buff file and giving it a horrified look. Craggs smiled warmly at her.

"Don't fret, Miss Duff, don't fret," he said soothingly in his deep, rich tones. "Just knock and take it in."

As she did this he lowered his voice and told me that Miss Duff was a rather 'terrified temp' who was covering for the Headmaster's redoubtable secretary, Di Daley, while she was away on a fortnight's course (which 'naturally enough she is leading') on the administration of local voluntary work.

He settled himself comfortably into his leather chair, crossed his legs at the ankles, and gave me some details of the recent history of the school, accommodation, hours of work and holidays.

"And, of course, you will be expected to pitch in with other elements of the joy that is school-mastering such as with games for one thing - but you'll also want to set up some activity of your own. Tim drives us all on as I'm sure you'll appreciate, Mr Wentworth – he is the very incarnation of energy! What area of interest might you wish to offer that will develop and enrich the educational experience of the boys here?"

I gave him what I hope was a disarming smile as I inwardly groaned – this was a question I had not been prepared for. Rather desperately casting around for something to say, I recalled something I'd seen on Naylor's board.

"Field studies," I said simply. Luckily, that was enough. The words seemed to ignite Craggs and he uncrossed his legs and sat forward.

"Very good!" he said, nodding the while. "Very good. We are frightfully keen on pushing the boys' horizons beyond the mere provincial – even to say parochial - limits of what have been those imposed by the traditional public school approach to education, limits which stifle any originality and flair, limits which merely mould the plasticity of character of the young mind rather than – I'm sorry, am I boring you?"

"Not at all," I replied hurriedly, tearing my eyes from the extraordinary painting of a bare lady that I had just noticed displayed for all and sundry to see just to the side of his desk. "No, no – I'm all for studying fields and all that," I assured him. He looked at his watch.

"We are just about finished now, I think, Mr Wentworth. What happens now is that one of the boys will give you a tour of the school for twenty minutes or so. At 12 o'clock you and the other candidate, Mr Benson-Briars, will meet the Head of Biology and sit in with his sixth form class for about half an hour. Then, before luncheon, both you and Mr Benson-Briars will lead a coaching session with the first fifteen rugger team. Lunch will be at the Headmaster's house and then you'll be free to go." He stood up and nodded towards the looming figure of a boy that had appeared in the doorway. "Mason here will show you around the school and I look forward to seeing you later for our meal."

"Isn't she a beauty - can I carry it for you, sir?" asked this Mason enthusiastically as we walked down the stairs from Craggs' office and out into the grounds. I thought it heartless to deny him this liberty and tucked my hands in my pockets as we wandered along. I must say that the lawns and flowerbeds were stunning and did their best to soften the untidy range of nondescript buildings that Mason dutifully named and provided a few details about. Things like "And this is the Gym-stroke-Library. During gym lessons we use the shelves for climbing, as parallel bars, as balancing beams, and the spaces in between for exercise areas such as press-ups in 'History', stretches in 'Literature', star-jumps in 'Physics'. In the evening, of course, it is purely a library…and that is where we make our lunch if it's raining or cold," He swept an arm towards a small tarpaulin-covered paved area on which there were a number of camping stoves. He explained that every boy had his own mess-tin and in it they would boil up water ready to heat the 'ration-bag' each was issued with by the matrons. He added that the school hoped to have its own dining hall and kitchen within the next few years. I asked him a question that had been gnawing away in my mind since one of Craggs' remarks about the programme for the rest of the day. It was making me a little anxious.

"Is the rugger team doing well?" I was hoping that my lack of expertise in this particular sport would not be unmasked. My poor eyesight precluded me from taking an active role in the rugger at Beckham Grange but I had instead turned myself into rather a demon of a linesman, developing all sorts of extra flourishes and wiggles of the flag to ginger up the rather limited range that more ordinary practitioners were wont to employ (and which, no doubt, gave rise to the jealousy that prompted some of the more negative reactions to my touch-line work).

"We are all frightfully keen," said Mason guardedly. "Our coach, Mr Longhorn, is taking us on a tour of the West Country before the season starts – which is why we are having an extra session before lunch this morning."

"Will Mr Longhorn be there for that session?" I asked innocently.

"Oh no, sir – he's teaching then. It will be just you and the other gentleman coaching us, sir," Mason said earnestly. I felt very relieved at this – there would be no-one there to witness any small flaws I might reveal. He immediately reversed this by adding: "But the Head of P.E. will be watching – and he is an England Schoolboy selector. And now here we are at the Biology Department. Thanks for this - and see you for rugger in a while, sir."

Before me were a couple of distressed prefabricated huts slumped on four courses of poorly-pointed brickwork. Out of the door of the nearer hut bounded a lithe, middle-aged, sandy-haired figure with a huge grin on his warm and pleasant face.

"You must be Wentworth! Welcome, welcome! Come in, come in, come in! Jack Natter's the name. Head of Bilge, ha, ha. Have you met Benson-Briars here? Thank you, Mason, off you go! Let's get on, get on, get on! Just stick it over there and we'll join the boys!" The man was like friendly whirlwind, sweeping Benson-Briars and me (after the merest hint of a friendly exchange of glances and smiles between us) into the classroom and settling us onto a couple of stools that completed a ring of people around four cheap tables pushed together. Besides we three adults, there were seven boys none of whom looked either at ease or intelligent.

"Thought we'd avail ourselves of the latest from you two founts, you know, founts!" shouted Natter, beaming around at Benson-Briars and me, then at the boys. "Have a sort of seminar – seminar no less, ha, ha – on what's newest and best. Smack up to date, the latest, the latest! Currently, we've been studying muscle – you know, sliding-filaments, sarcomere, T-system, all that, all that! Thought you chaps could chip in with, no, better still, better still, could flex your muscles on muscles!" This witty sally brought an appreciative laugh from everyone and the mood became relaxed all of a sudden. I felt very much at ease and sat back with an almost audible sigh as I waited for Natter to take the floor. Then it dawned on me that Natter was gesturing at me with an 'out with it' sort of signal. I felt my blood chill as I realised I was being thrust into the lime-light. The few stray names of things like 'myosin', 'troponin', 'Z-lines' and 'A-bands' whirled chaotically in my mind. I couldn't find any meaning in them.

"Perhaps one of the boys could say something about antagonistic muscles," said Benson-Briars pleasantly. Though I was grateful for his stepping into the silence that had been growing rather terribly as they waited for my tongue to unlock, I thought he'd committed something of a howler with this. Clearly, we were the ones expected to hold forth rather than putting the ball in the boys' court like this.

A spotty chap on the other side of the square told him that a muscle could only contract in length and therefore, to be restretched to its full extent, another muscle had to pull on it – hence all muscles were arranged in antagonistic pairs: when one contracts, the other relaxes. I nodded my head sagely – the boy knew his stuff.

"But what about the diaphragm?" objected Benson-Briars. "That's a muscle with no antagonistic pair to restretch it…" He raised his eyebrows and smiled around the ring of puzzled faces. What a chump the man was! Setting himself up to look foolish at what I knew was simply O-level standard stuff that any simpleton could explain. I grasped the moment.

"Of course, none of you boys should be tricked by the subtlety of Mr Benson-Briars's misdirection. Naturally, the muscles which work antagonistically to the diaphragm are the intercostals. As they contract to lift the ribcage, this creates a negative pressure in the thorax which sucks up the diaphragm." I tried not to look triumphant of this correction of my rival. Though some of the boys were looking at Natter with slightly worried expressions, Benson-Briars seemed blissfully unaware and, in my humble opinion, stupidly pressed on with trying to involve the boys. I let him dig his own grave.

"Now just take spiders, boys. Have you ever wondered why their legs collapse and curl up when you kill one? Well, it's because they have no extensor muscles in their legs, only flexor ones. No antagonistic pairs at work there." At this point he stretched his arm out straight and then bent his elbow "Flex", his wrist "Flex", his knuckles, "Flex" and his digits, "Flex". We were all watching this with some fascination. "But no – "and here he matched actions to words as he brought his arm back to gun-barrel straightness, "Extensor, extensor, extensor, extensor." He paused and looked searchingly at the boys. "What do you think causes their legs to straighten if it isn't muscle?"

"But it must be muscle, sir!" objected one of the boys after a time. "There needs to be a force…" here he tailed off and then a light dawned and he suddenly became excited. "No, it must be a squeezing pressure!" he burst out with something like delight.

"You're right," coaxed Benson-Briars. "Keep going – what's your name?"

"Temms, sir. Well, if the legs are filled with fluid, then as the flexor contracts it will raise the fluid pressure…and then, once the flexor stops contracting, the fluid pressure squeezes the leg straight again – no extensor needed!"

"Brilliant, Temms, brilliant!" chipped in Natter. "He's right isn't he Mr Benson-Briars?"

"Quite right," said Benson-Briars with a broad smile. "Isn't it interesting how this one group of arthropods uses both muscle and elevated fluid pressure in locomotion? Can you think of any more uses made in organisms of elevated fluid pressures?"

This question really animated the boys and they were soon feverishly vying with each other to impress Benson-Briars with their knowledge. Things like 'ultrafiltration in the Malpighian corpuscle', 'translocation in the phloem', 'stomatal regulation' and 'tissue fluid formation' were called out and Benson-Briars spent some time teasing out how these things worked.

While all this was going on it gave me plenty of time to gaze around at the walls to see what the department had that might be of interest to me. This didn't take long. There were the usual rows of jars containing pale gruesome specimens in formalin; some skeletons of small mammals rather amateurishly glued together; a few drab, torn and dusty posters depicting organs of the human body. Out of the window I noticed that the sun was shining through the leaves of an oak tree. My mind was wandering pleasantly to the thoughts of the summer to come and a hotter sun piercing through sultry air and the verdure of tropical trees when I became aware of Natter's insistent voice saying:

"Enough, boys, enough! 'Fraid we haven't been letting Mr Wentworth get much of a word in but time's up, you know. Time gentlemen please! Just a clap for these gentlemen, boys, a good clap!" Natter himself led the applause from the boys and I acknowledged it with a small bow before Benson-Briars and I made for the door.

"They're good lads, good lads," said Natter happily.

"Tell them I think they did you proud," said Benson-Briars.

"I will, I will indeed!" replied Natter, obviously very pleased by this. "Here's Mason back to take you to the killing fields. Not a rugger fan, you know, best of luck with it! And I'll see you both at lunch! Oh, and don't forget this, will you now. Couldn't catch a cold myself, ha, ha!"

"We all admired your performance in the 'Varsity match last year, sir," said Mason to Benson-Briars as we walked up to Dyke's Meadow, a large expanse of close-clipped turf now, out of season, basking unbruised and restful under the sky. "I thought you were unlucky to be pipped by that break-away try Cambridge scored in the last minute." I might have guessed Benson-Briars was an Oxford man – he had that quiet authority, self-possessed swagger and smirking superciliousness that that lot all seem to share. Still, I thought I was pretty far ahead of him in the job stakes so far: I'd impressed the Headmaster and the Nethermaster and Benson-Briars had really shot himself in the foot in the session with the sixth form Biology group.

A group of boys was playing 'touch' as we breasted the slope and a beefy, genial giant of a man came and shook hands.

"Martin Starr, Head of Games," he told us. He must have been a boxer in his day – his nose had been so frequently and so badly broken that whichever way he turned, it appeared to be in profile. "Take ten or fifteen minutes each with them will you gents? Just so I can see you can pass muster on the games front. Why don't you go first George?"

"I'd rather go second," I said at the same time as Benson-Briars was saying "Of course Uncle Martin." This muddle was quickly unravelled for me: Starr and Benson-Briars knew each other from when the latter had had a trial with the England Under-16 Group. Unsurprisingly, neither of them had been aware that we shared the first name.

Starr and I watched as Benson-Briars called in the players, rapidly marshalled them and told them what the practice would be about: a short drill session then a 'real action' set-up to use the drilled skills in scoring a try. He split them into small groups and, in a grid marked off with coloured ropes, coached them in the techniques of 'power-driving', 'contact-offloading', 'decoy-running' and 'double-crushing'. All nonsense to me but Starr kept grunting approvingly. The boys all looked grimly determined and, in the final 'real action' smashed into each other with sickening ferocity leaving one of their number to touch down in triumph. Starr gave a ragged cheer before turning to me. "Your turn now, Mr Hemingway. I'll hold that for you if you like. Well done, George!" he cried, clapping Benson-Briars on the back.

I decided not to play into their hands. "It's Wentworth, actually, Mr Starr. For my session I need four dozen bean-bags. Will you get them for me?" Unfortunately, he didn't trot off immediately to get them himself so removing his knowledgeable eye from my coaching performance. Instead, he waved Mason over and, pressing his enormous bunch of keys into his hand, ordered him to 'double on down to Willy's Store' to collect the bean-bags. Swallowing hard, I walked slowly up to the players, one of whom was ruefully rubbing his elbow – from the gruff chit-chat it seemed that he had hurt it by jabbing it into a hard-headed prop called Pugh. Suddenly, an idea came to me to fill in the time until the bean-bags arrived. The rubbed elbow had put me in mind of an Old Beckhamian professional tennis coach who had given a Founder's Day talk on a new-fangled fad called 'sports psychology' four or five years previously. Thinking on my feet, I adapted it.

"Sit down, boys. I'm going to coach your minds rather than your bodies in this first part of the session." Dutifully, they all sat cross-legged at my feet and looked up expectantly. I started conversationally:

"A lot of the game is played in the mind – look at the mood of determination you chaps engendered in that 'reaction session' just now. Without that mental state, you'd have been just a weak set of pansies, don't you know? When you face your opponent over the net, I mean at the other end of the court, no field, pitch, yes, pitch, what you have to think as that you are invincible. Every movement you make is machine-like, oiled, fluid, hypnotic, irresistible. You can strike with the speed of a cobra, spin, swerve, lob like a champion at Wimbledon, or Twickenham or whatnot. Your muscles, yes, those muscles are like steel bands, surging and swelling like mountainous tides as, in their antagonistic pairs, they impart precision and power, momentum and mystery to those synovial joints that will sweep your skeleton over the turf to drive a penetrating backhand or a fearsome volley, or a tough tackle, or one of your mauly things. And think of grace and beauty, yes, the grace of the arc of the ball, the beauty of a man running at speed to, to try, to try and, to try and score a try!" I finished with this magnificent flourish and punched the air. In all modesty, I can say that the boys were thunderstruck by my performance. Starr was slowly shaking his head in wonder and Benson-Briars's eyebrows were half-way up his forehead in consternation at what must have been an unpleasant surprise for him.

At this moment of triumph, Mason came puffing back up the hill with a sack containing the bean-bags and emptied them at my feet.

"There you are, sir. Forty-eight bean-bags"

"Right, boys," I said to them as they struggled to their feet. "I want you to make a grid 10 yards by 10 yards using these pretty ropes." They got on with this while I explained to Starr that the practice I had in mind developed poise, agility and handling skills. By this time the grid and the boys were ready. "Now, each of you, let's see, there are sixteen. Right, each of you puts a bean-bag on his head and stands in the grid. Do that now." They complied and stood grinning at each other. "Now the object of this exercise is for you to move smoothly around the grid. You must keep moving at all times. That is the first rule. A second rule is that you must not touch another player. Nor must you touch the bean-bag on your head or anyone else's head." I chuckled to myself. "Now comes the tricky bit. Every 5 seconds or so, I will toss one of you one of these bean-bags"

- I nudged the heap of the remaining 32 bags with my toe – "and you must catch and pass these new bags amongst each other without either dropping one or losing the bean-bag on your head. Every bag that hits the floor," here I paused for effect, "will mean the whole squad having to do a lap of the pitch as a punishment. That is one lap for every bag on the ground, boys." Seeing their scowls I lightened the tone. "Of course, that means a *maximum* of 48 laps," I assured them with a grin. "Off you go!"

As the boys moved cautiously around in the grid I included Starr and Benson-Briars in the conspiracy. "This is impossible," I murmured to them. "I heard that the most that our University team could manage was thirty bags before there was a general collapse. We're in for some fun!" I began lobbing an extra bean-bag into the crowd of boys after counts of five. A couple of minutes of this bending and lobbing (rather like a keeper throwing fish to seals, I thought) produced, rather puzzlingly, no dropped bag – the ground in the grid was empty as the boys continued milling around seemingly intent on balancing their own bag on their head. I started counting to five more quickly, positively showering the boys with bean-bags. Still they kept it up. Amazed, I lobbed the last two bags into the group and waited. Nothing dropped at all. Starr blew a whistle and the boys walked over.

"Well done, lads, well done. Lots of poise, agility and superb handling skills to impress Mr Windworth, here. Off and change now – oh, and Mason, make sure Willy gets all the bean-bags back won't you?" With this he slapped Mason's rather protuberant behind. Mason grinned back at him and then he and the other boys swaggered merrily down the slope. I was totally bemused.

"I think the boys did you proud there, Uncle Martin," said Benson-Briars.

Starr agreed and said "And now it's troughing time, I believe. I wonder if we'll get salmon – or perhaps a nice piece of trout." He led us to the Headmaster's House for luncheon reciting a fairly impressive list of fish possibilities that we might be about to enjoy.

In fact, there was soup, pork and spotted dick. Starr didn't look at all disappointed by this - which I thought a bit odd.

To my chagrin, the conversation during the meal was almost totally hogged by Benson-Briars after 'Tim' Naylor had asked him to explain to us why he was available to come and replace the 'shade of Sorenson' (the teacher who was 'lost in the Scotch mist' Natter whispered to me). Apparently, Benson-Briars had been due to be a part of a 6-month expedition to the Himalayas to study the physiological effects of cold and high altitude on the human body. It was to include an attempt to reach the summit of Everest. However, the leader had suffered a number of injuries in a car accident and so the expedition had been forced to be postponed until the next window of opportunity in two years' time. While he bragged about all this in reply to various animated and adulatory questions, I tucked in heartily to the food – which was both toothsome and plentiful. I sometimes found it difficult to reach the decanter to replenish my glass but Natter and Starr were most helpful in this regard.

At 2 o'clock, Naylor wiped his mouth on his napkin and, throwing it briskly onto the table, stood up and announced:
"Heartfelt thanks to Mr Benson-Briars and Mr Wentworth for their company and I'm sure we all enjoyed meeting them today. But, we must get on with the enterprise of education in this afternoon's classes, gentlemen, so, loath as I am to break up this assembly, let us to arms!" At this, I pushed back my chair and hauled myself to my feet. I stumbled a little as I caught a foot against the chair-leg and, aiming to catch the corner of the table to steady myself, unaccountably missed it and fell heavily to the floor. A second unfortunate thing was that I had tucked a corner of the table-cloth into my trousers when I had tucked my napkin there. Thus, as I tumbled over, everything on the table that could fall over – decanters, glasses, candelabra, vases of flowers – did fall over with quite a bit of noise and mess.

"Never mind, Mr Wentworth, never mind!" carolled Natter as he helped me up and handed me my glasses back. "Could have happened to anyone."

I shook hands all round and made for the door.

"You nearly forgot this," said Starr with a smile. I took it from him and, after a few steps found to my horror that the other end had somehow snagged the gaudy Chinese vase that stood in the hallway. It crashed to smithereens on the parquet. I thought for an instant that Starr was grinning but, on closer examination, his expression was of real concern. Craggs unhooked me and I trudged to the front of Carriage House to get my taximeter cab. The driver turned out to be the same grumpy individual who had brought me up from the station earlier and he refused to take me as he'd found the lining of his roof 'all marked and torn' after my ride.

Feeling quite dispirited now, I walked slowly down the hill to the train station and, deciding against the exploration of London that I had thought of making, travelled straight back here. A further unsettling event came when I idly started leafing through the Independent Schools Register and Review and looked up Sixokes since there seemed nothing better to do. For a second, I actually could not believe my eyes. Frantically, I checked the entry again – yes, it was 'Sixokes School' – and, then checked this was the same edition – yes, on the front was 'Property of B.U. Careers Centre – not to be removed'. How could I have missed those three vital words? I could scarcely believe it. I groaned aloud at the memory of Naylor's face. Repeated consultation could not change the lines back to what I thought they had said that morning. The quote persisted in reading (my italics): 'Sixokes is *far from being* a tin-pot tramp steamer struggling in the wake of its mighty neighbour, the majestic cruise liner that is Tinbridge School.' And then going on: 'Rather, under the resourceful and inspirational leadership of its Headmaster, V. K. Naylor, Sixokes is now close to outpacing that grand old lady by opening up exciting new horizons in the great voyage of discovery that is Education. Indeed, it hardly stretches the metaphor to regard

Naylor and Sixokes as pioneering in the tradition of Magellan and his ship, the *Trinidad*.'

At least Mother was out 'gallivanting with the girls' this evening so I won't have to tell her anything until the morning. Perhaps after a good night's sleep things will look brighter.

Saturday 10th July 1967

Brighter indeed – I've got the job! They must have made the decision early in the afternoon and caught that evening's post because here in front of me is the Headmaster's letter - exquisitely hand-written, of course:

> '*Dear George,*
>
> *I would be delighted if you would accept the post of Biology teacher here from September. We were all extremely impressed by you. I think you will find the experience of teaching most rewarding and know that the staff and boys here will all benefit from your knowledge, ability and character.*
>
> *I enclose the bumf needed for the Bursar but there is no necessity for you to complete those details immediately – all you need do is accept!*
>
> *Best wishes,*
>
> *Tim*
> *(V.K.Naylor)*'

I wrote back immediately.

> 'Dear Tim,
>
> I am delighted to accept the post of Biology teacher at your school from September.
>
> I am going abroad for a month from the start of next week and so will be out of communication for that time but will bring the bumf – fully-completed of course – with me on the 30th August.
>
> Yours sincerely,
>
> George
>
> (G.G.Wentworth)
>
> P.S. apologies for mixing up the Register and Review quote!'

I dropped this in the post-box and bought a bottle of champagne to share with Mother in celebration. Needless to say, she was cock-a-hoop at the news.

*   *   *

Monday 30th August 1967

Di Daley fixed me with something of a gimlet eye. "You were the one with the eight-foot fishing rod," she said with what some might have called an accusing tone. I ignored it and silently blessed Uncle Reggie – perhaps it was the rod that tipped the balance in my favour in the contest between me and Benson-Briars. She went on: "Of course, there's nothing to be done about it now but, just so you know, it was down to my stand-in that you are here today." Having uttered this very gnomic statement, she went into Naylor's study. What could she mean? How could anything that the timorous Miss Duff could have

- 196 -

said or done made any difference? Then it dawned on me: she had put the letters to me and to Benson-Briars in the wrong envelopes... Well, perhaps that is just fate, I thought to myself.

Glancing through the door I saw Naylor clutching his head in his hands as Di Daley was saying something to him. Watch out, Mr Naylor, I reflected. Here I am on the first rung of the ladder towards running my own school – you may well experience my feet on your shoulders as I rise above you. Watch out indeed!

Naylor appeared in front of me, smiled and shook my hand. "We'll start in the bilges shall we, Mr Wentworth?" he said pleasantly.

The voyage had begun.

Episode 19

From his diary

Saturday 12 July 1990

It was an odd sensation going back to my *alma mater* after all these years. Usually, I am the most incurious of men but there had been something about the invitation to the Beckham Grange Gala Dinner that had struck a chord of nostalgia that acted like the call of a Siren. After twenty-five years, what would the old place be like – and indeed, what life stories might my contemporaries have to tell? I took a taxi from my hotel and asked to be dropped at the school gates.

I noted with approval that there actually were some gates hanging on the gateposts now – a fancy bit of wrought iron work picked out in the school colours which looked positively jolly in the evening sunlight. There was a dedication to some worthy governor who presumably had stumped up the cash for them. The dedication, I thought, was rather equivocal: he was lauded for his integrity, diligence and tireless contribution, etc., etc., and then described as 'a man of rare wisdom' which reminded me of a similar ambivalence that Tony Cobberly had pointed out to me. In a review of Richard Hansum's poetry, Ted Hughes was asked for a comment on Hansum's famous description of an autumn leaf as 'marcelled and marcescent'. Hughes replied that he found it 'rather precious' which, of course, could have been damning or approving. Musing thus brought me to the end of the drive and a sensation of the end of the present.

I felt I had been whisked back in time as I passed through the smaller-than-remembered portals of Main School. Walking towards Hall I passed a placard spiked into the lawn and about three-foot square with 'Give!' on it in bold black letters on a white background. A few yards further on was a second placard which was twice the size. 'Give!!' it said. A few more yards walking and there was a third, truly enormous placard announcing 'Give!!!'

I passed into Hall which had been bedecked with banners proclaiming 'Raise the Roof Old Beckhamians!' Avoiding these ocular assaults, I focused instead on the dim, grim oil paintings of past Masters. There was only one new one: 'Flogger' Fredericks swinging his formidable ashplant while striding purposefully across the grass of the Quad with his bouncing fox-terrier at his heels.

"Shets!" called a voice behind me. I recognized it instantly: 'Squeaky' Berresfford. He came towards me and wrung my hand. He was immaculate in white tie and tails with some sort of decoration in his lapel and dropped a little in my estimation: honours and medals are so pretentious. He looked me up and down with delight on his face. "You've not grown a bit!" he roared. "Come over and join the others."

I shook several hands of people with familiar faces in unfamiliar bodies. We were just slipping back into a mutual easiness when a bustling stranger in a frothy, frilled, pink dress-shirt with a lime-green bowtie and cummerbund shoved his way unceremoniously into our circle and rattled a red plastic bucket around.

I appreciated his effort to blend in by using the School colours (it called to mind the fact that I had lost my old school tie in the visitors' changing room in the pavilion at Tinbridge School) which were a background of sober navy blue with the thinnest of lines of pink and green – what Joff Brown always laughed off as the Master's predilection for crab and avocado cocktails. I believe the more prosaic reason was that during the austerity years in the early part of the century, the very pragmatic governors chose to adopt a new uniform (out went the toppers, stiff wing collars and striped trousers!). They chose this combination of colours merely because there was a job lot of the ties and blazers available at a knock-down price from a failed school in a Southern State of the USA which the suppliers were happy to off-load at below cost. Be that as it may, this strange man announced himself.

"Dig deep, gentlemen!" he brayed with a menacing grin and a strong South African accent. "Warren Grobius Luger is the name: 'Luger' by name and 'Straight Shooter' by nature!" He paused for a reaction but got none. "I'm the FDP for the Roof Appeal and I want your cash!" He rattled his bucket around for a second time. I peered into its depths and noted the handful of brown coins at the bottom.

"Hardly enough for a small tile there I'd have thought." I said dubiously.

Swiftly, he turned towards me, obviously delighted in having provoked a response.

"That's your mistake, sir, your mistake!"

He reached out and took my lapel with a burning intensity in his eyes.

"You must know the 'sprat to catch a mackerel' adage, well, once I've got the mackerel, I'll use it to catch a codfish! …And then I'll use the codfish to catch a … marlin!"

By this time, the rest of the group was eyeing this stranger with looks of condescension and amusement. He ploughed on somewhat desperately.

"Then a marlin for…for a shark! And a shark for, well a shark for… a whale!" he finished with a triumphant shout and another firm rattle of his bucket. There was a pause. Suddenly the mood of the circle slipped into one of conspiracy: we were Insiders and here was an Outsider.

Solemnly, his idea was taken literally.

"I'm not exactly sure you could fit a whale into that bucket..." murmured Westering. "Well," drawled Berresfford thoughtfully, "I suppose a whale could be used to replace the roof. I suppose the skin must be waterproof and, if properly flensed – I believe 'flensing' is the right term – there would already be a good layer of blubber to act as insulation. And I dare say the flukes would act as a novel sort of awning over the rather undistinguished portico currently in position..."

"I'm a bit worried by your programme, actually," said Crubey. "So far as I know, whales don't actually eat sharks and so your whole baiting system might not get you the whaleskin roof you are after..."

"And what about the bones – would the kitchen staff use them for some sort of soup for the boys..."

"Perhaps there could be scrimshanking sessions..."

Defeated, Luger gazed desperately beyond our circle and, on catching sight of the entry of the Master's Party, scurried towards it.

"What a loathsome oik," said Phipps, voicing a general opinion.

"Yes, he talked to me earlier," said Clooney with a hint of a curl to his lip. "We were both offered a tray of those canapé things. He made some remark about 'getting my teeth into the rich blex' and I thought he was talking about that fishy pink goo smeared on the crackers that we'd chosen to eat. Far from it. After a couple of minutes talking at cross purposes it transpired that he was eyeing up Sammy Ngogo's Nigerian party on the other side of the room."

"Good Lord! Is that really Pokey Ponsford!" exclaimed Berresfford nodding towards the bent and shambling grey-haired apparition that had just entered the room with a palsied and hesitant step.

Before any of us had the chance to make a comment, Luger produced a tremendous clangour on a couple of hand bells and bellowed:

"Gentlemen, The Master of Beckham Grange!"

The Master gave a cursory gaze around Hall and uttered a few anodyne words of welcome and the sincere hope that we would all have an enjoyable evening while 'dipping our hands into our no doubt deep and well-lined pockets' to provide the momentum to achieve the £200 000 target to replace the roof before it collapsed. While he was speaking I noticed Berresfford edge over to Pokey Ponsford and, gripping him gently by the arm, steer him back to our group. After the desultory applause, we bagged a table for ten and settled ourselves down. Just for the record, in clockwise order sat: Pokey Ponsford, 'Sunny' Westering, Ngogo, Crubey, Berresfford, Phipps, Homerton-Teste, myself, Chert, Clooney.

I soon discovered that being both a bachelor and a Biology teacher at a top independent school were far more interesting and exciting than anything that Chert (a 'technical development director at an up-and-coming machine parts firm') or Homerton-Teste (an 'assistant audit clerk' at one of the major branches of some bank I'd never heard of) had to offer. Their account of devoted wives and the exploits of their tedious children just churned the dreariness that I have come to expect from those who embark on the married life. As they swapped photographs of family groups across me, I forked up some of the stringy cabbage that accompanied a couple of grey slices of a 'baron of beef' as the menu described it, and my glance fell on Berresfford who was listening to Crubey with a pained expression. It was the whiff of the boiled cabbage combined with the sight of his pursed lips that violently swept my mind back just over twenty-five years to that stupendous moment when I had last seen him – that last moment before he was summarily sacked by 'Flogger' and sent home by the early morning train. It came flooding back with an immediacy and clarity that was quite uncanny...

Two and a half decades ago on that charged evening in May, the story began on the grass of the Quad in the late afternoon. Well, actually, some more detail of what brought the four of us together there might be useful.

Berresfford had been elected as School Captain the previous September and had made the most of all the privileges that position had to offer while assiduously avoiding the great majority of the responsibilities. It was a huge surprise to us and to the new Master (Fredericks, of course) just what was written into the ancient constitution of the School about the rights the post of School Captain afforded and on which the triumphant Berresfford insisted. The first thing was that Berresfford was entitled to 'two rooms adjacent to the Master in order to fulfil his duties with greater efficacy'. Reluctantly, the Master felt honour-bound to move an understandably disgruntled Bursar and his secretary out of their erstwhile offices opposite his own suite of rooms for Berresfford's use. The place was done up rather sumptuously, it had to be said. Berresfford also tried to insist on his 'entitlement to carry a sword' and 'to stable and exercise a horse'. Fredericks balked at these and a compromise was finally reached such that he was allowed to have a sharpish letter-opener in his pencil-case and keep a gerbil in his study.

Miffed at being thwarted over the sword issue, Berresfford took to 'exercising' this gerbil on the Quad during the time when the rest of us were occupied with prep from which he, as School Captain, was exempt. Being Berresfford, he had named his gerbil Cedric (which, of course, was the Master's first name) and would spend twenty minutes or so shouting things like 'Roll over, Cedric!', 'Sit up and beg, Cedric!', 'You naughty boy, Cedric!' at the innocent little creature as it sat in a small portable cage washing its face.

Anyway, on that late afternoon in May, I had been sent on an errand by the prep-super – Pokey Ponsford, as it happened – and entered the Quad at the same time as Mamzel Durand walked into it (though 'walked' is rather too prosaic a word to describe her languorous, graceful, hip-swinging gait) from the other corner. Like the majority of the other boys, I was in awe of this new French mistress with her sultriness, gorgeous curves, sudden smiles and, above all else, her being a female and under thirty years of age.

Berressfford seemed to have none of the shyness that turned the rest of us into gibbering idiots whenever Mamzel spoke to us with the fascinating lilt and honeyed promise that is the French accent. He waved her over to admire Cedric. As she bent over the cage he said something to her and she laughed and tapped him reprovingly on the shoulder. Then he looked up and, seeing me hovering, called:

"Shets, get over here at the double!" The School Captain's word being law, I trotted over. "Now just you watch how clever and obedient to his master's voice Cedric is, Mamzel," he said, lifting the bemused gerbil out of the cage and setting him on the grass where he began sniffing around. "You stand over there, Shets and I'll go over here…" We moved so that we were both about 5 yards from Cedric who had hopped a bit and was now doing a bit more sniffing. "Now, both Shets and I will call Cedric to come to us and I'll bet you anything you like that he'll come to me," said Berressfford giving Mamzel a winning smile. She smiled back and a dimple winked in her cheek.

Before we had a chance to test Cedric, a blur of black and white hurtled across the Quad. It was Biffer, the Master's new dog (bought to replace his former one, a chocolate Labrador shot so tragically by S-S Jones). The Master himself then dashed into the Quad calling out for Biffer to stop but to no avail. Fortunately, Cedric proved alert to the danger and with a whisk of his tail, scurried off the grass and into the House. Mamzel Durand grabbed Biffer who squirmed deliciously in her arms as the Master reached us.

"Uh, sorry about that Berressfford, not very bright those terriers, not so easy to command."

Berressfford met his eye but said nothing.

"Thank you Mamzel, very quick thinking," he went on, plucking the wriggling Biffer from her. "I dare say your pet will be on its way to your room you know, Berressfford."

The Master looked around at the three of us and there was one of those awkward pauses that happen – when two or more people all know that now is the time to separate but all think that there is something to be said first - but there never is. The tableau stuck in my mind: me, the Master, Berresfford, and Mamzel Durand frozen in that moment of awkwardness. How could any of us know that in just a few hours the four of us would be in another tableau where no words could ever do justice to the emotions of the moment?

Which brings me neatly to the cabbage-and-pursed-lips-inspired recollection.

It was past eleven o'clock later that evening when I started walking down the pitch-dark corridor in which were the doors to the Master's and Berresfford's rooms. There was a small slit of light coming from the underside of each though of different shades: a buttery yellow from the former, a rich pink from the latter. I was tiptoeing along as, technically, this was out of bounds for me at this hour. I had a right and proper excuse of course (Mr Brown had undertaken to help polish up my oral French with me in his rooms after supper when I had gone up to check on my beetles. We had got really absorbed in it and not noticed how late the hour had reached) but I didn't want to have to explain all this and was hoping to get back to the dorm without encountering anyone. It was my innate love of animals that was my undoing.

As I neared the Master's door a sort of 'sixth sense' told me that there was something living and breathing in the darkness ahead. I froze and felt pins and needles prickling my palms. There was a faint sound not two paces from me. My heart galloped. The sound was repeated and then I saw it: the gerbil had hopped forwards and was sniffing at the gap under the Master's door. Horrified, I thought he was about to crawl underneath and meet his death in the jaws of Biffer. Without thinking I yelled his name: "Cedric!"

Almost immediately, two smart steps sounded on the floorboards on the other side of the door. The Master flung it open and light poured out into the corridor. Both of us stared not at each other but at the figure of a dressing-gowned Berresfford petrified in a pace, clutching a bottle of champagne in one hand and, in the other, a small box inscribed with the words: 'Gents' Assorted French Letters'.

The Master's mind obviously worked at a speed far superior to mine (which, I must admit, seemed to have seized up completely). He stepped swiftly across the corridor and threw open the door to Berresfford's rooms to reveal Mamzel Durant lying full-length in the bed and eyeing us lazily as she lifted the sheet to cover her chest. That was when Berresfford's lips pursed and, I suppose, imprinted the image of the three of them indelibly in my mind along with the immemorial cabbaginess of the smell of the House.

The Master was, well, masterful. He ordered Berresfford into his study and brusquely told Mamzel to go and pack her things. Then he turned to me. He leaned over and, in a commanding whisper, threatened me with immediate expulsion if I mentioned any of this to anyone else before talking to him again in his study at 8 a.m. Then he dismissed me and, like Cedric the gerbil before me, I scurried hurriedly down the corridor seeking a sanctuary.

Just before 8 o'clock I presented myself at the Master's study. I was awe-struck at the state of Berresfford's rooms as I glanced through the open door: they were empty of everything. Even the carpet and curtains had been removed.

"Ah, Wentworth. Come in and shut the door."

Naturally enough, I was expecting a flogging. But to my surprise and delight, all I got was a jawing after I'd hurriedly explained why I'd been in the corridor late at night. Satisfied with my innocence, I was briskly told that Berresfford and Mamzel Durant had both decided to leave the school forthwith. Clearly, there might be some speculation about this coincidence but he, the Master, would scotch any of that by announcing in a special assembly that Mamzel had returned to France to nurse a sick parent who had taken a turn for the worse and that Berresfford had been called to Argentina by his guardian to take up a post in the diplomatic service there with immediate effect – a post that had excellent potential for a great career. Flogger fixed me with his terrible eye.

"All I need from you, Wentworth, is a vow of silence. I ask this not for my sake, nor for the sake of the characters of Berresfford or Mamzel Durant. No, I ask it for the sake of your school, for the sake of Beckham Grange."

With a lump in my throat, I choked out my willingness to do anything for the sake of the school.

"Mind you do," he said. He picked up his ashplant and tapped it a couple of times against his shoe. "Mind you do." Then he opened the door and let me out.

I came out of this reverie to find myself gazing at Berresfford and, behind him on the wall, the painting of Fredericks and Biffer. The memory had been so vivid I still felt a surge of pride in my chest at being trusted to such an extent by the Master.

While I had been reliving those dramatic events of a quarter of a century past, stories were circulating as coffee was being poured. I took little notice of them, floating as I still was on the swells of yesteryear. But soon my attention was alerted by Crubey beginning:

"Do you remember that afternoon when the Bishop of Birmingham came to give a talk?" This caught my ear because I distinctly remembered that day because it was the first time I had plucked up the courage to ask a question publicly – in front of the whole school – and of a bishop to boot! Naturally, nowadays I am always one of the first to throw an interesting interrogative to a speaker when the opportunity arises but then, well, I was a little on the shy side.

It was the anniversary of the founding of the school and, by long tradition, a guest speaker gave a short speech after lunch and the rest of the afternoon was then free time for everyone. The weather was perfect: a hot bold sun hoisted high in a clear azure sky. The whole school had settled in the pews of the chapel and the Master introduced the Bishop of Birmingham who patted the edges of the pages of his speech, gripped the sides of the lectern and beamed at us knowing he was going to give us a treat. We were hushed.

"Don't I just!" exclaimed Clooney. "He just went on and on and on – it must have been for nearly a whole hour!"

"It was worse for me," said Crubey quietly. "I was in one of the back pews and right behind me was Pardoe. You'll remember what a clown Pardoe was?" He looked around the table and we all nodded – even Pokey. "Well, for nearly the whole of that blessed speech Pardoe leaned forward and, right in my ear, kept up a whispered sort of ecclesiastical sing-song repetition of every word the blessed Bishop uttered. This had two effects. The first was a huge, I mean really absolutely vast, irritation. The second was an inordinate desire to laugh out loud – I could almost feel the laughter gurgling just under the surface. Naturally, since silence and absolute stillness were required, I could do nothing to escape." We all shook our heads sympathetically at Crubey's ordeal. He went on:

'Thankfully, after an eternity, the Bishop drew to a close, and, just as we were all drawing breath ready to surge out into the free summer air, he asked if anyone had a question. I couldn't believe my eyes when I saw some blithering, blethering, bothersome cretin near the front put up his hand and ask the weakest, stupidest question. 'Please sir,' this vacuous imbecile said, 'Please sir, what made you become a bishop?' I could not believe what I had heard. The Bishop beamed and simpered, no doubt delighted that someone was still awake. In those unctuous tones we had all grown so weary of he replied: 'That is a very interesting question, my boy. Very interesting indeed. My answer to you is that, up in Heaven, God keeps a Great Book. And in this Great Book there are two columns and countless rows. In the first column of the Book are inscribed the names of every person in the world.' At this point, if you recall, he gazed benignly around the whole chapel before going on: 'The name of everyone here will be in that Great Book. In the second column will be the vocation that God has chosen for you. It may be 'soldier' or 'sailor', 'surgeon' or 'statesman', even, perhaps...' and here he turned archly and bowed towards old Chester, 'even a headmaster!' He paused for a laugh here but got nothing but a sullen silence. 'Well, next to my name in God's Great Book is written…'

'Wanker!'

When the laughter around the table had died away, Crubey continued his story.

"Of course, that wasn't the Bishop. It was Pardoe whispering it into my right ear. Though he was a clown, had the timing of a genius. I felt a great surge of laughter rising up in my chest – it was irresistible. Of course, at the same time I realised that I could not possibly laugh out loud in chapel in front of the Bishop. So instead I pretended to be having some sort of seizure and fell amongst the shoes and hassocks while choking with paroxysms of mirth. The noise had alerted everyone and, after a few seconds, through the tears blurring my eyes, who should I see but Joff Brown pushing his way towards me. You'll appreciate that the sight of his boobyish face with those buck teeth and slobbering lips did little to calm me. In fact, Pardoe made it even worse if that were possible by calling out to Brown: 'It's Crubey sir, I think he's dying sir, perhaps you should give him the kiss of life sir!'

Crubey sat back, enjoying his story and our appreciation of it. Perhaps Pokey Ponsford felt he owed it to the honour of the staff to try and find a butt amongst the boys. He turned to Berresfford and made an observation that would have been an impertinence from one person to another but is just the sort of thing that teachers feel they have the authority to ask of their ex-pupils.

"Berresfford, I know you won't mind my asking this," he said by way of preamble, "but we on the staff always thought there must be a story behind how you got to be School Captain because, as you know," he paused and smiled, clearly expecting this nicety to disarm what was coming. "Because, as I say, as you know, everyone was amazed when the Master announced your appointment." He paused again and began feebly tapping at his side plate, a mere echo of the insistent poking of the chest of the boy he was interrogating that we all remembered. "I remember Mr Dockery nearly swallowed his pipe when the news reached the staff room – and Mr Pym had to sit down as he felt so faint." He looked around the table before settling his eyes on Berresfford again. "You're among friends here…is there a story?"

We waited. Berresfford was smiling quietly to himself. He looked across at Westering, then across at me before swivelling his gaze back to our old physics teacher. "Yes, Pokey," (at his use of this familiarity we all felt some embarrassment and Ponsford himself looked put out). "There is indeed a small tale to be told." Seeing that we were all rapt, he removed some cellophane from a cigar that he had extracted from his dinner jacket and, with some deliberation, rolled it between his fingers before lighting it and exhaling a plume of smoke. The asthmatic Crubey coughed but said nothing.

"You'll remember that Fredericks had just started as Master and, to show he could change things if he wanted, decided that he would allow the boys themselves to select the School Captain?" We all nodded – the novelty had startled us all. He had announced this bombshell during the beginning of term assembly and had pointed towards the main door of the chapel. He drew our attention to the twenty-three identical black plastic boxes that were set out on the table in the passageway. Each box had a small slot in the top and the name of each member of the Top Sixth fixed to it. He told us that we all had one vote towards who was to be School Captain as he was persuaded that we would choose wisely and well. At the end, he got the teachers to give a plastic counter to each boy to drop into the box of their choice as we all filed out.

(Modesty prevented me dropping my counter into the box with my own name on it. I slipped it into Ngogo's as I knew he'd have no chance whatever of beating me.)

"You might also remember Shets' obsession with stationery," Berressfford went on, waving his cigar in my direction. "All those folders with subject dividers, the pen for every eventuality, the paper style and weight forever being re-sorted as they were re-catalogued, I could go on..." There was some light laughter around the table. "But the important item in my story is the dynotape machine that his mother had given him for Christmas and with which he stamped out labels for anything he could possibly attach a label to. I always half-expected to see one of his precious beetles lumbering along with a dynotape label stuck on its back saying *Beetlus boringus* or whatever..." There was more laughter at this sally and I began to feel just a little cross. It might have served as a warning to me for the enormity of another revelation to come from him later in the evening but, just then, I felt he was unnecessarily diminishing me.

"There is no such beetle, Berressfford," I said querulously. "And no doubt you know it. And as for labelling –"

'Yes," he cut in. "The labelling of those twenty-three identical black boxes." He had regained the attention of the table. "After that assembly where we all voted, those twenty-three boxes were taken to the Master's study. I'm sorry to have to admit to you that I obtained unofficial entry to the study while he was out walking that dumb brown mutt of his." He inspected the end of his cigar insouciantly, to all appearances not in the least guilty about anything at all. "I must also admit to having appropriated Shets' dynotape machine to produce duplicates of two of the names on those boxes," he added knocking off some ash into the remains of his coffee. "You see, what I had noticed was that the twenty-three names had all been stuck on those boxes with labels produced from an identical dynotape machine. Of course, they had been sealed in place with some sellotape which meant that any signs of tampering would be easily detected...but what they hadn't thought of was my plan. Using my trusty Italian letter-opener, I prised off the sellotape and dynotape from the two of the boxes and slipped the evidence into my pocket." He paused again and looked squarely into Westering's eyes. "I removed the names of 'Westering' and 'Berressfford'. And then stuck on the two names I had carefully brought with me as replacements and sellotaped over them so they looked indistinguishable from the originals. Then I left to await my election as School Captain."

He had been so stagey in all this rigmarole (and perhaps I had been just the slightest bit distracted by the reminder to that wonderful dynotape machine I'd had) that I was at a loss as to the point he was making.

"What were these names that you substituted for Westering and Berresfford then?" I asked with some asperity.

"Why 'Westering' and 'Berresfford' of course, Shets," he replied coolly. I shook my head at his asininity.

"You swapped the names, you bounder!" said Westering with some heat.

'Why naturally, Sunny – you were the most popular boy in the school by miles. You were bound to win," Berresfford explained kindly.

Pokey Ponsford was shaking his head slowly and making tutting noises while the rest of us sat there in appalled silence as we realised the duplicity of Berresfford's action. Sunny Westering's anger seemed to be seething inside him like a volcano preparing to erupt. Ngogo, ever the smoother of ruffled feathers and applier of oil to troubled waters, sought to change the subject.

"Mr Ponsford, sir. Perhaps you would be so good as to tell us why it is that the roof is suddenly so decrepit that the school needs such a large sum to replace it?"

Pokey gave a small guffaw and told us that the whole of the timber frame had undergone a routine inspection a few months back and had been found to be absolutely riddled with death-watch beetles. "The inspectors traced the source of the beetles to Mr Brown's rooms – apparently he had several old glass tanks in which the beetles were multiplying and then escaping up into the attics – and had been doing for twenty years or more!" He shook his head while still chuckling to himself. "I don't know what he was thinking of."

My mind was numbed – surely I couldn't have misidentified the beetles I'd given him to look after? Worse, much worse, was to come.

"Where is old Brown anyway?' asked Crubey. "I'd have thought he'd have come this evening." I, too, had thought this, had hoped this. Colour rose in Pokey's cheeks and he coughed apologetically but before he could say anything Homerton-Teste broke in with:

"Haven't you heard? Old Joff got sent down from Birmingham Crown Court last week. He got two years."

"Joff in jail!" exclaimed Crubey. "What on earth for?"

"Oh the usual," said Berresfford wearily. "Got caught fiddling with a boy."

I was thunderstruck at this news. It was at this moment that Berresfford turned to me and with the skill of an assassin with a stiletto, slid the following question between my ribs and into my heart:

"You were always rather thick with Joff weren't you Shets – were you ever one of his conquests?"

Suddenly, the lights appeared to dim in Hall and all sound faded away. I felt nauseous and, stumbling to my feet, hurried blindly out into the air. I scrabbled open the door of the nearest taxi and was taken back to my hotel. I could still hardly breathe as I crawled under the covers of the bed. And there I did something that I hadn't done since I was a small boy: I wept. I wept.

I wept.

Episode 20

From his diary

Thursday 7ᵗʰ January 2009

'Why must children have parents!' cried Roger Wood-Woode as he joined our group after what now passes for lunch. He slumped back in his chair and plied an exasperated hand over an exasperated head. 'I have just received a six-paragraph, point-by-point email seeking my justifications for assessing a boy's Chemistry homework as 'very good' rather than 'excellent' – and this after writing perfectly clear comments on the work itself: ones that even a child could understand!' He patted his forehead with a carefully-folded handkerchief ('ne'er sullied by emunctory emission!') before refreshing himself with some tea.

'Yes,' agreed Richard Hansum with his laconic drawl, 'Long gone are those halcyon days when parents left education in the hands of the experts.' He fussed with the position of his shirt-cuffs and went on. 'Now, on the basis of listening to a lot of half-baked educational theories from the latest loony-toons think-tank of unemployable academics, parents think they are justified in interfering whenever the fruit of their loins appears to be falling short of stellar performance at school.'

At this juncture I observed that one could despair about the bulk of one's pupils until one actually met the parents themselves at a parents' evening. Then, the explanation for the pupils' lack of ability, motivation, good sense and social skills sits four-square and abundantly clear in front of one.

'I don't see much of that, Dob, but we sporting types do have to put up with a lot from the parents on the touchline,' said Busby Beamish while topping up his beer-glass. 'There will always be at least one of them who is the greatest analyst, coach and manager that the national team has unaccountably overlooked.' He waved his drink in the general direction of Carriage House. 'And, I might add, it doesn't help when, after having spent hours and hours coaching the First Eleven into a subtle and silky passing game I have it undermined by one of our esteemed Executive Officers (a self-confessed 'sports virgin') coming along for five minutes and issuing shrill imprecations to 'hoof it up the middle': a phrase her husband, a keen Yeovil supporter, has taught her.'

'You're being too harsh, Busby,' said Hansum. 'Your boys could do with a bit more old-fashioned, raw-boned vim and vigour rather than that languid continental style you like to inflict on them...' He paused as we all burst out laughing at the very idea of Hansum being taken seriously about sport.

'I think we all know that parents should just pay the fees and steer well clear of us at all times,' I opined.

'Given that, I take it that you have not snapped up the free ticket on offer for this Saturday's Parents' Fancy Dress Ball then Dob?' asked Busby Beamish with a knowing smile.

This made me a little testy as he knew perfectly well that I do, in fact, have a ticket having agreed to make up the numbers on a table of Staff – it was Beamish himself who organised it. I had consented in a moment of relative weakness: Saturday evenings without a Scrabble match were just not the same. That and the chance to let off a bit of steam dancing, of course. The tickets being given to us free (rather than the hefty £100 face-value) made no difference. On the contrary, I was more of Hansum's kidney: he had rejected the invitation out of hand as 'an utterly patronising gesture - like asking the poor little governess to make up the numbers at dinner because the invited guest was suddenly unable to attend'.

I turned the conversation into another channel.

'I've got my costume. What are you coming as, Busby?'

'My guest and I are coming as a pair of black-and-white minstrels,' said Beamish with an air of insouciance calculated to provoke even further the collective intake of breath that greeted his announcement.

*   *   *

Sunday 10ᵗʰ January

After a good night's sleep, I now am sufficiently recruited and in the mood and frame of mind to set down exactly what happened at last night's débâcle at the Parents' Ball. I must say that, apart from the rain, the early part of the evening held only the promise of the continuation of all things good.

I was a touch late in arriving at the fabulous marquee set up on the football pitch next to the Multinational Centre and hurried down the drive past the line of massive, beetling-black 4 x 4s perched along the steep embankment – clearly, the mothers had driven to the Ball (the fathers all drive inappropriate sports cars) - though one or two contained a chauffeur stolidly gazing through a watery windscreen. Nigel Funnell, the Centre's legendary housemaster, clapped me on the back and pressed a glass of 'champagne' into my hand.

'Terrific outfit, Dob – stitch them all on yourself?' He was resplendent in a pirate costume complete with a stuffed parrot wired onto the shoulder. Several of his teeth had been blacked out and he bore a large and most realistic scar on his usually boyish cheek. 'Yo-ho-ho get it down your chest!' he roared, sinking his own bumper in a manly swig while brandishing a cutlass insistently until I emulated the feat. With a roar of 'Avast there you swab!' he waved over one of the MC boys who had been pressed into waiter service for the evening. He leant over me as the boy glumly stepped in our direction, forlorn in his duck trousers and striped vest, and *sotto voce* told me this one was a bit of a worry: 'He's the Último scholar from Angola – still gets homesick, poor lad.' Funnell snatched a couple of refills off the tray cackling 'Polly wants a cracker!' before sweeping off to menace a clot of parents dressed as Smurfs. I took another glass from the tray and spoke quietly to the boy – I gave him the old proverb of the flight of a mother's love being further and truer than your best spear. His face lit up immediately with a look of delight (I had spoken in Ki Mbundu) but at that moment I caught sight of Beamish and his guest arriving so, holding up a hand, I hurried towards them to join the crowd that was already being attracted to the startling pair.

I later found out that Beamish's guest was a retired but once-famous boxer with the name Chris Eubank. Both were in full minstrel rig but one was the negative of the other: Beamish's face was blackened with white eyelids and mouth; Eubank's was whitened with black eyelids and mouth: Beamish was in a white suit with black facings; Eubank was in a black suit with white facings: and so on in every detail. As I say, startling and, to my eye at least, grotesque. Funnell was soon capering around them gleefully singing a shanty interrupted by a lot of 'yo-ho-hoings' and abrupt tipping of glasses until the moment when the Head and her husband finally arrived, magnificently attired and made-up to be the spitting images of Sophia Loren and Carlo Ponti. There was spontaneous applause and, almost immediately afterwards, a call over a microphone for everyone to find their table as the entertainment was about to commence.

I suppose there can't be a 'top table' (Head and Husband as guests of honour and the Parents' Group Committee, of course, centrally positioned and on the edge of the dance floor) without there being 'less-top tables' but it was a trifle disappointing to find that the Staff table (number 17 out of 17) was positioned on the corner of the dance floor, just slightly behind the stage where the band was set up and right next to the side exit to the outside where a set of mobile lavatories was positioned. Nonetheless, we all settled down fairly cheerfully, tucked in the napkins, poured out the wine and soaked up the atmosphere. We were a merry bunch: Funnell and his wife, Eleanor (in a Hippy Chick costume); James Effitt and partner (he a Circus Strongman, she a Trapeze Artist); Beamish and Eubank (see above); Barbarella and her latest husband (he as the Honey Monster, she ingeniously arranged inside painted cloth, chicken wire and papier-mâché as a Sugar Puff); a History teacher I can't recall the name of (Dave, Kev, Tone? Anyway dressed as a Tommy); and myself, Pearly King in all his glory.

As a prelude to the meal the Parents' Group had organised for a very professional C & W band called *Clint Cody and the Hogwrestlers* to provide us with the music and calling for line-dancing. It was tremendous fun and all tables vied for space on the dance floor. After half an hour or so, the caller called the last song and, after the well-deserved applause, hoots of yee-hah and whistles, bid us 'A good-night for now unless any of y'all would care to sing for your supper!' Barbarella immediately clambered up onto the stage, seized the microphone and belted out *I'm on the Top of the World* as the Hogwrestlers gamely tried to keep up, apparently unsurprised by a giant warbling piece of breakfast cereal. Not to be outdone, Beamish and Eubank then borrowed a wash-board and harmonica to give us *Lickspittle Leavins* and a lively *Mammy!* I couldn't resist following this up with *My Old Man Said Follow the Van* clattering away with the old spoons. I think the parents just loved it as they all joined in by banging their own spoons on the table. Swiftly after I quitted the stage, the food began to be served.

Chris Eubank struck me as particularly interesting with displays of wit and erudition that I think even Richard Hansum would have admired and Nigel Funnell kept up a lively running joke with a nearby table which he had designated to the rest of us as 'underworld elements dripping with dodgy money'. Sallies such as 'how much did it cost to have the Range Rover armour-plated?' and 'managed to buy a football team yet?' kept nearly everyone amused. A rich source of humour was tapped by references to the fact that all of them were dressed as Keystone Kops. One thing we did notice was how swiftly they were sinking bottles of the most expensive wines available – mainly Krug champagne and Gevry-Chambertin – and following glasses of these up with shot after shot of glasses of scaldingly cold vodka (they insisted each of us join them for one as a toast to 'teachers with talent'). Even so, they did not get anywhere near as merry and jovial as we on the staff table did. Indeed, it was hard not to be aware of some rather sharp and bitter rivalry amongst them with occasional harsh-sounding words and gimlet-eyed looks being exchanged.

It was just as the plates from the main course were being cleared that the evening turned from conviviality to ugliness and disarray.

Quite innocently, I suppose I was the trigger for this. It happened just after I had visited the portable lavatory outside. The gents and the ladies were side-by-side and were rather up-market: painted in black with designations in gold lettering and adorned by the company name, *Bog Standard*. The insides were well-appointed but I did notice that one of the Kops from our neighbouring table was quite the worse for wear. He had washed his hands and was now bumping them fruitlessly on the underside of the condom dispenser having mistaken it for a hand-drier. When I tried to assist all I got was a mouthful of slushed and spiky words in what sounded like a Slavic tongue.

Back inside the marquee I went to the Kops' table to thank them again for their hospitality with the vodka and intending to perhaps hint at slowing down on the rate of imbibition. The patriarch of the group waved me to sit in an empty chair and passed me a couple of spoons and insisted on my giving a reprise of my performance earlier in the evening. While I did this, the too-hard drinker returned from the gents and weaved over to stand in a menacing sort of way a couple of feet behind me. Clearly, I was occupying his chair. When

I'd finished not trusting the specials like the old-time Koppers (with a nod around the table) and clanged the empty bottles as a final flourish, I made to stand up. Unfortunately, some of the buttons on my trousers and the back of my jacket had insinuated themselves into the interstices of the cane-work chair such that it rose with me and one of the legs must have caught Hard-Drinker's ankle and he began hopping and roaring in pain. He grabbed the chair and this tore off a volley of buttons which peppered his face with one of them lodging (rather comically it must be said) in his nostril. At least the patriarch found it hugely amusing and roared with laughter while shouting something at Hard-Drinker in their own language. Far from being similarly amused, the latter took an almighty swing at Patriarch and this precipitated a massive punch-up which soon spread as tables and chairs were upset and bodies and fists flew wildly from the epicentre. I had to admire Chris Eubank as he leaned languidly back on his chair and kept up a gloomy commentary on the 'sorry show of pugilistic finesse' as the array of hay-makers, cat-slingers and air-splitters was presented to his professional gaze.

A resourceful Parents' Group member had decided to run out for help from the security team stationed at the gates of the Multinational Centre. It was doubly unfortunate that a) he was dressed as a ghoul, and b) that an incoming taxi-driver was of a slightly nervous disposition and, on seeing in his headlights a long-chinned, dark-eyed mask of a face with black cloak swirling over the running black limbs, jumped on his brakes. The rain had made the drive greasy and the taxi skidded and slid off it and into one of the 4 x 4s perched on the embankment above the football pitch and the marquee. Perhaps the hand-brake had not been properly set, perhaps the chauffeur inside had engaged the engine for some extra warmth. Whatever, the car began to descend the bank. The chauffeur spun the steering wheel but this only had the effect of slewing the car broadside to the mud-slipping slope such that it crashed into both the ladies' and the gents' *Bog Standard*.

Here Fortune was more ambivalent but still not wholly favouring us. On the happy side, no-one was inside the lavatories or anywhere near the collision. On the less happy side were a couple of things: firstly, the power of the impact overturned the fairly flimsy structures and ruptured the container tanks within; and secondly, these tanks were nearly brim-full after having been used at our venue as well as an earlier Licensed Victuallers' Lunch. As a result, a wash of noisome human effluvia surged through the doorway and under the marquee flaps together with a truly appalling stench. Back to the happy side: at least this stopped the fighting.

I suppose that at such moments, the qualities that make themselves suitable for becoming Head of one of the world's great schools come to the fore. In a flash, she was on stage with the microphone and urging us to head for the Multinational Centre where 'perhaps we and the Hogwrestlers can continue with the party!' This with such calm demeanour and understated good-humour as she patted her beehive hairstyle that I must admit to more than a modicum of pride in our leader.

There was quite a scrimmage at the main door of the marquee (not greatly helped by Funnell crying 'Abandon Ship!' at the top of his voice. His pronunciation was equivocal.) and another at the entrance to the Multinational Centre as the dozens of us tried to effect an entry which, due to the security system just installed, meant MC boys frantically swiping their identity cards to keep the door opening. It was still raining hard.

By the time we had all squeezed inside it was clear that some people's footwear ought to have been left outside. Just as this realisation was making itself smelt, all the sprinklers were activated. Someone had lit up a cigarette in one of the lavatories in the building and, since smoking in the MC had been so rife, a smoke alarm and sprinkler system (always referred to as 'state of the art' but really just meaning 'new') had been fitted at the same time as the security one and was now earning its keep. Funnell dashed to the control board and began stabbing at buttons but to no avail. Luckily, all the exit doors had sprung open so we could swarm out easily onto the drive. All the rain and sprinkler water had had rather a damaging effect on Barbarella's costume: the golden glaze had been lost to reveal the orange undercoat and the papier-mâché was drooping in several places so that, as Beamish teased her, she was 'less like a Sugar Puff, more like a Cheesy Wotsit'.

There being little else I could usefully do, I bid them all goodnight, put my head down and came home without a dilly or a dally. Now I'll go out and burn the shoes, socks and suit before sending a cheque to *Cockney Kit*. I wonder how flammable the buttons will prove to be?

Episode 21

From his diary

Sunday 20ᵗʰ February 1996

Waking up in a double bed between the bride and groom the morning after their wedding seemed to come as an equal shock to all three of us. I am feeling calmer now and will use these pages to try to account for the circumstances which led up to this unlooked-for event.

Yesterday, the day dawned as bright, blue and breezy as anyone could hope and I'm sure that even the oft-jaundiced eyes of Tony Cobberly and Jean Masefield greeted the morn with unalloyed joy as a propitious augury for their nuptials as they stood tiptoe on the brink of middle-age matrimony. Having spent quite some time planning the (nightmarish!) logistics of getting to the village of Plodding, Norfolk from Sixokes, Kent by public transport, I was delighted when Busby Beamish phoned late on Friday offering me a lift in his car along with Richard Hansum and Casey McMann – apparently Busby's wife Maggie, who was to have occupied the fourth seat, had decided to go and visit her mother for a while which left a space for me. I must say that McMann was rather grudging about giving up the front seat to me after I explained about my tendency for being car-sick. He had a point about the lack of generosity of leg-room in the back but consoled himself by chain-smoking and blowing cloudy exhalations over my shoulder for the two hours or so that the journey took.

A topic of conversation in the car which seemed to fascinate the others was the approach that Beamish took to any woman he clapped eyes on.

'You mean that, for you, women fall into just two categories?' demanded McMann with asperity and some incredulity.

(I should interpolate here that the relations between Beamish and McMann were still a little frosty following the latter's presentation to the pupils and parents about a trip he was planning to take to Rome. McMann believed that Beamish tried to sabotage his slide-show but, as Beamish pointed out, there was no evidence for this accusation. That said, Beamish is notorious for being a practical joker: pouring an inch or so of custard into one of Phil Shikespier's walking boots that he had left overnight outside his tent on a D of E expedition, for instance; or the time he lobbed a mobile phone up into the rafters of the hall the evening before Speech Day and caused it to ring loudly and persistently and so cause an early abandonment of the set-piece speeches. Obviously, during his illustrated delivery of the educational possibilities of the trip, McMann was upset when he had said "And when we visit the Villa Borghese we will see this, a sight that almost brings me to my knees with wonder and delight..." and instead of a slide of Bernini's masterpiece *Aeneas and Anchises* up popped a photograph of the back of a Scotsman who had lifted his kilt to perform what I believe is called a 'full moon'. McCann carried it off with a shrug and a laugh before hurriedly moving on to his next slide (a Caravaggio) but inwardly he was seething.)

'Initially, that is,' confirmed Beamish as he moved out into the fast lane to cruise past a queue of huge foreign lorries. 'They are either *bedworthy* or *not bedworthy*. And in my experience, first impressions seem to prove pretty-well invariably correct.'

'You interest me, Busby' said Hansum thoughtfully. 'I can see why such a rough-and-ready summing up of potentiality could be appealing. But surely all of womanhood cannot be lumped into just two homogeneous masses as effectively as all that. Are there no further subtleties to your system?'

'Well naturally,' said Beamish, warming to his theme. 'It is the first cut that is perhaps a little crude but any female under 18 or older than 50 automatically falls into the *not bedworthy* category so they can safely be ignored as being of no interest to me. As do a whole lot of others between those ages for various reasons not just to do with their looks. That leaves me the time and leisure to address the *bedworthy* ones, those who have raised a blip on my beddability radar.'

'But that's appalling!' said McMann.

'But you're not me, Casey' rejoined Beamish with his winning insouciance. 'Life's too short to take a lot of other 'potentialities' as Richard has it, into consideration. Why not just cut to the chase?'

Before McMann could reply, Hansum quickly got in with a question.

'You said 'initially' just now, Beamish. Once the *not bedworthy* ones have dropped from your radar, on what do you focus your regard, as you say, at your time and leisure? I have a feeling that there is quite a science to what follows.'

Hansum was not wrong. Given his head Beamish launched into a lengthy and impassioned account as to what, for instance, would discriminate between a woman who was *eminently bedworthy* as opposed to one who was merely *extremely bedworthy*. I must say that I found the whole thing rather trivial – academic, in fact.

At the end of Beamish's exposition, Hansum drew attention to the 'simplistic subjectivity' involved.

'That's its beauty, Richard old man!' laughed Beamish gaily. 'Simple to use and, of course, viewing the world subjectively is what we all do in any case. Look, here we are – Plodding-in-the-Marsh. And, if I'm not mistaken, there is the handsome coaching inn that was so highly recommended by our blushing bridegroom Cobberly!' He took his hand off the steering wheel to point towards a large brick and flint thatched edifice crouching on the other side of the triangular green. With a spatter of pea-shingle, Beamish swept into the driveway that took us to the car park at the back of *The Huntsman* and we all debouched and stretched ourselves in the cool eastern air.

Beamish kept up a stream of lively chat with the young receptionist as we booked in. Except that I was not booked in: there was no record of my booking, despite my distinct memory of writing a letter weeks before when I received the invitation – a tasteful creamy card with neat italic script, a first-class production from the Copy Shop at school. Then a second memory dawned: I had given the letter to Mother to post and, doubtless, the dappy old bat had forgotten! Most likely it was even now residing at the bottom of the miscellaneous rubbish receptacle she calls her handbag. I was furious, particularly when I found out that all the rooms were taken and the nearest alternative hostelry was about twenty miles away. Beamish hustled me out of the receptionist's earshot and reassured me that I could easily 'doss down with one of the rest of us' and, trying to be philosophical about it, I agreed to make the best of a bad job.

In the bar, after the others had been to their rooms, Beamish explained to Hansum and McMann about my predicament and no one seemed at all pleased by the idea of my sharing a room with them. The two of them protested that Beamish, who, after all, had a double room, should be the one to entertain a guest. After a little time, Beamish suggested playing a knock-out game with coins called 'spoof' to decide on what he called 'the victim'. McMann lost and, borrowing his room key, I took my overnight bag up to his room and left it there.

By the time I got back to the bar, the room was filling up with more superbly-attired wedding guests. All were on the Masefield side of things – including Penny and Babs from the Copy Shop - with only the best man, Cobberly's brother Julius being with us from the 'groom's side'. Cobberly himself soon joined us in his grey morning suit and sipped soberly on a soda water while the rest of us quaffed gin and tonics.

In Beamish's words, since 'the match kicks off at 3' we four went up to change into our best bibs and tuckers at about half past two and then went straight off to the church. I can't recall anything of real note happening during the service: it seemed pretty typical to me. It wasn't too boring though which was a relief: so many weddings are dragged down by the religious part of the day. Once outside the church, we all perked up with the photographs being taken and, somewhat ludicrously, the bride and groom travelling about 50 yards from the church to *The Huntsman* in a pony and trap after having been showered with rose petals. (Hansum thought a Roman chariot would have struck a more apposite note and Beamish alluded to Cobberly now being accoutred with 'a fearsome battleaxe'.) We all (my guess was there were about 40 of us all told) trouped in their wake and, having formed up in a line to be 'greeted' by the new Mr and Mrs Cobberly, fell gratefully on the champagne.

I must say that Cobberly did us proud with the wines. Not only had he provided plenty of Pol Roger to start off with, he had some excellent Meursault with the salmon course and, of course, his favourite Margaux (a delightful Montbrison, no less) for the main course of Gressingham duck. The waiting staff circulated with it extremely freely too. Even the speeches didn't spoil things too much. Julius Cobberly kept his brief and witty; Cobberly himself expressed himself with unexpected grace and charm; even The Coaster (could I get used to calling her Jean Cobberly from now on?) said a few words of thanks which were not too threatening or leaden.

Ours was probably the liveliest table with the light banter of Beamish, the dry loquacity of McMann and the considered anecdotes of Hansum all keeping Penny and Babs royally entertained. The marquee was equipped with a small dance floor and, of course, I flung myself into it with my customary enthusiasm. One or two of the old dears I plucked from random tables were left rather breathless by my style (they couldn't summon up even enough air to say 'thank you' afterwards) but I certainly cut the biggest dash among the guests in that regard. It was thirsty work, however, and perhaps I refreshed myself rather too freely with the wine – but I was in good company there, I have to say.

Before I knew it, it was time for the bride and groom to depart. At first, I thought this a bit odd because, as we all knew, they were to spend their first night at *The Huntsman*. Hansum explained that there were two considerate reasons for their choosing to be driven off in a limousine at 9 o'clock. The first was to allow older guests to leave for home in good time – wedding etiquette forbidding departure prior to the Happy Couple. The second was that they were briefly visiting Jean's family home where an ancient aunt, too decrepit to get to the wedding itself, was to be greeted and regaled with the splendours of the day.

We then discovered Cobberly had arranged something thoughtful especially for us – in the bar were four bottles of Taylor's port and two bottles of cognac. We settled down to do them justice as the other guests called for coffees or retired to their rooms. An hour or so later I was feeling distinctly sleepy given the heat in the room and the exercise I had taken on the dance floor. At any event, my memory now begins to be just a little hazy. I think McMann left us quite early and I'm pretty sure Beamish left us to ply the receptionist with some of our port but I couldn't swear to it.

I do remember a bit of salacious speculation from Beamish about what both bride and groom could expect in terms of passion and expertise on their first night in bed together. What made this memorable was that Hansum actually descended to a level of coarseness in participating with this to a certain extent. He said:

'I'm sure Cobberly can be relied upon, in the words of the Immortal Bard, to put his ducat in her clack-dish.'

And with that he slumped sideways onto the sofa, and closed his eyes.

I thought this a good signal to retire myself. Beamish helped me up out of the deep armchair and accompanied me up the stairs. He told me that I was in luck because the receptionist had told him that a room had become available due to a cancellation – 'a princely one which you can have for the price of a single, Dob you lucky blighter.' He said the draw-back was that McMann had locked his door and so my bag was unavailable so I'd just have to go straight to bed and be re-united with my things at break of day.

By this time we were nearing the end of the corridor which was very gloomy indeed. Beamish fished the door key out of his pocket and, after watching me tussle with the lock, kindly opened it for me and, wishing me a pleasant good night, left me.

Switching on the lights, I registered that it was, indeed, sumptuously appointed with several vases of flowers all around the place. The double bed was extremely generous and quite bewitching in its attractiveness to my weary limbs. I removed my clothing, set it carefully on a chair, and, having to forego the suit of flannel pyjamas still packed in my bag in McMann's room, I extinguished the lights and slid under the vast puffiness of the duvet to the centre of the bed.

Well, that doesn't seem to have worked at all. I am still no nearer how it came to be that when I awoke (caused by the knock and then entry of the receptionist) on my left were the appalled waxy features of Tony Cobberly and on my right the horrified and florid face of The Coaster. The receptionist showed great presence of mind as Jean began to scream by throwing me a bathrobe which I quickly donned before snatching up my clothes and shoes and beating a retreat to McMann's room where I took refuge. Beamish poked his head around the door a short while later and to advise me to keep my head down until the Cobberlys had breakfasted and left for their holiday together in Belgium since they were both unwilling to be reminded of my existence at this juncture.

The journey back to Sixokes was more or less silent. Once here I had sharp words with Mother about the non-posting of my booking letter and ignored her for the rest of the day. I feel confident my being in bed with the Cobberlys on their wedding night will remain a secret between the three of us.

*   *   *

Wednesday 1ˢᵗ March

Quite by accident, I overheard Beamish talking to Penny and Babs in the Copy Shop earlier today. I am still quite cross with him and have every sympathy with McMann. This is what I heard:

Babs:	Of course, we heard the screaming but we daren't ask Jean what happened.
Penny:	Come on, Busby, tell us the secret. We saw you laughing with the receptionist. You must know!
Beamish:	Well, if you promise not to kiss and tell… You'll have seen Old Dobbin Wentworth get himself hopelessly drunk and make a right exhibition of himself on the dance-floor and, as you'll remember, he was going to have to doss down in McMann's room because, being Dob, he'd bungled the booking of a room for himself. I'd got friendly with the receptionist –

Penny: Yes, we noticed that. You were both looking rather tired in the morning…

Beamish: Enough of your disgraceful innuendos, young lady. I am as pure as the driven snow.

Babs: But you do drift a bit though, Busby.

Immoderate laughter

Beamish: Anyway, to get back to Dob. At about 10 o'clock that evening I persuaded that very helpful receptionist to give me the duplicate key to the bridal suite as it had struck me as amusing to park Dob in their room prior to the Happy Couple's return from their courtesy visit to the aged and respected aunt. I whipped up the stairs and, with what I admit is rather low cunning, unscrewed the light bulb in the corridor outside the suite. Then I went and collected Dob and hauled him to the room meanwhile spinning him a very plausible story about why he should be there. Like the port, he drank it all in.

            Inside the bridal suite, Dob dances out of his kit and burrows naked into the middle of the bed.

Babs: How can you know that? You weren't there.

Beamish: I have reconstructed the events from the known facts, my darling girl, so just shut up, lie back and prepare for something good. We have the sodden Dobbin snoring gently like a grampus in the bridal bed. The limousine containing The Coaster and Cobberly purrs into the car park and they enter *The Huntsman* together. It is easy to imagine that both are feeling nervous with anticipation.

Cobberly suggests a night-cap in the bar, fully aware of the necessity for a bit of Dutch (or, in his case, French) courage. But, as you both know, The Coaster, with that girlish giggle we all know and love, said that she would meet him in the room. However, on the way, she decided to drop in to your room to see you girls.

Penny: Yes – we told you that. It was a bit of a surprise when she popped in to our room for a cuppa. I thought she might have come for a bit of advice –

Beamish: And what would a virginal young thing like you know of the birds and bees?

Penny: Never you mind! Anyhow, just a bit of a chat about being newly-wed and how the day had gone. But what she really wanted to tell us at length was how the aunt was making them a gift of a house and a legacy of tens of thousands.

Beamish: Very interesting, I'm sure. But meanwhile, to continue my reconstruction, Cobberly has pottered solo into the bar where Hansum has woken up and got his second wind. The two of them have a bit of a chin-wag while downing a snifter of the fortifying cognac. Then, with a slap between the shoulders and some exhortation about his ducat's duty, Hansum sends Cobberly up to the bridal suite.

Cobberly, no doubt sparing an acid comment for the darkness in the corridor, with just a touch of trepidation, opens the door. It is widely known that the closest he has ever got to the more intimate parts of the female anatomy were in washing out the crevices in the Greek statues he unearths on his summer digs. Anyhow, in the dimness of the room he espies a form in the bed and, naturally enough, assumes it is the expectant bride. He is a little disheartened to hear that she is gently snoring rather than panting with anticipation. But he also feels some relief and decides to let her sleep. So, he doesn't switch on the lights and, tiptoeing about, brushes teeth etcetera and, in dashing new pyjamas, slips into bed with his bride.

Here, he thinks that honour requires him to do the gentlemanly thing and initiate some intimacy. He slides an exploratory hand onto his loved ones breasts. Rather disconcertingly, they turn out to be much smaller and more flabby than expected, and covered in a few curls of wiry chest hair.

Babs (laughing)
But that's –

Beamish: Just a touch of local colour, I'll admit. Anyway, no doubt like the inestimable Ruskin, our Cobberly gives a small shudder and turns over to fall asleep. Say ten minutes pass. Now along the corridor trips the bride having torn herself away from your sweet company and thoughts of material largesse are replaced by the spice of prospective physical intimacy – though, given her looks and demeanour, one doubts that any experience in that direction would be scant at best. She pauses at the door (perhaps, like her new husband, muttering a small curse about the lack of adequate lighting). She takes a deep breath. She enters.

Of course, in the dim light she too descries a shape in the bed; she too hears the gentle snoring; she too quickly and quietly prepares for bed and then slips between the sheets. Tentatively, she reaches out. She gets no response from her gentle chafing of the flaccid little chappy. She gives it up as a bad job and turns to make inroads into the great back-log of beauty sleep she is owed.

At day-break, the receptionist knocks with a tray of coffee and tea and –

At this point, the bell rang for the next lesson. In any case, I had heard enough: rather more than enough.

Episode 22

From his diary

Wednesday 28ᵗʰ June 1977

To those who have not given it any thought, a teacher who loses a whole class in the course of a trip has done something far worse than losing just the odd pupil. I can say this with the bitterness of my experience earlier today when I was subjected to quite a bit of vituperative comment from lots of parents - with even the Headmaster throwing in his two penn'orth of criticism – when I arrived back at Sixokes train station at the appointed time but minus all of pupils I was in charge of.

Naturally they were wrong. A little mature consideration discovers that it should be seen quite the other way round: one child going missing is a serious thing but, when multiples go missing, then the concern diminishes proportionally since it is most likely that those missing are together and hence safer. Thus, the whole group going missing is almost insignificant and, apart from the small inconvenience of late collection, something to be laughed off. I must say that my attempt to explain this met with no success at all – the parents, unlike their offspring, did not appreciate being told to shut up and listen to reason and my shrugging and prolonged chuckling just seemed to inflame them rather than helping persuade them to the sensible attitude towards the situation.

The sequence of events leading up to what the Headmaster intemperately called my 'dereliction' was perfectly innocuous: each event was, in itself, merely due to chance rather than anything for which I could be held to be responsible. In fact, none of it could have happened at all if the Headmaster himself hadn't dreamt up the idea of 'Enrichment Week' – ostensibly a plan to cover the widely-acknowledged fact that no academic work gets done in the last week of the summer term (all classes play Hangman or the like) and put in its place lots of courses and trips instead. Tony Cobberly, on hearing of the 'initiative' was typically blunt. "The 'enrichment' he means is aimed at the School: getting the parents to pay well over the odds for trips and courses will swell the Bursar's coffers nicely." I think Cobberly is too cynical here – to my mind the 'enrichment' is aimed at the parents – relieving them of the company of their offspring must provide the welcome peace and quiet for battery-recharging needed before the onslaught of the little blighters' demanding presence day in and day out for weeks on end during the holidays. Whichever is true, rather than the comfortable relaxation of the final week of term, it meant that we in Biology had to organise a field trip and, given that a couple of prime colleagues in the department were required elsewhere, we had to take the scrapings from other departments to help staff it: namely Gorval from Joggo and an *assistant* from the Tower of Babel, an odd little chap calling himself Brutin.

After Monday's and Tuesday's ecological work on our Dorset field trip, for today's morning session, the pupils were given what M. Brutin called 'carte libre': a free choice of joining whichever activity on offer they liked the look of. My own activity (excitingly billed as 'Fossil Fun') attracted just 6 of the pupils – which, at least, proved to be 50% more popular than Percy Gorval's rabbit population survey which involved counting and assessing numbers of rabbit pellets using quadrats. It was something of a surprise that as many as 4 pupils opted for it especially after he went into detail of how the pellets were to be assessed for 'time since deposition' by squeezing them between finger and thumb and then using a scale from 1 to

10 with 1 being 'plastic' and 10 being 'friable'. Be that as it may, our two small groups were put together in a minibus (which would later transport us back to Sixokes) and Gorval drove us from the Field Studies Centre to Charmouth.

We turned off the road and bumped over the unavoidable potholes in the unmade surface before Gorval pulled up just short of the low wall separating the beach from the small parking area. There were just a few other cars there and all, like us, facing the sea. The back and sides of the car park had as demarcation large white-painted stones set at intervals on the dusty turf. Though both warm and sunny, a stiff breeze was whipping the tops off the waves and tossing the rosy globes of thrift into a dancing frenzy. Cramming my sunhat more securely onto my head I agreed a time to meet back at the minibus with Gorval since we were heading in different directions. Showing good sense and forethought, Gorval rested the minibus keys on top of the back tyre under the wheel arch so that whichever group arrived back first could sit in comfort while waiting.

I dictated two or three paragraphs of introductory material to my group to note down in their books, pointing out the Sinemurian and Pliensbachian layers in the cliff faces as illustration and indicating where the likely good hunting spots amongst the mudstones were to be found. With a last instruction to be careful wielding their rock hammers as fragments might fly into eyes, I waved them off for individual hunting while I got going on my own. After an hour or so I whistled them all in and showed them my collection: a couple of ammonites (one pyritised, the other a yellow calcite), three different-sized belemnite guards, several crinoids, the tail of a fish and an ichthyosaur vertebra. With the exception of Mason, none of the pupils had collected any fossils at all – the only things they had amongst them were pebbles, some polished glass pieces and holdfasts from storm-blasted kelp. Pleasingly, Mason had found one or two duplicates of mine but also a very fine flint echinoid and a quite spectacular rolled ichthyosaur jaw both of which I appropriated.

Since we had half an hour or so to spare before our rendezvous back at the minibus, I agreed that we had time for a swim. All the boys except Temms quickly disrobed and, with wild cries, rushed into the spumy and tea-coloured waves. I slipped out of my socks, sandals, shorts and shirt a little more sedately and, putting my sunhat on top, weighted them all down with my bag of fossils into which I placed my glasses. I edged my way into the sea but, finding it much colder than expected, decided to take a more rapid plunge and so accelerated into a run and then dived like a porpoise into the surf. This proved to be a mistake. I had neglected to secure the drawstring in my bathing trunks and they were swept off me in the dive. Getting my head and shoulders above water I started looking and feeling around for my trunks but there was no sign. Mason was close by and, crouching down to preserve my dignity, I told him to help me hunt. "I'll get the others to help too, sir," he replied, shouting out about my predicament at the top of his voice. Despite what I suppose was all their best efforts, the trunks were nowhere to be found. I thought of sending one of them in to collect my shorts but Mason had a better idea: that I should borrow and wear Temms' trunks as Temms had decided not to swim. This seemed eminently sensible since I would then be decent on leaving the sea and would have something dry to change into. Though Temms is similar in height to me, he is not so solidly built and it was a pity that he had chosen to bring a pair of the skimpiest 'speedos' imaginable in a bright electric blue colour. I was hardly inconspicuous as I emerged from the bosom of the sea but I quickly quelled the cheers and shrieks of delight from the pupils.

After collecting my things, I scurried back to the bus leaving the pupils changing on the beach – it had been a struggle getting into the speedos and I wanted some privacy in what I anticipated (correctly) would be quite an ordeal in peeling the things back off. I retrieved the minibus keys and climbed into the back and, using a combination of brute strength and some contortion, eventually rolled the garment clear of my body. After a brisk rub-down with my towel, I dressed and whistled down the beach at the pupils to hurry up. Just as I turned away from the sea-wall, a gust of wind dashed the sunhat off my head and, with a skip or two in the dust, clean under the minibus. Down on my hands and knees I saw that – typically - it had found the most inaccessible place possible to come to rest.

I gave it a moment's thought but concluded that the hat would be out of reach of even Mason's simian arms and that shoving the diminutive Temms underneath would also be fruitless. I hit on a simpler solution: reverse the minibus. I had seen people driving and was aware of the rudiments so was in no doubt that the operation would be straight-forward. Behind the steering wheel I waggled the gear-stick as I had seen Gorval do to make sure it was in neutral. The engine fired up and, depressing the clutch, I smoothly shifted the gear into reverse. I was aware that the next part demanded a little coordination – raising the clutch pedal while depressing the accelerator pedal to effect the gentle backward motion required. Congratulating myself on it, I checked the mirrors to ensure it was all clear behind and, with a deep breath, moved both feet on the pedals.

I'm still not sure exactly what went wrong. It was probably that the sensitivity of my feet had been affected, numbed as they were from immersion in the Channel's waters - that and my socks sliding inside my sandals at this unpractised manoeuvre at a crucial moment. The upshot, however, was that in the resultant tangle of movements between feet, sandals and pedals, the minibus careered backwards at top speed. Before I had time to yank up the hand-brake there was quite a loud bang and the minibus stopped abruptly and the engine cut out. Just at this moment, all my pupils and Gorval's party arrived simultaneously. With a nonchalance I didn't really feel, I jumped out from the driver's seat and strode over to my sunhat and, dusting it down, told them I'd had to move the bus to retrieve it.

"But what was the noise, Mr Wentworth, sir?" asked Mason setting down the bag of rock hammers I'd put him in charge of. "Are you alright, sir?"

While he was saying this Gorval had marched himself to the back of the minibus and was looking underneath.

"You've smashed it into a rock, Wentworth. One of these." Gorval pointed at the nearest white-painted boundary stones along the edge of the car park. "Let's see if it's drivable." The minibus started easily and Gorval edged it forward a few feet to the accompaniment of some distressing grinding and clunking noises then came back to join us in a thoughtful ring around a fairly large oil-soaked circle of dust. A trail of smaller dark circles joined it to the vehicle. Gorval had another look underneath then with a grimace turned to me.

"Thought so, Dob old chap. You've sheared the diff."

Apparently, this made the minibus unroadworthy and I reflected on why it was that vehicle-manufacturers lacked the foresight to protect against the sort of minor collisions to be expected in day-to-day driving. Meanwhile Gorval went over to the telephone box to report in to our trip leader, Jack Natter. He was quite some time before coming back, rubbing his hands together.

"Here's the plan Mr Natter's arranged, everyone, so listen up. He's sending four taxis out to collect you pupils and Mr Wentworth and they'll take you to Sherborne station where you'll catch the train back to Sixokes. You'll be joined on the journey by M. Brutin. I'll stay here with the crippled old bus until a towing team arrives then, once it has been repaired – probably a couple of days work, I'd guess – I'll drive it back to school."

Natter was at the station and pressed information and tickets on me.

"Train's due in four minutes, don't you know, four minutes. The tickets go through to Sixokes – use them on the Tube. You'll catch the 17.44 from Waterloo East easily enough. I've phoned the school and Di Daley is ringing around to all the parents telling them to pick up at the station rather than the school at 18.15. Here's some cash to buy a meal for them all on the way back. Happy landings, happy landings!"

We were fortunate to collar two adjoining compartments and stowed our bags away on the racks above our heads. I left M.Brutin in charge of one compartment (he was already broaching his pale-blue pack of foul-smelling French cigarettes) and settled myself down in the corner seat of the next one with the other half of the boys. The sign below the sash window in the door had been defaced to read 'Do not clean soot off the window' and it took me back to dear old Joff Brown's Latin classes where the books he dealt out at the start of lessons had 'shortbread eating primer' on the front of every cover.

After a few minutes of settling to the rhythmical sounds and movement of a train that is always so soothing, I felt a rumble of hunger – all that sea air! I doled out cash to the boys and sent them off to the buffet car to buy their lunch. M. Brutin was half-way through his Gitane so I thought I'd save him a trip.

"Voulez-vous aimer un fromage sandwich, monsieur?" I essayed. He replied with that very odd French phrase 'well on top' and then enthusiastically rattled off an unintelligible list with plenty of Gallic gesturing which ended with something like 'Bel Paese, Roquefort, Crottin-Vieux, Brillat Savarin'.

On my return I handed him a waxed-paper plate with his sandwich.

"There you are, monsieur. A taste of our finest: British Rail Cheddar!"

With grave suspicion he lifted the bread to reveal a limp and lurid triangle of greasy tallow redolent of rancid butter and brine. He shuddered theatrically and passed the plate back to me with "Jamais, jamais!" I told him that cheese was all they had. He decided that he'd rather go without so I left him quite pleased to have the extra rations myself. After tucking in royally, I drifted off to sleep.

I was shaken awake by Mason with the information that Atkins was missing. Sure enough, there were now only four boys in the compartment with me. Stepping out into the corridor I checked next door: there was the assistant with the other five boys but none of them knew of the whereabouts of Atkins. Deeming it unlikely that not even the dim intellect of Atkins ('his brightness might be of use for a romantic dinner but would not help keep shipping off the rocks' as Hansum had put in his school report) would have prompted him to step off the train at one of the stations without the rest of us, I instructed them all to stay put while I searched the carriages between us and the engine while M. Brutin went the other way.

The search was fruitless with only the irritation of an officious woman threatening to call the guard after I had banged on a locked lavatory door demanding entry. After she'd opened it I tried to explain that I did not need the lavatory myself and was merely looking for a schoolboy but that did nothing to calm her – quite the reverse in fact.

Back in the corridor outside our compartments, M. Brutin spread his hands and reported no luck. But then he winked at me and jerked his head inwards and upwards. I followed the gesture to the bag-rack and noticed that it was now suspiciously over-burdened. Roughly pulling several of the bags down revealed the grinning Atkins. I was justifiably irate. I gave him a good clip round the ear and thundered at the rest of them (they must have been complicit in the rag) about their stupidity, their wasting the time of their betters, their general lack of consideration and their poor behaviour bringing the school into disrepute. I finished with "From now until we get back to Sixokes you will all be totally silent and totally obedient. Anything I tell you to do," at this moment I noticed the assistant, "or anything M. Brutin tells you to do, you will do instantly. Is that clear?" They merely looked cowed so I redoubled the volume. "Is that clear!"

"Yes, sir," they all murmured leaving me with an open goal.

"Didn't I tell you to remain totally silent! Five hundred lines each: 'Obedience to a teacher must be instantaneous and unswerving' handed in to me by the morning! Now get back to your places!"

We negotiated the section from Paddington to platform C at Waterloo East without mishap. Telling the boys to stay together and not to move, I checked the timetable. M. Brutin stood at my elbow gazing uncomprehendingly at the lines of figures. The time was 17.36. Naturally, my expertise quickly recognised that before our train arrived at the platform there would be a train to Hayes.

"Le train prochain?" enquired M. Brutin. As I turned to him I saw behind him that Mason was fooling around with one of the rock hammers pretending to chip away at the back of Atkins' head.

"Le prochain train mais un," I replied, then shouted "Mason – stop being an idiot, boy!"

Gratifyingly, he obeyed directly and I told M. Brutin that I was toddling off to wring out a kidney. Picking up my case and bag of fossils, I went to the Gents.

It was unlucky that, after carefully washing my hands, as I picked up the fossil bag, the rolled ichthyosaur jaw fell out and did some more rolling – under a closed door into one of the cubicles. It took a little time for the man inside to kick it back out to me. While this delay was going on I heard the Hayes train pull in. After stuffing the fossil back into the bag more securely, I left the Gents and turned to where the others should still be standing. They were gone. As the train pulled away I glanced into the last carriage – to see the unmistakeable figure of Mason (his ripped and safety-pinned pink punk jacket was unmissable) waving at me over the shoulders of the other boys and M. Brutin.

I accosted the guard on the platform with some urgency as he complacently tapped his green flag against his thigh.

"My group of school pupils have mistakenly taken the wrong train!"

"And have they no adult supervision, sir," he asked.

"No. Well, yes – but he's French!"

"Then it isn't an emergency, sir. If you'll calm down, I'll go and telephone their next station and tell the guard to disembark the party. They can catch the next up train to here and you can all go on to Sixokes together." He seemed very pleased with himself.

"But that will take ages –"

"Fifty three minutes," he put in suavely.

"But their parents will be worried to Hell. Can I phone through to the station master at Sixokes and get him to pass on a message at least?"

"Sorry, sir, no can do. As I've said, this is not an emergency and British Rail does not operate a messenger service."

Seeing that I was not in the mood to stand for this, he became more emollient.

"Tell you what, sir. You catch this." The 17.44 Sixokes train was at this moment pulling up at the platform. "You can deliver the message at Sixokes yourself and I'll look out for your party once they get back here. They'll be with you on the 18.44 arriving at precisely 19.18."

Reluctantly, I saw this as the best option available and climbed aboard.

Rehearsing my explanation to the expectant parents at Sixokes station, I went back over my conversation with M.Brutin at Waterloo puzzling over why he'd grasped the wrong end of the stick and regretting I'd spent more time in dry-tongued ogling at Mamzel Durand and less time polishing my French to a higher degree. As we slid past the dismal and familiar back gardens of Downton Green that heralded our arrival, the truth suddenly struck me: the idiomatic 'next train but one' had been lost on M. Brutin - and he might have mistook the 'mais un' for my addressing Mason!

I was delighted at my own perspicuity and swung with some confidence towards the parents as they called out 'Here he comes, here comes Mr Wentworth!' to each other. They crowded around me and, as luck would have it, we were joined by the Headmaster all togged up and with the three pupils he and his wife were taking on his outing to Covent Garden to see *La Bohème*. As indicated above, they all proved indifferent and ungrateful in equal measure.

I left them to it and came home and cheered myself up by starting to make a display cabinet to house my exciting new fossils. *C'est la vie!*

Episode 23

Email to Sixokes School Staff

Wednesday 25th May 2011

Given the number of gossips on the staff, no doubt you will have been presented with some lurid and sensational account of my being detained by the police over the weekend. Though, as you know, I am naturally a person who shies from parading my private life in front of all and sundry, I think it necessary to set the record straight in this matter. What follows is a faithful account of what some have come to see as a 'compromising position' for me – one, even, that threatens my position as a schoolmaster.

I can see why anyone unacquainted with my character (which, though not perhaps absolutely spotless, has certainly never been tarnished by even the slightest of scandals) might take the view that my appearing at the Accident and Emergency Department of the Kent and Sussex Hospital with my foreskin snagged on the braces on the teeth of a twelve-year-old girl was, at the very least, questionable. Once you have read the steps which led to this occurrence, you will, I feel sure, see that I am entirely blameless with respect to any impropriety and that it was merely a concatenation of unlucky events which could easily happen to anybody.

The first thing to which I would call your attention is what is acknowledged to be a high level of silliness and low level of any self-control in the girls of Lampardes boarding house. Certainly, when I accepted the invitation to the 'Summer Barbie' I went with some trepidation knowing that these creatures' spirits, usually held in some sort of check individually, could prove explosive when grouped – and especially when outside the confines of the classroom where, as you will know, I pride myself on the discipline I instil. Rumours of 'chases' and 'japes' in my lessons are all exaggerated well beyond what has been the normal latitude expected from, and granted to, youngsters at our School where a certain liveliness is encouraged.

A second thing was my having to wear an older pair of trousers than I had wanted; a pair with a zipper that was unreliable. My usual cavalry twills had become inadvertently soaked in slimy pond water during the Biology class when that idiot boy Mason decided - against all my instructions to the contrary I might add - to balance the tank right on the edge of the desk so that an unlucky stumble on his part upset the contents all over my legs. I was forthright in my criticism as you can well imagine.

Those of you familiar with the 'Summer Barbie' will know that, after the consumption of comestibles, there is always a game of 'Sardines' with which, as someone keen not to appear as any sort of stick-in-the-mud, I joined in. The pupils unanimously nominated me as 'it' for the first game and, as they hid their eyes, I hurried off while a hundred was counted. Perhaps my choice of hiding-place was unfortunate but it seemed eminently reasonable to choose a place that was roomy enough for my 'finders' to squeeze in beside me – which, by the end of the game, would amount to over twenty of us. Thus, rejecting the under-stairs cupboard and the san, I hit upon concealing myself in the spacious shade amongst the laurel bushes outside the main dormitories. What was unfortunate about this choice turned out to be twofold: a) while wriggling my way in commando-style under the branches, the zipper in my trousers worked itself open; b) a spiny but invisible piece of vegetation within this arbour made its vicious presence felt in a tender part of my anatomy. The pain necessitated swift action – the thorn had embedded itself quite deeply and so I squirmed over onto my back, pulled out my privy member and endeavoured to remove the offending item forthwith. It was at exactly this moment that Jessica Atkins, a notably-hysterical girl, crawled into the bushes. I suspect that she had not properly hidden her eyes during the hundred-count, otherwise how could she have discovered my hiding-place so quickly? Whatever brought her so speedily, she lost any poise or comportment that one might reasonably expect (notwithstanding my rather inelegant and embarrassing position) and was silly enough to open her mouth wide and emit a piercing scream causing me to clap my hands over my ears.

This Jessica Atkins, as you will be aware, sports the most alarming 'train-tracks' on her young teeth. It is beyond me why it is that so many parents find it necessary to have such things applied merely for the sake of something cosmetic. Of course, if some crookedness might conceivably lead to decay I can see the point. (Who, after all, would want to end up with a mouthful of poorly-fitting dentures which resemble nothing less than a crudely-sawn set of plywood pegs like those in the mouth of old Percy 'Awful' Gorval, long-since retired teacher of Joggo?) But I see no point whatever in having such things routinely fitted to young people who, at that age, already have to bear a good deal of personal physical ugliness.

Be that as it may, at the height of this piercing scream, Jessica was rammed from behind by another 'finder' (whose identity I never discovered) causing her to lurch forward and bury her head in my lap. This is how the snagging occurred. The screaming stopped as the girl fainted and, thankfully, the wise head of Cameron Cudgell then appeared asking if everything was alright. It was the work of a moment for this resourceful chap to get a blanket and a stretcher from the san and, once decently covered, have Jessica and I transferred to the Hospital.

Many people complain about the National Health Service and I can see why after the continuous stream of ribald and derogatory comments thrown my way by many anonymous voices on the other side of the screen as the operation to separate master and pupil was effected.

The stitching was uncomfortable but, as you saw, I was back at School behind my desk punctually on Monday. Jessica suffered no physical harm and, in my view, the extended period of 'counselling' she had to withstand will prove to do more harm than otherwise. Filling her up with a lot of psychological claptrap will only confuse what is already an imperfect brain. Her parents, I am told, have been fairly understanding about the whole thing and I hope, now that the truth is published, no more will be heard on this matter and we can get on as usual - not least, as the Head says, 'for the good of the School'.

Episode 24

Monday 18ᵗʰ June 2002

Though rather dubious about Busby Beamish's new-found enthusiasm for nineteenth century literature, I agreed to accompany him to a meeting of the Sixokes School Staff Jane Austen Appreciation Society if only to stir up memories of Mother who, of course, was addicted to the stuff of BBC costume dramas. Having witnessed parts of some of these, I've found it unnecessary to actually read the books (sticking to my tried and trusted Dick Francis) since they all follow the same formula: male and female protagonists initially thwarted in love get married in the end. Richard Hansum, when he heard we were going, dismissed Austen as 'vastly over-rated' and 'teeth-achingly saccharine' which I found a little surprising in a Man of Books but perhaps it's not taste but flavour that matters. Be that as it may, we joined the half-dozen or so other teachers in S6 (a classroom in which the perfume of over-heated and under-washed pupils lay heavy) and, after tea and biscuits were handed round, got under way with the president, Paul Happiman, introducing an illustrated talk by Adrian Witson. He called it *Bonnets and Beavers* and then went on for quite some time telling us about the types of head-gear mentioned in the books and, at intervals between distinguishing fabrics and explaining etiquette and fashioning, paraded himself up and down the classroom wearing some examples that he and his wife had made. Surprisingly, it wasn't totally uninteresting although I noticed that Beamish spent rather a lot of it trying to make eye-contact with Holly Stephen who had recently joined the English Department and whose beauty had caused quite a flutter among the younger male teachers. Beamish has never conceded he's far too old for such fare – quite apart from being married to boot!

Next, Jane Pensword read her own short story supposedly in the style of Austen 'though more Barbara Pym than Jane herself' entitled *Dancing With The Vicar*. I suppose I must have missed some nuances or other because nothing much happened and then she finished to tremendous applause from the others.

I nearly got up to leave when paper and pencils were handed out for a quiz but Beamish pressed me back to my seat whispering to me that I'd thank him for it later. It was of some consolation to see that there were only ten questions so, as the others were screwing up their faces and then feverishly writing down the names of the residences of the characters from the novels as demanded by Happiman the question-master, I surveyed the classroom walls and was gratified to spot three grammatical and two spelling errors in the pupils' work adorning them. Glancing at Beamish's answer sheet I observed he had written 'Pemberly' next to each of the ten numbers presumably hoping to score at least one mark. Ever the teacher, Happiman called on us to 'swap papers with your neighbour and pay attention as I call out the answers' then, when the marked papers were returned to us, said 'hands up anybody not scoring any marks at all' adding in a waggish way that this might entail 'being shown the door out of the SSSJAAS!' Beamish got a big laugh by shooting his hand up enthusiastically while I received wry smiles a few seconds later by tentatively half-raising mine. Happiman continued counting upwards until the last, highest-scoring arm was shyly held aloft by Holly Stephen. To another sustained round of applause, Happiman presented her with the Prize Cushion and she blushed, delighted and delightful.

At that moment I was unaware of any particular expression adorning my facial features but Happiman took it as one of keen curiosity and, plucking the cushion back, showed it to me and launched into a lengthy explanation:

"As I'm sure you know, George, Jane Austen's great-uncle Francis lived in The Red House very near to the School (where, of course, her great grandmother was a matron and housekeeper to the Master) and she would often visit the family for weeks at a time. I was fortunate enough to purchase this cushion when there was a house-clearance there a few months ago. You will see that it is hand-embroidered and you can just about make out the initials 'JA' in the bottom corner: the work of Jane herself!"

I examined it. Calling it 'home-made' or even 'homely' would be dishonest. It displayed a degree of clumsiness in execution that should have provoked hesitation in making it public even to close family. The unevenness of the letters spelling out 'Powell Park' showed poor planning in their spacing and the gross stitching to depict a delicate fallow deer in the foreground made it look like a sort of boss-eyed moose. Unaccountably, everyone else was regarding it as if it were a sacred relic as they gushed:

"Perhaps it supported Dear Jane's back on a long carriage journey!"

"Or it was laid beneath Dear Jane's head as she rested from her labours!"

"Or it was slipped onto a hard chair to ease Dear Jane's pliant buttocks!"

This last suggestion (from Beamish needless to say) met with the stony silence such irreverence warranted.

Happiman clapped his hands together to break the mood and announced that the planned SSSJAAS Outing to Godmersham Park 'the model for some details found in residences mentioned in *Mansfield* and *Pride*' would take place in the second week of the summer holidays and he hoped that we would all come along – 'in appropriate costume, naturally!' Beamish had been right, this had been worth waiting for: a rare opportunity to dress up. I noted the date carefully and came home while Beamish stayed behind to help Holly clear up the tea things.

*   *   *

Wednesday 12th July 2002

Thinking it best, I changed into my costume at School rather than walking in it through Sixokes High Street at a busy time of the morning. I must say that I was very pleased with the stylish figure I cut in my 'Mr Bingley Special' (from the theatrical costumier *Ravishing Strides*). The snug blue coat and patterned weskit surmounted a white shirt with flounced stock and a horse-head pin. These were complemented by pale breeches, highly-polished and tight-fitting riding boots and a gleaming top hat. Even Adrian Witson was impressed - though after his initial cries of praise he did lean forward to confide 'it's a pity your gibus is anachronistic' whatever that meant.

I dare say that the main house at Godmersham would have been impressive, sitting, as it did, under a clear blue English sky and surrounded by a very fine park with lake, trees and extensive rolling swards. Unfortunately, major renovation was underway and the whole front façade was swathed in plastic-shrouded scaffolding. Paul Happiman was not put out because, as he explained while we debouched from the school minibus and tugged our clothing back into a semblance of shape, today had been arranged privately for the SSSJAAS at an especially cut-price rate in light of the building-work. We trudged around in search of an entrance (nobly ignoring the catcalls and whistling from a group of smoking workmen sitting on a low wall by some outbuildings) until greeted by a leathery old dear with a shock of grey hair who turned out to be our hostess for the day. She introduced herself as Emma Knatchbull-Bowes and ushered us though a narrow door and corridor and, via a red-baize-covered door, into the main hall.

The first hour of 'The Austens at Godmersham Experience' consisted of a tour of the house together with cartloads of commentary from EK-B. Most of what she said went in one ear and out the other but I was struck by a couple of things. The first was that Jane Austen herself was thought by the Godmersham (and Sixokes) Austens to be deficient in social skills and as having a sour personality (as opposed to the more rustic Steventon Austens who, clearly lacking the sophistications of poise and polish, enjoyed her waspish observations on the foibles of others) which is why her older sister Cassandra was favoured as a visitor. The second was something I could use in a lesson on human biology to illustrate how times have changed with respect to human reproduction: Cassandra was invited to Godmersham to attend her aunt Elizabeth as a companion during confinements – more or less every year for each of her eleven offspring. There was no twelfth because 'Elizabeth the brood mare conked out at the age of 35' as our guide and hostess explained. That should make my Year Ten girls a bit more thankful. The final part of the tour was a viewing of some very undistinguished watercolours by said Cassandra and the opportunity to handle a brush that Jane had thrown at the head of the toddler William Austen after he had called her a 'scratchy old trout'.

We then made our way outside for the second element of the 'experience' which was to be a drive through the Park and along lanes to retrace the route followed by the Austens on their frequent visits to the neighbouring improbably-named Faggs. There were a couple of open-topped four-seater carriages each with two horses and a driver and, while Happiman, Jane Pensword, Penny Greensleeves and Jo Bostle clambered into the first, Witson, Holly Stephen, Beamish and I got into the second – not without quite a bit of by-play as Beamish adopted an elaborate courtly mien to hand Holly to her seat and arrange her cushion behind the small of her back. With the faintest crack of a whip and a 'sit tight everybody' we were off!

I must say that the plush seats were remarkably comfortable and the soothing pace set by our trotting pair of steeds just about perfect for travelling through the glories of the countryside. Witson and I admired it as we watched it gently recede behind us (the others being forward-facing). Beamish, no doubt attempting to impress with his smattering of knowledge, called out to the driver:

"This is what is known as a 'curricle' isn't it, Drives?"

The driver half-turned his head and with a short laugh said, "Bless you no, sir. It's a barouche." He followed this up with an extensive lecture on the differences between this and a brougham, a landau and a phaeton. We listened politely and at the end Beamish told him he'd be the perfect host for *Top Gear of Yesteryear* and added, sotto voce to the rest of us 'Here's a man who knows everything about nothing and nothing about anything' which sounded rather good at the time but now just seems strange.

It was as we were passing down a narrow shady lane that the mishap occurred. Holly had abruptly leant forward in her seat laughing at some remark that Beamish had made and I saw her cushion was about to slip to the floor. Thinking that I too could demonstrate courtliness as well as the next man, I swiftly got to my feet to reach out and save it. There was an abrupt thud as my top hat was swept from my head by a low-hanging branch of an oak. By the time we had impressed on the driver the necessity to stop, we had gone a good 50 yards more down the lane. He was unsympathetic, saying 'you ought to have sat tight like I told you, sir' as I climbed down and hurried back to retrieve my hat (recalling the rather large deposit I had left with *Ravishing Strides* against non-returns or damage). Disconcertingly, it was nowhere to be seen on the road. I thought I saw it in the ditch but, after stepping into the rank-smelling mud beneath a weft of coarse grass, it turned out to be just an old black plastic hand-bag.

After a few minutes Beamish sauntered back and then pointed upwards: there was the hat wedged in a fork in a branch of the tree.

Of course, it was a long way out of my reach and even Beamish jumping failed to get near it. I refused to let him attempt dislodging it by throwing stones and he refused to lift me on his shoulders as this would befoul his elegant clothing. Naturally, I could not remove my mud-daubed boots as I had left the necessary boot-jack at school. The driver came up to us at this point and Beamish asked him to back up the barouche. This simply had the effect of more derisive laughter: apparently a pair of horses cannot be persuaded to 'reverse'. He suggested instead that I 'shimmy along the branch'. Seeing no alternative, I shrugged my way out of my coat, handed it to Beamish and scrambled up the hedge and into the tree. The branch over the lane looked disconcertingly high as I gripped it between my legs and, hands forward, inched myself along. By this time Holly and Witson had come back and joined the others in vocal encouragements. They gave a heartening cheer when I plucked the hat from its woody bracket before dropping it down for Beamish to catch. Unlike the horses, I could do 'reverse' and was soon back along the branch and down into the lane dusting off my hands and grinning with self-satisfaction while basking in the congratulations of the others at my derring-do. We hurried back to our seats and the driver clattered us to Godmersham at a crisper pace so that we would get to dinner (scheduled for 'three o-clock on the dot and woe betide me if we're a minute late') with the others.

The fare served up was plain, nourishing and plentiful though there was a lot of groaning when the wine, 'authentically well-watered' was poured and found to be less than stimulating. Nonetheless, we were a cheery and chatty group thoroughly enjoying ourselves. After the flunkeys had cleared the table, EK-B organised a couple of dances and the sort of games the Austens indulged in. We all swung into Lord Wellington's Waltz and Lady Dashwood's Reel (though proper musicians would have been more in keeping than the taped recordings from a ghetto-blaster) before playing battledore and blind-man's buff. The final game was called 'bullet pudding'. This involved a large salver on which was a volcano-like cone of flour referred to as the 'pudding'. In the crater of the volcano was a round steel ball-bearing, the 'bullet' ('health and safety disallowing the lead ball that gives the game its name'). Using a knife, each player in turn had to slice into the 'pudding' and remove a bladeful of flour and put it on the side of the salver but without dislodging the 'bullet'. The player who does this loses and, as a penalty, has to retrieve the 'bullet' from the salver using mouth alone.

It was unlucky for me that, as I triumphantly removed a bladeful of flour from the cone and straightened up, my stomach jogged the edge of the table which caused a 'landslide' down which the 'bullet' slipped and which meant that I had lost. It was also unlucky that my face was still sweaty from the exertions of full-blooded dancing so that after retrieving the ball-bearing in my lips (quite difficult to do as the flour kept clogging up the front of my mouth), my face, apart from my eyes, was thickly covered. Apparently, this was side-splittingly funny especially when I replaced my horn-rim glasses. EK-B managed to jerk out a recommendation that I 'repair to the gents for a good wash'.

Ruefully, I had to admit that my face had a comic appearance when I surveyed myself in the full-length mirror in the 'Visitors' Jakes'. Furthermore, I now noticed that there was a bright green stain deep in the crotch of my fawn breeches which I had failed to see heretofore. This, no doubt, was caused by the alga (in the genus *Pleurococcus* if I'm any judge) encrusting the branch of the oak that I'd heroically slithered along to rescue my hat. The penalty clause from *Ravishing Strides*, and the oft-repeated admonishment from Mother about treating stains early, made me fill the hand-basin with hot water and, soaking a few handfuls of paper towels, scrub away between my legs. This seemed only to produce the effect of spreading the stain to a greater area though, to be fair, it was a paler green as it got further from 'ground zero'. This frenzied activity took a few minutes and, when I gave in to the obvious (I was making things worse rather than better), the water in the basin was cool and only faintly green. I pulled out the plug in preparation for getting more water with which to tackle my face. While I watched the vortex draining the basin my attention was drawn to a curious sensation: it felt as if my face were encased in plaster of Paris. I guessed that the flour-and-sweat paste had set – but that a brisk, soapy wash should do the trick.

My run of bad luck, however, continued. On opening the hot tap, no water issued forth. Ditto for the cold. I surmised (correctly as it turned out) that the water supply had been interrupted at just this juncture, by the building-work going on in the house. I would have to peel it off. Gripping a projecting piece of the white mask just above my left eye I gave a sharp tug and cursed as I removed an eyebrow along with a jagged tear of the sweat-flour face-pack. Further peeling was almost as equally painful so I switched to scrubbing with dry paper towels. This was less painful but also far less effective. Annoyingly, Beamish banged on the door at this moment to say that the minibus was all revved up and everyone was ready to go.

Reluctantly, I abandoned any further ablutions and went to say farewell to our hostess, EK-B. If she found anything amusing in the figure that hobbled (in those too-damn-tight boots) towards her, breeches pea-green stained from crotch to knees, face minus one eyebrow and leper-like with its blotches of raw pink and tanned skin with occasional bright white smears of flour, it never showed. Noblesse obliged, no doubt.

Episode 25

From his diary

Wednesday 28th November 1979

In the Staff Common Room this morning I recounted how my lesson on taste discrimination had been sabotaged by the idiocy of that boy Temms. My intention was to have the class work in pairs to devise an experiment to establish whether there was a significant taste difference between two types of cola (an idea I had pinched from Alex James). Prior to the lesson, I had carefully decanted the litre of each type into anonymous stoppered flasks labelled 'A' and 'B'. I told them to get into pairs and sort out a strategy for a fair test to establish if people really could 'taste the difference'. Knowing this would keep them occupied for a few minutes I slipped out to the prep room for a quick cup of tea and a couple of bourbons. Just as I was finishing these, I heard a good deal of excited cheering from the classroom and hastened in. There I saw Temms with flask 'A' upended above his mouth as he swallowed the last couple of mouthfuls of the cola. Apparently, he had risen to the challenge of 'down in one'. He managed to jerk this explanation out before going quiet and then green. A second or two later, the cola came spewing out of his mouth and between his ineffectual fingers to spray all over the teacher's desk – including my new copy of *Dinosaur Data* that I'd brought in to read as they were experimenting. I was livid: not only was my magazine ruined but so was the experiment – one could hardly 'taste the difference' with just a single cola. As a punishment for egging him on I made the whole class stand at the back of the room facing the wall in silence for the remainder of the lesson while the technicians gamely cleared up the mess. In addition, I gave Temms 500 lines: 'I must not regurgitate over dinosaurs.'

"You need a bit of cheering up, Dob," said Richard Hansum sympathetically, gently stirring the lemon slice in his favoured blend of teas in his personal bone china tea cup. He glanced across at Tony Cobberly. "How about coming along to the *Pro Probus* with us next week?"

"Yes," chimed in Cobberly. "It should prove apposite because, as you may know, we like to do some taste discriminating of our own on such occasions."

I was flattered. This was the first invitation I'd ever had to an evening with the legendary fine wine and dining group in their annual get-together. Like the food and the wine, the group was extremely select.

"Do you like claret?" asked Hansum. I was about to say that I preferred a drop of red when, luckily for me, Cobberly broke in, anxious to give me more information and so spared me some embarrassment.

"We focus on claret as the best of all red wines," he said, rather portentously in my opinion. "We select a particular region of Bordeaux for tasting and each diner brings a bottle for sampling. Last year we focused on St-Julien; the year before we crossed the two seas to try some Pomerols" - a glance at Hansum here - "and before that we in the heart of the Pauillacs." I nodded my head as intelligently as I could at all this gibberish as he waved his hands about while his lips went redder and wetter − it looked like he was drooling with the recollections. "This year's nomination for the evening is, in my estimation at least," here he gave a meaningful look towards Hansum, "the supreme argo." He raised both hands palms outwards to indicate there was no more to be said and, with a nod to us both, stalked out.

"Cobberly and I disagree about the best," explained Hansum. "He can't forgive me for giving him a Pétrus in a blind tasting which he confidently identified as a Latour."

I admit to feeling rather lost in all these bewildering names but Hansum was reassuring. "Just get your hands on a bottle of Cobberly's 'supreme argo' and you'll be fine, Dob old man." I thanked him and hurried off to the library to do some homework of my own.

I must say that I was extremely pleased to find that my scholarship skills have not deserted me. First I got hold of a dictionary to find out what 'argo' was. I came across 'argot' with its two meanings: the spur on a cock's foot or, generally, any such excrescence on the foot of an animal. That one seemed unlikely. The second 'argot' was a specialist or minority language. 'Latin, perhaps, or Greek?' I mused – but Cobberly, so proud of his classical languages, would never have allowed them to be classed as 'argots'. I tried again: 'argo' was referenced as 'Argo' – the ship in which Jason made his quest for the Golden Fleece. Again, not immediately pertinent to wines. On the other hand, Cobberly was Head of Classics and did enjoy intellectual teasing – perhaps this 'Argo' clue should be followed up?

I got the Britannica and turned to 'Jason and the Argonauts'. Rather dispiritingly, there were about 5 pages of closely-packed print on the subject but, as I leafed through the pages, I came across a map which, of course, immediately caught my eye. I looked at the dotted outline of Jason's voyage through the Aegean Sea and, call it intellectual instinct if you will, I was strangely attracted by the island of Chios, just a tiny speck of land. Putting off reading the 'Jason and the Argonauts' entry, I turned instead to 'Chios' – and struck gold! After some dull details about size, population and so forth, it said 'Chios was famous in the Ancient Greek world for its wine. Philip of Macedonia claimed that Chian wine was supreme'. This all fitted perfectly – and even chimed in with that remark Cobberly had made earlier about 'crossing seas'. I resolved to buy the best Chian wine I could find and so demonstrate to Cobberly and the rest that I knew my way around the wine world!

*   *   *

Saturday 1ˢᵗ December 1979

Drawing blanks on Chian wines on the shelves of both Waitrose and Tesco, I went into the off-licence next to the dry-cleaners in the High Street and confidently demanded a bottle of their best Chian. To my practiced eye the assistant behind the counter looked a feckless fool and, sure enough, he disclaimed any knowledge of such a wine even when prompted with the clue that it was a famous wine from the Aegean (though at his blank look at this I explained that this was a part of the Mediterranean). I instructed him to fetch the manager. Thankfully, the latter proved better-stocked with such straight-forward facts and, after glancing at my spelling out of 'Chian' on a slip of paper, and prompted by the lug of an assistant murmuring 'Mediterranean', he reached up to a shelf and pulled down a raffia-covered rounded flask of a bottle with the label 'Chianti Classico' on it. I felt absolutely bucked: the name was Cobberly all over! Better was to come. The manager pointed to the silhouette of a black cockerel on the seal of the bottle and informed me that this guaranteed a top-quality chianti. This surely was more of the Cobberly tease – I remembered the 'argot' that was the cock's spur. I was relishing the look on his face when I presented the group with the wine and regaled them all with my scholarship in the matter. Noticing my exuberant mood, the manager went on to tell me that the wine was very popular (which, of course, I already knew otherwise the *Pro Probus* would not be devoting an evening to sampling it) and not too expensive. Wishing to show that my largesse was equal to my finesse, I bought two bottles and took them home where I almost hugged myself in the delight of the treat in store.

*   *   *

Friday 7th December 1979

The *Pro Probus* gathered earlier this evening (in all good faith, it seems like days ago given the events outlined below. In fact, I should own up that it is now the early hours of Saturday the 8th) in a private room above *Le Coeur Anglais*, the best restaurant in town and conveniently situated just a couple of hundred yards from the School. The cream of the staff was there: Cobberly, of course, as founder and president; the sophisticated Hansum; suave and debonair Byron Craggs; the fresh-faced and dynamic Yanto Williams, our new Head of Chemistry; jewel of the Modern Languages department, Malcolm D'Orby; the clubbable Historian Johnny Ryott; puissant man of letters, Hugh Pollen; and the lively and sparkling Duncan Gownsend. I was the last to arrive (Mother had asked me to help her sort out some laundry issues) and the restaurateur, M. Nebout, ushered me upstairs and into the exclusive and intimate room where the others were already quaffing champagne. I took my bottles of chianti out of my shopping bag and put them (with some pride, it must be said) on the front of the small side-table on which there were already eight bottles of wine. M. Nebout handed me a bumper and I cheerily called good evening to one and all.

A few minutes later we settled at the table and the gastronomic feast began. A menu was provided at each place and I kept my copy so I can give some of the details. There were seven courses: a bonne bouche of foie gras and blue cheese on toasted brioche; scallops on a bed of parsnip and bacon; sea-bass and salsify; elderflower sorbet; gigot of lamb in a jus bordelais; brie, brebis, Roquefort and Port Salut; tarte tatin. Before me was a plain of white napery, a sweep of four glittering glasses and an uncountable number of sparkling knives and forks. Hansum was on one side, Pollen the other. Pollen gave me the history of the name '*Pro Probus*'. It was typical Cobberly.

Apparently, there had been an edict put out by a Roman Emperor called Domitian in AD92 which instructed that all vineyards outside Italy were to be extirpated. This edict was relaxed by the order of Emperor Probus in AD280 "which, of course, meant that Cobberly's claret was saved and hence the reason why we are all terribly pro Probus" he finished with a warm smile.

It was at this point that Cobberly stood up and formally welcomed me to the group and then walked over to the table on which the diners' wines were assembled.

"I will read out the various chateaux we are to sample," he said then stopped short and reached out a hand towards my two bottles. Turning to us with a rather roguish air, he laid hands on the two prominent protuberances of my rounded khaki-coloured raffia flasks. "These remind me of a visit to Cairo where I encountered an impressively-endowed stud camel," he said sorrowfully to some laughter and then looked at me. "Yours, Dob?" I nodded with a smile of self-depreciation.

"I think you'll like to hear –" I began quietly but got no further as a tumult of laughter drowned out the account of my researches that I had been about to deliver. When this eventually subsided, Cobberly quite kindly put me right by announcing that the 'non-testicular bottles' were all bona fide examples from the incomparably great Bordeaux region of Margaux. Putting on his reading glasses he read out the various chateaux we were to sample: d'Angludet, d'Issan, Labegorce-Zédé, Durfort-Vivens, Rausan-Ségla, Branc-Cantenac, Malescot St-Exupéry, and – his own contribution – Margaux itself. I kept quiet about my mistake and tucked into the excellent food. M. Nebout opened the bottles of Margaux with a great show of Gallic flourish and set them on the table just after the fish course (which had been accompanied by what Hansum had declared to be 'a very fine fumé') and we all began tasting.

I must say that this Margaux wine was very nice stuff indeed. Although I couldn't match the sort of pronouncements of the connoisseurs (apparently the Branc-Cantenac had 'lovely body but no beauty', and the Durfort-Vivens 'promised a return to generosity and depth' for instance) I relished every one and was careful to single out Cobberly's Chateau Margaux for particular praise after a careful sip. This was the last of the bottles to be sampled and, once all glasses had been drained, the *Pro Probus'* traditional toast was made. We rose to our feet and Tony Cobberly shouted "With the great King John, we say…" here he paused and all members cried: "*A bas la Grande Coutume!*" and to a man we flung our empty glasses over our shoulders to smash on the walls. A skivvy came in to sweep up the fragments while we resumed our seats and fell on the cheese. M. Nebout came up trumps with a couple of complimentary bottles of a sweet and fruity white wine called Barsac to accompany the apple tart and we all toasted the 'entente cordial'.

Over coffee anecdotes, amusing observations and recollections ebbed and flowed up and down the table. I felt that I owed the group something interesting. I cleared my throat and silence fell.

"Chucking those wine glasses after the King John toast put me in mind of a curiosity," I began and was encouraged to see all present turn to look at me. "If a man in a desert held out a pistol horizontally with one hand and, in the other, equally horizontal, held a bullet…" I paused to enhance the moment. There was a great silence. "If he fired the pistol and dropped the bullet in his hand at the same moment," I was almost whispering and paused again for several seconds before intoning: "both bullets would hit the ground at the exact same moment."

The silence held for several more seconds before Yanto Williams laughed out loud and shouted "Cobblers, Dob!" This prompted a good deal of general hilarity which made me peeved – particularly because Williams was a scientist like me and should know this was a fact (albeit one which the more recherché literary types would be unlikely to be acquainted with). I protested that it was true and it was at this point that Cobberly suggested that 'in the best tradition of science, we ask the world for an answer by performing the experiment'. Irritably, I pointed out that we didn't have a gun.

"But surely, this fact would hold true for any projectile, Dob?" he said smoothly. "If, for instance, a ball was dropped from the tower of Pisa at the same time that another ball was thrown sideways from it, then – if what you say is true – both balls would land at the same time?"

"Yes, yes," I said rather sharply. "But we aren't in Italy and don't have the balls."

"Oh, but we do," he said with a quiet smile and lifted my bottles of chianti, one in each hand. "We can chuck these off the tower of St Emilius – one dropped, the other thrown horizontally – and see if the world agrees with your assertion, Dob old man." I thought the whole thing rather silly and a waste of my wine but the rest all thought this would be a fine way to round off the evening. D'Orby was a churchwarden of St Emilius and had the key to the door to the tower with him. Williams, being a fearsome scrum-half in his day, volunteered to hurl a flask horizontally and Cobberly himself said that he would drop the other one on the countdown from D'Orby.

We all hurried through the night air to the churchyard. D'Orby, Cobberly and Williams went through the small oak door and climbed the tower while the rest of us strung ourselves out in a line on the path between the tower and the High Street to witness whether the crash of smashing bottles was indeed simultaneous or not. Knowing from experience just how powerful Williams's scrum-half pass was, I stationed myself furthest from the base of the tower – nearly on the street pavement, in fact.

It was a clear and silent night, the stars shining bleakly in the unutterable vastnesses of space as the Earth plummeted artlessly and helplessly through the darkness. The faint light from the window of the house nearby illuminated the clouds of vapour I gently exhaled while thinking of the spirit of Margaux that was being released into the fragrant Kentish air. Above me I heard indistinct voices and then D'Orby bellowed:

"Stands the world ready to reveal whether the Wentworth Assertion bears the Mark of Truth?" A few giggles followed and then Hansum shouted up:

"The World stands witness, oh Great Experimenters!"

There was a minute or so's pause (presumably as Williams and Cobberly positioned themselves on the tower) before D'Orby's rich tones called out:

"On the count of three, gentlemen: One…Two…Three!"

On the count of 'two' a police panda car hurtled around the corner of the High Street and, with wheels locked, skidded to a stop just a few yards from me. I heard the 'three' and, in the backwash of the car's headlights, glimpsed the flask of chianti hurtling towards us from the powerful hands of Yanto Williams. I leapt upwards, arms raised in an attempt to catch it but was unsuccessful: it struck the windscreen and both it and the flask shattered. In the blink of an eye, a policeman leapt out of the panda car and assaulted me – he wrenched my arm up my back, wrestled me out of the churchyard and slammed me over the bonnet and grunted: "Just stay calm, chummy, or I'll give you a proper duffing." The policeman who had been driving got out from behind the wheel with a large torch in one hand, a truncheon in the other, and rushed into the churchyard.

I felt glass under my cheek and smelt the fumes of wine. Though the position was tense, I am pleased to record that my mind worked coolly nonetheless. What was essential was that I protect my colleagues from getting caught as culprits in this idiotic escapade. All I had to do was think up a plausible set of circumstances (other than the true ones, of course) that would explain why bottles of wine were being thrown in a churchyard in the small hours such that one of them accidentally smashed the windscreen of a police car. The policeman pressing his weight onto my back urged me to speak.

"Right, chummy, where's your gear?"

This puzzled me and my mind froze.

"Come on, come on, we know you're up for having the lead away," he went on.

I was baffled and dumb-struck: what was he on about? He twisted my arm painfully.

"And what's with smashing up our panda?"

I realised I'd have to start extemporising.

"Well, officer, I was interested in testing a little theory I have about the parabolic nature of projectiles and, finding a wine-bottle or two in the grass decided to see if –"

He twisted my arm harder and said, "Don't play the monkey with me, chummy. Let's have a look at you." Roughly, he handcuffed my wrists behind my back, pulled me upright and, collecting a torch from inside the car, shone it directly into my face. I felt him relax somewhat: clearly, the fact that I was in full evening dress gave him pause.

"Name and address," he snapped. I told him.

The other policeman returned somewhat more slowly than he had left. "No sign of anyone else, John. Door to the roof and tower is securely locked. No sign of any damage," he said, eyeing me curiously. "I'll just check over there." He pointed towards the neighbouring house and strode across and knocked on its door. It was opened almost immediately by the Headmaster, naturally enough, and I overheard his mellifluous tones in snatches: "Heard voices... lead-thieves...valuable...wonderfully prompt.....bid you goodnight." Mercifully, the door closed.

I was relieved for my sake that the Headmaster had not noticed that it was me who had been apprehended by the constabulary; and for my colleagues' sakes that they had managed to melt away into the night. The handcuffs were chafing uncomfortably but, having heard that the arrest was due to a misapprehension, I felt sure that I would soon be freed and on my way home. This proved to be well wide of the mark.

"Reeks of booze!" said the one called John. "Have you been drinking?" he went on harshly. Though I thought to deprecate his lack of civility now it was clear I was no common thief, I thought it wiser merely to demonstrate the sophistication of my evening.

"Actually, I have been dining and wine-tasting," I announced airily. "I, and other bon-viveurs, have been exploring the delights of Margaux –"

"You mean a gang of you got boozed up and had a prozzie between you?" he interrupted coarsely, in an unpleasantly suggestive tone.

"Not in the least," I answered severely. "We had some champagne and a Pouilly fumé and then sampled eight bottles of claret rounding it off with a couple of Barsac." I thought this enviable listing of our fine wines would impress them favourably. I was wrong.

"Got you bang to rights, chummy. One: you are drunk; two, disorderly in throwing bottles about; three, criminal damage for smashing our windscreen; four, resisting arrest; and five, you are trespassing on church property." He turned with some satisfaction to the other policeman. "Radio in for another car, Geoff, and we'll get chummy into the cells and the charge sheets will cover our allocation for the night easily." He laughed. I say this in all honesty: he laughed.

I was overcome and hung my head: this was awful. It was the end of my career: I could not be a teacher – even in an independent prep school – if I had a criminal record. It would be intolerable to live on in Sixokes, open to ridicule and opprobrium from everyone who knew me. Mother would be horribly let down. My life was crashing down in pieces all around me. Then an angel in a most unlikely shape came to my rescue.

"Mr Wentworth, sir, as I live and breathe!" said Atkins. There he stood in his sergeant's uniform with a look of sheer delight on his – 'twas ever thus – bovine features. He had got out from the back-up panda car that had just arrived and looked genuinely pleased to see me. I thought this rather handsome of him, particularly as our last interview had been when he'd been my pupil in the Fifth Form and

I'd given him a detention for bullying Bradwell into consuming a whole roast chicken in the course of my lesson and (what caught him out) attempting to smuggle the bones into my dinosaur relics case. He turned to the arresting officers. "This must be a mistake, lads – Mr Wentworth's one of the finest. Taught me everything I know about Biology – which isn't much!" he roared with laughter. "Let's just turn him loose." The others took some persuading since this would mean missing their 'quota' of crimes but, eventually, Atkins won them over with the promise of an 'early knock' given that their panda car was out of commission and how he would cover their beats meantime. I was uncuffed and could only silently shake Atkins by the hand, thankful for the Sixokes Spirit that bound us together.

I feel harrowed, tired and dreadful.

Saturday 8th December

The hope that I had cherished about the events of yestereve being unknown were dashed as I walked into the Staff Common Room after breakfast to be greeted by cries of:
  "Chummy-monkey!"
  "Jail-bird!'
  "Lead-stripper!"
  "Plod-knocker!"
  "Minion of the Moon!"
  "Panda-smasher!"
  "Keeper of the camel's jewels!"

I had been wrong about the others melting away into the night – only Gownsend and Pollen had been quick enough to flee. Gownsend himself had caught the other bottle that Cobberly had dropped explaining he 'couldn't resist such a dolly at night' and, whipping it out from under his gown, lobbed it in my direction. Fortunately, it didn't break. The others had witnessed everything.

D'Orby, Williams and Cobberly had spotted the panda car's arrival just after the launching of the bottles and Williams had hurtled down the tower stairs to lock the door and then returned to the others to watch yours truly being man-handled from behind the castellations. Ryott had clambered up into a yew tree and I have to admit to a grudging admiration for Hansum and Craggs who, not fleet enough of foot to run or agile enough to climb, hit on the ruse of stretching themselves out on a couple of tombs as effigies and so went undetected in the brief torchlight that swept over them but were close enough to witness everything.

The Headmaster has sent around a memo about vigilance and security, meanwhile preening himself about the police commending his alert good-citizenship.

Episode 26

From his diary

Wednesday 14ᵗʰ February 1993

I was in the Copy Shop before the start of lessons this morning, sifting rather acquisitively through the new range of fancy bulldog clips that had just come in and pointing out to Busby Beamish how useful these might be in sorting different parts of one's notes, when one of the porters came and paused in the doorway with 'Oh my darlings, oh my darlings, oh my darling Valentines!' in a pleasant, if over-loud baritone. Having drawn sufficient attention to himself, he stepped forward crying 'Post!'. This caused some feminine squeals of excitement from Penny and Cheryl who always seemed to attract a good deal of attention from amongst the other staff. The new girl (whose name I had yet to learn), and the diminutive but formidable Jean Masefield, task-mistress of the secretarial staff, were far more sober about it. The porter, Dicky, fancies himself as something of a wag and adopted a sort of Father Christmasish bonhomie as he waved a carrier bag from Waitrose in front of himself.

"A lot of little goodies for St Valentine's for the girls!" he chirped.

"Come on, Dicky, pour them out," Beamish said, pretending to take some interest and pleasure in the business.

"If it's the usual mail, please just give it to us," said Jean wearily. "We've a busy schedule and-"

"And the first one is for..." Dicky paused theatrically before plucking a lurid pink card out of the bag. "...young Sandra!"

I must say that, like Jean Masefield, I found all this rather tiresome. Beamish continued his pretence however, grinning eagerly and encouragingly at Sandra. She opened the envelope.

"Read it out, Sandie," Penny called with a smile. "No secrets in here you know!"

Sandra frowned and read out:

> "'*Rose's are red*
> *Violet's are blue*
> *Daisy's are white*
> *I wonder what colour yours are?*' Signed with a big X."

Beamish, Penny and Cheryl guffawed but Jean had a very different attitude.

"Disgusting. I will not have my staff exposed to such filth. Let me see the envelope," she rasped out menacingly. Sandra handed it over and we all moved closer as she studied the handwriting.

"Let me have a look," said Dicky with an air of self-importance. "I know pretty well all the different hand-writing of the staff here." He set down the Waitrose bag next to Beamish who had been rather edged out as the others had closed in, and drew out his pince-nez (an affectation typical of the man) before taking the envelope from Jean to peer at the 'For Sandra' in the best Sherlockian style. He spent some time about it, fingering the flap of the envelope, then, plucking the card from Sandra, turned it over and over. After all this detective stuff, he stood up straight, drew in a deep breath and said:

"If you ask me-"

Busby Beamish interrupted him.

"Here's some more evidence, Hercule!" He held up an oblong cardboard box in the same shade of lurid pink as Sandra's card. "But this one's got 'For Jean' written on it."

He handed it to Dicky who, after some slapstick glancing from box to envelope and back again nodded slowly.

"Different pen, of course," he said. "But definitely the same fist."

"Oh, do open it Ms Masefield!" pleaded Penny.

Jean took the box from Dicky with some distaste. "I hardly like to," she said. "Given the lewd nature of Sandra's card, who knows what this might be."

At this moment Beamish leaned over her and brought his mouth near her ear. He whispered very quietly and, apart from Jean herself, I'm pretty sure I alone heard what he said.

"I noticed Tony Cobberly slipping a couple of pink items into the post last night, Jean," he intoned. "He looked a little furtive too..."

Jean's slab-like cheeks quivered a little and they went a little ruddier than usual. She prised open the box with her rough, grimy and forceful fingers.

"It's a mug for tea," she said softly.

As the other ladies cooed with congratulations I decided I had had enough of all the gushing and walked out – and anyway, I was already just a little late for my first lesson with the Fifth Form.

I quelled the row they were making by a stately pacing into the lab bearing aloft an enamel tray covered with an old tea-cloth in the manner of a cleric reverently stepping up to the altar with some religious doodah. I laid it down gently on the front bench and looked around. I had their attention – that rapt anticipation of 'teacher has something special for us' that so many other teachers report.

Well, I say I had their attention – all, that is, except that great oaf Mason who was gazing down into his own lap. He didn't notice as, with fleet and silent steps, I went and stood on the other side of his bench.

"Care to share with the rest of us what is so fascinating, Mason," I enquired innocently. Mason leaned forward with a start.

"Oh, no sir, sorry sir!" he said.

"Just stand up will you please," I asked with a pleasant smile. He pressed his lips together but, after the shortest interval to convey his reluctance, lifted his heavy frame off the stool. A Valentine's card dropped from the folds of his trousers onto the bench. I picked it up and, turning to the class, read it aloud:

"Bet you're built like a horse. HT"

After the roars of laughter had died away, I looked up into the discomfiture on Mason's face.

"Why are they all laughing, Mason? It's gibberish to me. Can you explain?" I asked sweetly as I looked around the room once again, taking in the guilty delight on the faces of the other pupils as they looked from Mason and me towards the red-faced Hannah Thorpe sitting right at the front of the room next to Temms.

"It's a joke card from one of the other boys, Mr Wentworth sir," said Mason in a clear and steady voice. "You see, they've been ribbing me about my interest in what we're doing in Classics with Mr Cobberly at the moment, sir. I really like it - the stories in the *Odyssey*, sir. Mr Cobberly really brings them to life and, one lesson, I got a bit carried away with the romance of it all: the triremes retreating along the coast and the Trojan horse being swept into the heart of the city, all for the sake of the love of a beautiful woman: Helen of Troy, sir. That's the HT – Helen of Troy."

"I don't believe a word of it!" I said. But I had to inwardly acknowledge that he'd been very plausible. I could sense the admiration for him that was coming from the other pupils. Knowing it would be a waste of time probing any further to find the truth in the case, I hurried back to the enamel tray telling them all to gather round.

When they were quite ready, I paused for a moment and then, with one of my witticisms, whisked away the tea-towel:

"Not the heart of a city, Mason – but the heart of an ox!"

Temms, who was right at the front, recoiled and went a little green around the gills. He looked at the heart with a mixture of fascination and revulsion.

"What are you going to do with it, sir?" he asked.

"Cut it open to show you," I answered briskly.

"It looks full of something," he said slowly. "It's not going to spurt out blood is it sir?"

"Of course not, boy. Just watch."

With my customary dexterity, I sliced the heart open with deft and skilful darts of the scalpel. Having laid ventricles and atria bare, I lifted it up towards Temms.

"There you are, Temms, quite empty of anything."

He fell back with a thud. There's always one. I got Mason and Miss Thorpe to carry him out into the fresh air while the others walked slowly back to their places and got on with copying the notes on the structure of the heart into their exercise books.

After a hearty lunch (pun fully intended!), I went up to the Masters' Common Room to relax. I was awakened by the sound of Richard Hansum chuckling to himself over a stapled sheaf of papers.

"What's so funny?" asked Busby Beamish as he sank into the chair next to Hansum and settled his can of lager and glass of whisky on the scarred oak coffee table.

"It's Cobberly's opening chapters of a detective novel he's writing. It's called *The Blue Stockings*. He's given it to me so I can advise him about it. Apparently, it's been rejected by half a dozen publishers already and he is mystified as to why. The trouble is, it's a sort of Chandleresque novel – you know, written in the first person with the detective being a hard-nosed tough guy with an instinct for trouble and a slick line in dialogue – and, every time this detective figures in the action (and, as an action figure, he figures pretty well constantly), the image of old Cobberly floats into my mind and this, though phenomenologically fascinating, means I can't take the book at all seriously."

He paused and leafed back through a few sheets of the manuscript.

"I mean, just listen to this." He settled his half-moon spectacles more securely on the end of his nose and read with a very creditable American accent: 'She was good-looking in what I guess you'd call an obvious kind of way. But that was just the kind of way I like my women to look' – I mean, it's a good enough line but what looms ineluctably in my mind's eye is Cobberly gazing fondly towards that pyknic frump the Coaster, and hitching up his gown in that way that he has."

"I see what you mean," I said, chuckling myself. The conceit that the socially inept Cobberly was secretly in love with the severe and redoubtable Jean Masefield, was a long-running source of amusement for Hansum. Beamish sipped some whisky and chased it down with a good swallow of lager.

"Give us a shufty, old man," he said holding out one hand while belching softly into the other. Hansum passed the manuscript to him and leaned back into the worn buttoned leather of his chair, crossed one knee over the other and linked his hands behind his head.

"Do you know, the Coaster nearly smiled at me this morning? It was a chilling experience. I'd gone into the Copy Shop to collect some ink and paper when that starchy new girl brought in four mugs of tea on a tray (no doubt both cheap and tin) for their 'elevenses'. Being in a light-hearted and playful mood for some reason, I clapped my hands and announced that I would guess from the style of the mug which tea was for whom. There was a shapely bright pink one with 'hot and sweet' written on it in bulbous purple letters and, of course, I handed that one to Penny with what I hope was a lascivious wink; the next had a picture of a cowboy rodeo-rider on a bucking bronco, hat clutched aloft and with 'wild horses wouldn't drag me away' on it in playbill font and I handed that one to Cheryl and said something about the great Hector's flashing helmet. That left one for the Coaster and one for the new girl. I eyed the two mugs ruminatively and stroked my chin. One was fluted bone china with a vile chocolate-box painting of a country cottage on it; the other was just plain, white, thick and ugly. I looked from the new girl to the Coaster and then back at the mugs. Making up my mind, I seized the china mug and handed it to the new girl saying she looked as pretty and fresh as a cottage garden. I turned back to face the Coaster. There was an ominous silence. 'And, of course,' I said with a smile, 'This one must be for me!' It got a huge laugh from the girls – mainly due to relief, I feel sure – and a sort of ghastly twitch of the lips from the Coaster that could, with some imagination, be described as a smile."

"Actually," said Beamish looking up from a page that he'd been smoothing thoughtfully, "The pink one with 'hot and sweet' on it belongs to the Coaster herself." Hansum looked astonished. I smiled inwardly at Beamish's insouciance.

"I'm sure it was a secret Valentine's Day gift from Cobberly," Beamish went on airily and, after a furtive glance at me, quickly turned back to the manuscript. "But what do you make of this for snappy sex talk? Our hero has just pulled the aforementioned good-looking girl from the sinking car and they stand close - face to face, I'm supposing – and she kicks off with:
'- You're kind of sweet
- Hard-boiled?
- Maybe a good egg.
- Not too much of the curate about me anyhow.
- A little goes a long way.
- Like a speeding bullet.
- You gunning for me?
- Other way round, precious – you're like a shot to the heart.
She reached up and hooked a finger behind my ear. Her face turned up to me in supplication. Her eyes were closed. I never like to disappoint.'

"I mean," said Beamish as he shook his head slowly from side to side. "What on earth was that cross-talk all about? And if our hero's ears are anything like Cobberly's she's in for a surprise – I'm sure he's got a mouse nesting in each of them."

"Yes," agreed Hansum, complacently smoothing the fine waves of his own coiffure. "Poor Cobberly is one of those men who, as they age, find their timid tresses retreat from the scalp to find refuge in nostrils and ears."

At this moment, Cobberly himself appeared through the door and he came over and stood in front of us with an exasperated expression. He lifted up the folds of the tatty master's gown he invariably wore in school, and let them fall again in a gesture of despair.

"Another rejection, Hansum! I'm going to abandon the whole enterprise unless you advise me otherwise," he said.

"I'm afraid my approaching my publishers won't be much good – far too arty for this sort of thing," said Hansum equably.

"I know – I've telephoned them, just as I have telephoned all the others. I tell you that all publishers fall into one of three categories: they are fools who do not recognise merit; or they are simply self-serving concerned only with their own little position; or they do not have the competence to perform their job adequately."

He looked at each of us but got no comment. He tossed his head, plucked once more at the folds of his gown, and then swept, petulant and aggrieved, from our sight.

Slowly, I heaved myself up out of my chair. It was well past the time to go and teach. As I ambled over to the Biology department I reflected on Cobberly's assessment of publishers and had to agree that he had a point – had not my own excellent *Fascinating Fossil Facts For Five-Year-Olds* been summarily rejected and dismissed with 'as dull and lifeless as a coprolite'?

On a whim I dropped in at the Copy Shop on the off-chance of seeing Jean Masefield gazing lovingly at her 'hot and sweet' mug. Curiously, though the mug sat on her desk (on a round cork coaster, I noticed) the Copy Shop, almost always the churning hub of the school was, like my dissected heart from the morning, quite, quite empty.

A Sort of Epilogue

Afterwords

Before writing this, I was in something of a quandary. I think Wentworth might well have allowed me to add a final section to the collection of episodes that have preceded it if he had lived. On the other hand, he might well *not* have allowed it given the views on story-telling that I outline below. The thing that finally swayed me was that he did, after all, entrust me with the editorship of all his written material. This implies some faith in my judgement. And in that judgement, the circumstances surrounding the genesis of what has become *Writing Lines*, together with the very Wentworthian (I think I can confidently conjure that term after all the time I spent ploughing through his words) way in which he left this world, are worthy of an episode in the collection. Should you decide otherwise, you are free to simply rip out this section and hurl it from you in disgust (I have asked the printer to put in perforations to the pages here to make this easier for you to achieve without damaging the rest of the book[1]).

*   *   *

The facts of Wentworth's life are simple. He was born on April 1st 1946 in Birmingham in the house where he lived for the first 18 years of his life: 62, Starling Road, Edgbaston. His prep school was in Handsworth. From there he went as a boarder to Beckham

---

[1] Though she says this 'extra' cannot apply to the cheapest editions.

Grange, near Ludlow, and then took his degree in biological sciences at Birmingham University. He joined Sixokes School as a biology teacher in September 1967 and taught there until his retirement in July 2011. Throughout this time he lived at 28, Powell Road, Sixokes[2] and died there on November 5th 2011. He was an only child and always close to his mother, Elizabeth (1926 – 99) who came to 'keep house' for him in Sixokes in 1974 until her death. He never married (I deliberately eschew 'life-long bachelor' as I am aware that this phrase is used by professional obituarists to mean 'an incontinent and indiscriminate male homosexual') and showed very little interest in forming relationships at all: the episodes containing references to Monica Stimpson, Mary Boyne and, at a pinch, Dotty Benson, are the only ones in all his papers with any hints in that direction. He had few interests, with none of these amounting to expertise[3] or passion. His person, his character, his life were all wholly unremarkable: he was, just like us, very ordinary indeed.

* * *

All of that sort of detail, Wentworth would have hated. Here is why.

* * *

I was sitting alone and at a loose end in the Staff Room one rain-lashed Tuesday afternoon in June 2011 (Games having been cancelled) when Wentworth came in drying his head with a large spotted handkerchief.

---

[2] I follow Wentworth in lightly disguising most of the names of places and individuals in and around the school where he actually worked in order to provide a cast-iron defence against any accusations of libel that might arise from his writings.

[3] Except, perhaps, the skill and enthusiasm for assembling flat-pack furniture which he would happily employ for anyone who asked - including the sturdy Bübo executive office desk on which I am writing this.

"Piss-poor weather!" he said, looking at me. I think these were the first words he had ever spoken directly to me - this despite my having been a teacher at the School with him for over ten years. "Stuart isn't it?"

"Yes, Stuart," I agreed. "Tony - Tony Stuart," I added, just to eliminate any confusion. Wentworth settled himself into his disgraceful leather armchair in the corner of the room near to me, sighed and, now vigorously polishing his round horn-rimmed glasses with the handkerchief, said:

"Tea?"

"Why not?" I replied and went to the kitchen and soon returned with two cups. Surprisingly, Wentworth was still wide awake.

"You're the chappie who keeps sending round those newsletter things aren't you? You know, Jane Austen and all that?" he asked, sipping his tea appreciatively. I bent my head modestly to acknowledge the truth of this. "Don't look at them myself," he said. "Went on the first outing but it wasn't for me all that sort of stuff. Far too busy to do much extra reading." He paused and I waited, wondering about what all this unwonted talk might lead up to. Putting down his cup and saucer and absently rubbing with a thumb at some of the tea that had dripped onto his tie, he gave me a quick, sharp look.

"I've decided that you might well fit the bill as my editor," he announced quietly.

"Your editor?"

"Don't sound so bloody surprised," he snapped. "As you know, I have been at the School since 1967 and have kept diaries and letters and so on in which the richness of all that experience is there ready to be mined." He sat back in his chair and smoothed his sparse and grizzled hair. "I flatter myself that I am well-regarded and well-respected by hundreds – if not thousands – of ex-pupils, let alone all the parents and other teachers who have been acquainted with me over the years. I feel certain that they would welcome the opportunity of reading my memoirs."

There was a longish pause as he waited for me to say something.

"Why not just write them then?" I asked innocently.

"Because, young man, I want my life-story to be like life itself. I also want some objectivity in it so the reader sees me warts and all, so to speak – none of that self-aggrandisation and false modesty you read in all those autobiographies. To that end, I need an editor to select episodes from my life for me. You can be that editor," he concluded gravely.

I had nothing projected for the summer holidays and thought this might be diverting – after all, Wentworth was a major figure of fun in the school, legendary for his escapades and mishaps – so said that I was game. He handed me the key to his garage and told me that all the material was stored there. After that, he sank back and closed his eyes. Our first interview was over.

* * *

Our second and final interview was in his kitchen with a large pot of tea at the end of the half-term holiday in early November. My wife had dropped me off with the boxes of books and papers I was returning and I carried them in and deposited them on the floor of the garage through which I passed on my way into Wentworth's kitchen. (Apparently it was his idiosyncrasy to enter and leave his house via the garage rather than the perfectly serviceable front door.) I had with me in my briefcase the episodes that I had chosen to illustrate his life, each neatly stapled with a cover sheet with the episode number on it. I was slightly apprehensive about what he would make of my selection as I took them out and laid them in a small neat stack on the table. I needn't have been because he showed no interest in reading them. The conversation went something like this.

Wentworth	I'm not going to ask you if you found the opportunity of getting that unique insight into my life interesting. That goes without saying. How many episodes have you culled from the wealth of material on offer?
Me	Twenty-six.

Long pause

Wentworth   Twenty-six! Is that fucking all? I suppose these episodes are lengthy?

Me   Oh no. They vary a fair bit. Say about three thousand words per episode on average.

Long sigh from Wentworth. Long pause

Wentworth   I see.

Me   I've got pretty much the whole spectrum of your life covered and I've arranged them in their chronological order so now all we need do is pad it out with some details of you and your life to weave them together to produce a rounded story –

Wentworth   No.

Me   But without –

Wentworth   No. Fuck off with all that. Just listen. As I mentioned before, I want the story of my life to be like life itself. I don't want some crappy pseudish biography loaded with dreary footnotes.[4] I remember listening in to Richard Hansum and Hugh Pollen when they were discussing how Conrad and Ford Maddox Ford wrote. Though I've not read anything by them myself, I was struck by their approach. Apparently, they argued that, in life, we meet people and form an impression. As we meet them again, or as we hear about them from others, that impression deepens, or is modified, or even proved to be greatly mistaken. So, they imitated this in their novels in their aim to be more realistic, more true to life.

Me   Well, that's in fiction where the action –

---

[4] I disagree with Wentworth about this as I often find footnotes a piquant relish to the fare on offer in the main text.

Wentworth   And I have decided that this should be the model for my memoirs. There will be no chronological order, no linking notes. Each of the episodes separately will provide a partial reflection of me and my life and, when all have been read, will reveal something like the whole truth.

Me   But that will be terribly confusing and –

Wentworth   Of course, they will have to be arranged in some sort of sequence when you send them off for publication -

Me   About that, I'm not so sure whether –

Wentworth   So we will decide that now. Let me see, twenty-six episodes…twenty-six… playing cards!

Wentworth hurries from the kitchen and returns with a pack of playing cards and a felt-tip pen. He sorts the cards into red and black pushing the latter to one side. With the pen he writes on the red cards. Then he shuffles them.

Wentworth   I want the order to be random – that should take away any sort of 'authorial bias'. You will rearrange your episodes in this order…

He turns the first card. It is the queen of hearts with '22' written on it.

Wentworth   The first episode in the book will be your episode twenty-two. Well, what are you waiting for? Do it!

I take out episode twenty-two from the stack and, borrowing his felt-tip pen, cross out the 'twenty-two' and put '1'. Wentworth rapidly lays out the rest of the cards and then looks across at me expectantly. I work through the stack, renumbering.

Me   Now, you said something about publication?

Wentworth   I don't trust those fellows who go into publishing. To quote Tony Cobberly, an old colleague of mine, all publishers fall into one of three categories: tits, shits or wankers. I've given it some thought and will trust to the taste and power of the reader.[5]

Long pause

           I can see by your blank expression you haven't a clue how I can get masses of readers without getting a publisher. My plan is to make the readers do the work of getting it published…

Me   You're right, I am being rather dense here –

Wentworth No apology needed. I must say that it took a bit of genius on my part to come up with it. What you are going to do is first of all is use the pool of talent and influence on the school staff. You will send them a couple of episodes every term – in the order the cards have now dictated.

---

[5] I was unable to get to the bottom of Wentworth's antipathy to publishers. One sort of clue to it might be something I found tucked right at the bottom of one of the boxes of material he had given me. A folded sugar-paper poster enclosed a flat black cardboard box. On the poster, in childish paintwork, were depicted three figures holding hands (one perhaps representing Wentworth, the others two black girls in yellow dresses) and the words 'We love you Mr Wentwort' (they had miscalculated the space available and the final 'h' hung like a roosting bat to the last 't' of his name) and then 'Akunge and Meera'. In the box was a silver medal with an elephant on one side and the words 'Order of the Elephant (Third Class)' on the other. Inside the lid of the box was a citation: 'Awarded to George Gordon Wentworth to honour the time and love he gave to the children in the Orphan's Hospital of Luanda every summer for over four decades.' After this, there is some small print which indicated the class distinctions – from 'First class' for 'Politicians' through military, civilian, judiciary, arts and music, science and technology, medicine, academic, entertainment and finally, 'Tenth Class – Journalists and Publishers'. Presumably, Wentworth had bought the medal in a junk-shop for some fancy dress party or other and the idea of Publishers being tenth-rate made a strong negative impression on him. This is the only (very tentative) explanation I can offer.

Me	How will they know what you want them to do with them? Should I put in an introduction, or something about the significance of each –
Wentworth	For fuck's sake - weren't you listening! I don't want anything like that! Just the episodes in the order I have told you!
Me	Alright, yes, yes, I'll do that. But what do you hope –
Wentworth	Look, I know there are a fair few dead-beats and duffers on the Sixokes School staff now, but there are also quite a few who are discerning with regard to good writing. I'd guess 25 or 30 or so. Each of these will no doubt appreciate the merit of the episodes they receive as time goes on and will start spreading the word to others. These ripples will widen and, again no doubt, will eventually reach a publisher who, given that something is already obviously popular and appreciated, will seize the opportunity of getting the rights to publish the memoirs more widely. Now do you see?
Me	Well...I suppose it's one way...
Wentworth	And I've got a back-up plan too.
Me	Would a vanity publisher –
Wentworth	Just shut up and listen a minute! If, after the, what is it...four or five years of drip-feeding of the episodes to the Sixokes staff hasn't had the publishers leaping, then you can throw some more pebbles into the pond. Get 500 paperback copies printed off in the Copy Shop and post them out to random Old Sixokians. With the sort of massive ripple effect that results from that, there's bound to be a publisher who recognises a winner when he sees it!
Me	Well, that sounds easy enough. Shall I leave you these to read before I start sending them round?

Wentworth No – I wrote them didn't I? I couldn't give a gnat's ballock[6] about your selection. I'll let my words speak for me. I take it they are all my words and you haven't tried to put in stuff of your own?

Me No, not at all. It's all you – apart from some letters that were in the boxes.

Wentworth That's alright then. I dare say you must be going?

I finish my tea and put the stack of episodes into my briefcase. Wentworth accompanies me through the door from the kitchen into the garage. I gesture at the three cardboard boxes on the floor.

Me There's everything. Do you want a hand putting them away?

Wentworth Now there's a thought…What should I?…I know!

Me Yes?

Wentworth Yes! Yes! Those episodes will be all the world will get! I'll get rid of the lot and all that will stand will be the episodes that you, a pretty ordinary Joe Public, have seen as representative! Excellent! And then the whole thing will be my Complete Words!

Me You mean you're going to chuck them all away?

Wentworth That's exactly what I'm going to do! Goodbye to all this!

I'm afraid that it was at this moment that the Wentworthian train of unlucky events which led to a truly Wentworthian end – literally,

---

[6] Though never appearing in his 'complete words' I have no doubt that this is the spelling Wentworth would have employed. He was an ardent and scrupulous pedant with respect to English usage (once 'correcting' my own use of the preterite) almost always excusing his strictures on the grounds of "safeguarding the purity of English from mucky-fingered ignorance". I found his pedantry profoundly myopic. So, for instance, he was probably the last man in Britain to insist on a circumflex over the 'o' in 'hotel' while never actually using English to express anything apt, illuminating or original.

the end of Wentworth – shunted out of the station and along the track of destiny as a result of my own curiosity and intended helpfulness.

High up on one of the shelves above his impressive workbench in the garage were a dozen or so dusty brown bottles of the type that you see in laboratories. Wentworth saw me looking at them and told me they were samples of Group I and Group II metals that his old friend Yanto Williams, the head of Chemistry, had let him have. I hadn't a clue what these were since I had thankfully opted out of 'science' with its simplicity, stinks and smugness at the earliest possible moment. He told me that they were 'better than fireworks' and that he had meant to 'put on a show for the neighbours' children' but that they had moved out 'leaving just an old biddy who is best avoided' before he'd had the chance.

"They sound dangerous," I observed.

"Of course they are – if they are in the wrong hands," he said. "But I must get on, you know." He turned to go.

"Shall I get rid of the boxes of your papers for you?" I asked. "I know you don't have a car and I can easily take them to the recycling centre for you – I can bring my car around tomorrow afternoon if you like?"

He nodded and sketched a wave over his head.

"Take them, take them." Then he fixed me with a look. "They must be destroyed. All I want are those twenty-six episodes."

I assured him that the recycling of paper would probably lead to the unselected words getting rendered into egg-boxes or cardboard.

"I suppose it all comes back to eggs," he muttered and left the garage shutting the door between it and the kitchen behind him.

These were almost certainly the last words he ever spoke.

I stood for a moment or two considering those bottles of dangerous metals. They must be a massive fire risk, let alone the risk to any 'wrong hands' getting hold of them. Wasn't it stupid of Wentworth to have them just sitting on a shelf in his garage? Wouldn't it be negligent of me to ignore that stupidity? Obviously, Wentworth wasn't a man to reason with (and he clearly had a dim view of my own intellect) and so I made the fateful decision to put the bottles in the boxes with his papers – hidden underneath a few sheaves – and quietly get rid of the danger at the recycling centre the next day. That done, I dusted off my hands and went out through the garage door, closed and locked it, and walked home.

*　　　*　　　*

The circumstances relating to Wentworth's sudden death came out at the inquest. Having given my evidence and heard all the rest of it, I have a pretty clear picture of what must have happened on that November morning.

Wentworth's neighbour, Dotty Benson, saw him from her bedroom window carrying three cardboard boxes to the top of the garden at about ten o'clock. She said this interested her as she had objected before to Wentworth's frequent bonfires and was thinking that, if he were to light a fire, there was no point in her opening any of her windows. My guess is that Wentworth had decided that he couldn't really trust me to get rid of his papers and so needed to do it properly and certainly himself. (My wife thinks that I am blaming myself too much, that Wentworth probably heard or saw reference to Bonfire Night on the news and this made him think of having a fire – no shadow of a lack of confidence in me at all. Perhaps she is right.)

Whatever the reason, Dotty Benson then reported seeing him strike several matches but failing to get the papers in the boxes to light. (This again might be due to me: I had left the papers in our cellar while working on them over the previous months and the cellar, I know, is rather damp.) She says he walked purposefully ('stanked' was her more colourful term) back into his house and soon returned with a petrol can. He unscrewed it and began pouring the contents over the boxes. "Then there was a terrific 'whoomph' and a great sheet of flame," said Dotty, "and the petrol can was lifted up in his hand and hit him a horrible thump on the forehead." Wentworth fell forward onto the burning boxes.

The Chief Fire Officer of Sixokes Brigade was questioned about this during his evidence – it seemed that the coroner was ruling out suicide – and said that falling forwards could be explained by Wentworth having been knocked unconscious by the petrol can and, given that there had been an explosive start to the fire, the inrushing oxygen in the air would have pushed him into it. He also took the opportunity to point out the folly of pouring petrol onto material you had already dropped lighted matches into.

Dotty Benson was shocked and reaching for her mobile phone to call for help when there was an even greater explosion and a terrifically bright light for several seconds 'like masses of flashes from cameras all at the same time but all the colours of the rainbow'. This caused the new wooden fence separating her property from Wentworth's to catch fire too. The Fire Officer related this fiercer explosion to the bottles of metals I had secreted in the boxes. The sodium, potassium, magnesium, lithium, rubidium and so on provided incandescent heat and light. The heat was so intense that practically all of Wentworth's body was consumed. All that was left of him were his feet and ankles.

The coroner was satisfied that identification of the body could be established as that of Wentworth by Dotty Benson's eye-witness testimony and my acknowledging that I had seen Wentworth wearing the diamond-patterned socks and ancient brogues on the feet on previous occasions.

The verdict was death by misadventure.

*   *   *

Unsurprisingly perhaps, (without telling me) Wentworth had appointed me as executor of his will and this put me into a bit of a difficult position with respect to what to do with his remains (or, I suppose, the remains of his remains). The will was quite clear: he wanted his body left to medical science and, any parts once finished with, then incinerated. The ashes from this were to be collected and buried under an ash sapling in the grounds of Sixokes School. (Showing his customary leaden wit he put in brackets that, once this ash had grown and taken up the nutrients from his ashes and later put forth seeds which themselves would grow, he would pass 'from ashes to ashes'.) He was adamant about having no religious ceremony.

The difficulty began when I phoned Guy's Hospital about a dead body for research. When they heard that the body in question consisted of just feet, they said they would have no use for them. I tried pointing out that some student might be grateful for some extra material to practise on that might have good examples of things like verrucae or bunions or hammer toes but they got rather impatient and asked if this was a hoax call. Stymied by this, I went to the funeral director's to see about a cremation.

By coincidence, the assistant director was an Old Sixokian who had known Wentworth well: James 'Monumental' Mason (the nickname was one of Hansum's). Gravely, he shook my hand.

"Cremation? Just to finish off the job, I suppose," he said. "A full-sized coffin would be a bit of a waste of space (though I'm not implying anything about the deceased, I'll have you know)," he said with a wink. "We do have baby coffins. We could put the feet in those. Trouble is they are all distinctively white and would be hard to fit the feet in neatly – and it would look a bit like a final joke about his titchiness, wouldn't it? I suppose we could use a couple of shoe boxes – I notice he took size 5s." I wanted to laugh but somehow, being surrounded by photographs advertising styles of wreaths, headstones and coffins made that seem inappropriate. "And you'll get hardly any ashes, of course – be like a pinch of snuff with just the feet to work with."

I had an idea and suggested it to Mason.

"Not just irregular, Mr Stuart, absolutely illegal. Human remains cannot be disposed of except through the designated authorities," he said, adopting a nasal tone. I suppose I must have looked crestfallen. He went on in his usual voice. "But, you'll remember that I was one who didn't always toe the line, Mr Stuart, sir. Didn't always come to heel. You wait here and I'll bring in the immortal soles." He ducked through a doorway covered by a red velvet curtain to return a couple of minutes later with a plain brown paper carrier bag. He opened it a little to show me Wentworth's feet in their slightly charred socks and shoes all neatly sealed in transparent plastic. "Now, so long as you keep schtum and do what you say, then I'll deal with the necessary paperwork here and no-one will be any the wiser. Just keep them in a freezer until the time comes. And don't get cold feet yourself!"

*   *   *

A couple of weeks later, a small crowd assembled on the edge of Dyke's Meadow, the large sports ground in Sixokes School. We had just listened to a dreadful peroration by Old Busby Beamish (who had recently suffered a stroke), clinging feebly to his zimmer-frame, on *Wentworth – The Man* which was rambling, dreary and shot through with factual inaccuracies. His long-suffering wife[7], Maggie, had to keep wiping the drool off his chin as he maundered on and on. At one point he referred to Wentworth's bequests to some hospital somewhere (which Beamish's slurring voice totally obscured) and 'Help the Aged'. Jean Cobberly, always one to match her dead husband for sharpness and bitterness of tongue, murmured quite loudly: 'Yes, help the aged – to the ovens!'

---

[7] Here I do use the term as per the professional obituarists.

This rather heartless comment may well have provoked a deeply-tanned, tough-looking old woman in a severe grey suit with a small brooch with MSF in fiery red letters in the lapel to shake her head. She then tugged a large white handkerchief from her sleeve and mopped her face before giving her nose a viscous blow and turning and forcing her way through the rest of us and striding briskly away. Later, I asked around but no-one had a clue who she was.

But now the time had come for the Head Gardener to place the ash sapling into the hole that had been prepared for it. A step or two away was a small brass marker set into the ground (where it was sure to prove a painful hazard to unwary ankles in the future, I noted) with the inscription:

In commemoration of G G Wentworth
(1946 – 2011)
Employed here as a teacher for 44 years

I sighed with relief as the sapling was put in place and heaped around with spadefuls of soil which were then stamped into place. I had got away with it.

The previous evening I had removed Wentworth's feet from the bottom of the freezer, taken them out of the plastic and put them into the paper carrier bag that Mason had given me. I had thought about defrosting them first but had decided the difficulty of getting them into the microwave, together with the possibility of my wife coming in and finding me apparently cooking feet, was too risky. (I hadn't told her of my plan so as not to implicate her in what was, after all, a crime.) Then, just after midnight, I sneaked into the School grounds with the bag, a torch and a spade. Even with the torch, finding the hole in Dyke's Meadow where the ash sapling was to be planted wasn't easy. In fact, it was my unwary ankle that the brass Wentworth marker was the first to claim as a victim. I dug a hole in the hole and then fished out Wentworth's feet for burial. Should they be placed standing or lying? I tossed the sixpence he had left me: standing it was. I earthed over the feet and crept home relatively confident that the spirit of his wishes about his remains had been honoured.

The end of it all was marked by a couple of sopranos (Temms and Atkins) from the School choir leading the singing of Wentworth's favourite hymn, *Jerusalem*. As the words *"And did those feet…"* rose uncertainly into the heavens I suddenly and surprisingly found my eyes swarming with tears. I felt something like love.

March 2012
Sevenoaks

Lightning Source UK Ltd.
Milton Keynes UK
UKOW02f1051151016

285333UK00001B/60/P